MY FAVORITE SCIENCE FICTION STORY

edited by
Martin H. Greenberg

DAW BOOKS, INC.
DONALD A. WOLLHEIM, FOUNDER
375 Hudson Street, New York, NY 10014
ELIZABETH R. WOLLHEIM
SHEILA E. GILBERT
PUBLISHERS

Cover art by Angus McKie

DAW Book Collectors No. 1115.

DAW Books are distributed by Penguin Putnam Inc.

First Printing, March 1999
1 2 3 4 5 6 7 8 9

THEIR FAVORITE SCIENCE FICTION STORIES

"There's a lot wrong with science fiction. One of the things that's right about it is Barry Malzberg, easily the finest writer of his era."

—Mike Resnick on "A Galaxy Called Rome"
by Barry Malzberg.

"There aren't many short stories, in SF or out of it, as beautifully done as this. That doesn't mean it's merely exquisite. Real beauty has strength and 'Black Charlie' is, in its quiet way, as strong a story as you'll ever find."

—Poul Anderson on "Black Charlie"
by Gordon R. Dickson

" Every writer has a story about which he thinks, "Damn, I wish I'd written that one." 'The Ugly Chickens' is mine.'

—Harry Turtledove on "The Ugly Chickens"
by Howard Waldrop

"This story scared the spit out of me when I was a kid. It's a disturbing, dreadful, wonderful story. My favorite, in fact."

—Connie Willis on "Lot" by Ward Moore

"In a little more than a score of pages, Smith give us a vast and wondrous world, true love, cosmic justice, and great cat-values. You could not ask (nor get) more from most trilogies."

—Lois McMaster Bujold on "The Ballad of Lost C'mell"
by Cordwainer Smith

"For me it is an unforgetable masterpiece. May you find it as moving and strange and wonderful as I did. . . ."

—Robert Silverberg on "Common Time"
by James Blish

More Masterful Science Fiction Anthologies Brought to You by DAW:

ACKNOWLEDGMENTS

"The Man Who Lost the Sea" by Theodore Sturgeon. Copyright ©1956, renewed by the Theodore Sturgeon Literary Trust. Reprinted by permission of the Executrix of the author's Estate, Noel Sturgeon.

"The Last Command" by Keith Laumer. Copyright ©1966 by Condé Nast Publications, renewed 1993 by Baen Books. Reprinted by permission of Baen Books.

"Day Million" by Frederik Pohl. Copyright ©1966 by Frederik Pohl. Reprinted by permission of the author.

"The Little Black Bag" by C.M. Kornbluth. Copyright ©1950 by C.M. Kornbluth. Reprinted by permission of the agent for the author's Estate, Richard Curtis, Richard Curtis Associates, Inc.

"A Galaxy Called Rome" by Barry N. Malzberg. Copyright ©1975 by Mercury Press, Inc. Reprinted by permission of the author.

"Diabologic" by Eric Frank Russell. Copyright ©1955 by Eric Frank Russell. Reprinted by permission of the agent for the author's Estate, Joshua Bilmes, JABberwocky Literary Agency, P.O. Box 4558, Sunnyside, NY, 11104-0558.

"Untouched by Human Hands" by Robert Sheckley. Copyright ©1956 by Robert Sheckley. Reprinted by permission of the author.

"Black Charlie" by Gordon R. Dickson. Copyright ©1954 by Galaxy Publishing Corporation, renewed copyright ©1982 by Gordon R. Dickson. Reprinted by permission of the author.

"The Ugly Chickens" by Howard Waldrop. Copyright ©1980 by Terry Carr. Reprinted by permission of the author.

"The Mathenauts" by Norman Kagan. Copyright ©1965 by Galaxy Publishing Corporation, renewed 1987 by the author. Reprinted by permission of the author and his agent, Dianna Collier, Collier Associates, P.O. Box 21361, West Palm Beach, FL 33416 USA.

"Lot" by Ward Moore. Copyright ©1953, 1981 by the Estate of Ward Moore. Reprinted by permission of the author's Estate and the Estate's agent, Virginia Kidd, Virginia Kidd Agency, Inc.

"The Ballad of Lost C'mell" by Cordwainer Smith. Copyright ©1962 by Galaxy Publications. Reprinted by the agent for the author's Estate, Barry Malzberg, Scott Meredith Literary Agency.

"A Martian Odyssey" by Stanley G. Weinbaum. Copyright ©1964 by Margaret Weinbaum. Reprinted by permission of the agent for the author's Estate, Forrest J. Ackerman, 2495 Glendower Ave., Hollywood, CA 90027-1110.

"Common Time" by James Blish. Copyright © 1953, renewed 1981 by James Blish. Reprinted by permission of the Executrix for the author's Estate, Judith Ann Lawrence Blish.

"The Engine at Heartspring's Center" by Roger Zelazny. Copyright ©1974 by Roger Zelazny. Reprinted by permission of the agent for the author's Estate, Kirby McCauley, The Pimlico Agency, Inc.

"Nerves" by Lester del Rey. Copyright ©1942 by Street & Smith Publications. Reprinted by the agent for the author's Estate, Barry Malzberg, Scott Meredith Literary Agency.

"The Only Thing We Learn" by C.M. Kornbluth. Copyright ©1949 by C. M. Kornbluth. Reprinted by permission of the agent for the author's Estate, Richard Curtis, Richard Curtis Associates, Inc.

CONTENTS

INTRODUCTION

Ever since the beginning of recorded time, mankind has always told stories. From the first caveman silhouetted by the flickering firelight of his cave as he described that day's hunting, to parents reading to their children at bedtime; from minstrels and bards to the thousands of people working today in fiction, journalism, or film; we have always been tellers of tales.

While many people chronicle the events and history of life as we know it, a select group of writers prefer to look beyond the mundane, to use what we know already and imagine what the future might be like. Of course, we're referring to science fiction writers.

The *Writer's Encyclopedia* defines science fiction as ". . . literature involving elements of science and techonology as a basis of conflict, or as the setting for a story. The science and technology are generally extrapolations of existing scientific fact, and most (though not all) science fiction stories take place in the future." Admittedly, this is a broad overview of a field that now encompasses hard science fiction, space opera, military science fiction, alternate history, and several other subgenres. But no matter what type of science fiction these writers choose to write about—from interstellar empires and laser pistols, to a world where the Romans did conquer the Earth, to a logically rigorous account of the first human settlement on Mars—there will always be readers and writers who want to know what's around the corner. But, since time travel hasn't been invented yet, science fiction writers have to find out the hard way; by making the future up.

But to get to the future, first we must take a quick look at the past. Most scholars believe science fiction's roots stretch back to about 175 A.D., when a Greek named Lucian of Somostrata wrote a story called *True History*, a fanciful tale of a ship that journeyed to the Moon, carried there by a giant whirlwind. These ancient roots took slowly, however, and it wasn't until the publication of Mary Shelley's *Frankenstein: or, The Modern Prometheus* in 1818 that science fiction began to achieve greater prominence. Robert Louis Stevenson's *Dr. Jekyll and Mr. Hyde* and Jules Verne's *20,000 Leagues Under the Sea* expanded the boundaries of science fiction, then called "scientific romance." H.G. Wells removed the romance in his seminal novel *War of the Worlds*. His chilling tale of invaders from outer space terrified thousands, and caused a citywide panic when broadcast over the radio in New York.

In 1926, science fiction took a huge step forward with the appearance of *Amazing Stories,* the first magazine devoted to science fiction and fantastic literature. It was the age of the pulps, and with it came the launch of hundreds of magazines, often combining science fiction with detective stories and other genres. Although many of these magazines didn't last more than one or two issues, their proliferation helped achieve the next step in science fiction's evolution: the Golden Age.

In the 1950s, writers such as Isaac Asimov, Robert Heinlein, and Arthur C. Clarke were turning more and more to the conclusion that science fiction was a literature of ideas. Editors such as John W. Campbell and H.L. Gold were demanding more rigorous science fiction that was based on facts. They expected plausible explanations for the scientific wonders that authors came up with. And authors such as Cordwainer Smith, Lester del Rey, C.M. Kornbluth, Eric Frank Russell, and James Blish delivered stories that gave those explanations. Magazines such as *The Magazine of Fantasy and Science Fiction, Galaxy, If,* and dozens of others flourished.

Toward the end of the 1950s and early in the 1960s, with the advent of the Cold War, the science fiction genre declined. People were too concerned with worrying whether or not there would be a tomorrow to wonder what it would actually look like. Dozens of markets dried up for lack of readers, and dozens of writers grew dissatisfied with how the genre seemed to be stagnating. Fresh blood was needed.

In the latter half of the 1960s and the early 1970s, the revolution started. Authors such as Anne McCaffrey, Roger Zelazny, Keith Laumer, Vonda McIntyre, Ursula K. Le Guin, Harlan Ellison, Robert Silverberg, and Philip K. Dick brought science fiction out of its doldrums and into the New Wave.

Combining rich characterization with imaginative use of language, and often skillfully blending elements of science fiction, fantasy, and mystery into a brand new synthesis, they revitalized the genre and pushed the boundaries of what was considered science fiction.

All of which brings us to science fiction today, from the 1980s to the present. With so many advances in science and technology, what would have been considered amazing even forty years ago is now commonplace. Many of the grand ideas of early science fiction—Martians, traveling to the Moon, colonizing other planets—have been partially or totally overtaken by mankind's incredible accomplishments and discoveries. Yet our inexorable progress has also opened up entirely new worlds of adventure. The decoding of DNA, the power of the computer, and the possibilities of virtual reality are just three of the scientific fields that have only appeared in the last forty years. These are the new horizons for writers to explore, the new springboards that launch thousands of ideas each year. Authors such as Jonathan Lethem, Patricia Cadigan, Lois McMaster Bujold, Lucius Shepard, Connie Willis, and Octavia Butler are pushing the genre into the future. If you noticed that this last list of authors contained more women than men, that's not coincidental. The past three decades have also seen a tremendous increase in women writing science fiction using their own names and voices, not having to resort to ambiguous names (Andre Norton), or pseudonyms (Alice Sheldon writing as James Tiptree, Jr.).

And yet, we cannot forget the past, and the foundation that was built over the past two hundred years that raised the science fiction genre from its obscure gothic beginnings to the respected literary form it is today. As each new generation of writers appears, the links to the authors of past decades grows slightly more tenuous. With everyone eagerly looking toward the future, sometimes it is too easy to overlook the past, to leave behind ideas that now seem quaint or outdated while we focus our attention on the exciting, unknowable future.

With this in mind, we've asked some of the most innovative authors of this generation to look back over the vast body of short science fiction stories and choose their favorites, the one story that inspired each of them as an author, or the one with a message that spoke so clearly and powerfully that the memory of its impact remains to this day. Luminaries such as Anne

McCaffrey, Robert Silverberg, Arthur C. Clarke, Gregory Benford, Marion Zimmer Bradley, Andre Norton, and many others have picked the one piece of fiction that is their favorite science fiction story.

As usual, whenever a group of writers (or any group of people, for that matter, but writers especially) are asked to choose one item from a group, the results are as varied and interesting as the people themselves. One of the first alien contact stories is included here, with a fully realized and detailed alien, not the faceless, implacable invaders of H.G. Wells. A gripping tale of life after nuclear war from the viewpoint of an everyday family is also included. Space exploration, time travel, military science fiction, nuclear physics—all are examined here in some of the finest stories of the past century.

The authors who have selected the stories that make up this collection have also provided a brief commentary which explains why they chose each story. Again, the reasons for including these stories are as far-ranging as the stories themselves. So come explore the genre's past and the strange and wondrous future that was envisioned in stories that today's premier science fiction writers have chosen as their favorites.

I am not really sure if I *do* have a favorite story—but if I did, it would be Theodore Sturgeon's "The Man Who Lost the Sea."

I am fond of this for several reasons—first of all, it perfectly describes the moment of panic which every diver knows at least once in his career (some unlucky ones *only* know it once . . .), and its construction is also technically fascinating.

But the real reason is that, I suspect, it inspired my *own* favorite short story "Transit of Earth," and even though every detail is different, it describes exactly the same situation.

—Arthur C. Clarke

THE MAN WHO LOST THE SEA

by Theodore Sturgeon

Say you're a kid, and one dark night you're running along the cold sand with this helicopter in your hand, saying very fast *witchy-witchy-witchy.* You pass the sick man and he wants you to shove off with that thing. Maybe he thinks you're too old to play with toys. So you squat next to him in the sand and tell him it isn't a toy, it's a model. You tell him look here, here's something most people don't know about helicopters. You take a blade of the rotor in your fingers and show him how it can move in the hub, up and down a little, back and forth a little, and twist a little, to change pitch. You start to tell him how this flexibility does away with the gyroscopic effect, but he won't listen. He doesn't want to think about flying, about helicopters, or about you, and he most especially does not want explanations about anything by anybody. Not now. Now, he wants to think about the sea. So you go away.

The sick man is buried in the cold sand with only his head and his left arm showing. He is dressed in a pressure suit and looks like a man from Mars. Built into his left sleeve is a combination timepiece and pressure gauge, the gauge with a luminous blue indicator which makes no sense, the clockhands luminous red. He can hear the pounding of surf and the soft swift pulses of his pumps. One time long ago when he was swimming, he went too deep and stayed down too long and came up too fast, and when he came to it was like this: they said, "Don't move, boy. You've got the bends. Don't even *try* to move." He had tried anyway. It hurt. So now, this time, he lies in the sand without moving, without trying.

His head isn't working right. But he knows clearly that it isn't working right, which is a strange thing that happens to people in shock sometimes. Say you were that kid, you could say how it was, because once you woke up lying in the gym office in high school and asked what had happened. They explained how you tried something on the parallel bars and fell on your head. You understood exactly, though you couldn't remember falling. Then a minute later you asked again what had happened and they told you. You understood it. And a minute later . . . forty-one times they told you, and you understood. It was just that no matter how many times they pushed it into your head, it wouldn't stick there; but all the while you *knew* that your head would start working again in time. And in time it did. . . . Of course, if you were that kid, always explaining things to people and to yourself, you wouldn't want to bother the sick man with it now.

Look what you've done already, making him send you away with that angry shrug of the mind (which, with the eyes, are the only things which will move just now). The motionless effort costs him a wave of nausea. He has felt seasick before but he has never *been* seasick, and the formula for that is to keep your eyes on the horizon and stay busy. Now! Then he'd better get busy—now; for there's one place especially not to be seasick in, and that's locked up in a pressure suit. Now!

So he busies himself as best he can, with the seascape, landscape, sky. He lies on high ground, his head propped on a vertical wall of black rock. There is another such outcrop before him, whip-topped with white sand and with smooth flat sand. Beyond and down is valley, salt-flat, estuary; he cannot yet be sure. He is sure of the line of footprints, which begin behind him, pass to his left, disappear in the outcrop shadows, and reappear beyond to vanish at last into the shadows of the valley.

Stretched across the sky is old mourning cloth with starlight burning holes in it, and between the holes the black is absolute—wintertime, mountaintop sky-black.

(Far off on the horizon within himself, he sees the swell and crest of approaching nausea; he counters with an undertow of weakness, which meets and rounds and settles the wave before it can break. Get busier. *Now.*)

Burst in on him, then, with the X-15 model. That'll get him. Hey, how about this for a gimmick? Get too high for the thin air to give you any control, you have these little jets in the wingtips, see? and on the sides of the *empennage*: bank, roll, yaw, whatever, with squirts of compressed air.

But the sick man curls his sick lip: oh, git, kid, git, will you?—that has nothing to do with the sea. So you git.

Out and out the sick man forces his view, etching all he sees with a meticulous intensity, as if it might be his charge, one day, to duplicate all this. To his left is only starlit sea, windless. In front of him across the valley, rounded hills with dim white epaulettes of light. To his right, the jutting corner of the black wall against which his helmet rests. (He thinks the distant moundings of nausea becalmed, but he will not look yet. So he scans the sky, black and bright, calling Sirius, calling Pleiades, Polaris, Ursa Minor, calling that . . . that . . . why, it *moves.* Watch it: Yes, it moves! It is a fleck of light, seeming to be wrinkled, fissured rather like a chip of boiled cauliflower in the sky. (Of course, he knows better than to trust his own eyes just now.) But that movement . . .

As a child he had stood on cold sand in a frosty Cape Cod evening, watching Sputnik's steady spark rise out of the haze (madly, dawning a little north of west); and after that he had sleeplessly wound special coils for his receiver, risked his life restraining high antennas, all for the brief capture of an unreadable *tweetle-eep-tweetle* in his earphones from Vanguard, Explorer, Lunik, Discoverer, Mercury. He knew them all (well some people collect match covers, stamps) and he knew especially that unmistakable steady sliding in the sky.

This moving fleck was a satellite, and in a moment, motionless, uninstrumented but for his chronometer and his part-brain, he will know which one. (He is grateful beyond expression—without that sliding chip of light, there were only those footprints, those wandering footprints, to tell a man he was not alone in the world.)

Say you were a kid, eager and challengeable and more than a little bright, you might in a day or so work out a way to measure the period of satellite with nothing but a timepiece and a brain; you might eventually see that the shadow in the rocks ahead had been there from the first only because of the light from the rising satellite. Now if you check the time exactly at the moment when the shadow on the sand is equal to the height of the outcrop, and time it again when the light is at the zenith and the shadow gone, you will multiply this number of minutes by eight—think why, now; horizon to zenith is one-fourth of the orbit, give or take a little, and halfway up the sky is half that quarter—and you will then know this satellite's period. You know all the periods—ninety minutes, two, two-and-a-half hours; with that and the appearance of this bird, you'll find out which one it is.

But if you were that kid, eager or resourceful or whatever, you wouldn't jabber about it to the sick man, for not only does he not want to be bothered with you, he's thought of all that long since and is even now watching the shadows for that triangular split second of measurement. *Now!* His eyes drop to the face of his chronometer; 0400, near as makes no never mind.

He has minutes to wait now—ten? . . . thirty? . . . twenty-three?—while this baby moon eats up its slice of shadowpie; and that's too bad, the waiting, for though the inner sea is calm there are currents below, shadows that shift and swim. Be busy. Be busy. He must not swim near that great invisible amoeba whatever happens: its first cold pseudopod is even now reaching for the vitals.

Being a knowledgeable young fellow, not quite a kid any more, wanting to help the sick man too, you want to tell him everything you know about the cold-in-the-gut, that reaching invisible surrounding implacable amoeba. You know all about it—listen, you want to yell at him, don't let that touch of cold bother you. Just know what it is, that's all. Know what it is that is touching your gut. You want to tell him, listen:

Listen, this is how you met the monster and dissected it. Listen, you were skin-diving in the Grenadines, a hundred tropical shoal-water islands; you had a new blue snorkel mask, the kind with a face plate and breathing tube all in one, and new blue flippers on your feet, and a new blue spear gun—all this new because you'd only begun, you see; you were a beginner, aghast with pleasure at your easy intrusion into this underwater otherworld. You'd been out in a boat, you were coming back, you'd just reached the mouth of the little bay, you'd taken the notion to swim the rest of the way. You'd said as much to the boys and slipped into the warm silky water. You brought your gun.

Not far to go at all, but then beginners find wet distances deceiving. For the first five minutes or so it was only delightful, the sun hot on your back and the water so warm it seemed not to have any temperature at all and you were flying. With your face under the water, your mask was not so much attached as part of you, your wide blue flippers trod away yards, your gun rode all but weightless in your hand, the taut rubber sling making an occasional hum as your passage plucked it in the sunlit green. In your ears crooned the breathy monotone of the snorkel tube, and through the invisible disk of plate glass you saw wonders. The bay was shallow—ten, twelve feet or so—and sandy, with great growths of brain-, bone-, and fire-coral, intricate waving sea fans, and fish—such fish! Scarlet and green and aching azure, gold and rose and slate-color studded with sparks of enamel blue, pink and peach and silver. And that *thing* got into you, that . . . monster.

There were enemies in this otherworld: the sand-colored spotted sea snake with his big ugly head and turned-down mouth, who would not retreat but lay watching the intruder pass; and the mottled moray with jaws like bolt cutters; and somewhere around, certainly, the barracuda with his undershot face and teeth turned inward so that he must take away whatever he might strike. There were urchins—the plump white sea egg with its thick fur of sharp quills and the black ones with the long slender spines that would break off in unwary flesh and fester there for weeks; and filefish and stonefish with their poisoned barbs and lethal meat; and the stingaree who could drive his spike through a leg bone. Yet these were not *monsters,* and could not matter to you, the invader churning along above them all. For you were above them in so many ways—armed, rational, comforted by the close shore (ahead the beach, the rocks on each side) and by the presence of the boat not too far behind. Yet you were . . . attacked.

At first it was uneasiness, not pressing, but pervasive, a contact quite as intimate as that of the sea; you were sheathed in it. And also there was the touch—the cold inward contact. Aware of it at last, you laughed: for Pete's sake, what's there to be scared of?

The monster, the amoeba.

You raised your head and looked back in air. The boat had edged in to the cliff at the right; someone was giving a last poke around for lobster. You waved at the boat; it was your gun you waved, and emerging from the water it gained its latent ounces so that you sank a bit, and as if you had no snorkel on, you tipped your head back to get a breath. But tipping your head back plunged the end of the tube under water; the valve closed; you drew in a hard lungful of nothing at all. You dropped your face under; up came the tube; you got your air, and along with it a bullet of seawater which struck you somewhere inside the throat. You coughed it out and floundered, sobbing as you sucked in air, inflating your chest until it hurt, and the air you got seemed no good, no good at all, a worthless devitalized inert gas.

You clenched your teeth and headed for the beach, kicking strongly and knowing it was the right thing to do; and then below and to the right you saw a great bulk mounding up out of the sand floor of the sea. You knew it was only the reef, rocks and coral and weed, but the sight of it made you scream; you didn't care what you knew. You turned hard left to avoid it, fought by as if it would reach for you, and you couldn't get air, couldn't get air, for all the unobstructed hooting of your snorkel tube. You couldn't bear the mask, suddenly, not for another second, so you shoved it upward clear of your mouth and rolled over, floating on your back and opening your mouth to the sky and breathing with a sort of quacking noise

It was then and there that the monster well and truly engulfed you, mantling you round and about within itself—formless, borderless, the illimitible amoeba. The beach, mere yards away, and the rocky arms of the bay, and the not too distant boat—these you could identify but no longer distinguish, for they were all one and the same thing . . . the thing called unreachable.

You fought that way for a time, on your back, dangling the gun under and behind you and straining to get enough warm sun-stained air into your chest. And in time some particles of sanity began to swirl in the roil of your mind, and to dissolve and tint it. The air pumping in and out of your square-grinned frightened mouth began to be meaningful at last, and the monster relaxed away from you.

You took stock; saw surf, beach, a leaning tree. You felt the new scene with your body as the rollers humped to become breakers. Only a dozen firm kicks brought you to where you could roll over and double up; your shin struck coral with a lovely agony and you stood in foam and waded ashore. You gained the wet sand, hard sand, and ultimately with two more paces powered by bravado, you crossed high-water mark and lay in the dry sand, unable to move.

You lay in the sand, and before you were able to move or to think, you were able to feel a triumph—a triumph because you were alive and knew that much without thinking at all.

When you *were* able to think, your first thought was of the gun, and the first move you were able to make was to let go at last of the thing. You had nearly died because you had not let it go before; without it you would not have been burdened and you would not have panicked. You had (you began to understand) kept it because someone else would have had to retrieve it—easily enough—and you could not have stood the laughter. You had almost died because They might laugh at you.

This was the beginning of the dissection, analysis, study of the monster. It began then; it had never finished. Some of what you had learned from it was merely important; some of the rest—vital.

You had learned, for example, never to swim farther with a snorkel than you could swim back without one. You learned never to burden yourself with the unnecessary in an emergency; even a hand or a foot might be as expendable as a gun; pride was expendable, dignity was. You learned never to dive alone, even if they laugh at you, even if you have to shoot a fish yourself and say afterwards "we" shot it. Most of all, you learned that fear has many fingers, and one of them—a simple one, made of too great a concentration of carbon dioxide in your blood, as from too rapid breathing in and out of the same tube—is not really fear at all but feels like fear, and can turn into panic and kill you.

Listen, you want to say, listen, there isn't anything wrong with such an experience or with all the study it leads to, because a man who can learn enough from it could become fit enough, cautious enough, foresighted, modest, teachable enough to be chosen, to be qualified for——

You lose the thought, or turn it away, because the sick man feels that cold touch deep inside, feels it right now, feels it beyond ignoring, above and beyond anything that you, with all your experience and certainty, could explain to him even if he would listen, which he won't. Make him, then; tell him the cold touch is some simple explainable thing like anoxemia, like gladness even: some triumph that he will be able to appreciate when his head is working right again.

Triumph? Here he's alive after . . . whatever it is, and that doesn't seem to be triumph enough, though it was in the Grenadines, and that other time, when he got the bends, saved his own life, saved two other lives. Now, somehow, it's not the same: there seems to be a reason why just being alive afterwards isn't a triumph.

Why not triumph? Because not twelve, not twenty, not even thirty minutes is it taking the satellite to complete its eighth-of-an-orbit: fifty minutes are gone, and still there's a slice of shadow yonder. It is this, *this* which is placing the cold finger upon his heart, and he doesn't know why, he doesn't know why, he *will* not know why; he is afraid he shall when his head is working again . . .

Oh, where's the kid? Where is any way to busy the mind, apply it to something, anything else but the watch hand which outruns the moon? Here, kid: come over here—what you got there?

If you were the kid, then you'd forgive everything and hunker down with your new model, not a toy, not a helicopter or a rocket-plane, but the big one, the one that looks like an overgrown cartridge. It's so big even as a model that even an angry sick man wouldn't call it a toy. A giant cartridge, but watch: the lower four-fifths is Alpha—all muscle—over a million pounds thrust. (Snap it off, throw it away.) Half the rest is Beta—all brains—it puts you on your way. (Snap it off, throw it away.) And now look at the polished fraction which is left. Touch a control somewhere and see—see? it has wings—wide triangular wings. This is Gamma, the one with wings, and on its back is a small sausage; it is a moth with a sausage on its back. The sausage (click! it comes free) is Delta. Delta is the last, the smallest: Delta is the way home.

What will they think of next? Quite a toy. Quite a toy. Beat it, kid. The satellite is almost overhead, the sliver of shadow going—going—almost gone and . . . gone.

Check: 0459. Fifty-nine minutes?, give or take a few. Times eight . . . 472 . . . is, uh, seven hours fifty-two minutes.

Seven hours fifty-two minutes? Why there isn't a satellite round earth with a period like that. In all the solar systems there's only . . .

The cold finger turns fierce, implacable.

The east is paling and the sick man turns to it, wanting the light, the sun, an end to questions whose answers couldn't be looked upon. The sea stretches endlessly out to the growing light, and endlessly, somewhere out of sight, the surf roars. The paling east bleaches the sandy hilltops and throws the line of footprints into aching relief. That would be the buddy, the sick man knows, gone for help. He cannot at the moment recall who the buddy is, but in time he will, and meanwhile the footprints make him less alone.

The sun's upper rim thrusts itself above the horizon with a flash of green, instantly gone. There is no dawn, just the green flash and then a clear white blast of unequivocal sunup. The sea could not be whiter, more still, if it were frozen and snow-blanketed. In the west, stars still blaze, and overhead the crinkled satellite is scarcely abashed by the growing light. A formless jumble in the valley below begins to resolve itself into a sort of tent-city, or installation of some kind, with tube-like and sail-like buildings. This would have meaning for the sick man if his head were working right. Soon, it would. Will. (Oh . . .)

The sea, out on the horizon just under the rising sun, is behaving strangely, for in that place where properly belongs a pool of unbearable brightness, there is instead a notch of brown. It is as if the white fire of the sun is drinking dry the sea—for look, look! the notch becomes a bow and the bow a crescent, racing ahead of the sunlight, white sea ahead of it and behind it a cocoa-dry stain spreading across and down toward where he watches.

Beside the finger of fear which lies on him, another finger places itself, and another, making ready for that clutch, that grip, that ultimate insane squeeze of panic. Yet beyond that again, past that squeeze when it comes, to be savored if the squeeze is only fear and not panic, lies triumph—triumph, and a glory. It is perhaps this which constitutes his whole battle: to fit himself, prepare himself to bear the utmost that fear could do, for if he can do that, there is a triumph on the other side. But . . . not yet. Please, not yet awhile.

Something flies (or flew, or will fly—he is a little confused on this point) toward him, from the far right where the stars still shine. It is not a bird and it is unlike any aircraft on earth, for the aerodynamics are wrong. Wings so wide and so fragile would be useless, would melt and tear away in any of earth's atmosphere but the outer fringes. He sees then (because he prefers to see it so) that it is the kid's model, or part of it, and for a toy, it does very well indeed.

It is the part called Gamma, and it glides in, balancing, parallels the sand and holds away, holds away slowing, then settles, all in slow motion, throwing up graceful sheet fountains of fine sand from its skids. And it runs along the ground for an impossible distance, letting down its weight by the ounce and stingily the ounce, until *look out* until a skid *look out* fits itself into a bridged crevasse *look out, look out!* and still moving on, it settles down to the struts. Gamma then, tired, digs her wide left wingtip carefully into the racing sand, digs it in hard; and as the wing breaks off, Gamma slews, sidles, slides slowly, pointing her other triangular tentlike wing at the sky, and broadside crushes into the rocks at the valley's end.

As she rolls smashing over, there breaks from her broad back the sausage, the little Delta, which somersaults away to break its back upon the rocks, and through the broken hull, spill smashed shards of graphite from the moderator of her power pile. *Look out! Look out!* and at the same instant from the finally checked mass of Gamma there explodes a doll, which slides and tumbles into the sand, into the rocks and smashed hot graphite from the wreck of Delta.

The sick man numbly watches this toy destroy itself: what will they think of next—and with a gelid horror prays at the doll lying in the raging rubble of the atomic pile: *don't stay there, man—get away! get away! that's hot, you know?* But it seems like a night and a day and half another night before the doll staggers to its feet and, clumsy in its pressure-suit, runs away up the valley-side, climbs a sand-topped outcrop, slips, falls, lies under a slow cascade of cold ancient sand until, but for an arm and the helmet, it is buried.

The sun is high now, high enough to show the sea is not a sea, but brown plain with the frost burned off it, as now it burns away from the hills, diffusing in air and blurring the edges of the sun's disk, so that in a very few minutes there is no sun at all, but only a glare in the east. Then the valley below loses its shadows, and like an arrangement in a diorama, reveals the form and nature of the wreckage below: no tent-city this, no installation, but the true real ruin of Gamma and the eviscerated hulk of Delta. (Alpha was the muscle, Beta the brain; Gamma was a bird, but Delta, Delta was the way home.)

And from it stretches the line of footprints, to and by the sick man, above to the bluff, and gone with the sandslide which had buried him there. Whose footprints?

He knows whose, whether or not he knows that he knows, or wants to or not. He knows what satellite has (give or take a bit) a period like that (want it exactly?—it's 7.66 hours). He knows what world has such a night, and such a frosty glare by day. He knows these things as he knows how spilled radio-actives will pour the crash and mutter of surf into a man's earphones.

Say you were that kid: say, instead, at least, that you are the sick man, for they are the same; surely then you can understand why of all things, even while shattered, shocked, sick, with radiation calculated (leaving) radiation computed (arriving) and radiation past all bearing (lying in the wreckage of Delta) you would want to think of the sea. For no farmer who fingers the soil with love and knowledge, no poet who sings of it, artist, contractor, engineer, even child bursting into tears at the inexpressible beauty of a field of daffodils—none of these is as intimate with Earth as those who live on, live with, breathe and drift in its seas. So of these things you must think; with these you must dwell until you are less sick and more ready to face the truth.

The truth, then, is that the satellite fading here is Phobos, that those footprints are your own, that there is no sea here, that you have crashed and are killed and will in a moment be dead. The cold hand ready to squeeze and still your heart is not anoxia or even fear, it is death. Now, if there is something more important than this, now is the time for it to show itself.

The sick man looks at the line of his own footprints, which testify that he is alone, and at the wreckage below, which states that there is no way back, and at the white east and the mottled west and the paling bleek-like satellite above. Surf sounds in his ears. He hears his pumps. He hears what is left of his breathing. The cold clamps down and folds him round past measuring, past all limits.

Then he speaks, cries out: then with joy he takes his triumph at the other side of death, as one takes a great fish, as one completes a skilled and mighty task, rebalances at the end of some great daring leap; and as he used to say "we shot a fish" he uses no "I":

"God," he cries, dying on Mars, "God, we made it!"

Keith Laumer was the epitome, in looks and temperament, of a military man: he was not the least bit a sentimental writer. As we know, he took the mickey out of the diplomatic corps with his Retief yarns. He also wrote very good future militaristic novels. He was always a good read.

But in this story, he showed another side of himself which punched all my buttons; the sound of taps, the flag-draped coffin. It has a very simple theme: the responsibility of command.

"The Last Command" was so powerful in my eyes, that I asked Keith if I could have the television rights, which he did grant me. I have never had such a perfect vision of how a story could be turned into a half-hour show. It would have had to be made in England to give it the right tone . . . but I could see exactly how I should start it, what scenes should be included, and how the final shot ought to provoke tears from every viewer. I don't know if Keith ever realized what an impact that yarn had . . . on me, as well as others.

I have never had a chance to write a scenario for "The Last Command," but with today's computer graphics, it'd be a snap. So I unquestionably recommend that for inclusion in *My Favorite Science Fiction Story.*

—Anne McCaffrey

THE LAST COMMAND

by Keith Laumer

I come to awareness, sensing a residual oscillation traversing my hull from an arbitrarily designated heading of 035. From the damping rate I compute that the shock was of intensity 8.7, emanating from a source within the limits 72 meters/46 meters. I activate my primary screens, trigger a return salvo. There is no response. I engage reserve energy cells, bring my secondary battery to bear—futilely. It is apparent that I have been ranged by the Enemy and severely damaged.

My positional sensors indicate that I am resting at an angle of 13 degrees 14 seconds, deflected from a base line at 21 points from median. I attempt to right myself, but encounter massive resistance. I activate my forward scanners, shunt power to my IR microstrobes. Not a flicker illuminates my surroundings. I am encased in utter blackness.

Now a secondary shock wave approaches, rocks me with an intensity of 8.2. It is apparent that I must withdraw from my position—but my drive trains remain inert under full thrust. I shift to base emergency power, try again. Pressure mounts; I sense my awareness fading under the intolerable strain; then, abruptly, resistance falls off and I am in motion.

It is not the swift maneuvering of full drive, however; I inch forward, as if restrained by massive barriers. Again I attempt to penetrate the surrounding darkness, and this time perceive great irregular outlines shot through with fracture planes. I probe cautiously, then more vigorously, encountering incredible densities.

I channel all available power to a single ranging pulse, direct it upward. The indication is so at variance with all experience that I repeat the test at a new angle. Now I must accept the fact: I am buried under 207.6 meters of solid rock!

I direct my attention to an effort to orient myself to my uniquely desperate situation. I run through an action-status checklist of thirty thousand items, feel dismay at the extent of power loss. My main cells are almost completely drained, my reserve units at no more than .4 charge. Thus my sluggishness is explained. I review the tactical situation, recall the triumphant announcement from my commander that the Enemy forces are annihilated, that all resistance has ceased. In memory, I review the formal procession; in company with my comrades of the Dinochrome Brigade, many of us deeply scarred by Enemy action, we parade before the Grand Commandant, then assemble on the depot ramp. At command, we bring our music storage cells into phase and display our Battle Anthem. The nearby star radiates over a full spectrum, unfiltered by atmospheric haze. It is a moment of glorious triumph. Then the final command is given—

The rest is darkness. But it is apparent that the victory celebration was premature. The Enemy has counterattacked with a force that has come near to immobilizing me. The realization is shocking, but the .1 second of leisurely introspection has clarified my position. At once, I broadcast a call on Brigade Action wavelength:

"Unit LNE to Command, requesting permission to file VSR."

I wait, sense no response, call again, using full power. I sweep the enclosing volume of rock with an emergency alert warning. I tune to the all-units band, await the replies of my comrades of the Brigade. None answers. Now I must face the reality: I alone have survived the assault.

I channel my remaining power to my drive and detect a channel of reduced density. I press for it and the broken rock around me yields reluctantly. Slowly, I move forward and upward. My pain circuitry shocks my awareness center with emergency signals; I am doing irreparable damage to my overloaded neural systems, but my duty is clear: I must seek and engage the Enemy.

Emerging from behind the blast barrier, Chief Engineer Pete Reynolds of the New Devonshire Port Authority pulled off his rock mask and spat grit from his mouth.

"That's the last one; we've bottomed out at just over two hundred yards. Must have hit a hard stratum down there."

"It's almost sundown," the paunchy man beside him said shortly. "You're a day and a half behind schedule."

"We'll start backfilling now, Mr. Mayor. I'll have pilings poured by oh-nine hundred tomorrow, and with any luck the first section of pad will be in place in time for the rally."

"I'm . . ." The mayor broke off, looked startled. "I thought you told me that was the last charge to be fired . . ."

Reynolds frowned. A small but distinct tremor had shaken the ground underfoot. A few feet away, a small pebble balanced atop another toppled and fell with a faint clatter.

"Probably a big rock fragment falling," he said. At that moment, a second vibration shook the earth, stronger this time. Reynolds heard a rumble and a distant impact as rock fell from the side of the newly blasted excavation. He whirled to the control shed as the door swung back and Second Engineer Mayfield appeared.

"Take a look at this, Pete!" Reynolds went across to the hut, stepped inside. Mayfield was bending over the profiling table.

"What do you make of it?" he pointed. Superimposed on the heavy red contour representing the detonation of the shaped charge that had completed the drilling of the final pile core were two other traces, weak but distinct.

"About .1 intensity," Mayfield looked puzzled. "What . . ."

The tracking needle dipped suddenly, swept up the screen to peak at .21, dropped back. The hut trembled. A stylus fell from the edge of the table. The red face of Mayor Daugherty burst through the door.

"Reynolds, have you lost your mind? What's the idea of blasting while I'm standing out in the open? I might have been killed!"

"I'm not blasting," Reynolds snapped. "Jim, get Eaton on the line, see if they know anything." He stepped to the door, shouted.

A heavyset man in sweat-darkened coveralls swung down from the seat of a cable-lift rig. "Boss, what goes on?" he called as he came up. "Damn near shook me out of my seat!"

"I don't know. You haven't set any trim charges?"

"No, boss. I wouldn't set no charges without your say-so."

"Come on." Reynolds started out across the rubble-littered stretch of barren ground selected by the Authority as the site of the new spaceport. Halfway to the open mouth of the newly blasted pit, the ground under his feet rocked violently enough to make him stumble. A gout of dust rose from the excavation ahead. Loose rock danced on the ground. Beside him, the drilling chief grabbed his arm.

"Boss, we better get back!"

Reynolds shook him off, kept going. The drill chief swore and followed. The shaking of the ground went on, a sharp series of thumps interrupting a steady trembling.

"It's a quake!" Reynolds yelled over the low rumbling sound. He and the chief were at the rim of the core now.

"It can't be a quake, boss," the latter shouted. "Not in these formations!"

"Tell it to the geologists . . ." The rock slab they were standing on rose a foot, dropped back. Both men fell. The slab bucked like a small boat in choppy water.

"Let's get out of here!" Reynolds was up and running. Ahead, a fissure opened, gaped a foot wide. He jumped it, caught a glimpse of black depths, a glint of wet clay twenty feet below—

A hoarse scream stopped him in his tracks. He spun, saw the drill chief down, a heavy splinter of rock across his legs. He jumped to him, heaved at the rock. There was blood on the man's shirt. The chief's hands beat the dusty rock before him.

Then other men were there, grunting, sweaty hands gripping beside Reynolds'. The ground rocked. The roar from under the earth had risen to a deep, steady rumble. They lifted the rock aside, picked up the injured man and stumbled with him to the aid shack.

The mayor was there, white-faced.

"What is it, Reynolds? If you're responsible—"

"Shut up!" Reynolds brushed him aside, grabbed the phone, punched keys.

"Eaton! What have you got on this temblor?"

"Temblor, hell." The small face on the four-inch screen looked like a ruffled hen. "What in the name of Order are you doing out there? I'm reading a whole series of displacements originating from that last core of yours! What did you do, leave a pile of trim charges lying around?"

"It's a quake. Trim charges, hell! This thing's broken up two hundred yards of surface rock. It seems to be traveling north-northeast—"

"I see that; a traveling earthquake!" Eaton flapped his arms, a tiny and ridiculous figure against a background of wall charts and framed diplomas. "Well . . . do something, Reynolds! Where's Mayor Daugherty?"

"Underfoot!" Reynolds snapped, and cut off.

Outside, a layer of sunset-stained dust obscured the sweep of level plain. A rock-dozer rumbled up, ground to a halt by Reynolds. A man jumped down.

"I got the boys moving equipment out," he panted. "The thing's cutting a trail straight as a rule for the highway!" He pointed to a raised roadbed a quarter-mile away.

"How fast is it moving?"

"She's done a hundred yards; it hasn't been ten minutes yet!"

"If it keeps up another twenty minutes, it'll be into the Intermix!"

"Scratch a few million cees and six months' work then, Pete!"

"And Southside Mall's a couple miles farther."

"Hell, it'll damp out before then!"

"Maybe. Grab a field car, Dan."

"Pete!" Mayfield came up at a trot. "This thing's building! The centroid's moving on a heading of 022—"

"How far subsurface?"

"It's rising; started at two-twenty yards, and it's up to one-eighty!"

"What have we stirred up?" Reynolds stared at Mayfield as the field car skidded to a stop beside them.

"Stay with it, Jim. Give me anything new. We're taking a closer look." He climbed into the rugged vehicle.

"Take a blast truck—"

"No time!" He waved and the car gunned away into the pall of dust.

The rock car pulled to a stop at the crest of the three-level Intermix on a lay-by designed to permit tourists to enjoy the view of the site of the proposed port, a hundred feet below. Reynolds studied the progress of the quake through field glasses. From this vantage point, the path of the phenomenon was a clearly defined trail of tilted and broken rock, some of the slabs twenty feet across. As he watched, the fissure lengthened.

"It looks like a mole's trail." Reynolds handed the glasses to his companion, thumbed the Send key on the car radio.

"Jim, get Eaton and tell him to divert all traffic from the Circular south of Zone Nine. Cars are already clogging the right-of-way. The dust is visible from a mile away, and when the word gets out there's something going on, we'll be swamped."

"I'll tell him, but he won't like it!"

"This isn't politics! This thing will be into the outer pad area in another twenty minutes!"

"It won't last—"

"How deep does it read now?"

"One-five!" There was a moment's silence. "Pete, if it stays on course, it'll surface at about where you're parked!"

"Uh-huh. It looks like you can scratch one Intermix. Better tell Eaton to get a story ready for the press."

"Pete—talking about newshounds," Dan said beside him. Reynolds switched off, turned to see a man in a gay-colored driving outfit coming across from a battered Monojag sportster which had pulled up behind the rock car. A big camera case was slung across his shoulder.

"Say, what's going on down there?" he called.

"Rock slide," Reynolds said shortly. "I'll have to ask you to drive on. The road's closed . . ."

"Who're you?" The man looked belligerent.

"I'm the engineer in charge. Now pull out, brother." He

turned back to the radio. "Jim, get every piece of heavy equipment we own over here, on the double." He paused, feeling a minute trembling in the car. "The Intermix is beginning to feel it," he went on. "I'm afraid we're in for it. Whatever that thing is, it acts like a solid body boring its way through the ground. Maybe we can barricade it."

"Barricade an earthquake?"

"Yeah . . . I know how it sounds . . . but it's the only idea I've got."

"Hey . . . what's that about an earthquake?" The man in the colored suit was still there. "By gosh, I can feel it—the whole bridge is shaking!"

"Off, mister—now!" Reynolds jerked a thumb at the traffic lanes where a steady stream of cars was hurtling past. "Dan, take us over to the main track. We'll have to warn this traffic off . . ."

"Hold on, fellow," the man unlimbered his camera. "I represent the New Devon *Scope.* I have a few questions—"

"I don't have the answers," Pete cut him off as the car pulled away.

"Hah!" the man who had questioned Reynolds yelled after him. "Big shot! Think you can . . ." His voice was lost behind them.

In a modest retirees' apartment block in the coast town of Idlebreeze, forty miles from the scene of the freak quake, an old man sat in a reclining chair, half dozing before a yammering Tri-D tank.

". . . Grandpa," a sharp-voiced young woman was saying. "It's time for you to go in to bed."

"Bed? Why do I want to go to bed? Can't sleep anyway . . ." He stirred, made a pretense of sitting up, showing an interest in the Tri-D. "I'm watching this show."

"It's not a show, it's the news," a fattish boy said disgustedly. "Ma, can I switch channels—"

"Leave it alone, Bennie," the old man said. On the screen, a panoramic scene spread out, a stretch of barren ground across which a furrow showed. As he watched, it lengthened.

". . . Up here at the Intermix we have a fine view of the whole curious business, lazangemmun," the announcer chattered. "And in our opinion it's some sort of publicity stunt staged by the Port Authority to publicize their controversial Port project—"

"Ma, can I change channels?"

"Go ahead, Bennie—"

"Don't touch it," the old man said. The fattish boy reached for the control, but something in the old man's eyes stopped him.

"The traffic's still piling up here," Reynolds said into the phone. "Damn it, Jim, we'll have a major jam on our hands—"

"He won't do it, Pete! You know the Circular was his baby—the super all-weather pike that nothing could shut down. He says you'll have to handle this in the field—"

"Handle, hell! I'm talking about preventing a major disaster! And in a matter of minutes, at that!"

"I'll try again—"

"If he says no, divert a couple of the big ten-yard graders and block it off yourself. Set up field 'arcs, and keep any cars from getting in from either direction."

"Pete, that's outside your authority!"

"You heard me!"

Ten minutes later, back at ground level, Reynolds watched the boom-mounted polyarcs swinging into position at the two roadblocks a quarter of a mile apart, cutting off the threatened section of the raised expressway. A hundred yards from where he stood on the rear cargo deck of a light grader rig, a section of rock fifty feet wide rose slowly, split, fell back with a ponderous impact. One corner of it struck the massive pier supporting the extended shelf of the lay-by above. A twenty-foot splinter fell away, exposing the reinforcing-rod core.

"How deep, Jim?" Reynolds spoke over the roaring sound coming from the disturbed area.

"Just subsurface now, Pete! It ought to break through—" His voice was drowned in a rumble as the damaged pier shivered, rose up, buckled at its midpoint and collapsed, bringing down with it a large chunk of pavement and guard rail, and a single still-glowing light pole. A small car that had been parked on the doomed section was visible for an instant just before the immense slab struck. Reynolds saw it bounce aside, then disappear under an avalanche of broken concrete.

"My God, Pete—" Dan blurted. "That damned fool newshound—"

"Look!" As the two men watched, a second pier swayed, fell backward into the shadow of the span above. The roadway sagged, and two more piers snapped. With a bellow like a burst dam, a hundred-foot stretch of the road fell into the roiling dust cloud.

"Pete!" Mayfield's voice burst from the car radio. "Get out of there! I threw a reader on that thing and it's chattering . . ."

Among the piled fragments, something stirred, heaved, rising up, lifting multi-ton pieces of the broken road, thrusting them aside like so many potato chips. A dull blue radiance broke through from the broached earth, threw an eerie light on the shattered structure above. A massive, ponderously irresistible shape thrust forward through the ruins. Reynolds saw a great blue-glowing profile emerge from the rubble like a surfacing submarine, shedding a burden of broken stone, saw immense treads ten feet wide claw for purchase, saw the mighty flank brush a still standing pier, send it crashing aside.

"Pete . . . what . . . what is it—?"

"I don't know." Reynolds broke the paralysis that had gripped him. "Get us out of here, Dan, fast! Whatever it is, it's headed straight for the city!"

I emerge at last from the trap into which I had fallen, and at once encounter defensive works of considerable strength. My scanners are dulled from lack of power, but I am able to perceive open ground beyond the barrier, and farther still, at a distance of 5.7 kilometers, massive walls. Once more I transmit the Brigade Rally signal; but as before, there is no reply. I am truly alone.

I scan the surrounding area for the emanations of Enemy drive units, monitor the EM spectrum for their communications. I detect nothing; either my circuitry is badly damaged, or their shielding is superb.

I must now make a decision as to possible courses of action. Since all my comrades of the Brigade have fallen, I compute that the walls before me must be held by Enemy forces. I direct probing signals at the defenses, discover them to be of unfamiliar construction, and less formidable than they appear. I am aware of the possibility that this may be a trick of the Enemy; but my course is clear.

I re-engage my driving engines and advance on the Enemy fortress.

"You're out of your mind, Father," the stout man said. "At your age—"

"At your age, I got my nose smashed in a brawl in a bar on Aldo," the old man cut him off. "But I won the fight."

"James, you can't go at this time of night . . ." an elderly woman wailed.

"Tell them to go home." The old man walked painfully toward his bedroom door. "I've seen enough of them for today."

"Mother, you won't let him do anything foolish?"

"He'll forget about it in a few minutes; but maybe you'd better go now and let him settle down."

"Mother . . . I really think a home is the best solution."

"Yes, Grandma," the young woman nodded agreement. "After all, he's past ninety—and he has his veteran's retirement . . ."

Inside his room, the old man listened as they departed. He went to the closet, took out clothes, began dressing.

City Engineer Eaton's face was chalk-white on the screen.

"No one can blame me," he said. "How could I have known—"

"Your office ran the surveys and gave the PA the green light," Mayor Daugherty yelled.

"All the old survey charts showed was 'Disposal Area.' " Eaton threw out his hands. "I assumed—"

"As City Engineer, you're not paid to make assumptions! Ten minutes' research would have told you that was a 'Y' category area!"

"What's 'Y' category mean?" Mayfield asked Reynolds. They were standing by the field comm center, listening to the dispute. Nearby, boom-mounted Tri-D cameras hummed, recording the progress of the immense machine, its upper turret rearing forty-five feet into the air, as it ground slowly forward across smooth ground toward the city, dragging behind it a trailing festoon of twisted reinforcing iron crusted with broken concrete.

"Half-life over one hundred years," Reynolds answered shortly. "The last skirmish of the war was fought near here.

Apparently this is where they buried the radioactive equipment left over from the battle."

"But, that was more than seventy years ago—"

"There's still enough residual radiation to contaminate anything inside a quarter mile radius."

"They must have used some hellish stuff." Mayfield stared at the dull shine half a mile distant.

"Reynolds, how are you going to stop this thing?" The mayor had turned on the PA Engineer.

"Me stop it? You saw what it did to my heaviest rigs: flattened them like pancakes. You'll have to call out the military on this one, Mr. Mayor."

"Call in Federation forces? Have them meddling in civic affairs?"

"The station's only sixty-five miles from here. I think you'd better call them fast. It's only moving at about three miles per hour, but it will reach the south edge of the Mall in another forty-five minutes."

"Can't you mine it? Blast a trap in its path?"

"You saw it claw its way up from six hundred feet down. I checked the specs; it followed the old excavation tunnel out. It was rubble-filled and capped with twenty-inch compressed concrete."

"It's incredible," Eaton said from the screen. "The entire machine was encased in a ten-foot shell of reinforced armocrete. It had to break out of that before it could move a foot!"

"That was just a radiation shield; it wasn't intended to restrain a Bolo Combat Unit."

"What *was,* may I inquire?" the mayor glared.

"The units were deactivated before being buried," Eaton spoke up, as if he were eager to talk. "Their circuits were fused. It's all in the report—"

"The report you should have read somewhat sooner," the mayor snapped.

"What . . . what started it up?" Mayfield looked bewildered. "For seventy years it was down there, and nothing happened!"

"Our blasting must have jarred something," Reynolds said shortly. "Maybe closed a relay that started up the old battle reflex circuit."

"You know something about these machines?" the mayor asked.

"I've read a little."

"Then speak up, man. I'll call the station, if you feel I must. What measures should I request?"

"I don't know, Mr. Mayor. As far as I know, nothing on New Devon can stop that machine now."

The mayor's mouth opened and closed. He whirled to the screen, blanked Eaton's agonized face, punched in the code for the Federation Station.

"Colonel Blane!" he blurted as a stern face came onto the screen. "We have a major emergency on our hands! I'll need everything you've got! This is the situation—"

I encounter no resistance other than the flimsy barrier, but my progress is slow. Grievous damage has been done to my main-drive sector due to overload during my escape from the trap; and the failure of my sensing circuitry has deprived me of a major portion of my external receptivity. Now my pain circuits project a continuous signal to my awareness center; but it is my duty to my commander and to my fallen comrades of the Brigade to press forward at my best speed; but my performance is a poor shadow of my former ability.

And now at last the Enemy comes into action! I sense aerial units closing at supersonic velocities; I lock my lateral batteries to them and direct salvo fire; but I sense that the arming mechanisms clatter harmlessly. The craft sweep over me, and my impotent guns elevate, track them as they release detonants that spread out in an envelopmental pattern which I, with my reduced capabilities, am powerless to avoid. The missiles strike; I sense their detonations all about me; but I suffer only trivial damage. The enemy has blundered if he thought to neutralize a Mark XXVIII Combat Unit with mere chemical explosives! But I weaken with each meter gained.

Now there is no doubt as to my course. I must press the charge and carry the walls before my reserve cells are exhausted.

From a vantage point atop a bucket rig four hundred yards from the position the great fighting machine had now reached, Pete Reynolds studied it through night glasses. A battery of beamed polyarcs pinned the giant hulk, scarred and rust-scaled, in a pool of blue-white light. A mile and a half beyond it, the walls of the Mall rose sheer from the garden setting.

"The bombers slowed it some," he reported to Eaton via scope. "But it's still making better than two miles per hour. I'd say another twenty-five minutes before it hits the main ring-wall. How's the evacuation going?"

"Badly! I get no cooperation! You'll be my witness, Reynolds, I did all I could—"

"How about the mobile batteries; how long before they'll be in position?" Reynolds cut him off.

"I've heard nothing from Federation Central—typical militaristic arrogance, not keeping me informed—but I have them on my screens. They're two miles out—say three minutes."

"I hope you made your point about N-heads."

"That's outside my province!" Eaton said sharply. "It's up to Brand to carry out this portion of the operation!"

"The HE Missiles didn't do much more than clear away the junk it was dragging," Reynolds' voice was sharp.

"I wash my hands of responsibility for civilian lives," Eaton was saying when Reynolds shut him off, changed channels.

"Jim, I'm going to try to divert it," he said crisply. "Eaton's sitting on his political fence; the Feds are bringing artillery up, but I don't expect much from it. Technically, Brand needs Sector OK to use nuclear stuff, and he's not the boy to stick his neck out—"

"Divert it how? Pete, don't take any chances—"

Reynolds laughed shortly. "I'm going to get around it and drop a shaped drilling charge in its path. Maybe I can knock a tread off. With luck, I might get its attention on me, and draw it away from the Mall. There are still a few thousand people over there, glued to their Tri-Ds. They think it's all a swell show."

"Pete, you can't walk up on that thing! It's hot . . ." He broke off. "Pete—there's some kind of nut here—he claims he has to talk to you; says he knows something about that damned juggernaut. Shall I send . . . ?"

Reynolds paused with his hand on the cut-off switch. "Put him on," he snapped. Mayfield's face moved aside and an ancient, bleary-eyed visage stared out at him. The tip of the old man's tongue touched his dry lips.

"Son, I tried to tell this boy here, but he wouldn't listen—"

"What have you got, old-timer?" Pete cut in. "Make it fast."

"My name's Sanders. James Sanders. I'm . . . I was with the Planetary Volunteer Scouts, back in '71—"

"Sure, dad," Pete said gently. "I'm sorry, I've got a little errand to run—"

"Wait . . ." The old man's face worked. "I'm old, son—too damned old. I know. But bear with me. I'll try to say it straight. I was with Hayle's squadron at Toledo. Then afterwards, they shipped us . . . but hell, you don't care about that! I keep wandering, son; can't help it. What I mean to say is—I was in on that last scrap, right here at New Devon—only we didn't call it New Devon then. Called it Hellport. Nothing but bare rock and Enemy emplacements . . ."

"You were talking about the battle, Mr. Sanders," Pete said tensely. "Go on with that part."

"Lieutenant Sanders," the oldster said. "Sure, I was Acting Brigade Commander. See, our major was hit at Toledo—and after Tommy Chee stopped a sidewinder . . ."

"Stick to the point, Lieutenant!"

"Yes, sir!" the old man pulled himself together with an obvious effort. "I took the Brigade in; put out flankers, and ran the Enemy into the ground. We mopped 'em up in a thirty-three-hour running fight that took us from over by Crater Bay all the way down here to Hellport. When it was over, I'd lost six units, but the Enemy was done. They gave us Brigade Honors for that action. And then . . ."

"Then what?"

"Then the triple-dyed yellow-bottoms at Headquarters put out the order the Brigade was to be scrapped; said they were too hot to make decon practical. Cost too much, they said! So after the final review . . ." He gulped, blinked. "They planted 'em deep, two hundred meters, and poured in special High-R concrete."

"And packed rubble in behind them," Reynolds finished for him. "All right, Lieutenant, I believe you! But what started that machine on a rampage?"

"Should have known they couldn't hold down a Bolo Mark XXVIII!" The old man's eyes lit up. "Take more than a few million tons of rock to stop Lenny when his battle board was lit!"

"Lenny?"

"That's my old Command Unit out there, son. I saw the markings on the 3-D. Unit LNE of the Dinochrome Brigade!"

"Listen!" Reynolds snapped out. "Here's what I intend to try . . ." he outlined his plan.

"Ha!" Sanders snorted. "It's quite a notion, mister, but Lenny won't give it a sneeze."

"You didn't come here to tell me we were licked," Reynolds cut in. "How about Brand's batteries?"

"Hell, son, Lenny stood up to point-blank Hellbore fire on Toledo, and—"

"Are you telling me there's nothing we can do?"

"What's that? No, son, that's not what I'm saying . . ."

"Then what!"

"Just tell these johnnies to get out of my way, mister. I think I can handle him."

At the field Comm hut, Pete Reynolds watched as the man who had been Lieutenant Sanders of the Volunteer Scouts pulled shiny black boots over his thin ankles, and stood. The blouse and trousers of royal blue polyon hung on his spare frame like wash on a line. He grinned, a skull's grin.

"It doesn't fit like it used to, but Lenny will recognize it. It'll help. Now, if you've got that power pack ready . . ."

Mayfield handed over the old-fashioned field instrument Sanders had brought in with him.

"It's operating, sir—but I've already tried everything I've got on that infernal machine; I didn't get a peep out of it."

Sanders winked at him. "Maybe I know a couple of tricks you boys haven't heard about." He slung the strap over his bony shoulder and turned to Reynolds.

"Guess we better get going, mister. He's getting close."

In the rock car Sanders leaned close to Reynolds' ear. "Told you those Federal guns wouldn't scratch Lenny. They're wasting their time."

Reynolds pulled the car to a stop at the crest of the road, from which point he had a view of the sweep of ground leading across to the city's edge. Lights sparkled all across the towers of New Devon. Close to the walls, the converging fire of the ranked batteries of infinite repeaters drove into the glowing bulk of the machine, which plowed on, undeterred. As he watched, the firing ceased.

"Now, let's get in there, before they get some other scheme going," Sanders said.

The rock car crossed the rough ground, swung wide to come

up on the Bolo from the left side. Behind the hastily rigged radiation cover, Reynolds watched the immense silhouette grow before him.

"I knew they were big," he said. "But to see one up close like this—" He pulled to a stop a hundred feet from the Bolo.

"Look at the side ports," Sanders said, his voice crisper now. "He's firing anti-personnel charges—only his plates are flat. If they weren't, we wouldn't have gotten within half a mile." He unclipped the microphone and spoke into it:

"Unit LNE, break off action and retire to ten-mile line!"

Reynolds' head jerked around to stare at the old man. His voice had rung with vigor and authority as he spoke the command.

The Bolo ground slowly ahead. Sanders shook his head, tried again.

"No answer, like that fella said. He must be running on nothing but memories now . . ." He reattached the microphone and before Reynolds could put out a hand, had lifted the anti-R cover and stepped off on the ground.

"Sanders—get back in here!" Reynolds yelled.

"Never mind, son. I've got to get in close. Contact induction." He started toward the giant machine. Frantically, Reynolds started the car, slammed it into gear, pulled forward.

"Better stay back," Sanders' voice came from his field radio. "This close, that screening won't do you much good."

"Get in the car!" Reynolds roared. "That's hard radiation!"

"Sure; feels funny, like a sunburn, about an hour after you come in from the beach and start to think maybe you got a little too much." He laughed. "But I'll get to him . . ."

Reynolds braked to a stop, watched the shrunken figure in the baggy uniform as it slogged forward, leaning as against a sleet-storm.

"I'm up beside him," Sanders' voice came through faintly on the field radio. "I'm going to try to swing up on his side. Don't feel like trying to chase him any farther."

Through the glasses, Reynolds watched the small figure, dwarfed by the immense bulk of the fighting machine as he tried, stumbled, tried again, swung up on the flange running across the rear quarter inside the churning bogie wheel.

"He's up," he reported. "Damned wonder the track didn't get him before . . ."

Clinging to the side of the machine, Sanders lay for a moment, bent forward across the flange. Then he pulled himself up, wormed his way forward to the base of the rear quarter turret, wedged himself against it. He unslung the communicator, removed a small black unit, clipped it to the armor; it clung, held by a magnet. He brought the microphone up to his face.

In the Comm shack Mayfield leaned toward the screen, his eyes squinted in tension. Across the field Reynolds held the glasses fixed on the man lying across the flank of the Bolo. They waited.

The walls are before me, and I ready myself for a final effort, but suddenly I am aware of trickle currents flowing over my outer surface. Is this some new trick of the Enemy? I tune to the wave-energies, trace the source. They originate at a point in contact with my aft port armor. I sense modulation, match receptivity to a computed pattern. And I hear a voice:

"Unit LNE, break it off, Lenny. We're pulling back now, boy! This is Command to LNE; pull back to ten miles. If you read me, Lenny, swing to port and halt."

I am not fooled by the deception. The order appears correct, but the voice is not that of my Commander. Briefly I regret that I cannot spare energy to direct a neutralizing power flow at the device the Enemy has attached to me. I continue my charge.

"Unit LNE! Listen to me, boy; maybe you don't recognize my voice, but it's me! You see—some time has passed. I've gotten old. My voice has changed some, maybe. But it's me! Make a port turn, Lenny. Make it now!"

I am tempted to respond to the trick, for something in the false command seems to awaken secondary circuits which I sense have been long stilled. But I must not be swayed by the cleverness of the Enemy. My sensing circuitry has faded further as my energy cells drain; but I know where the Enemy lies. I move forward, but I am filled with agony, and only the memory of my comrades drives me on.

"Lenny, answer me. Transmit on the old private band—the one we agreed on. Nobody but me knows it, remember?"

Thus the Enemy seeks to beguile me into diverting precious power. But I will not listen.

"Lenny—not much time left. Another minute and you'll be into the walls. People are going to die. Got to stop you, Lenny. Hot here. My God, I'm hot. Not breathing too well, now. I can feel it; cutting through me like knives. You took a load of

Enemy power, Lenny; and now I'm getting my share. Answer me, Lenny. Over to you . . ."

It will require only a tiny allocation of power to activate a communication circuit. I realize that it is only an Enemy trick, but I compute that by pretending to be deceived, I may achieve some trivial advantage. I adjust circuitry accordingly, and transmit:

"Unit LNE to Command. Contact with Enemy defensive line imminent. Request supporting fire!"

"Lenny . . . you can hear me! Good boy, Lenny! Now make a turn, to port. Walls . . . close . . ."

"Unit LNE to Command. Request positive identification; transmit code 685749."

"Lenny—I can't . . . don't have code blanks. But it's me . . ."

"In absence of recognition code, your transmission disregarded." *I send. And now the walls loom high above me. There are many lights, but I see them only vaguely. I am nearly blind now.*

"Lenny—less'n two hundred feet to go. Listen, Lenny. I'm climbing down. I'm going to jump down, Lenny, and get around under your force scanner pickup. You'll see me, Lenny. You'll know me then."

The false transmission ceases. I sense a body moving across my side. The gap closes. I detect movement before me, and in automatic reflex fire anti-P charges before I recall that I am unarmed.

A small object has moved out before me, and taken up a position between me and the wall behind which the Enemy conceal themselves. It is dim, but appears to have the shape of a man . . .

I am uncertain. My alert center attempts to engage inhibitory circuitry which will force me to halt, but it lacks power. I can override it. But still I am unsure. Now I must take a last risk, I must shunt power to my forward scanner to examine this obstacle more closely. I do so, and it leaps into greater clarity. It is indeed a man—and it is enclothed in regulation blues of the Volunteers. Now, closer, I see the face, and through the pain of my great effort, I study it . . .

"He's backed against the wall," Reynolds said hoarsely. "It's still coming. Fifty feet to go—"

"You were a fool, Reynolds!" the mayor barked. "A fool to stake everything on that old dotard's crazy ideas!"

"Hold it!" As Reynolds watched, the mighty machine slowed, halted, ten feet from the sheer wall before it. For a moment it sat, as though puzzled. Then it backed, halted again, pivoted ponderously to the left and came about.

On its side, a small figure crept up, fell across the lower gun deck. The Bolo surged into motion, retracing its route across the artillery-scarred gardens.

"He's turned it," Reynolds let his breath out with a shuddering sigh. "It's headed out for open desert. It might get twenty miles before it finally runs out of steam."

The strange voice that was the Bolo's came from the big panel before Mayfield:

Command . . . Unit LNE reports main power cells drained, secondary cells drained; now operating at .037 percent efficiency, using Final Emergency Power. Request advice as to range to be covered before relief maintenance available."

"It's a long, long way, Lenny . . . " Sanders' voice was a bare whisper. *"But I'm coming with you . . . "*

Then there was only the crackle of static. Ponderously, like a great, mortally stricken animal, the Bolo moved through the ruins of the fallen roadway, heading for the open desert.

"That damned machine," the mayor said in a hoarse voice. "You'd almost think it was alive."

"You would at that," Pete Reynolds said.

"Day Million" is an odd story, full of fun and sly self-referentiality. I love it for its wry, sarcastic voice, and the curious authority of its teller, who presents himself as a cultural interpreter between the distant future and now. He doesn't have a lot of respect for "now."

I picked this story immediately, when the editors queried me, because, coincidentally, an interviewer a few days before had asked what my favorite sf story was, and I instantly came up with "Day Million." There are lots of older stories by Asimov, Bradbury, Clarke, and Heinlein, that rang my chimes with a definite bong! when I was young. But I read "Day Million" as an adult who was studying the craft of writing and trying to make a living at it, and it was exactly the kind of thing I wanted to write—satisfying as science fiction but not *just* that. Stylistically original; experimental but still accessible.

In a very short span it created characters and a world unlike anything I'd ever seen, and it reads as if the author had a rollicking good time doing it.

—Joe Haldeman

DAY MILLION

by Frederik Pohl

On this day I want to tell you about, which will be about ten thousand years from now, there were a boy, a girl, and a love story.

Now, although I haven't said much so far, none of it is true. The boy was not what you and I would normally think of as a boy, because he was a hundred and eighty-seven years old. Nor was the girl a girl, for other reasons. And the love story did not entail that sublimation of the urge to rape, and concurrent postponement of the instinct to submit, which we at present understand in such matters. You won't care much for this story if you don't grasp these facts at once. If, however, you will make the effort you'll likely enough find it jam-packed, chock-full and tiptop-crammed with laughter, tears and poignant sentiment which may, or may not, be worthwhile. The reason the girl was not a girl was that she was a boy.

How angrily you recoil from the page! You say, who the hell wants to read about a pair of queers? Calm yourself. Here are no hot-breathing secrets of perversion for the coterie trade. In fact, if you were to see this girl you would not guess that she was in any sense a boy. Breasts, two; reproductive organs, female. Hips, callipygean; face hairless, supraorbital lobes nonexistent. You would term her female on sight, although it is true that you might wonder just what species she was a female of, being confused by the tail, the silky pelt and the gill slits behind each ear.

Now you recoil again. Cripes, man, take my word for it. This is a sweet kid, and if you, as a normal male, spent as much as an hour in a room with her you would bend heaven and Earth to get her in the sack. Dora—we will call her that; her "name" was omicron-Dibase seven-group-totter-oot S Doradus 5314, the last part of which is a color specification corresponding to a shade of green—Dora, I say, was feminine, charming and cute. I admit she doesn't sound that way. She was, as you might put it, a dancer. Her art involved qualities of intellection and expertise of a very high order, requiring both tremendous natural capacities and endless practice; it was performed in null gravity and I can best describe it by saying that it was something like the performance of a contortionist and something like classical ballet, maybe resembling Danilova's dying swan. It was also pretty damned sexy. In a symbolic way, to be sure; but face it, most of the things we call "sexy" are symbolic, you know, except perhaps an exhibitionist's open clothing. On Day Million when Dora danced, the people who saw her panted, and you would too.

About this business of her being a boy. It didn't matter to her audiences that genetically she was a male. It wouldn't matter to you, if you were among them, because you wouldn't know it—not unless you took a biopsy cutting of her flesh and put it under an electron microscope to find the XY chromosome—and it didn't matter to them because they didn't care. Through techniques which are not only complex but haven't yet been discovered, these people were able to determine a great deal about the aptitudes and easements of babies quite a long time before they were born—at about the second horizon of cell division, to be exact, when the segmenting egg is becoming a free blastocyst—and then they naturally helped those aptitudes along. Wouldn't we? If we find a child with an aptitude for music we give him a scholarship to Juilliard. If they found a child whose aptitudes were for being a woman, they made him one. As sex had long been dissociated from reproduction this was relatively easy to do and caused no trouble, and no, or at least very little, comment.

How much is "very little"? Oh, about as much as would be caused by our own tampering with divine will by filling a tooth. Less than would be caused by wearing a hearing aid. Does it still sound awful? Then look closely at the next busty babe you meet and reflect that she may be a Dora, for adults who are genetically male but somatically females are far from unknown even in our own time. An accident of environment in the womb overwhelms the blueprints of heredity. The difference is that with us it happens only by accident and we don't know about it except rarely, after close study; whereas the people of Day Million did it often, on purpose, because they wanted to.

Well, that's enough to tell you about Dora. It would only confuse you to add that she was seven feet tall and smelled of peanut butter. Let us begin our story.

On Day Million, Dora swam out of her house, entered a transportation tube, was sucked briskly to the surface in its flow of water and ejected in its plume of spray to an elastic platform in front of her—ah—call it her rehearsal hall. "Oh, hell!" she cried in pretty confusion, reaching out to catch her balance and finding herself tumbled against a total stranger, whom we will call Don.

They met cute. Don was on his way to have his legs renewed. Love was the farthest thing from his mind. But when, absentmindedly taking a shortcut across the landing platform for submarinites and finding himself drenched, he discovered his arms full of the loveliest girl he had ever seen, he knew at once they were meant for each other. "Will you marry me?" he asked. She said softly, "Wednesday," and the promise was like a caress.

Don was tall, muscular, bronze and exciting. His name was no more Don than Dora's was Dora, but the personal part of it was Adonis in tribute to his vibrant maleness, and so we will call him Don for short. His personality color code, in angstrom units, was 5290, or only a few degrees bluer than Dora's 5314—a measure of what they had intuitively discovered at first sight: that they possessed many affinities of taste and interest.

I despair of telling you exactly what it was that Don did for a living—I don't mean for the sake of making money, I mean for the sake of giving purpose and meaning to his life, to keep him from going off his nut with boredom—except to say that it involved a lot of traveling. He traveled in interstellar spaceships. In order to make a spaceship go really fast, about thirty-one male and seven genetically female human beings had to do certain things, and Don was one of the thirty-one. Actually, he contemplated options. This involved a lot of exposure to radiation flux—not so much from his own station in the propulsive system as in the spillover from the next stage, where a genetic female preferred selections, and the subnuclear particles making the selections she preferred demolished themselves in a shower of quanta. Well, you don't give a rat's ass for that, but it meant that Don had to be clad at all times in a skin of light, resilient, extremely strong copper-colored metal. I have already mentioned this, but you probably thought I meant he was sunburned.

More than that, he was a cybernetic man. Most of his ruder parts had been long since replaced with mechanisms of vastly more permanence and use. A cadmium centrifuge, not a heart, pumped his blood. His lungs moved only when he wanted to speak out loud, for a cascade of osmotic filters rebreathed oxygen out of his own wastes. In a way, he probably would have looked peculiar to a man from the twentieth century, with his glowing eyes and seven-fingered hands. But to himself, and of course to Dora, he looked mighty manly and grand. In the course of his voyages Don had circled Proxima Centauri, Procyon and the puzzling worlds of Mira Ceti; he had carried agricultural templates to the planets of Canopus and brought back warm, witty pets from the pale companion of Aldebaran. Blue-hot or red-cool, he had seen a thousand stars and their ten thousand planets. He had, in fact, been traveling the star lanes, with only brief leaves on Earth, for pushing two centuries. But you don't care about that, either. It is people who make stories, not the circumstances they find themselves in, and you want to hear about these two people. Well, they made it. The great thing they had for each other grew and flowered and burst into fruition on Wednesday, just as Dora had promised. They met at the encoding room, with a couple of well-wishing friends apiece to cheer them on, and while their identities were being taped and stored they smiled and whispered to each other and bore the jokes of their friends with blushing repartee. Then they exchanged their mathematical analogues and went away, Dora to her dwelling beneath the surface of the sea and Don to his ship.

It was an idyll, really. They lived happily ever after—or anyway, until they decided not to bother any more and died.

Of course, they never set eyes on each other again.

Oh, I can see you now, you eaters of charcoal-broiled steak, scratching an incipient bunion with one hand and holding this story with the other, while the stereo plays d'Indy or Monk. You don't believe a word of it, do you? Not for a minute. People wouldn't live like that, you say with a grunt as you get up to put fresh ice in a drink.

And yet there's Dora, hurrying back through the flushing commuter pipes toward her underwater home (she prefers it there; has had herself somatically altered to breathe the stuff). If I tell you with what sweet fulfillment she fits the recorded analogue of Don into the symbol manipulator, hooks herself in and turns herself on . . . if I try to tell you any of that you will simply stare. Or glare; and grumble, what the hell kind of love-making is this? And yet I assure you, friend, I really do assure you that Dora's ecstasies are as creamy and passionate as any of James Bond's lady spies', and one hell of a lot more so than anything you are going to find in "real life." Go ahead, glare and grumble. Dora doesn't care. If she thinks of you at all, her thirty-times-great-great-grandfather, she thinks you're a pretty primordial sort of brute. You are. Why, Dora is farther removed from you than you are from the australopithecines of five thousand centuries ago. You could not swim a second in the strong currents of her life. You don't think progress goes in a straight line, do you? Do you recognize that it is an ascending, accelerating, maybe even exponential curve? It takes hell's own time to get started, but when it goes it goes like a bomb. And you, you Scotch-drinking steak eater in your relaxacizing chair, you've just barely lighted the primacord of the fuse. What is it now, the six or seven hundred thousandth day after Christ? Dora lives in Day Million. Ten thousand years from now. Her body fats are polyunsaturated, like Crisco. Her wastes are hemodialyzed out of her bloodstream while she sleeps—that means she doesn't have to go to the bathroom. On whim to pass a slow half-hour, she can command more energy than the entire nation of Portugal can spend today, and use it to launch a weekend satellite or remold a crater on the moon. She loves Don very much. She keeps his every gesture, mannerism, nuance, touch of hand, thrill of intercourse, passion of kiss stored in symbolic-mathematical form. And when she wants him, all she has to do is turn the machine on and she has him.

And Don, of course, has Dora. Adrift on a sponson city a few hundred yards over her head, or orbiting Arcturus fifty light-years away, Don has only to command his own symbol-manipulator to rescue Dora from the ferrite files and bring her to life for him, and there she is; and rapturously, tirelessly they love all night. Not in the flesh, of course; but then his flesh has been extensively altered and it wouldn't really be much fun. He doesn't need the flesh for pleasure. Genital organs feel nothing. Neither do hands or breasts, or lips; they are only receptors, accepting and transmitting impulses. It is the brain that feels; it is the interpretation of those impulses that make agony or orgasm, and Don's symbol-manipulator gives him the analogue of cuddling, the analogue of kissing, the analogue of wild, ardent hours with the eternal, exquisite and incorruptible analogue of Dora. Or Diane. Or sweet Rose, or laughing Alicia; for to be sure, they have each of them exchanged analogues before, and will again.

Rats, you say, it looks crazy to me. And you—with your after-shave lotion and your little red car, pushing papers across a desk all day and chasing tail all night—tell me, just how the hell do you think you would look to Tiglath-Pileser, say, or Attila the Hun?

C.M. Kornbluth was not only a close friend but a greatly admired colleague. When he died, shockingly prematurely, the field of science fiction lost one of its most graceful and inventive writers. By his mid-thirties Cyril had given us dozens of wonderful stories—"The Marching Morons," "The Luckiest Man in Denv," "Gomez," and many more—but the list ended there, because that was when he ran to catch a train one morning and dropped dead of a heart attack on the station platform.

Of all his stories, "The Little Black Bag" is my favorite. My reasons are personal; I feel I can claim a little bit of responsibility for the story's existence. One day at lunch Cyril complained to me that he didn't have an idea for a new story. I was able to remind him that, some time earlier, he had said he'd like to do something about future medical instruments accidentally arriving in our present. "Oh," he said, blinking at me, "right." And he went away, and the next time I saw him he was bearing the finished manuscript of "The Little Black Bag."

—Frederik Pohl

THE LITTLE BLACK BAG

by C.M. Kornbluth

Old Dr. Full felt the winter in his bones as he limped down the alley. It was the alley and the back door he had chosen rather than the sidewalk and the front door because of the brown paper bag under his arm. He knew perfectly well that the flat-faced, stringy-haired women of his street and their gap-toothed, sour-smelling husbands did not notice if he brought a bottle of cheap wine to his room. They all but lived on the stuff themselves, varied with whiskey when pay checks were boosted by overtime. But Dr. Full, unlike them, was ashamed. One of the neighborhood dogs—a mean little black one he knew and hated, with its teeth always bared and always snarling with menace—hurled at his legs through a hole in the board fence that lined his path. Dr. Full flinched, then swung his leg in what was to have been a satisfying kick to the animal's gaunt ribs. But the winter in his bones weighed down the leg. His foot failed to clear a half-buried brick, and he sat down abruptly, cursing. When he smelled unbottled wine and realized his brown paper package had slipped from under his arm and smashed, his curses died on his lips. The snarling black dog was circling him at a yard's distance, tensely stalking, but he ignored it in the greater disaster.

With stiff fingers as he sat on the filth of the alley, Dr. Full unfolded the brown paper bag's top, which had been crimped over, grocer-wise. The early autumnal dusk had come; he could not see plainly what was left. He lifted out the jug-handled top of his half gallon, and some fragments, and then the bottom of the bottle. Dr. Full was far too occupied to exult as he noted that there was a good pint left. He had a problem, and emotions could be deferred until the fitting time.

The dog closed in, its snarl rising in pitch. He set down the bottom of the bottle and pelted the dog with the curved triangular glass fragments of its top. One of them connected, and the dog ducked back through the fence, howling. Dr. Full then placed a razor-like edge of the half-gallon bottle's foundation to his lips and drank from it as though it were a giant's cup. Twice he had to put it down to rest his arms, but in one minute he had swallowed the pint of wine.

He thought of rising to his feet and walking through the alley to his room, but a flood of well-being drowned the notion. It was, after all, inexpressibly pleasant to sit there and feel the frost-hardened mud of the alley turn soft, or seem to, and to feel the winter evaporating from his bones under a warmth which spread from his stomach through his limbs.

A three-year-old girl in a cut-down winter coat squeezed through the same hole in the board fence from which the black dog had sprung its ambush. Gravely she toddled up to Dr. Full and inspected him with her dirty forefinger in her mouth. Dr. Full's happiness had been providentially made complete; he had been supplied with an audience.

"Ah, my dear," he said hoarsely. And then: "Preposserous accusation. 'If that's what you call evidence,' I should have told them, 'you better stick to your doctoring.' I should have told them: 'I was here before your County Medical Society. And the License Commissioner never proved a thing on me. So, gennulmen, doesn't it stand to reason? I appeal to you as fellow memmers of a great profession—' "

The little girl, bored, moved away, picking up one of the triangular pieces of glass to play with as she left. Dr. Full forgot her immediately, and continued to himself earnestly: "But so help me, they *couldn't* prove a thing. Hasn't a man got any *rights?*" He brooded over the question, of whose answer he was so sure, but on which the Committee on Ethics of the County Medical Society had been equally certain. The winter was creeping into his bones again, and he had no money and no more wine.

Dr. Full pretended to himself that there was a bottle of whiskey somewhere in the fearful litter of his room. It was an old and cruel trick he played on himself when he simply had to be galvanized into getting up and going home. He might freeze there in the alley. In his room he would be bitten by bugs and would cough at the moldy reek from his sink, but he would not freeze and be cheated of the hundreds of bottles of wine that he still might drink, the thousands of hours of glowing content he still might feel. He thought about that bottle of whiskey—was it back of a mounded heap of medical journals? No; he had looked there last time. Was it under the sink, shoved well to the rear, behind the rusty drain? The cruel trick began to play itself out again. Yes, he told himself with mounting excitement, yes, it might be! Your memory isn't so good nowadays, he told himself with rueful good fellowship. You know perfectly well you might have bought a bottle of whiskey and shoved it behind the sink drain for a moment just like this.

The amber bottle, the crisp snap of the sealing as he cut it, the pleasurable exertion of starting the screw cap on its threads, and then the refreshing tangs in his throat, the warmth in his stomach, the dark, dull happy oblivion of drunkenness—they became real to him. You *could* have, you know! You *could* have! he told himself. With the blessed conviction growing in his mind—It *could* have happened, you know! It *could* have!—he struggled to his right knee. As he did, he heard a yelp behind him, and curiously craned his neck around while resting. It was the little girl; who had cut her hand quite badly on her toy, the piece of glass. Dr. Full could see the rilling bright blood down her coat, pooling at her feet.

He almost felt inclined to defer the image of the amber bottle for her, but not seriously. He knew that it was there, shoved well to the rear under the sink, behind the rusty drain where he had hidden it. He would have a drink and then magnanimously return to help the child. Dr. Full got to his other knee and then his feet, and proceeded at a rapid totter down the littered alley toward his room, where he would hunt with calm optimism at first for the bottle that was not there, then with anxiety, and then with frantic violence. He would hurl books and dishes about before he was done looking for the amber bottle of whiskey, and finally would beat his swollen knuckles against the brick wall until old scars on them opened and his thick old blood oozed over his hands. Last of all, he would sit down somewhere on the floor, whimpering, and would plunge into the abyss of purgative nightmare that was his sleep.

After twenty generations of shilly-shallying and "we'll cross that bridge when we come to it," genus homo had bred himself into an impasse. Dogged biometricians had pointed out with irrefutable logic that mental subnormals were out-breeding mental normals and supernormals, and that the process was occurring on an exponential curve. Every fact that could be mustered in the argument proved the biometricians' case, and led inevitably to the conclusion that genus homo was going to wind up in a preposterous jam quite soon. If you think that had any effect on breeding practices, you do not know genus homo.

There was, of course, a sort of masking effect produced by that other exponential function, the accumulation of technological devices. A moron trained to punch an adding machine seems to be a more skillful computer than a medieval mathematician trained to count on his fingers. A moron trained to operate the twenty-first century equivalent of a linotype seems to be a better typographer than a Renaissance printer limited to a few fonts of movable type. This is also true of medical practice.

It was a complicated affair of many factors. The supernormals "improved the product" at greater speed than the subnormals degraded it, but in smaller quantity because elaborate training of their children was practiced on a custom-made basis. The fetish of higher education had some weird avatars by the twentieth generation: "colleges" where not a member of the student body could read words of three syllables; "universities" where such degrees as "Bachelor of Typewriting," "Master of Shorthand," and "Doctor of Philosophy (Card Filing)" were conferred with the traditional pomp. The handful of supernormals used such devices in order that the vast majority might keep some semblance of a social order going.

Some day the supernormals would mercilessly cross the bridge; at the twentieth generation they were standing irresolutely at its approaches wondering what had hit them. And the ghosts of twenty generations of biometricians chuckled malignantly.

It is a certain Doctor of Medicine of this twentieth generation that we are concerned with. His name was Hemingway—John Hemingway, B.Sc., M.D. He was a general practitioner, and did not hold with running to specialists with every trifling ailment. He often said as much, in approximately these words: "Now, uh, what I mean is you got a good old G.P. See what I mean? Well, uh, now a good old G.P. don't claim he knows all about lungs and glands and them things, get me? But you got a G.P., you got, uh, you got a, well, you got a . . . *all-around man!* That's what you got when you got a G.P.—you got a all-around man."

But from this, do not imagine that Dr. Hemingway was a poor doctor. He could remove tonsils or appendixes, assist at practically any confinement and deliver a living, uninjured infant, correctly diagnose hundreds of ailments, and prescribe and administer the correct medication or treatment for each. There was, in fact, only one thing he could not do in the medical line, and that was violate the ancient canons of medical ethics. And Dr. Hemingway knew better than to try.

Dr. Hemingway and a few friends were chatting one evening when the event occurred that precipitates him into our story. He had been through a hard day at the clinic, and he wished his physicist friend Walter Gillis, B.Sc., M.Sc., Ph.D., would shut up so he could tell everybody about it. But Gillis kept rambling on, in his stilted fashion: "You got to hand it to old Mike; he don't have what we call the scientific method, but you got to hand it to him. There this poor little dope is, puttering around with some glassware and I come up and I ask him, kidding of course, 'How's about a time-travel machine, Mike?' "

Dr. Gillis was not aware of it, but "Mike" had an I.Q. six times his own, and was—to be blunt—his keeper. "Mike" rode herd on the pseudo-physicists in the pseudo-laboratory, in the guise of a bottle washer. It was a social waste—but as has been mentioned before, the supernormals were still standing at the approaches to a bridge. Their irresolution led to many such preposterous situations. And it happens that "Mike," having grown frantically bored with his task, was malevolent enough to—but let Dr. Gillis tell it:

"So he gives me these here tube numbers and says, 'Series circuit. Now stop bothering me. Build your time machine, sit down at it and turn on the switch. That's all I ask, Dr. Gillis—that's all I ask.' "

"Say," marveled a brittle and lovely blonde guest, "you remember real good, don't you, doc?" She gave him a melting smile.

"Heck," said Gillis modestly, "I always remember good. It's what you call an inherent facility. And besides I told it quick to my secretary, so she wrote it down. I don't read so good, but I sure remember good, all right. Now, where was I?"

Everybody thought hard, and there were various suggestions:

"Something about bottles, doc?"

"You was starting a fight. You said 'time somebody was traveling.' "

"Yeah—you called somebody a swish. Who did you call a swish?"

"Not swish—*switch.*"

Dr. Gillis' noble brow grooved with thought, and he declared: "Switch is right. It was about time travel. What we call travel through time. So I took the tube numbers he gave me and I put them into the circuit builder; I set it for 'series' and there it is—my time-traveling machine. It travels things through time real good." He displayed a box.

"What's in the box?" asked the lovely blonde.

Dr. Hemingway told her: "Time travel. It travels things through time."

"Look," said Gillis, the physicist. He took Dr. Hemingway's little black bag and put in on the box. He turned on the switch and the little black bag vanished.

"Say," said Dr. Hemingway, "that was, uh, swell. Now bring it back."

"Huh?"

"Bring back my little back bag."

"Well," said Dr. Gillis, "they don't come back. I tried it backwards and they don't come back. I guess maybe that dummy Mike give me a bum steer."

There was wholesale condemnation of "Mike" but Dr.

Hemingway took no part in it. He was nagged by a vague feeling that there was something he would have to do. He reasoned: "I am a doctor, and a doctor has got to have a little black bag. I ain't got a little black bag—so ain't I a doctor no more?" He decided that this was absurd. He *knew* he was a doctor. So it must be the bag's fault for not being there. It was no good, and he would get another one tomorrow from that dummy Al, at the clinic. Al could find things good, but he was a dummy—never liked to talk sociable to you.

So the next day Dr. Hemingway remembered to get another little black bag from his keeper—another little black bag with which he could perform tonsillectomies, appendectomies, and the most difficult confinements, and with which he could diagnose and cure his kind until the day when the supernormals could bring themselves to cross that bridge. Al was kinda nasty about the missing little black bag, but Dr. Hemingway didn't exactly remember what had happened, so no tracer was sent out, so—

Old Dr. Full awoke from the horrors of the night to the horrors of the day. His gummy eyelashes pulled apart convulsively. He was propped against a corner of his room, and something was making a little drumming noise. He felt very cold and cramped. As his eyes focused on his lower body, he croaked out a laugh. The drumming noise was being made by his left heel, agitated by fine tremors against the bare floor. It was going to be the D.T.s again, he decided dispassionately. He wiped his mouth with his bloody knuckles, and the fine tremor coarsened; the snare-drum beat became louder and slower. He was getting a break this fine morning, he decided sardonically. You didn't get the horrors until you had been tightened like a violin string, just to the breaking point. He had a reprieve, if a reprieve into his old body with the blazing, endless headache just back of the eyes and the screaming stiffness in the joints was anything to be thankful for.

There was something or other about a kid, he thought vaguely. He was going to doctor some kid. His eyes rested on a little black bag in the center of the room, and he forgot about the kid. "I could have sworn," said Dr. Full, "I hocked that two years ago!" He hitched over and reached the bag, and then realized it was some stranger's kit, arriving here he did not know how. He tentatively touched the lock and it snapped open and lay flat, rows and rows of instruments and medications tucked into loops in its four walls. It seemed vastly larger open than closed. He didn't see how it could possibly fold up into that compact size again, but decided it was some stunt of the instrument makers. Since his time—that made it worth more at the hock shop, he thought with satisfaction.

Just for old times' sake, he let his eyes and fingers rove over the instruments before he snapped the bag shut and headed for Uncle's. More than a few were a little hard to recognize—exactly that is. You could see the things with blades for cutting, the forceps for holding and pulling, the retractors for holding fast, the needles and gut for suturing, the hypos—a fleeting thought crossed his mind that he could peddle the hypos separately to drug addicts.

Let's go, he decided, and tried to fold up the case. It didn't fold until he happened to touch the lock, and then it folded all at once into a little black bag. Sure have forged ahead, he thought, almost able to forget that what he was primarily interested in was its pawn value.

With a definite objective, it was not too hard for him to get to his feet. He decided to go down the front steps, out the front door, and down the sidewalk. But first—

He snapped the bag open again on his kitchen table, and pored through the medication tubes. "Anything to sock the autonomic nervous system good and hard," he mumbled. The tubes were numbered, and there was a plastic card which seemed to list them. The left margin of the card was a rundown of the systems—vascular, muscular, nervous. He followed the last entry across to the right. There were columns for "stimulant," "depressant," and so on. Under "nervous system" and "Depressant" he found the number 17, and shakily located the little glass tube which bore it. It was full of pretty blue pills and he took one.

It was like being struck by a thunderbolt.

Dr. Full had so long lacked any sense of well-being except the brief glow of alcohol that he had forgotten its very nature. He was panic-stricken for a long moment at the sensation that spread through him slowly, finally tingling in his fingertips. He straightened up, his pains gone and his leg tremor stilled.

That was great, he thought. He'd be able to *run* to the hock shop, pawn the little black bag, and get some booze. He started down the stairs. Not even the street, bright with mid-morning sun, into which he emerged, made him quail. The little black bag in his left hand had a satisfying, authoritative weight. He was walking erect, he noted, and not in the somewhat furtive crouch that had grown on him in recent years. A little self-respect, he told himself, that's what I need. Just because a man's down doesn't mean—

"Docta, please-a come wit'!" somebody yelled at him, tugging his arm. "Da litt-la girl, she's-a burn' up!" It was one of the slum's innumerable flat-faced, stringy-haired women, in a slovenly wrapper.

"Ah, I happen to be retired from practice—" he began hoarsely, but she would not be put off.

"In by here, Docta!" she urged, tugging him to a doorway. "You come look-a da litt-la girl. I got two dolla, you come look!" That put a different complexion on the matter. He allowed himself to be towed through the doorway into a messy, cabbage-smelling flat. He knew the woman now, or rather knew who she must be—a new arrival who had moved in the other night. These people moved at night, in motorcades of battered cars supplied by friends and relations, with furniture lashed to the tops, swearing and drinking until the small hours. It explained why she had stopped him: she did not yet know he was old Dr. Full, a drunken reprobate whom nobody would trust. The little black bag had been his guarantee, outweighing his whiskery face and stained black suit.

He was looking down on a three-year-old girl who had, he rather suspected, just been placed in the mathematical center of a freshly changed double bed. God knew what sour and dirty mattress she usually slept on. He seemed to recognize her as he noted a crusted bandage on her right hand. Two dollars, he thought— An ugly flush had spread up her pipe-stem arm. He poked a finger into the socket of her elbow, and felt little spheres like marbles under the skin and ligaments roll apart. The child began to squall thinly; beside him, the woman gasped and began to weep herself.

"Out," he gestured briskly at her, and she thudded away, still sobbing.

Two dollars, he thought— Give her some mumbo jumbo, take the money and tell her to go to a clinic. Strep, I guess, from that stinking alley. It's a wonder any of them grow up. He put down the little black bag and forgetfully fumbled for his key, then remembered and touched the lock. It flew open, and he selected a bandage shears, with a blunt wafer for the lower jaw. He fitted the lower jaw under the bandage, trying not to hurt the kid by its pressure on the infection, and began to cut. It was amazing how easily and swiftly the shining shears snipped through the crusty rag around the wound. He hardly seemed to be driving the shears with fingers at all. It almost seemed as though the shears were driving his fingers instead as they scissored a clean, light line through the bandage.

Certainly have forged ahead since my time, he thought—sharper than a microtome knife. He replaced the shears in their loop on the extraordinarily big board that the little black bag turned into when it unfolded, and leaned over the wound. He whistled at the ugly gash, and the violent infection which had taken immediate root in the sickly child's thin body. Now what can you do with a thing like that? He pawed over the contents of the little black bag, nervously. If he lanced it and let some of the pus out, the old woman would think he'd done something for her and he'd get the two dollars. But at the clinic they'd want to know who did it and if they got sore enough they might send a cop around. Maybe there was something in the kit—

He ran down the left edge of the card to "lymphatic" and read across to the column under "infection." It didn't sound right at all to him; he checked again, but it still said that. In the square to which the line and column led were the symbols: "IV-g-3cc." He couldn't find any bottles marked with Roman numerals, and then noticed that that was how the hypodermic needles were designated. He lifted number IV from its loop, noting that it was fitted with a needle already and even seemed to be charged. What a way to carry those things around! So—three cc. of whatever was in hypo number IV out to do something or other about infections settled in the lymphatic system—which, God knows, this one was. What did the lowercase "g" mean, though? He studied the glass hypo and saw letters engraved on what looked like a rotating disk at the top of the barrel. They ran from "a" to "i," and there was an index line engraved on the barrel on the opposite side from the calibrations.

Shrugging, old Dr. Full turned the disk until "g" coincided with the index line, and lifted the hypo to eye level. As he pressed in the plunger he did not see the tiny thread of fluid squirt from the tip of the needle. There was a sort of dark mist for a moment about the tip. A closer inspection showed that the cut across the bias of the shaft, but the cut did not expose an oval hole. Baffled, he tried pressing the plunger again. Again *something* appeared around the tip and vanished. "We'll settle this," said the doctor. He slipped the needle into the skin of his forearm. He thought at first that he had missed—that the point had glided over the top of his skin instead of catching and slipping under it. But he saw a tiny blood-spot and realized that somehow he just hadn't felt the puncture. Whatever was in the barrel, he decided, couldn't do him any harm if it lived up to its billing—and if it could come out through a needle that had no hole. He gave himself three cc. and twitched the needle out. There was the swelling—painless, but otherwise typical.

Dr. Full decided it was his eyes or something, and gave three cc. of "g" from hypodermic IV to the feverish child. There was no interruption to her wailing as the needle went in and the swelling rose. But a long instant later, she gave a final gasp and was silent.

Well, he told himself, cold with horror, you did it that time. You killed her with that stuff.

Then the child sat up and said: "Where's my mommy?"

Incredulously, the doctor seized her arm and palpated the elbow. The gland infection was zero, and the temperature seemed normal. The blood-congested tissues surrounding the wound were subsiding as he watched. The child's pulse was stronger and no faster than a child's should be. In the sudden silence of the room he could hear the little girl's mother sobbing in her kitchen, outside. And he also heard a girl's insinuating voice:

"She gonna be O.K., doc?"

He turns and saw a gaunt-faced, dirty-blonde sloven of perhaps eighteen leaning in the doorway and eyeing him with amused contempt. She continued: "I heard about you, *Doctor* Full. So don't go try and put the bite on the old lady. You couldn't doctor up a sick cat."

"Indeed?" he rumbled. This young person was going to get a lesson she richly deserved. "Perhaps you would care to look at my patient?"

"Where's my mommy?" insisted the little girl, and the blonde's jaw fell. She went to the bed and cautiously asked: "You O.K. now, Teresa? You all fixed up?"

"Where's my mommy?" demanded Teresa. Then, accusingly, she gestured with her wounded hand at the doctor. "You *poke* me!" she complained, and giggled pointlessly.

"Well—" said the blonde girl, "I guess I got to hand it to you, doc. These loud-mouth women around here said you didn't know your . . . I mean, didn't know how to cure people. They said you ain't a real doctor."

"I *have* retired from practice," he said. "But I happened to be taking this case to a colleague as a favor, your good mother noticed me, and—" a deprecating smile. He touched the lock of the case and it folded up into the little black bag again.

"You stole it," the girl said flatly.

He sputtered.

"Nobody'd trust you with a thing like that. It must be worth plenty. You stole that case. I was going to stop you when I come in and saw you working over Teresa, but it looked like you wasn't doing her any harm. But when you give me that line about taking that case to a colleague I know you stole it. You gimme a cut or I go to the cops. A thing like that must be worth twenty—thirty dollars."

The mother came timidly in, her eyes red. But she let out a whoop of joy when she saw the girl sitting up and babbling to herself, embraced her madly, fell on her knees for a quick prayer, hopped up to kiss the doctor's hand, and then dragged him into the kitchen, all the while rattling in her native language while the blonde girl let her eyes go cold with disgust. Dr. Full allowed himself to be towed into the kitchen, but flatly declined a cup of coffee and a plate of anise cakes and St. John's Bread.

"Try him on some wine, ma," said the girl sardonically.

"Hyass! Hyass!" breathed the woman delightedly. "You like-a wine, docta?" She had a carafe of purplish liquid before him in an instant, and the blonde girl snickered as the doctor's hand twitched out at it. He drew his hand back, while there grew in his head the old image of how it would smell and then taste and then warm his stomach and limbs. He made the kind of calculation at which he was practiced; the delighted woman would not notice as he downed two tumblers, and he could overawe her through two tumblers more with his tale of Teresa's narrow brush with the Destroying Angel, and then—why, then it would not matter. He would be drunk.

But for the first time in years, there was a sort of counter-image: a blend of the rage he felt at the blonde girl to whom he was so transparent, and of pride at the cure he had just effected. Much to his own surprise, he drew back his hand from the carafe and said, luxuriating in the words: "No, thank you. I don't believe I'd care for any so early in the day." He covertly watched the blonde girl's face, and was gratified at her surprise. Then the mother was shyly handing him two bills and saying: "Is no much-a money, docta—but you come again, see Teresa?"

"I shall be glad to follow the case through," he said. "But now excuse me—I really must be running along." He grasped the little black bag firmly and got up; he wanted very much to get away from the wine and the older girl.

"Wait up, doc," said she, "I'm going your way." She followed him out and down the street. He ignored her until he felt her hand on the black bag. Then old Dr. Full stopped and tried to reason with her:

"Look, my dear. Perhaps you're right. I might have stolen it. To be perfectly frank, I don't remember how I got it. But you're young and you can earn your own money—"

"Fifty-fifty," she said, "or I go to the cops. And if I get another word outta you, it's sixty-forty. And you know who gets the short end, don't you, doc?"

Defeated, he marched to the pawnshop, her impudent hand still on the handle with his, and her heels beating out a tattoo against his stately tread.

In the pawnshop, they both got a shock.

"It ain't standard," said Uncle, unimpressed by the ingenious lock. "I ain't nevva seen one like it. Some cheap Jap stuff, maybe? Try down the street. This I nevva could sell."

Down the street they got an offer of one dollar. The same complaint was made: "I ain't a collecta, mista—I buy stuff that got resale value. Who could I sell this to, a Chinaman who don't know medical instruments? Everyone of them looks funny. You sure you didn't make these yourself?" They didn't take the one-dollar offer.

The girl was baffled and angry; the doctor was baffled too, but triumphant. He had two dollars, and the girl had a half-interest in something nobody wanted. But, he suddenly marveled, the thing had been all right to cure the kid, hadn't it?

"Well," he asked her, "do you give up? As you see, the kit is practically valueless."

She was thinking hard. "Don't fly off the handle, doc. I don't get this, but something's going on all right . . . would those guys know good stuff if they saw it?"

"They would. They make a living from it. Wherever this kit came from—"

She seized on that, with a devilish faculty she seemed to have of eliciting answers without asking questions. "I thought so. You don't know either, huh? Well, maybe I can find out for you. C'mon in here. I ain't letting go of that thing. There's money in it—some way, I don't know how, there's money in it." He followed her into a cafeteria and to an almost-empty corner. She was oblivious to stares and snickers from the other customers as she opened the little black bag—it almost covered a cafeteria table—and ferreted through it. She picked out a retractor from a loop, scrutinized it, contemptuously threw it down, picked out a speculum, threw it down, picked out the lower half of an O. B. forceps, turned it over, close to her sharp young eyes—and saw what the doctor's dim old ones could not have seen.

All old Dr. Full knew was that she was peering at the neck of the forceps and then turned white. Very carefully, she placed the half of the forceps back in its loop of cloth and then replaced the retractor and the speculum. "Well?" he asked. "What did you see?"

" 'Made in U.S.A.,' " she quoted hoarsely. " 'Patent Applied for July 2450.' "

He wanted to tell her she must have misread the inscription, that it must be a practical joke, that—

But he knew she had read correctly. Those bandage shears: they *had* driven his fingers, rather than his fingers driving them. The hypo needle that had no hole. The pretty blue pill that had struck him like a thunderbolt.

"You know what I'm going to do?" asked the girl, with sudden animation. "I'm going to go to charm school. You'll like that, won't ya, doc? Because we're sure going to be seeing a lot of each other."

Old Dr. Full didn't answer. His hands had been playing idly with that plastic card from the kit on which had been printed the rows and columns that had guided him twice before. The card had a slight convexity; you could snap the convexity back and forth from one side to the other. He noted, in a daze, that with each snap a different text appeared on the cards. *Snap.* "The knife with the blue dot in the handle is for tumors only.

Diagnose tumors with your Instrument Seven, the Swelling Tester. Place the Swelling Tester—" *Snap.* "An overdose of the pink pills in Bottle 3 can be fixed with one white pill from Bottle—" *Snap.* "Hold the suture needle by the end without the hole in it. Touch it to one end of the wound you want to close and let go. After it has made the knot, touch it—" *Snap.* "Place the top half of the O.B. Forceps near the opening. Let go. After it has entered and conformed to the shape of—" *Snap.*

The slot man saw "FLANNERY 1—MEDICAL" in the upper left corner of the hunk of copy. He automatically scribbled "trim to .75" on it and skimmed it across the horseshoe-shaped copy desk to Piper, who had been handling Edna Flannery's quack-exposé series. She was a nice youngster, he thought, but like all youngsters she overwrote. Hence, the "trim."

Piper dealt back a city hall story to the slot, pinned down Flannery's feature with one hand and began to tap his pencil across it, one tap to a word, at the same steady beat as a teletype carriage traveling across the roller. He wasn't exactly reading it this first time. He was just looking at the letters and words to find out whether, as letters and words, they conformed to *Herald* style. The steady tap of his pencil ceased at intervals as it drew a black line ending with a stylized letter "d" through the word "breast" and scribbled in "chest" instead, or knocked down the capital "E" in "East" to lower case with a diagonal, or closed up a split word—in whose middle Flannery had bumped the space bar of her typewriter—with two curved lines like parentheses rotated through ninety degrees. The thick black pencil zipped a ring around the "30," which, like all youngsters, she put at the end of her stories. He turned back to the first page for the second reading. This time the pencil drew lines with the stylized "d's" at the end of them through adjectives and whole phrases, printed big "Ls" to mark paragraphs, hooked some of Flannery's own paragraphs together with swooping recurved lines.

At the bottom of "FLANNERY ADD 2—MEDICAL" the pencil slowed down and stopped. The slot man, sensitive to the rhythm of his beloved copy desk, looked up almost at once. He saw Piper squinting at the story, at a loss. Without wasting words, the copy reader skimmed it back across the Masonite horseshoe to the chief, caught a police story in return and buckled down, his pencil tapping. The slot man read as far as the fourth add, barked at Howard, on the rim: "Sit in for me," and stumped through the clattering city room toward the alcove where the managing editor presided over his own bedlam.

The copy chief waited his turn while the make-up editor, the pressroom foreman, and the chief photographer had words with the M.E. When his turn came, he dropped Flannery's copy on his desk and said: "She says this one isn't a quack."

The M.E. read:

"FLANNERY 1—MEDICAL, by Edna Flannery, *Herald* Staff Writer.

"The sordid tale of medical quackery which the *Herald* has exposed in this series of articles undergoes a change of pace today which the reporter found a welcome surprise. Her quest for the facts in the case of today's subject started just the same way that her exposure of one dozen shyster M.D.s and faith-healing phonies did. But she can report for a change that Dr. Bayard Full is, despite unorthodox practices which have drawn the suspicion of the rightly hypersensitive medical associations, a true healer living up to the highest ideals of his profession.

"Dr. Full's name was given to the *Herald*'s reporter by the ethical committee of a county medical association, which reported that he had been expelled from the association on July 18, 1941, for allegedly 'milking' several patients suffering from trivial complaints. According to sworn statements in the committee's files, Dr. Full had told them they suffered from cancer, and that he had a treatment which would prolong their lives. After his expulsion from the association, Dr. Full dropped out of their sight—until he opened a midtown 'sanitarium' in a brownstone front which had for years served as a rooming house.

"The *Herald*'s reporter went to that sanitarium, on East 89th Street, with the full expectation of having numerous imaginary ailments diagnosed and of being promised a sure cure for a flat sum of money. She expected to find unkempt quarters, dirty instruments, and the mumbo-jumbo paraphernalia of the shyster M.D. which she had seen a dozen times before.

"She was wrong.

"Dr. Full's sanitarium is spotlessly clean, from its tastefully furnished entrance hall to its shining, white treatment rooms. The attractive, blonde receptionist who greeted the reporter was soft-spoken and correct, asking only the reporter's name, address, and the general nature of her complaint. This was given, as usual, as 'nagging backache.' The receptionist asked the *Herald*'s reporter to be seated, and a short while later conducted her to a second-floor treatment room and introduced her to Dr. Full.

"Dr. Full's alleged past, as described by the medical society spokesman, is hard to reconcile with his present appearance. He is a clear-eyed, white-haired man in his sixties, to judge by his appearance—a little above middle height and apparently in good physical condition. His voice was firm and friendly, untainted by the ingratiating whine of the shyster M.D. which the reporter has come to know too well.

"The receptionist did not leave the room as he began his examination after a few questions as to the nature and location of the pain. As the reporter lay face down on a treatment table the doctor pressed some instrument to the small of her back. In about one minute he made this astounding statement: 'Young woman, there is no reason for you to have any pain where you say you do. I understand they're saying nowadays that emotional upsets cause pains like that. You'd better go to a psychologist or psychiatrist if the pain keeps up. There is no physical cause for it, so I can do nothing for you.'

"His frankness took the reporter's breath away. Had he guessed she was, so to speak, a spy in his camp? She tried again: 'Well, doctor, perhaps you'd give me a physical checkup, I feel run down all the time, besides the pains. Maybe I need a tonic.' This is never-failing bait to shyster M.D.s—an invitation for them to find all sorts of mysterious conditions wrong with a patient, each of which 'requires' an expensive treatment. As explained in the first article of this series, of course, the reporter underwent a thorough physical checkup before she embarked on her quack hunt, and was found to be in one hundred percent perfect condition, with the exception of a 'scarred' area at the bottom tip of her left lung resulting from a childhood attack of tuberculosis and a tendency toward 'hyperthyroidism'—overactivity of the thyroid gland which makes it difficult to put on weight and sometimes causes a slight shortness of breath.

"Dr. Full consented to perform the examination, and took a number of shining, spotlessly clean instruments from loops in a large board literally covered with instruments—most of them unfamiliar to the reporter. The instrument with which he approached first was a tube with a curved dial in its surface and two wires that ended on flat disks growing from its ends. He placed one of the disks on the back of the reporter's right hand and the other on the back of her left. 'Reading the meter,' he called out some number which the attentive receptionist took down on a ruled form. The same procedure was repeated several times, thoroughly covering the reporter's anatomy and thoroughly convincing her that the doctor was a complete quack. The reporter had never seen any such diagnostic procedure practiced during the weeks she put in preparing for this series.

"The doctor then took the ruled sheet from the receptionist, conferred with her in low tones, and said: 'You have a slightly overactive thyroid, young woman. And there's something wrong with your left lung—not seriously, but I'd like to take a closer look.'

"He selected an instrument from the board which, the reporter knew, is called a 'speculum'—a scissorlike device which spreads apart body openings such as the orifice of the ear, the nostril, and so on, so that a doctor can look in during an examination. The instrument was, however, too large to be an aural or nasal speculum but too small to be anything else. As the *Herald*'s reporter was about to ask further questions, the attending receptionist told her: 'It's customary for us to blindfold our patients during lung examinations—do you mind?' The reporter, bewildered, allowed her to tie a spotlessly clean bandage over her eyes, and waited nervously for what would come next.

"She still cannot say exactly what happened while she was blindfolded—but X rays confirm her suspicions. She felt a cold sensation at her ribs on the left side—a cold that seemed to enter inside her body. Then there was a snapping feeling, and the cold sensation was gone. She heard Dr. Full say in a matter-of-fact voice: 'You have an old tubercular scar down there. It isn't doing any particular harm, but an active person like you needs all the oxygen she can get. Lie still and I'll fix it for you.'

"Then there was a repetition of the cold sensation, lasting for a longer time. 'Another batch of alveoli and some more vascular glue,' the *Herald*'s reporter heard Dr. Full say, and the receptionist's crisp response to the order. Then the strange sensation departed and the eye bandage was removed. The reporter saw no scar on her ribs, and yet the doctor assured her: 'That did it. We took out the fibrosis—and a good fibrosis it was, too; it walled off the infection so you're still alive to tell the tale. Then we planted a few clumps of alveoli—they're the little gadgets that get the oxygen from the air you breathe into your blood. I won't monkey with your thyroxin supply. You've got used to being the kind of person you are, and if you suddenly found yourself easygoing and all the rest of it, chances are you'd only be upset. About the backache: just check with the county medical society for the name of a good psychologist or psychiatrist. And look out for quacks; the woods are full of them.'

"The doctor's self-assurance took the reporter's breath away. She asked what the charge would be, and was told to pay the receptionist fifty dollars. As usual, the reporter delayed paying until she got a receipt signed by the doctor himself, detailing the services for which it paid. Unlike most, the doctor cheerfully wrote: 'For removal of fibrosis from left lung and restoration of alveoli,' and signed it.

"The reporter's first move when she left the sanitarium was to head for the chest specialist who had examined her in preparation for this series. A comparison of X rays taken on the day of the 'operation' and those taken previously would, the *Herald*'s reporter then thought, expose Dr. Full as a prince of shyster M.D.s and quacks.

"The chest specialist made time on his crowded schedule for the reporter, in whose series he has shown a lively interest from the planning stage on. He laughed uproariously in his staid Park Avenue examining room as she described the weird procedure to which she had been subjected. But he did not laugh when he took a chest X ray of the reporter, developed it, dried it, and compared it with the ones he had taken earlier. The chest specialist took six more X rays that afternoon, but finally admitted that they all told the same story. The *Herald*'s reporter has it on his authority that the scar she had eighteen days ago from her tuberculosis is now gone and has been replaced by healthy lung tissue. He declared that this is a happening unparalleled in medical history. He does not go along with the reporter in her firm conviction that Dr. Full is responsible for the change.

"The *Herald*'s reporter, however, sees no two ways about it. She concludes that Dr. Bayard Full—whatever his alleged past may have been—is now an unorthodox but highly successful practitioner of medicine, to whose hands the reporter would trust herself in any emergency.

"Not so is the case of 'Rev.' Annie Dimsworth—a female harpy who, under the guise of 'faith' preys on the ignorant and suffering who come to her sordid 'healing parlor' for help and remain to feed 'Rev.' Annie's bank account, which now totals up to $53,238.64. Tomorrow's article will show, with photostats of bank statements and sworn testimony that—"

The managing editor turned down "FLANNERY LAST ADD—MEDICAL" and tapped his front teeth with a pencil, trying to think straight. He finally told the copy chief: "Kill the story. Run the teaser as a box." He tore off the last paragraph—the "teaser" about "Rev." Annie—and handed it to the desk man, who stumped back to his Masonite horseshoe.

The make-up editor was back, dancing with impatience as he tried to catch the M.E.'s eye. The interphone buzzed with the red light which indicated that the editor and publisher wanted to talk to him. The M.E. thought briefly of a special series on this Dr. Full, decided nobody would believe it and that he probably was a phony anyway. He spiked the story on the "dead" hook and answered his interphone.

Dr. Full had become almost fond of Angie. As his practice had grown to engross the neighborhood illnesses, and then to a corner suite in an uptown taxpayer building, and finally to the sanitarium, she seemed to have grown with it. Oh, he thought, we have our little disputes—

The girl, for instance, was too much interested in money. She had wanted to specialize in cosmetic surgery—removing wrinkles from wealthy old women and whatnot. She didn't realize, at first, that a thing like this was in their trust, that they were the stewards and not the owners of the little black bag and its fabulous contents.

He had tried, ever so cautiously, to analyze them, but without success. All the instruments were slightly radioactive, for instance, but not quite so. They would make a Geiger-Mueller counter indicate, but they would not collapse the leaves of an electroscope. He didn't pretend to be up on the latest developments, but as he understood it, that was just plain *wrong*. Under the highest magnification there were lines on the instruments' superfinished surfaces: incredibly fine lines, engraved in random hatchments which made no particular sense. Their magnetic properties were preposterous. Sometimes the instruments were strongly attracted to magnets, sometimes less so, and sometimes not at all.

Dr. Full had taken X rays in fear and trembling lest he disrupt whatever delicate machinery worked in them. He was *sure* they were not solid, that the handles and perhaps the blades must be mere shells filled with busy little watchworks—but the X rays showed nothing of the sort. Oh, yes—and they were always sterile, and they wouldn't rust. Dust *fell* off them if you shook them: now, that was something he understood. They ionized the dust, or were ionized themselves, or something of the sort. At any rate, he had read of something similar that had to do with phonograph records.

She wouldn't know about that, he proudly thought. She kept the books well enough, and perhaps she gave him a useful prod now and then when he was inclined to settle down. The move from the neighborhood slum to the uptown quarters had been her idea, and so had the sanitarium. Good, good, it enlarged his sphere of usefulness. Let the child have her mink coats and her convertible, as they seemed to be calling roadsters nowadays. He himself was too busy and too old. He had so much to make up for.

Dr. Full thought happily of his Master Plan. She would not like it much, but she would have to see the logic of it. This marvelous thing that had happened to them must be handed on. She was herself no doctor; even though the instruments practically ran themselves, there was more to doctoring than skill. There were the ancient canons of the healing art. And so, having seen the logic of it, Angie would yield; she would assent to his turning over the little black bag to all humanity.

He would probably present it to the College of Surgeons, with as little fuss as possible—well, perhaps a *small* ceremony, and he would like a souvenir of the occasion, a cup or a framed testimonial. It would be a relief to have the thing out of his hands, in a way; let the giants of the healing art decide who was to have its benefits. No, Angie would understand. She was a goodhearted girl.

It was nice that she had been showing so much interest in the surgical side lately—asking about the instruments, reading the instruction card for hours, even practicing on guinea pigs. If something of his love for humanity had been communicated to her, old Dr. Full sentimentally thought, his life would not have been in vain. Surely she would realize that a greater good would be served by surrendering the instruments to wiser hands than theirs, and by throwing aside the cloak of secrecy necessary to work on their small scale.

Dr. Full was in the treatment room that had been the brownstone's front parlor; through the window he saw Angie's yellow convertible roll to a stop before the stoop. He liked the way she looked as she climbed the stairs; neat, not flashy, he thought. A sensible girl like her, she'd understand. There was somebody with her—a fat woman, puffing up the steps, overdressed and petulant. Now, what could she want?

Angie let herself in and went into the treatment room, followed by the fat woman. "Doctor," said the blonde girl gravely, "may I present Mrs. Coleman?" Charm school had not taught her everything, but Mrs. Coleman, evidently *nouveau riche,* thought the doctor, did not notice the blunder.

"Miss Aquella told me *so* much about you, doctor, and your remarkable system!" she gushed.

Before he could answer, Angie smoothly interposed: "Would you excuse us for just a moment, Mrs. Coleman?"

She took the doctor's arm and led him into the reception hall. "Listen," she said swiftly, "I know this goes against your grain, but I couldn't pass it up. I met this old thing in the exercise class at Elizabeth Barton's. Nobody else'll talk to her there. She's a widow. I guess her husband was a black marketeer or something, and she has a pile of dough. I gave her a line about how you had a system of massaging wrinkles out. My idea is, you blindfold her, cut her neck open with the Cutaneous Series knife, shoot some Firmol into the muscles, spoon out some of that blubber with an Adipose Series curette and spray it all with Skintite. When you take the blindfold off she's got rid of a wrinkle and doesn't know what happened. She'll pay five hundred dollars. Now, don't say 'no,' doc. Just this once, let's do it my way, can't you? I've been working on this deal all along too, haven't I?"

"Oh," said the doctor, "very well." He was going to have to tell her about the Master Plan before long anyway. He would let her have it her way this time.

Back in the treatment room, Mrs. Coleman had been thinking things over. She told the doctor sternly as he entered: "Of course, your system is permanent, isn't it?"

"It is, madam," he said shortly. "Would you please lie down there? Miss Aquella, get a sterile three-inch bandage for Mrs. Coleman's eyes." He turned his back on the fat woman to avoid conversation, and pretended to be adjusting the lights. Angie blindfolded the woman, and the doctor selected the instruments he would need. He handed the blonde girl a pair of retractors, and told her: "Just slip the corners of the blades in as I cut—" She gave him an alarmed look, and gestured at the reclining woman. He lowered his voice: "Very well. Slip in the corners and rock them along the incision. I'll tell you when to pull them out."

Dr. Full held the Cutaneous Series knife to his eyes as he adjusted the little slide for three centimeters depth. He sighed a little as he recalled that its last use had been in the extirpation of an "inoperable" tumor of the throat.

"Very well," he said, bending over the woman. He tried a tentative pass through her tissues. The blade dipped in and flowed through them, like a finger through quicksilver, with no wound left in the wake. Only the retractors could hold the edges of the incision apart.

Mrs. Coleman stirred and jabbered; "Doctor, that felt so peculiar! Are you sure you're rubbing the right way?"

"Quite sure, madam," said the doctor wearily. "Would you please try not to talk during the massage?"

He nodded at Angie, who stood ready with the retractors. The blade sank in to its three centimeters, miraculously cutting only the dead horny tissues of the epidermis and the live tissue of the dermis, pushing aside mysteriously all major and minor blood vessels and muscular tissue, declining to affect any system or organ except the one it was—tuned to, could you say? The doctor didn't know the answer, but he felt tired and bitter at this prostitution. Angie slipped in the retractor blades and rocked them as he withdrew the knife, then pulled to separate the lips of the incision. It bloodlessly exposed an unhealthy string of muscle, sagging in a dead-looking loop from blue-gray ligaments. The doctor took a hypo. Number IX, pre-set to "g," and raised it to his eye level. The mist came and went; there probably was no possibility of an embolus with one of these gadgets, but why take chances? He shot one cc. of "g"—identified as "Firmol" by the card—into the muscle. He and Angie watched as it tightened up against the pharynx.

He took the Adipose Series curette, a small one, and spooned out yellowish tissue, dropping it into the incinerator box, and then nodded to Angie. She eased out the retractors and the gaping incision slipped together into unbroken skin, sagging now. The doctor had the atomizer—dialed to "Skintite"—ready. He sprayed, and the skin shrank up into the new firm throat line.

As he replaced the instruments, Angie removed Mrs. Coleman's bandage and gaily announced: "We're finished! And there's a mirror in the reception hall—"

Mrs. Coleman didn't need to be invited twice. With incredulous fingers she felt her chin, and then dashed for the hall. The doctor grimaced as he heard her yelp of delight, and Angie turned to him with a tight smile. "I'll get the money and get her out," she said. "You won't have to be bothered with her any more."

He was grateful for that much.

She followed Mrs. Coleman into the reception hall, and the doctor dreamed over the case of instruments. A ceremony, certainly—he was *entitled* to one. Not everybody, he thought, would turn such a sure source of money over to the good of humanity. But you reached an age when money mattered less, and when you thought of these things you had done that *might* be open to misunderstanding if, just if, there chanced to be any of that, well, that judgment business. The doctor wasn't a religious man, but you certainly found yourself thinking hard about some things when your time drew near—

Angie was back, with a bit of paper in her hands. "Five hundred dollars," she said matter-of-factly. "And you realize, don't you, that we could go over her an inch at a time—at five hundred dollars an inch?"

"I've been meaning to talk to you about that," he said.

There was bright fear in her eyes, he thought—but why?

"Angie, you've been a good girl and an understanding girl, but we can't keep this up forever, you know."

"Let's talk about it some other time," she said flatly. "I'm tired now."

"No—I really feel we've gone far enough on our own. The instruments—"

"Don't say it, doc!" she hissed. "Don't say it, or you'll be sorry!" In her face there was a look that reminded him of the hollow-eyed, gaunt-faced, dirty blonde creature she had been. From under the charm-school finish there burned the guttersnipe whose infancy had been spent on a sour and filthy mattress, whose childhood had been play in the littered alley, and whose adolescence had been the sweat-shops and the aimless gatherings at night under the glaring street lamps.

He shook his head to dispel the puzzling notion. "It's this way," he patiently began. "I told you about the family that invented the O. B. forceps and kept them a secret for so many generations, how they could have given them to the world but didn't?"

"They knew what they were doing," said the guttersnipe flatly.

"Well, that's neither here nor there," said the doctor, irritated. "My mind is made up about it. I'm going to turn the instruments over to the College of Surgeons. We have enough money to be comfortable. You can even have the house. I've been thinking of going to a warmer climate, myself." He felt peeved with her for making the unpleasant scene. He was unprepared for what happened next.

Angie snatched the little black bag and dashed for the door, with panic in her eyes. He scrambled after her, catching her arm, twisting it in a sudden rage. She clawed at his face with her free hand, babbling curses. Somehow, somebody's finger touched the little black bag, and it opened grotesquely into the enormous board, covered with shining instruments, large and small. Half a dozen of them joggled loose and fell to the floor.

"*Now* see what you've done!" roared the doctor, unreasonably. Her hand was still viselike on the handle, but she was standing still, trembling with choked-up rage. The doctor bent stiffly to pick up the fallen instruments. Unreasonable girl! he thought bitterly. Making a scene—

Pain drove in between his shoulderblades and he fell face down. The light ebbed. "Unreasonable girl!" he tried to croak. And then: "They'll know I tried, anyway—"

Angie looked down on his prone body, with the handle of the Number Six Cautery Series knife protruding from it. "—will cut through all tissues. Use for amputations before you spread on the Re-Gro. Extreme caution should be used in the vicinity of vital organs and major blood vessels or nerve trunks—"

"I didn't mean to do that," said Angie, dully, cold with horror. Now the detective would come, the implacable detective who would reconstruct the crime from the dust in the room. She would run and turn and twist, but the detective would find her out and she would be tried in a courtroom before a judge and jury; the lawyer would make speeches, but the jury would convict her anyway, and the headlines would scream: "BLONDE KILLER GUILTY!" and she'd maybe get the chair, walking down a plain corridor where a beam of sunlight struck through the dusty air, with an iron door at the end of it. Her mink, her convertible, her dresses, the handsome man she was going to meet and marry—

The mist of cinematic clichés cleared, and she knew what she would do next. Quite steadily, she picked the incinerator box from its loop in the board—a metal cube with a different-textured spot on one side. "—to dispose of fibroses or other unwanted matter, simply touch the disk—" You dropped something in and touched the disk. There was a sort of soundless whistle, very powerful and unpleasant if you were too close, and a sort of lightless flash. When you opened the box again, the contents were gone. Angie took another of the Cautery Series knives and went grimly to work. Good thing there wasn't any blood to speak of— She finished the awful task in three hours.

She slept heavily that night, totally exhausted by the wringing emotional demands of the slaying and the subsequent horror. But in the morning, it was as though the doctor had never been there. She ate breakfast, then dressed with care. Nothing out of the ordinary, she told herself. Don't do one thing different from the way you would have done it before. After a day or two, you can phone the cops. Say he walked out spoiling for a drunk, and you're worried. But don't rush it, baby—*don't rush it.*

Mrs. Coleman was due at 10:00 A.M. Angie had counted on being able to talk the doctor into at least one more five-hundred-dollar sessions. She'd have to do it herself now—but she'd have to start sooner or later.

The woman arrived early. Angie explained smoothly: "The doctor asked me to take care of the massage today. Now that he has the tissue-firming process beginning, it only requires somebody trained in his methods—" As she spoke, her eyes swiveled to the instrument case—open! She cursed herself for the single flaw as the woman followed her gaze and recoiled.

"What are those things!" she demanded. "Are you going to cut me with them? I *thought* there was something fishy—"

"Please, Mrs. Coleman," said Angie, "please, *dear* Mrs.

Coleman—you don't understand about the . . . the massage instruments!"

"Massage instruments my foot!" squabbled the woman shrilly. "That doctor *operated* on me. Why, he might have killed me!"

Angie wordlessly took one of the smaller Cutaneous Series knives and passed it through her forearm. The blade flowed like a finger through quicksilver, leaving no wound in its wake. *That* should convince the old cow!

It didn't convince her, but it did startle her. "What did you do with it? The blade folds up into the handle—that's it!"

"Now look closely, Mrs. Coleman," said Angie, thinking desperately of the five hundred dollars. "Look very closely and you'll see that the, uh, the sub-skin massager simply slips beneath the tissues without doing any harm, tightening and firming the muscles themselves instead of having to work through layers of skin and adipose tissue. It's the secret of the doctor's method. Now, how can outside massage have the effect that we got last night?"

Mrs. Coleman was beginning to calm down. "It *did* work, all right," she admitted, stroking the new line of her neck. But your arm's one thing and my neck's another! Let me see you do that with your neck!"

Angie smiled—

Al returned to the clinic after an excellent lunch that had almost reconciled him to three more months he would have to spend on duty. And then, he thought, and then a blessed year at the blessedly super-normal South Pole working on his speciality—which happened to be telekinesis exercises for ages three to six. Meanwhile, of course, the world had to go on and of course he had to shoulder his share in the running of it.

Before settling down to desk work he gave a routine glance at the bag board. What he saw made him stiffen with shocked surprise. A red light was on next to one of the numbers—the first since he couldn't think when. He read off the number and murmured "O.K., 674,101. That fixes *you*." He put the number on a card sorter and in a moment the record was in his hand. Oh, yes—Hemingway's bag. The big dummy didn't remember how or where he had lost it; none of them ever did. There were hundreds of them floating around.

Al's policy in such cases was to leave the bag turned on. The things practically ran themselves, it was practically impossible to do harm with them, so whoever found a lost one might as well be allowed to use it. You turn it off, you have a social loss—you leave it on, it may do some good. As he understood it, and not very well at that, the stuff wasn't "used up." A temporalist had tried to explain it to him with little success that the prototypes in the transmitter *had been transducted* through a series of point-events of transfinite cardinality. Al had innocently asked whether that meant prototypes had been stretched, so to speak, through all time, and the temporalist had thought he was joking and left in a huff.

"Like to see him do this," thought Al darkly, as he telekinized himself to the combox, after a cautious look to see that there were no medics around. To the box he said: "Police chief," and then to the police chief: "There's been a homicide committed with Medical Instrument Kit 674,101. It was lost some months ago by one of my people, Dr. John Hemingway. He didn't have a clear account of the circumstances."

The police chief groaned and said: "I'll call him in and question him." He was to be astonished by the answers, and was to learn that the homicide was well out of his jurisdiction.

Al stood for a moment at the bag board by the glowing red light that had been sparked into life by a departing vital force giving, as its last act, the warning that Kit 674,101 was in homicidal hands. With a sigh, Al pulled the plug and the light went out.

"Yah," jeered the woman. "You'd fool around with my neck, but you wouldn't risk your own with that thing!"

Angie smiled with serene confidence a smile that was to shock hardened morgue attendants. She set the Cutaneous Series knife to three centimeters before drawing it across her neck. Smiling, knowing the blade would cut only the dead horny tissue of the epidermis and the live tissue of the dermis, mysteriously push aside all major and minor blood vessels and muscular tissue—

Smiling, the knife plunging in and its microtomesharp metal shearing through major and minor blood vessels and muscular tissue and pharynx, Angie cut her throat.

In the few minutes it took the police, summoned by the shrieking Mrs. Coleman, to arrive, the instruments had become crusted with rust, and the flasks which had held vascular glue and clumps of pink, rubbery alveoli and spare gray cells and coils of receptor nerves held only black slime, and from them when opened gushed the foul gases of decomposition.

There's a lot wrong with science fiction. One of the things that's right about it is Barry Malzberg, easily the finest writer of his era. And in "A Galaxy Called Rome," Barry uses a science fiction story as a unique vehicle for criticizing the field.

In frequent asides to the audience, he explains exactly what he is doing with the story of Lena Thomas and her spaceship, and why. But—and here is the devastating part—he also points out how, as an artist, he would *like* to attack the story, and hints at the commercial restraints that prevent him from doing so.

So what you really have is two stories in one: a generic space adventure, better written than most; and a mordant, cynical commentary showing you how even brilliant authors make the choices that turns their fiction into generic space adventures. It's perhaps even more meaningful today, in a market filled with Trekbooks and Wookiebooks and 5-volume trilogies, than when it was written.

—Mike Resnick

A GALAXY CALLED ROME

by Barry N. Malzberg

In memory of John W. Campbell

I

This is not a novelette but a series of notes. The novelette cannot be truly written because it partakes of its time, which is distant and could be perceived only through the idiom and devices of that era.

Thus the piece, by virtue of these reasons and others too personal even for this variety of true confession, is little more than a set of constructions toward something less substantial . . . and, like the author, it cannot be completed.

II

The novelette would lean heavily upon two articles by the late John Campbell, for thirty-three years the editor of

Astounding/Analog, which were written shortly before his untimely death on July 11, 1971, and appeared as editorials in his magazine later that year, the second being perhaps the last piece which will ever bear his by-line. They imagine a black galaxy which would result from the implosion of a neutron star, an implosion so mighty that gravitational forces unleashed would contain not only light itself but space and time; and *A Galaxy Called Rome* is his title, not mine, since he envisions a spacecraft that might be trapped within such a black galaxy and be unable to get out . . . because escape velocity would have to exceed the speed of light. All paths of travel would lead to this galaxy, then, none away. A galaxy called Rome.

III

Conceive then of a faster-than-light spaceship which would tumble into the black galaxy and would be unable to leave. Tumbling would be easy, or at least inevitable, since one of the characteristics of the black galaxy would be its *invisibility,* and there the ship would be. The story would then pivot on the efforts of the crew to get out. The ship is named *Skipstone.* It was completed in 3892. Five hundred people died so that it might fly, but in this age life is held even more cheaply than it is today.

Left to my own devices, I might be less interested in the escape problem than that of adjustment. Light housekeeping in an anterior sector of the universe; submission to the elements, a fine, ironic literary despair. This is not science fiction, however. Science fiction was created by Hugo Gernsback to show us the ways out of technological impasse. So be it.

IV

As interesting as the material was, I quailed even at this series of notes, let alone a polished, completed work. My personal life is my black hole, I felt like pointing out (who would listen?); my daughters provide more correct and sticky implosion than any neutron star, and the sound of the pulsars is as nothing to the music of the paddock area at Aqueduct racetrack in Ozone Park, Queens, on a clear summer Tuesday. "Enough of these breathtaking concepts, infinite distances, quasar leaps, binding messages amid the arms of the spiral nebula," I could have pointed out. "I know that there are those who find an ultimate truth there, but I am not one of them. I would rather dedicate the years of life remaining (my melodramatic streak) to an understanding of the agonies of this middle-class town in northern New Jersey; until I can deal with those, how can I comprehend Ridgefield Park, to say nothing of the extension of fission to include progressively heavier gases?" Indeed, I almost abided to this until it occurred to me that Ridgefield Park would forever be as mysterious as the stars and that one could deny infinity merely to pursue a particular that would be impenetrable until the day of one's death.

So I decided to try the novelette, at least as this series of notes, although with some trepidation, but trepidation did not unsettle me, nor did I grieve, for my life is merely a set of notes for a life, and Ridgefield Park merely a rough working model of Trenton, in which, nevertheless, several thousand people live who cannot discern their right hands from their left, and also much cattle.

V

It is 3895. The spacecraft *Skipstone*, on an exploratory flight through the major and minor galaxies surrounding the Milky Way, falls into the black galaxy of a neutron star and is lost forever.

The captain of this ship, the only living consciousness of it, is its commander, Lena Thomas. True, the hold of the ship carries five hundred and fifteen of the dead sealed in gelatinous fix who will absorb unshielded gamma rays. True, these rays will at some time in the future hasten their reconstitution. True, again, that another part of the hold contains the prostheses of seven skilled engineers, male and female, who could be switched on at only slight inconvenience and would provide Lena not only with answers to any technical problems which would arise but with companionship to while away the long and grave hours of the *Skiptone*'s flight.

Lena, however, does not use the prosthesis, nor does she feel the necessity to. She is highly skilled and competent, at least in relation to the routine tasks of this testing flight, and she feels that to call for outside help would only be an admission of weakness, would be reported back to the bureau, and lessen her potential for promotion. (She is right; the bureau has monitored every cubicle of this ship, both visually and biologically: she can see or do nothing which does not trace to a printout; they would not think well of her if she was dependent upon outside assistance.) Toward the embalmed she feels somewhat more; her condition rattling in the hold of the ship as it moves on tachyonic drive seems to approximate theirs: although they are deprived of consciousness, that quality seems to be almost irrelevant to the condition of hyperspace; and if there were any way that she could bridge their mystery, she might well address them. As it is, she must settle for imaginary dialogues and for long, quiescent periods when she will watch the monitors, watch the rainbow of hyperspace, the collision of the spectrum, and say nothing whatsoever.

Saying nothing will not do, however, and the fact is that Lena talks incessantly at times, if only to herself. This is good because the story should have much dialogue; dramatic incident is best impelled through straightforward characterization, and Lena's compulsive need, now and then, to state her condition and its relation to the spaces she occupies will satisfy this need.

In her conversation, of course, she often addresses the embalmed. "Consider," she says to them, some of them dead eight hundred years, others dead weeks, all of them stacked in the hold in relation to their status in life and their ability to hoard assets to pay for the process that will return them their lives, "consider what's going on here," pointing through the hold, the colors gleaming through the portholes onto her wrist, colors dancing in the air, her eyes quite full and maddened in this light, which does not indicate that she is mad but only that the condition of hyperspace itself is insane, the Michelson-Morley effect having a psychological as well as physical reality here. "Why it could be *me* dead and in the hold and all of you here in the dock watching the colors spin, it's all the same, all the same faster than light," and indeed the twisting and sliding effects of the tachyonic drive are such that at the moment of speech what Lena says is true.

The dead live; the living are dead, all slides and becomes jumbled together as she has noted; and were it not that their objective poles of consciousness were fixed by years of training and discipline, just as hers are transfixed by a different kind of training and discipline, she would press the levers to eject the dead one by one into the larger coffin of space, something which is indicated only as an emergency procedure under the gravest of terms and which would result in her removal from the bureau immediately upon her return. The dead are precious cargo; they are, in essence, paying for the experiments and must be handled with the greatest delicacy. "I will handle you with the greatest delicacy," Lena says in hyperspace, "and I will never let you go, little packages in my little prison," and so on, singing and chanting as the ship moves on somewhat in excess of one million miles per second, always accelerating; and yet, except for the colors, the nausea, the disorienting swing, her own mounting insanity, the terms of this story, she might be in the IRT Lexington Avenue local at rush hour, moving slowly uptown as circles of illness move through the fainting car in the bowels of summer.

VI

She is twenty-eight years old. Almost two thousand years in the future, when man has established colonies on forty planets in the Milky Way, has fully populated the solar system, is working in the faster-than-light experiments as quickly as he can to move through other galaxies, the medical science of that day is not notably superior to that of our own, and the human life span has not been significantly extended, nor have the diseases of mankind which are now known as congenital been eradicated. Most of the embalmed were in their eighties or nineties; a few of them, the more recent deaths, were nearly a hundred, but the average life span still hangs somewhat short of eighty, and most of these have died from cancer, heart attacks, renal failure, cerebral blowout, and the like. There is some irony in the fact that man can have at least established a toehold in his galaxy, can have solved the mysteries of the FTL drive and yet finds the fact of his own biology as stupefying as he has throughout history, but every sociologist understands that those who live in a culture are least qualified to criticize it (because they have fully assimilated the codes of the culture, even as to criticism), and Lena does not see this irony any more than the reader will have to in order to appreciate the deeper and more metaphysical irony of the story, which is this: that greater speed, greater space, greater progress, greater sensation has not resulted in any definable expansion of the limits of consciousness and personality and all that the FTL drive is to Lena is an increasing entrapment.

It is important to understand that she is merely a technician; that although she is highly skilled and has been trained through the bureau for many years for her job as pilot, she really does not need to possess the technical knowledge of any graduate scientists of our own time . . . that her job, which is essentially a probe-and-ferrying, could be done by an adolescent; and that all of her training has afforded her no protection against the boredom and depression of her assignment.

When she is done with this latest probe, she will return to Uranus and be granted a six-month leave. She is looking forward to that. She appreciates the opportunity. She is only twenty-eight, and she is tired of being sent with the dead to tumble through the spectrum for weeks at a time, and what she would very much like to be, at least for a while, is a young woman. She would like to be at peace. She would like to be loved. She would like to have sex.

VII

Something must be made of the element of sex in this story, if only because it deals with a female protagonist (where asepsis will not work); and in the tradition of modern literary science fiction, where some credence is given to the whole range of human needs and behaviors, it would be clumsy and amateurish to ignore the issue. Certainly the easy scenes can be written and to great effect: Lena masturbating as she stares through the port at the colored levels of hyperspace; Lena dreaming thickly of intercourse as she unconsciously massages her nipples, the ship lunging deeper and deeper (as she does not yet know) toward the black galaxy; the black galaxy itself as some ultimate vaginal symbol of absorption whose Freudian overcast will not be ignored in the imagery of this story . . . indeed, one can envision Lena stumbling toward the evictors at the depths of her panic in the black galaxy to bring out one of the embalmed, her grim and necrophiliac fantasies as the body is slowly moved upwards on its glistening slab, the way that her eyes will look as she comes to consciousness and realizes what she has become . . . oh, this would be a very powerful scene indeed, almost anything to do with sex in space is powerful (one must also conjure with the effects of hyperspace upon the orgasm; would it be the orgasm which all of us know and love so well or something entirely different, perhaps detumescence, perhaps exaltation?), and I would face the issue squarely, if only I could, and in line with the very real need of the story to have powerful and effective dialogue.

"For God's sake," Lena would say at the end, the music of her entrapment squeezing her, coming over her, blotting her toward extinction, "for God's sake, all we ever needed was a fuck, that's all that sent us out into space, that's all that it ever meant to us, I've got to have it, got to have it, do you understand?" jamming her fingers in and out of her aqueous surfaces. . . .

But of course this would not work, at least in the story which I am trying to conceptualize. Space *is* aseptic; that is the secret of science fiction for forty-five years; it is not deceit or its adolescent audience or the publication codes which have deprived most of the literature of the range of human sexuality but the fact that in the clean and abysmal spaces between the stars sex, that demonstration of our perverse and irreplaceable humanity, would have no role at all. Not for nothing did the astronauts return to tell us their vision of otherworldness, not for nothing did they stagger in their thick landing gear as they walked toward the colonels' salute, not for nothing did all of those marriages, all of those wonderful kids undergo such terrible strains. There is simply no room for it. It does not fit. Lena would understand this. "I never thought of sex," she would say, "never thought of it once, not even at the end when everything was around me and I was dancing."

VIII

Therefore it will be necessary to characterize Lena in some other way, and that opportunity will only come through the moment of crisis, the moment at which the *Skipstone* is drawn into the black galaxy of the neutron star. This moment will occur fairly early in the story, perhaps five or six hundred words deep (her previous life on the ship and impressions of hyperspace will come in expository chunks interwoven between sections of ongoing action), and her only indication of what has happened will be when there is a deep, lurching shiver in the gut of the ship where the embalmed lay and then she feels herself falling.

To explain this sensation it is important to explain normal hyperspace, the skip-drive which is merely to draw the curtains and to be in a cubicle. There is no sensation of motion in hyperspace, there could not be, the drive taking the *Skipstone* past any concepts of sound or light and into an era where there is no language to encompass nor glands to register. Were she to draw the curtains (curiously similar in their frills and pastels to what we might see hanging today in lower-middle-class homes of the kind I inhabit), she would be deprived of any sensation, but of course she cannot; she must open them to the portholes, and through them she can see the song of the colors to which I have previously alluded. Inside, there is a deep and grievous wretchedness, a feeling of terrible loss (which may explain why Lena thinks of exhuming the dead) that may be ascribed to the effects of hyperspace upon the corpus; but these sensations can be shielded, are not visible from the outside and can be completely controlled by the phlegmatic types who comprise most of the pilots of these experimental flights. (Lena is rather phlegmatic herself. She reacts more to stress than some of her counterparts but well within the normal range prescribed by the bureau, which admittedly does a superficial check.)

The effects of falling into the black galaxy are entirely different however, and it is here where Lena's emotional equipment becomes completely unstuck.

IX

At this point in the story great gobs of physics, astronomical, and mathematic data would have to be incorporated, hopefully in a way which would furnish the hard-science basis of the story without repelling the reader.

Of course one should not worry so much about the repulsion of the reader; most who read science fiction do so in pursuit of exactly this kind of hard speculation (most often they are disappointed, but then most often they are, after a time, unable to tell the difference), and they would sit still much longer for a lecture than would, say, readers of the fiction of John Cheever, who could hardly bear sociological diatribes wedged into the everlasting vision of Gehenna which is Cheever's gift to his admirers. Thus it would be possible without awkwardness to make the following facts known, and these facts could indeed be set off from the body of the story and simply told like this:

It is posited that in other galaxies there are such as neutron stars, stars of four or five hundred times the size of our own or "normal" suns, which in their continuing nuclear process, burning and burning to maintain their light, will collapse in a mere ten to fifteen thousand years of difficult existence, their hydrogen fusing to helium then nitrogen and then to even heavier elements until with an implosion of terrific force, hungering for power which is no longer there, they collapse upon one another and bring disaster.

Disaster not only to themselves but possibly to the entire galaxy which they inhabit, for the gravitational force created by the implosion would be so vast as to literally seal in light. Not only light but sound and properties of all the stars in that great tube of force . . . so that the galaxy itself would be sucked into the funnel of gravitation created by the collapse and be absorbed into the flickering and desperate heart of the extinguished star.

It is possible to make several extrapolations from the fact of the neutron stars—and of the neutron stars themselves we have no doubt; many nova and supernova are now known to have been created by exactly this effect; not *ex*- but *im*plosion—and some of them are these:

(a) The gravitational forces created, like great spokes wheeling out from the star, would drag in all parts of the galaxy within their compass; and because of the force of that gravitation, the galaxy would be invisible. . . . These forces would, as has been said, literally contain light.

(b) The neutron star, functioning like a cosmic vacuum cleaner, might literally destroy the universe. Indeed, the universe may be in the slow process at this moment of being destroyed as hundreds of millions of its suns and planets are being inexorably drawn toward these great vortexes. The process would be *slow,* of course, but it is seemingly inexorable. One neutron star, theoretically, could absorb the universe. There are many more than one.

(c) The universe may have, obversely, been *created* by such an implosion, throwing out enormous cosmic filaments that, in a flickering instant of time which is as eons to us but an instant to the cosmologists, are now being drawn back in. The universe may be an accident.

(d) Cosmology aside, a ship trapped in such a vortex, such a "black," or invisible, galaxy, drawn toward the deadly source of the neutron star would be unable to leave it through normal faster-than-light drive . . . because the gravitation would absorb light, it would be impossible to build up any level of acceleration (which would at some point not exceed the speed of light) to permit escape. If it were possible to emerge from the field, it could only be done by an immediate switch to tachyonic drive without accelerative buildup . . . a process which could drive the occupant insane and which would, in any case, have no clear destination. The black hole of the dead star is a literal vacuum in space . . . one could fall through the hole, but where, then, would one go?

(e) The actual process of being in the field of the dead star might well drive one insane.

For all of these reasons Lena does not know that she has fallen into the galaxy called Rome until the ship simply does so. And she would instantly and irreparably become insane.

X

The technological data having been stated, the crisis of the story—the collapse into the galaxy—having occurred early on, it would now be the obligation of the writer to describe the actual sensations involved in falling into the black galaxy. Since little or nothing is known of what these sensations would be—other than that it is clear that the gravitation would suspend almost all physical laws and might well suspend time itself, time only being a function of physics—it would be easy to lurch into a surrealistic mode here; Lena could see monsters slithering on the walls, two-dimensional monsters that is, little cutouts of her past; she could reenact her life *in full consciousness* from birth until death; she could literally be turned inside out anatomically and perform in her imagination or in the flesh gross physical acts upon herself; she could live and die a thousand times in the lightless, timeless expanse of the pit. . . . All of this could be done within the confines of the story, and it would doubtless lead to some very powerful material. One could do it picaresque fashion, one perversity or lunacy to a chapter—that is to say, the chapters spliced together with more data on the gravitational excesses and the fact that neutron stars (this is interesting) are probably the pulsars which we have identified, stars which can be detected through sound but not by sight from unimaginable distances. The author could do this kind of thing and do it very well indeed; he has done it literally hundreds of times before, but this, perhaps, would be in disregard of Lena. She has needs more imperative than those of the author or even those of the editors. She is in terrible pain. She is suffering.

Falling, she sees the dead; falling, she hears the dead; the dead address her from the hold, and they are screaming, "Release us, release us, we are alive, we are in pain, we are in torment"; in their gelatinous flux, their distended limbs sutured finger and toe to the membranes which hold them, their decay has been reversed as the warp into which they have fallen has reversed time; and they are begging Lena from a torment which they cannot phrase, so profound is it; their voices are in her head, pealing and banging like oddly shaped bells. "Release us!" they scream; "we are no longer dead, the trumpet has sounded!" and so on and so forth, but Lena literally does not know what to do. She is merely the ferryman on this dread passage; she is not a medical specialist; she knows nothing of prophylaxis or restoration, and any movement she made to release them from the gelatin which holds them would surely destroy their biology, no matter what the state of their minds.

But even if this were not so, even if she could by releasing them give them peace, she cannot because she is succumbing to her own responses. In the black hole, if the dead are risen, then the risen are certainly the dead; she dies in this space, Lena does; she dies a thousand times over a period of seventy thousand years (because there is no objective time here, chronology is controlled only by the psyche, and Lena has a thousand full lives and a thousand full deaths), and it is terrible, of course, but it is also interesting because for every cycle of death there is a life, seventy years in which she can meditate upon her condition in solitude; and by the two hundredth death, the fourteen thousandth year or more (or less, each of the lives is individual, some of them long, others short), Lena has come to an understanding of exactly where she is and what has happened to her. That it has taken her fourteen thousand years to reach this understanding is in one way incredible, and yet it is a kind of miracle as well because in an infinite universe with infinite possibilities, all of them reconstituted for her, it is highly unlikely that even in fourteen thousand years she would stumble upon the answer, had it not been for the fact that she is unusually strong-willed and that some of the personalities through which she has lived are highly creative and controlled and have been able to do some serious thinking. Also there is a carryover from life to life, even with the differing personalities, so that she is able to make use of preceding knowledge.

Most of the personalities are weak, of course, and not a few are insane, and almost all are cowardly, but there is little residue; even in the worst of them there is enough residue to carry forth the knowledge, and so it is in the fourteenth thousandth year, when the truth of it has finally come upon her and she realizes what has happened to her and what is going on and what she must do to get out of there, and so it is (then) that she summons all of the strength and will which are left to her and stumbling to the console (she is in her sixty-eighth year of this life and in the personality of an old, sniveling, whining man, an ex-ferryman himself), she summons one of the prostheses, the master engineer, the controller. All of this time the dead have been shrieking and clanging in her ears, fourteen thousand years of agony billowing from the hold and surrounding her in sheets like iron; and as the master engineer, exactly as he was when she last saw him fourteen thousand years and two weeks ago emerges from the console, the machinery whirring slickly, she gasps in relief, too weak even to respond with pleasure to the fact that in this condition of antitime, antilight, anticausality the machinery still works. But then it would. The machinery always works, even in this final and most terrible of all the hard-science stories. It is not the machinery which fails but its operators or, in extreme cases, the cosmos.

"What's the matter?" the master engineer says.

The stupidity of this question, its naiveté and irrelevance in the midst of the hell she has occupied, stuns Lena, but she realizes even through the haze that the master engineer would, of course, come without memory of circumstances and would have to be apprised of background. This is inevitable. Whining and sniveling, she tells him in her old man's voice what has happened.

"Why that's terrible!" the master engineer says. "That's

really terrible," and lumbering to a pothole, he looks out at the black galaxy, the galaxy called Rome, and one look at it causes him to lock into position and then disintegrate, not because the machinery has failed (the machinery never fails, not ultimately) but because it has merely recreated a human substance which could not possibly come to grips with what has been seen outside that porthole.

Lena is left alone again, then, with the shouts of the dead carrying forward.

Realizing instantly what has happened to her—fourteen thousand years of perception can lead to a quicker reaction time, if nothing else—she addresses the console again, uses the switches and produces three more prostheses, all of them engineers barely subsidiary to the one she has already addressed. (Their resemblance to the three comforters of Job will not be ignored here, and there will be an opportunity to squeeze in some quick religious allegory, which is always useful to give an ambitious story yet another level of meaning.) Although they are not quite as qualified or definitive in their opinions as the original engineer, they are bright enough by far to absorb her explanation, and this time her warnings not to go to the portholes, not to look upon the galaxy, are heeded. Instead, they stand there in rigid and curiously mortified postures, as if waiting for Lena to speak.

"So you see," she says finally, as if concluding a long and difficult conversation, which in fact she has, "as far as I can see, the only way to get out of this black galaxy is to go directly into tachyonic drive. Without any accelerative buildup at all."

The three comforters nod slowly, bleakly. They do not quite know what she is talking about, but then again, they have not had fourteen thousand years to ponder this point. "Unless you can see anything else," Lena says, "unless you can think of anything different. Otherwise, it's going to be infinity in here, and I can't take much more of this, really. Fourteen thousand years is enough."

"Perhaps," the first comforter suggests softly, "perhaps it is your fate and your destiny to spend infinity in this black hole. Perhaps in some way you are determining the fate of the universe. After all, it was you who said that it all might be a gigantic accident, eh? Perhaps your suffering gives it purpose."

"And then too," the second lisps, "you've got to consider the dead down there. This isn't very easy for them, you know, what with being jolted alive and all that, and an immediate vault into tachyonic would probably destroy them for good. The bureau wouldn't like that, and you'd be liable for some pretty stiff damages. No, if I were you I'd stay with the dead," the second concludes, and a clamorous murmur seems to arise from the hold at this, although whether it is one of approval or of terrible pain is difficult to tell. The dead are not very expressive.

"Anyway," the third says, brushing a forelock out of his eyes, averting his glance from the omnipresent and dreadful portholes, "there's little enough to be done about this situation. You've fallen into a neutron star, a black funnel. It is utterly beyond the puny capacities and possibilities of man. I'd accept my fate if I were you." His model was a senior scientist working on quasar theory, but in reality he appears to be a metaphysician. "There are corners of experience into which man cannot stray without being severely penalized."

"That's very easy for you to say," Lena says bitterly, her whine breaking into clear glissando, "but you haven't suffered as I have. Also, there's at least a theoretical possibility that I'll get out of here if I do the buildup without acceleration."

"But where will you land?" the third says, waving a trembling forefinger. "And when? All rules of space and time have been destroyed here; only gravity persists. You can fall through the center of this sun, but you do not know where you will come out or at what period of time. It is inconceivable that you would emerge into normal space in the time you think of as contemporary."

"No," the second says. "I wouldn't do that. You and the dead are joined together now; it is truly your fate to remain with them. What is death? What is life? In the galaxy called Rome all roads lead to the same, you see; you have ample time to consider these questions, and I'm sure that you will come up with something truly viable, of much interest."

"Ah, well," the first says, looking at Lena, "if you must know, I think that it would be much nobler of you to remain here; for all we know, your condition gives substance and viability to the universe. Perhaps you *are* the universe. But you're not going to listen anyway, and so I won't argue the point. I really won't," he says rather petulantly and then makes a gesture to the other two; the three of them quite deliberately march to a porthole, push a curtain aside and look out upon it. Before Lena can stop them—not that she is sure she would, not that she is sure that this is not exactly what she was willed—they have been reduced to ash.

And she is left alone with the screams of the dead.

XI

It can be seen that the satiric aspects of the scene above can be milked for great implication, and unless a very skillful controlling hand is kept upon the material, the piece could easily degenerate into farce at this moment. It is possible, as almost any comedian knows, to reduce (or elevate) the starkest and most terrible issues to scatology or farce simply by particularizing them; and it will be hard not to use this scene for a kind of needed comic relief in what is, after all, an extremely depressing tale, the more depressing because it has used the largest possible canvas on which to imprint its messages that man is irretrievably dwarfed by the cosmos. (At least, that is the message which it would be easiest to wring out of the material; actually I have other things in mind, but how many will be able to detect them?)

What will save the scene and the story itself, around this point, will be the lush physical descriptions of the black galaxy, the neutron star, the altering effects they have had upon perceived reality. Every rhetorical trick, every typographical device, every nuance of language and memory which the writer has to call upon will be utilized in this section describing the appearance of the black hole and its effects upon Lena's (admittedly distorted) consciousness. It will be a bleak vision, of course, but not necessarily a hopeless one; it will demonstrate that our concepts of "beauty" or "ugliness" or "evil" or "good" or "love" or "death" are little more than metaphors, semantically limited, framed in by the poor receiving equipment in our heads; and it will be suggested that, rather than showing us a different or alternative reality, the black hole may only be showing us the only reality we know, but *extended,* infinitely extended so that the story may give us, as good science fiction often does, at this point some glimpse of possibilities beyond ourselves, possibilities not to be contained in word rates or the problems of editorial qualification. And also at this point of the story it might be worthwhile to characterize Lena in a "warmer" and more "sympathetic" fashion so that the reader can see her as a distinct and admirable human being, quite plucky in the face of all her disasters and fourteen thousand years, two hundred lives. This can be done through conventional fictional technique: individuation through defining idiosyncrasy, tricks of speech, habits, mannerisms, and so on. In common everyday fiction we could give her an affecting stutter, a dimple on her left breast, a love of policemen, fear of red convertibles, and leave it at that; in this story, because of its considerably extended theme, it will be necessary to do better than that, to find originalities of idiosyncrasy which will, in their wonder and suggestion of panoramic possibility, approximate the black hole . . . but no matter. No matter. This can be done; the section interweaving Lena and her vision of the black hole will be the flashiest and most admired but in truth the easiest section of the story to write, and I am sure that I would have no trouble with it whatsoever if, as I said much earlier, this were a story instead of a series of notes for a story, the story itself being unutterably beyond our time and space and devices and to be glimpsed only in empty little flickers of light much as Lena can glimpse the black hole, much as she knows the gravity of the neutron star. These notes are as close to the vision of the story as Lena herself would ever get.

As this section ends, it is clear that Lena has made her decision to attempt to leave the black galaxy by automatic boost to tachyonic drive. She does not know where she will emerge or how, but she does know that she can bear this—no longer.

She prepares to set the controls, but before this it is necessary to write the dialogue with the dead.

XII

One of them presumably will appoint himself as the spokesman of the many and will appear before Lena in this new space as if in a dream. "Listen here," this dead would say, one born in 3361, dead in 3401, waiting eight centuries for exhumation to a society that can rid his body of leukemia (he is bound to be disappointed), "you've got to face the facts of the situation here. We can't just leave in this way. Better the death we know than the death you will give us."

"The decision is made," Lena says, her fingers straight on the controls. "There will be no turning back."

"We are dead now," the leukemic says. "At least let this death continue. At least in the bowels of this galaxy where there is no time we have a kind of life or at least that nonexistence of which we have always dreamed. I could tell you many of the things we have learned during these fourteen thousand years, but they would make little sense to you, of course. We have learned resignation. We have had great insights. Of course all of this would go beyond you."

"Nothing goes beyond me. Nothing at all. But it does not matter."

"Everything matters. Even here there is consequence, causality, a sense of humanness, one of responsibility. You can suspend physical laws, you can suspend life itself, but you cannot separate the moral imperatives of humanity. There are absolutes. It would be apostasy to try and leave."

"Man must leave," Lena says, "man must struggle, man must attempt to control his conditions. Even if he goes from worse to obliteration, that is still his destiny." Perhaps the dialogue is a little florid here. Nevertheless, this will be the thrust of it. It is to be noted that putting this conventional viewpoint in the character of a woman will give another of those necessary levels of irony with which the story must abound if it is to be anything other than a freak show, a cascade of sleazy wonders shown shamefully behind a tent . . . but irony will give it legitimacy. "I don't care about the dead," Lena says. "I only care about the living."

"Then care abut the universe," the dead man says, "care about that, if nothing else. By trying to come out through the center of the black hole, you may rupture the seamless fabric of time and space itself. You may destroy everything. Past and present and future. The explosion may extend the funnel of gravitational force to infinite size, and all of the universe will be driven into the hole."

Lena shakes her head. She knows that the dead is merely another one of her tempters in a more cunning and cadaverous guise. "You are lying to me," she says. "This is merely another effect of the galaxy called Rome. I am responsible to myself, only to myself. The universe is not at issue."

"That's a rationalization," the leukemic says, seeing her hesitation, sensing his victory, "and you know it as well as I do. You can't be an utter solipsist. You aren't God, there is no God, not here, but if there was it wouldn't be you. You must measure the universe about yourself."

Lena looks at the dead and the dead looks at her; and in that confrontation, in the shade of his eyes as they pass through the dull lusters of the neutron star effect, she sees that they are close to a communion so terrible that it will become a weld, become a connection . . . that if she listens to the dead for more than another instant, she will collapse within those eyes as the *Skipstone* has collapsed into the black hole; and she cannot bear this, it cannot be . . . she must hold to the belief, that there is some separation between the living and the dead and that there is dignity in that separation, that life is not death but something else because, if she cannot accept that, she denies herself . . . and quickly then, quickly before she can consider further, she hits the controls that will convert the ship instantly past the power of light; and then in the explosion of many suns that might only be her heart she hides her head in her arms and screams.

And the dead screams with her, and it is not a scream of joy but not of terror either. . . . It is the true natal cry suspended between the moments of limbo, life and expiration, and their shrieks entwine in the womb of the *Skipstone* as it pours through into the redeemed light.

XIII

The story is open-ended, of course.

Perhaps Lena emerges into her own time and space once more, all of this having been a sheath over the greater reality. Perhaps she emerges into an otherness. Then again, she may never get out of the black hole at all but remain and live there, the *Skipstone* a planet in the tubular universe of the neutron star, the first or last of a series of planets collapsing toward their deadened sun. If the story is done correctly, if the ambiguities are prepared right, if the technological data are stated well, if the material is properly visualized . . . well, it does not matter then what happens to Lena, her *Skipstone* and her dead. Any ending will do. Any would suffice and be emotionally satisfying to the reader.

Still, there is an inevitable ending.

It seems clear to the writer, who will not, cannot write this story, but if he did he would drive it through to this one conclusion, the conclusion clear, implied really from the first and bound, bound utterly, into the text.

So let the author have it.

XIV

In the infinity of time and space, all is possible, and as they are vomited from that great black hole, spilled from this anus of a neutron star (I will not miss a single Freudian implication if I can), Lena and her dead take on this infinity, partake of the vast canvas of possibility. Now they are in the Antares Cluster flickering like a bulb; here they are at the heart of Sirius the Dog Star, five hundred screams from the hold; here gain in ancient Rome watching Jesus trudge up carrying the cross of Calvary . . . and then again in another unimaginable galaxy dead across from the Milky Way a billion light-years in span with a hundred thousand habitable planets, each of them with its Calvary . . . and they are not, they are not yet satisfied.

They cannot, being human, partake of infinity; they can partake only of what they know. They cannot, being created from the consciousness of the writer, partake of what he does not know but what is only close to him. Trapped within the consciousness of the writer, the penitentiary of his being, as the writer is himself trapped in the *Skipstone* of his mortality, Lena and her dead emerge in the year 1975 to the town of Ridgefield Park, New Jersey, and there they inhabit the bodies of its fifteen thousand souls, and there they are, there they are yet, dwelling amid the refineries, strolling on Main Street, sitting in the Rialto theater, shopping in the supermarkets, pairing off and clutching one another in the imploded stars of their beds on this very night at this very moment, as that accident, the author, himself one of them, has conceived them.

It is unimaginable that they would come, Lena and the dead, from the heart of the galaxy called Rome to tenant Ridgefield Park, New Jersey . . . but more unimaginable still that from all the Ridgefield Parks of our time we will come and assemble and build the great engines which will take us to the stars and some of the stars will bring us death and some bring life and some will bring nothing at all but the engines will go on and on and so—after a fashion, in our fashion—will we.

The dry humor so well displayed in the work of British writers can be the base of fiction which is seldom if ever forgotten by the reader who is lucky enough to chance upon it. I first read "Diabologic" years ago. I returned to read it in one of the anthologies in which it happily appeared several times thereafter. As a writer, my admiration for the work of Eric Frank Russell stands very high and I cherish the volumes I have been able to obtain. The only difficulty is that there is so little of it to amuse one—some novels and a handful of short stories—but always to be treasured and reenjoyed as the years pass.

Humor is not an easy subject in any field and requires more than the usual skill of a writer to make a fine example such as this. I preserve my Russells carefully and *that* is logical.

—Andre Norton

DIABOLOGIC

by Eric Frank Russell

He made one circumnavigation to put the matter beyond doubt. That was standard space-scout technique; look once on the approach, look again all the way around. It often happened that second and closer impressions contradicted first and more distant ones. Some perverse factor in the probability sequence frequently caused the laugh to appear on the other side of a planetary face.

Not this time, though. What he'd observed coming in remained visible right around the belly. This world was occupied by intelligent life of a high order. The unmistakable markings were there in the form of dockyards, railroad marshaling grids, power stations, spaceports, quarries, factories, mines, housing projects, bridges, canals, and a hundred and one other signs of a life that spawns fast and vigorously.

The spaceports in particular were highly significant. He counted three of them. None held a flightworthy ship at the moment he flamed high above them, but in one was a tubeless vessel undergoing repair. A long, black, snouty thing about the size and shape of an Earth-Mars tramp. Certainly not as big and racy-looking as a Sol-Sirius liner.

As he gazed down through his tiny control-cabin's armor-glass, he knew that this was to be contact with a vengeance. During long, long centuries of human expansion, more than seven hundred inhabitable worlds had been found, charted, explored and, in some cases, exploited. All contained life. A minority held intelligent life. But up to this moment nobody had found one other lifeform sufficiently advanced to cavort among the stars.

Of course, such a discovery had been theorized. Human adventuring created an exploratory sphere that swelled into the cosmos. Sooner or later, it was assumed, that sphere must touch another one at some point within the heavenly host. What would happen then was anybody's guess. Perhaps they'd fuse, making a bigger, shinier biform bubble. Or perhaps both bubbles would burst. Anyway, by the looks of it the touching-time was now.

If he'd been within reach of a frontier listening-post, he'd have beamed a signal detailing this find. Even now it wasn't too late to drive back for seventeen weeks and get within receptive range. But that would mean seeking a refueling dump while he was at it. The ship just hadn't enough for such a double run plus the return trip home. Down there they had fuel. Maybe they'd give him some and maybe it would suit his engines. And just as possibly it would prove useless.

Right now he had adequate power reserves to land here and eventually get back to base. A bird in the hand is worth two in the bush. So he tilted the vessel and plunged into the alien atmosphere, heading for the largest spaceport of the three.

What might be awaiting him at ground level did not bother him at all. The Terrans of today were not the nervy, apprehensive Terrans of the earthbound and lurid past. They had become space-sophisticated. They had learned to lounge around with a carefree smile and let the other lifeforms do the worrying. It lent an air of authority and always worked. Nothing is more intimidating than an idiotic grin worn by a manifest non-idiot.

Quite a useful weapon in the diabological armory was the knowing smirk.

His landing created a most satisfactory sensation. The planet's point-nine Earth-mass permitted a little extra dexterity in handling the ship. He swooped it down, curved it up, dropped tail-first, stood straddle-legged on the tail-fins, cut the braking blast and would not have missed centering on a spread handkerchief by more than ten inches.

They seemed to spring out of the ground the way people do when cars collide on a deserted road. Dozens of them, hundreds. They were on the short side, the tallest not exceeding five feet. Otherwise they differed from his own pink-faced, blue-eyed type no more than would a Chinese covered in fine gray fur.

Massing in a circle beyond range of his jet-rebound, they stared at the ship, gabbled, gesticulated, nudged each other, argued, and generally behaved in the manner of a curious mob that has discovered a deep, dark hole with strange noises issuing therefrom. The noteworthy feature about their behavior was that none were scared, none attempted to get out of reach, either openly or surreptitiously. The only thing about which they were wary was the chance of a sudden blast from the silent jets.

He did not emerge at once. That would have been an error—and blunderers are not chosen to pilot scout-vessels. Pre-exit rule number one is that air must be tested. What suited that crowd outside would not necessarily agree with him. Anyway, he'd have checked air even if his own mother had been smoking a cigar in the front row of the audience.

The Schrieber analyzer required four minutes in which to suck a sample through the Pitot tube, take it apart, sneer at the bits, make a bacteria count and say whether its lord and master could condescend to breathe the stuff.

He sat patiently while it made up its mind. Finally the needle on its half-red, half-white dial crawled reluctantly to mid-white. A fast shift would have pronounced the atmosphere socially acceptable. Slowness was the Schrieber's way of saying that his lungs were about to go slumming. The analyzer was and always had been a robotic snob that graded alien atmospheres on the caste system. The best and cleanest air was Brahman, pure Brahman. The worst was Untouchable.

Switching it off, he opened the inner and outer air-lock doors, sat in the rim with his feet dangling eighty yards above ground level. From this vantage-point he calmly surveyed the mob, his expression that of one who can spit but not be spat upon. The sixth diabological law states that the higher, the fewer. Proof: the sea gull's tactical advantage over man.

Being intelligent, those placed by unfortunate circumstances eighty yards deeper in the gravitational field soon appreciated their state of vertical disadvantage. Short of toppling the ship or climbing a polished surface, they were impotent to get at him. Not that any wanted to in any inimical way. But desire grows strongest when there is the least possibility of satisfaction. So they wanted him down there, face to face, merely because he was out of reach.

To make matters worse, he turned sidewise and lay within the rim, one leg hitched up and hands linked around the knee, then continued looking at them in obvious comfort. They had to stand. And they had to stare upward at the cost of a crick in the neck. Alternatively, they could adjust their heads and eyes to a crickless level and endure being looked at while not looking. Altogether, it was a hell of a situation.

The longer it lasted the less pleasing it became. Some of them shouted at him in squeaky voices. Upon those he bestowed a benign smile. Others gesticulated. He gestured back and the sharpest among them weren't happy about it. For some strange reason that no scientist had ever bothered to investigate, certain digital motions stimulate special glands in any part of the cosmos. Basic diabological training included a course in what was known as signal-deflation, whereby the yolk could be removed from an alien ego with one wave of the hand.

For a while the crowd surged restlessly around, nibbling the gray fur on the backs of their fingers, muttering to each other, and occasionally throwing sour looks upward. They still kept clear of the danger zone, apparently assuming that the specimen reclining in the lock-rim might have a companion at the controls. Next, they became moody, content to do no more than scowl futilely at the tail-fins.

That state of affairs lasted until a convoy of heavy vehicles arrived and unloaded troops. The newcomers bore riot sticks and handguns, and wore uniforms the color of the stuff hogs roll in. Forming themselves into three ranks, they turned right at a barked command, marched forward. The crowd opened to make way.

Expertly, they stationed themselves in an armed circle separating the ship from the horde of onlookers. A trio of officers paraded around and examined the tail-fins without going nearer than was necessary. Then they backed off, stared up at the air-lock rim. The subject of their attention gazed back with academic interest.

The senior of the three officers patted his chest where his heart was located, bent and patted the ground, forced pacific innocence into his face as again he stared at the arrival high above. The tilt of his head made his hat fall off, and in turning to pick it up he trod on it.

This petty incident seemed to gratify the one eighty yards higher because he chuckled, let go the leg he was nursing, leaned out for a better look at the victim. Red-faced under his furry complexion, the officer once more performed the belly and ground massage. The other understood this time. He gave a nod of gracious assent, disappeared into the lock. A few seconds later a nylon ladder snaked down the ship's side and the invader descended with monkey-like agility.

Three things struck the troops and the audience immediately he stood before them, namely, the nakedness of his face and hands, his greater size and weight, and the fact that he carried no visible weapons. Strangeness of shape and form was to be expected. After all, they had done some space-roaming themselves and knew of lifeforms more outlandish. But what sort of creature has the brains to build a ship and not the sense to carry means of defense?

They were essentially a logical people.

The poor saps.

The officers made no attempt to converse with this specimen from the great unknown. They were not telepathic, and space-experience had taught them that mere mouth-noises are useless until one side or the other has learned the meanings thereof. So by signs they conveyed to him their wish to take him to town where he would meet others of their kind more competent to establish contact. They were pretty good at explaining with their hands, as was natural for the only other lifeform that had found new worlds.

He agreed to this with the same air of a lord consorting with the lower orders that had been apparent from the start. Perhaps he had been unduly influenced by the Schrieber. Again the crowd made way while the guard conducted him to the trucks. He passed through under a thousand eyes, favored them with deflatory gesture number seventeen, this being a nod that acknowledged their existence and tolerated their vulgar interest in him.

The trucks trundled away leaving the ship with air-lock open, ladder dangling and the rest of the troops still standing guard around the fins. Nobody failed to notice that touch, either. He hadn't bothered to prevent access to the vessel. There was nothing to prevent experts looking through it and stealing ideas from another space-going race.

Nobody of that caliber could be so criminally careless. Therefore, it would not be carelessness. Pure logic said the ship's designs were not worth protecting from the stranger's viewpoint because they were long out of date. Or else they were unstealable because they were beyond the comprehension of a lesser people. Who the heck did he think they were? By the Black World of Khas, they'd show him!

A junior officer climbed the ladder, explored the ship's interior, came down, reported no more aliens within, not even a pet *lansim,* not a pretzel. The stranger had come alone. This item of information circulated through the crowd. They didn't care for it too much. A visit by a fleet of battleships bearing ten thousand they could understand. It would be a show of force worthy of their stature. But the casual arrival of one, and only one, smacked somewhat of the dumping of a missionary among the heathens of the twin worlds of Morantia.

Meanwhile, the trucks rolled clear of the spaceport, speeded up through twenty miles of country, entered a city. Here, the leading vehicle parted company from the rest, made for the western suburbs, arrived at a fortress surrounded by huge walls. The stranger dismounted and promptly got tossed into the clink.

The result of that was odd, too. He should have resented incarceration, seeing that nobody had yet explained the purpose of it. But he didn't. Treating the well-clothed bed in his cell as if it were a luxury provided as recognition of his rights, he sprawled on it full length, boots and all, gave a sigh of deep satisfaction and went to sleep. His watch hung close by his ear and compensated for the constant ticking of the auto-pilot, without which slumber in space was never complete.

During the next few hours guards came frequently to look at him and make sure that he wasn't finagling the locks or disintegrating the bars by means of some alien technique. They had not searched him and accordingly were cautious. But he snored on, dead to the world, oblivious to the ripples of alarm spread through a spatial empire.

He was still asleep when Parmith arrived bearing a load of picture books. Parmith, elderly and myopic, sat by the bedside and waited until his own eyes became heavy in sympathy and he found himself considering the comfort of the carpet. At that point he decided he must either get to work or lie flat. He prodded the other into wakefulness.

They started on the books. *Ah* is for *ahmud* that plays in the grass. *Ay* is for *aysid* that's kept under glass. *Oom* is for *oomtuck* that's found in the moon. *Uhm* is for *uhmlak,* a clown or buffoon. And so on.

Stopping only for meals, they were at it the full day and progress was fast. Parmith was a first-class tutor, the other an excellent pupil able to learn with remarkable speed. At the end of the first long session they were able to indulge in a brief and simple conversation.

"I am called Parmith. What are you called?"

"Wayne Hillder."

"Two callings?"

"Yes."

"What are many of you called?"

"Terrans."

"We are called Vards."

Talk ceased for lack of enough words and Parmith left. Within nine hours he was back accompanied by Gerka, a younger specimen who specialized in reciting words and phrases again and again until the listener could echo them to perfection. They carried on for another four days, working into late evening.

"You are not a prisoner."

"I know," said Wayne Hillder, blandly self-assured.

Parmith looked uncertain. "How do you know?"

"You would not dare to make me one."

"Why not?"

"You do not know enough. Therefore you seek common speech. You must learn from me—and quickly."

This being too obvious to contradict, Parmith let it go by and said, "I estimated it would take about ninety days to make you fluent. It looks as if twenty will be sufficient."

"I wouldn't be here if my kind weren't smart," Hillder pointed out.

Gerka registered uneasiness; Parmith was disconcerted.

"No Vard is being taught by us," he added for good measure. "Not having got to us yet."

Parmith said hurriedly, "We must get on with this task. An important commission is waiting to interview you as soon as you can converse with ease and clarity. We'll try again this *fth-* prefix that you haven't got quite right. Here's a tongue-twister to practice on. Listen to Gerka."

"*Fthon deas fthleman fathangafth,*" recited Gerka, punishing his bottom lip.

"*Futhong deas—*"

"*Fthon,*" corrected Gerka. "*Fthon deas fthlemanfthangafth.*"

"It's better in a civilized tongue. Wet evenings are gnatless *futhong—*"

"*Fthon!*" insisted Gerka, playing catapults with his mouth.

The commission sat in an ornate hall containing semicircular rows of seats rising in ten tiers. There were four hundred present. The way in which attendants and minor officials fawned around them showed that this was an assembly of great importance.

It was, too. The four hundred represented the political and military power of a world that had created a space-empire extending through a score of solar systems and controlling twice as many planets. Up to a short time ago they had been, to the best of their knowledge and belief, the lords of creation. Now there was some doubt about it. They had a serious problem to settle, one that a later Terran historian irreverently described as "a moot point."

They ceased talking among themselves when a pair of guards arrived in charge of Hillder, led him to a seat facing the tiers. Four hundred pairs of eyes examined the stranger, some curiously, some doubtfully, some challengingly, many with unconcealed antagonism.

Sitting down, Hillder looked them over much as one looks into one of the more odorous cages at the zoo. That is to say, with faint distaste. Gently, he rubbed the side of his nose with a forefinger and sniffed. Deflatory gesture number twenty-two, suitable for use in the presence of massed authority. It brought its carefully calculated reward. Half a dozen of the most bellicose characters glared at him.

A frowning, furry-faced oldster stood up, spoke to Hillder as if reciting a well-rehearsed speech. "None but a highly intelligent and completely logical species can conquer space. It being self-evident that you are of such a kind, you will appreciate our position. Your very presence compels us to consider the ultimate alternatives of cooperation or competition, peace or war."

"There are no two alternatives to anything," Hillder asserted. "There is black and white and a thousand intermediate shades. There is yes and no and a thousand ifs, buts, or maybes. For example: you could move farther out of reach."

Being tidy-minded, they didn't enjoy watching the thread of their logic being tangled. Neither did they like the resultant knot in the shape of the final suggestion. The oldster's frown grew deeper, his voice sharper.

"You should also appreciate your own position. You are one among countless millions. Regardless of whatever may be the strength of your kind, you, personally, are helpless. Therefore, it is for us to question and for you to answer. If our respective positions were reversed, the contrary would be true. That is logical. Are you ready to answer our questions?"

"I am ready."

Some showed surprise at that. Others looked resigned, taking it for granted that he would give all the information he saw fit and suppress the rest.

Resuming his seat, the oldster signaled to the Vard on his left, who stood up and asked, "Where is your base-world?"

"At the moment I don't know."

"You don't know?" His expression showed that he had expected awkwardness from the start. "How can you return to it if you don't know where it is?"

"When within its radio-sweep I pick up its beacon. I follow that."

"Aren't your space-charts sufficient to enable you to find it?"

"No."

"Why not?"

"Because," said Hillder, "it isn't tied to a primary. It wanders around."

Registering incredulity, the other said, "Do you mean that it is a planet broken loose from a solar system?"

"Not at all. It's a scout-base. Surely you know what that is?"

"I do not," snapped the interrogator. "What is it?"

"A tiny, compact world equipped with all the necessary contraptions. An artificial sphere that functions as a frontier outpost."

There was a deal of fidgeting and murmuring among the audience as individuals tried to weigh the implications of this news.

Hiding his thoughts, the questioner continued, "You define it as a frontier outpost. That does not tell us where your home-world is located."

"You did not ask about my home-world. You asked about my base-world. I heard you with my own two ears."

"Then where is your home-world?"

"I cannot show you without a chart. Do you have charts of unknown regions?"

"Yes." The other smiled like a satisfied cat. With a dramatic flourish he produced them, unrolled them. "We obtained them from your ship."

"That was thoughtful of you," said Hillder, disappointingly pleased. Leaving his seat he placed a fingertip on the topmost chart and said, "There! Good old Earth!" Then he returned and sat down.

The Vard stared at the designated point, glanced around at his fellows as if about to make some remark, changed his mind and said nothing. Producing a pen he marked the chart, rolled it up with the others.

"This world you call Earth is the origin and center of your empire?"

"Yes."

"The mother-planet of your species?"

"Yes."

"Now," he went on, firmly, "how many of your kind are there?"

"Nobody knows."

"Don't you check your own numbers?"

"We did once upon a time. These days, we're too scattered around." Hillder pondered a moment, added helpfully, "I can tell you that there are four billions of us spread over three planets in our own solar system. Outside of those the number is a guess. We can be divided into the rooted and the rootless and the latter can't be counted. They won't let themselves be counted because somebody might want to tax them. Take the grand total as four billions plus."

"That tells us nothing," the other objected. "We don't know the size of the plus."

"Neither do we," said Hillder, visibly awed at the thought of it. "Sometimes it frightens us." He surveyed the audience. "If nobody's ever been scared by a plus, now's the time."

Scowling, the questioner tried to get at it another way. "You say you are scattered. Over how many worlds?"

"Seven hundred fourteen at last report. That's already out of date. Every report is eight to ten planets behind the times."

"And you have mastery of that huge number?"

"Whoever mastered a planet? Why, we haven't yet dug into the heart of our own, and I doubt that we ever shall." He shrugged, finished, "No, we just amble around and maul them a bit. Same as you do."

"You mean you exploit them?"

"Put it that way if it makes you happy."

"Have you encountered no opposition at any time?"

"Feeble, friend, feeble," said Hillder.

"What did you do about it?"

"That depended upon circumstances. Some folk we ignored, some we smacked, some we led toward the light."

"What light?" asked the other, baffled.

"That of seeing things our way."

It was too much for a paunchy specimen in the third row. Coming to his feet he spoke in acidulated tones. "Do you expect *us* to see things your way?"

"Not immediately," Hillder said.

"Perhaps you consider us incapable of—"

The oldster who had first spoken now arose and interjected, "We must proceed with this inquisition logically or not at all. That means one line of questioning at a time and one questioner at a time." He gestured authoritatively toward the Vard with the charts. "Carry on, Thormin."

Thormin carried on for two solid hours. Apparently he was an astronomical expert, because all his questions bore more or less on that subject. He wanted details of distances, velocities, solar classifications, planetary conditions, and a host of similar items. Willingly, Hillder answered all that he could, pleaded ignorance with regard to the rest.

Eventually Thormin sat down and concentrated on his notes in the manner of one absorbed in fundamental truth. He was succeeded by a hard-eyed individual named Grasud, who for the last half-hour had been fidgeting with impatience.

"Is your vessel the most recent example of its type?"

"No."

"There are better models?"

"Yes," agreed Hillder.

"Very much better?"

"I wouldn't know, not having been assigned one yet."

"Strange, is it not," said Grasud pointedly, "that an old-type ship should discover us while superior ones have failed to do so?"

"Not at all. It was sheer luck. I happened to head this way. Other scouts, in old or new ships, boosted other ways. How many directions are there in deep space? How many radii can be extended from a sphere?"

"Not being a mathematician, I—"

"If you *were* a mathematician," Hillder interrupted, "you would know that the number works out at 2n." He glanced over the audience, added in tutorial manner, "The factor of two being determined by the demonstrable fact that a radius is half a diameter and 2n being defined as the smallest number that makes one boggle."

Grasud boggled as he tried to conceive it, gave it up, said, "Therefore, the total number of your exploring vessels is of equal magnitude?"

"No. We don't have to probe in every direction. It is necessary only to make for visible stars."

"Well, aren't there stars in every direction?"

"If distance is disregarded, yes. But one does not disregard distance. One makes for the nearest yet-unexplored solar systems and thus cuts down repeated jaunts to a reasonable number."

"You are evading the issue," said Grasud. "How many ships of your type are in actual operation?"

"Twenty."

"Twenty?" He made it sound anticlimactic. "Is that all?"

"It's enough, isn't it? How long do you expect us to keep antiquated models in service?"

"I am not asking about out-of-date vessels. How many scout-ships of all types are functioning?"

"I don't really know. I doubt whether anyone knows. In addition to Earth's fleets, some of the most advanced colonies are running expeditions of their own. What's more, a couple of allied lifeforms have learned things from us, caught the fever and started poking around. We can no more take a complete census of ships than we can of people."

Accepting that without argument, Grasud went on, "Your vessel is not large by our standards. Doubtless you have others of greater mass." He leaned forward, gazed fixedly. "What is the comparative size of your biggest ship?"

"The largest I've seen was the battleship *Lance.* Forty times the mass of my boat."

"How many people does it carry?"

"It has a crew numbering more than six hundred but in a pinch it can transport three times that."

"So you know of at least one ship with an emergency capacity of about two thousands?"

"Yes."

More murmurings and fidgetings among the audience. Disregarding them, Grasud carried on with the air of one determined to learn the worst.

"You have other battleships of equal size?"

"Yes."

"How many?"

"I don't know. If I did, I'd tell you. Sorry."

"You may have some even bigger?"

"That is quite possible," Hillder conceded. "If so, I haven't seen one yet. But that means nothing. One can go through a lifetime and not see everything. If you calculate the number of seeable things in existence, deduct the number already viewed, the remainder represents the number yet to be seen. And if you study them at the rate of one per second it would require—"

"I am not interested," snapped Grasud, refusing to be bollixed by alien argument.

"You should be," said Hillder. "Because infinity minus umpteen millions leaves infinity. Which means that you can take the part from the whole and leave the whole still intact. You can eat your cake and have it. Can't you?"

Grasud flopped into his seat, spoke moodily to the oldster,

"I seek information, not a blatant denial of logic. His talk confuses me. Let Shahding have him."

Coming up warily, Shahding started on the subject of weapons, their design, mode of operation, range, and effectiveness. He stuck with determination to this single line of inquiry and avoided all temptations to be sidetracked. His questions were astute and penetrating. Hillder answered all he could, freely, without hesitation.

"So," commented Shahding, toward the finish, "it seems that you put your trust in force-fields, certain rays that paralyze the nervous system, bacteriological techniques, demonstrations of number and strength, and a good deal of persuasiveness. Your science of ballistics cannot be advanced after so much neglect."

"It could never advance," said Hillder. "That's why we abandoned it. We dropped fiddling around with bows and arrows for the same reason. No initial thrust can outpace a continuous and prolonged one. Thus far and no farther shalt thou go." Then he added by way of speculative afterthought, "Anyway, it can be shown that no bullet can overtake a running man."

"Nonsense!" exclaimed Shahding, having once ducked a couple of slugs himself.

"By the time the bullet has reached the man's point of departure, the man has retreated," said Hillder. "The bullet then has to cover that extra distance but finds the man has retreated farther. It covers that, too, only to find that again the man is not there. And so on and so on."

"The lead is reduced each successive time until it ceases to exist," Shahding scoffed.

"Each successive advance occupies a finite length of time, no matter how small," Hillder pointed out. "You cannot divide and subdivide a fraction to produce zero. The series is infinite. An infinite series of finite time-periods totals an infinite time. Work it out for yourself. The bullet does not hit the man because it cannot get to him."

The reaction showed that the audience had never encountered this argument before or concocted anything like it of their own accord. None were stupid enough to accept it as serious assertion of fact. All were sufficiently intelligent to recognize it as logical or pseudo-logical denial of something self-evident and demonstrably true.

Forthwith they started hunting for the flaw in this alien reasoning, discussing it between themselves so noisily that Shahding stood in silence waiting for a break. He posed like a dummy for ten minutes while the clamor rose to a crescendo. A group in the front semicircle left their seats, knelt and commenced drawing diagrams on the floor while arguing vociferously and with some heat. A couple of Vards in the back tier showed signs of coming to blows.

Finally the oldster, Shahding and two others bellowed a united "Quiet!"

The investigatory commission settled down with reluctance, still muttering, gesturing, showing each other sketches on pieces of paper. Shahding fixed ireful attention on Hillder, opened his mouth in readiness to resume.

Beating him to it, Hillder said casually, "It sounds silly, doesn't it? But anything is possible, anything at all. A man can marry his widow's sister."

"Impossible," declared Shahding, able to dispose of that without abstruse calculations. "He must be dead for her to have the status of a widow."

"A man married a woman who died. He then married her sister. He died. Wasn't his first wife his widow's sister?"

Shahding shouted, "I am not here to be tricked by the tortuous squirmings of an alien mind." He sat down hard, fumed a bit, said to his neighbor, "All right, Kadina, you can have him and welcome."

Confident and self-assured, Kadina stood up, gazed authoritatively around. He was tall for a Vard, and wore a well-cut uniform with crimson epaulettes and crimson-banded sleeves. For the first time in a while there was silence. Satisfied with the effect he had produced, he faced Hillder, spoke in tones deeper, less squeaky than any heard so far.

"Apart from the petty problems with which it has amused you to baffle my compatriots," he began in an oily manner, "you have given candid, unhesitating answers to our questions. You have provided much information that is useful from the military viewpoint."

"I am glad you appreciate it," said Hillder.

"We do. Very much so," Kadina bestowed a craggy smile that looked sinister. "However, there is one matter that needs clarifying."

"What is that?"

"If the present situation were reversed, if a lone Vard-scout was subject to intensive cross-examination by an assembly of your lifeform, and if he surrendered information as willingly as you have done . . ." He let it die while his eyes hardened, then growled, "We would consider him a traitor to his kind! The penalty would be death."

"How fortunate I am not to be a Vard," said Hillder.

"Do not congratulate yourself too early," Kadina retorted. "A death sentence is meaningless only to those already under such a sentence."

"What are you getting at?"

"I am wondering whether you are a major criminal seeking sanctuary among us. There may be some other reason. Whatever it is, you do not hesitate to betray your own kind." He put on the same smile again. "It would be nice to know *why* you have been so cooperative."

"That's an easy one," Hillder said, smiling back in a way that Kadina did not like. "I am a consistent liar."

With that, he left his seat and walked boldly to the exit. The guards led him to his cell.

He was there three days, eating regular meals and enjoying them with irritating gusto, amusing himself writing figures in a little notebook, as happy as a legendary space-scout named Larry. At the end of that time a ruminative Vard paid a visit.

"I am Bulak. Perhaps you remember me. I was seated at the end of the second row when you were before the commission."

"Four hundred were there," Hillder reminded. "I cannot recall all of them. Only the ones who suffered." He pushed forward a chair. "But never mind. Sit down and put your feet up—if you do have feet inside those funny-looking boots. What can I do for you?"

"I don't know."

"You must have come for some reason, surely?"

Bulak looked mournful. "I'm a refugee from the fog."

"What fog?"

"The one you've spread all over the place." He rubbed a fur-coated ear, examined his fingers, stared at the wall. "The commission's main purpose was to determine relative standards of intelligence, to settle the prime question of whether your kind's cleverness is less than, greater than, or equal to our own.

Upon that and that alone depends our reaction to contact with another space-conqueror."

"I did my best to help, didn't I?"

"Help?" echoed Bulak as if it were a new and strange word. "Help? Do you call it that? The true test should be that of whether your logic has been extended farther than has ours, whether your premises have been developed to more advanced conclusions."

"Well?"

"You ended up by trampling all over the laws of logic. A bullet cannot kill anybody. After three days fifty of them are still arguing about it, and this morning one of them proved that a person cannot climb a ladder. Friends have fallen out, relatives are starting to hate the sight of each other. The remaining three hundred fifty are in little better state."

"What's troubling them?" inquired Hillder with interest.

"They are debating veracity with everything but brickbats," Bulak informed, somewhat as if compelled to mention an obscene subject. "You are a consistent liar. Therefore the statement itself must be a lie. Therefore you are not a consistent liar. The conclusion is that you can be a consistent liar only by not being a consistent liar. Yet you cannot be a consistent liar without being consistent."

"That's bad," Hillder sympathized.

"It's worse," Bulak gave back. "Because if you really are a consistent liar—which logically is a self-contradiction—none of your evidence is worth a sack of rotten *muna*-seeds. If you have told us the truth all the way through, then your final claim to be a liar must also be true. But if you are a consistent liar then none of it is true."

"Take a deep breath," advised Hillder.

"But," continued Bulak, taking a deep breath, "since that final statement must be untrue, all the rest may be true." A wild look came into his eyes and he started waving his arms around. "But the claim to consistency makes it impossible for any statement to be assessed as either true or untrue because, on analysis, there is an unresolvable contradiction that—"

"Now, now," said Hillder, patting his shoulder. "It is only natural that the lower should be confused by the higher. The trouble is that you've not yet advanced far enough. Your thinking remains a little primitive." He hesitated, added with the air of making a daring guess, "In fact it wouldn't surprise me if you still think *logically.*"

"In the name of the Big Sun," exclaimed Bulak, "how *else* can we think?"

"Like us," said Hillder. "But only when you're mentally developed." He strolled twice around the cell, said by way of musing afterthought, "Right now you couldn't cope with the problem of why a mouse when it spins."

"Why a mouse when it spins?" parroted Bulak, letting his jaw hang down.

"Or let's try an easier one, a problem any Earth-child could tackle.

"Such as what?"

"By definition an island is a body of land entirely surrounded by water?"

"Yes, that is correct."

"Then let us suppose that the whole of this planet's northern hemisphere is land and all the southern hemisphere is water. Is the northern half an island? Or is the southern half a lake?"

Bulak gave it five minutes' thought. Then he drew a circle on a sheet of paper, divided it, shaded the top half and contemplated the result. In the end he pocketed the paper and got to his feet.

"Some of them would gladly cut your throat but for the possibility that your kind may have a shrewd idea where you are and be capable of retribution. Others would send you home with honors but for the risk of bowing to inferiors."

"They'll have to make up their minds someday," Hillder commented, refusing to show concern about which way it went.

"Meanwhile," Bulak continued morbidly, "we've had a look over your ship, which may be old or new according to whether or not you have lied about it. We can see everything but the engines and remote controls, everything but the things that matter. To determine whether they're superior to ours we'd have to pull the vessel apart, ruining it and making you a prisoner."

"Well, what's stopping you?"

"The fact that you may be bait. If your kind has great power and is looking for trouble, they'll need a pretext. Our victimization of you would provide it. The spark that fires the powder-barrel." He made a gesture of futility. "What can one do when working utterly in the dark?"

"One could try settling the question of whether a green leaf remains a green leaf in complete absence of light."

"I have had enough," declared Bulak, making for the door. "I have had more than enough. An island or a lake? Who cares? I am going to see Mordafa."

With that he departed, working his fingers around while the fur quivered on his face. A couple of guards peered through the bars in the uneasy manner of those assigned to keep watch upon a dangerous maniac.

Mordafa turned up next day in the mid-afternoon. He was a thin, elderly, and somewhat wizened specimen with incongruously youthful eyes. Accepting a seat, he studied Hillder, spoke with smooth deliberation.

"From what I have heard, from all that I have been told, I deduce a basic rule applying to lifeforms deemed intelligent."

"You deduce it?"

"I have to. There is no choice about the matter. All the lifeforms we have discovered so far have not been truly intelligent. Some have been superficially so, but not genuinely so. It is obvious that you have had experiences that may come to us sooner or later but have not arrived yet. In that respect we may have been fortunate, seeing that the results of such contact are highly speculative. There's just no way of telling."

"And what is this rule?"

"That the governing body of any lifeform such as ours will be composed of power-lovers rather than of specialists."

"Well, isn't it?"

"Unfortunately, it is: Government falls into the hands of those who desire authority and escapes those with other interests." He paused, went on, "That is not to say that those who govern us are stupid. They are quite clever in their own particular field of mass-organization. But by the same token they are pathetically ignorant of other fields. Knowing this, your tactic is to take advantage of their ignorance. The weakness of authority is that it cannot be diminished and retain strength. To play upon ignorance is to dull the voice of command."

"Hm!" Hillder surveyed him with mounting respect. "You're the first one I've encountered who can see beyond the end of his nose."

"Thank you," said Mordafa. "Now the very fact that you have taken the risk of landing here alone, and followed it up by confusing our leaders, proves that your kind has developed a technique for a given set of conditions and, in all probability, a series of techniques for various conditions."

"Go on," urged Hillder.

"Such techniques must be created empirically rather than theoretically," Mordafa continued. "In other words, they result from many experiences, the correcting of many errors, the search for workability, the effort to gain maximum results from minimum output." He glanced at the other. "Am I correct so far?"

"You're doing fine."

"To date we have established foothold on forty-two planets without ever having to combat other than primitive life. We may find foes worthy of our strength on the forty-third world, whenever that is discovered. Who knows? Let us assume for the sake of argument that intelligent life exists on one in every forty-three inhabitable planets."

"Where does that get us?" Hillder prompted.

"I would imagine," said Mordafa thoughtfully, "that the experience of making contact with at least six intelligent life-forms would be necessary to enable you to evolve techniques for dealing with their like elsewhere. Therefore your kind must have discovered and explored not less than two hundred fifty worlds. That is an estimate in minimum terms. The correct figure may well be that stated by you."

"And I am not a consistent liar?" asked Hillder, grinning.

"That is beside the point, if only our leaders would hold on to their sanity long enough to see it. You may have distorted or exaggerated for purposes of your own. If so, there is nothing we can do about it. The prime fact holds fast, namely, that your space-venturings must be far more extensive than ours. Hence you must be older, more advanced, and numerically stronger."

"That's logical enough," conceded Hillder, broadening his grin.

"Now don't start on me," pleaded Mordafa. "If you fool me with an intriguing fallacy I won't rest until I get it straight. And that will do neither of us any good."

"Ah, so your intention is to do me good?"

"Somebody has to make a decision, seeing that the top brass is no longer capable of it. I am going to suggest that they set you free with our best wishes and assurances of friendship."

"Think they'll take any notice?"

"You know quite well they will. You've been counting on it all along." Mordafa eyed him shrewdly. "They'll grab at the advice to restore their self-esteem. If it works, they'll take the credit. If it doesn't, I'll get the blame." He brooded a few seconds, asked with open curiosity, "Do you find it the same elsewhere, among other peoples?"

"Exactly the same," Hillder assured him. "And there is always a Mordafa to settle the issue in the same way. Power and scapegoats go together like husband and wife."

"I'd like to meet my alien counterparts someday." Getting up, he moved to the door. "If I had not come along, how long would you have waited for your psychological mixture to congeal?"

"Until another of your type chipped in. If one doesn't arrive of his own accord, the powers-that-be lose patience and drag one in. The catalyst mined from its own kind. Authority lives by eating its vitals."

"That is putting it paradoxically," Mordafa observed, making it sound like a mild reproof. He went away.

Hillder stood behind the door and gazed through the bars in its top half. The pair of guards leaned against the opposite wall and stared back.

With amiable pleasantness, he said to them, "No cat has eight tails. Every cat has one tail more than no cat. Therefore every cat has nine tails."

They screwed up their eyes and scowled.

Quite an impressive deputation took him back to the ship. All the found hundred were there, about a quarter of them resplendent in uniforms, the rest in their Sunday best. An armed guard juggled guns at barked command. Kadina made an unctuous speech full of brotherly love and the glorious shape of things to come. Somebody presented a bouquet of evil-smelling weeds and Hillder made mental note of the difference in olfactory senses.

Climbing eighty yards to the lock, Hillder looked down. Hadina waved an officious farewell. The crowd chanted, "Hurrah!" in conducted rhythm. He blew his nose on a handkerchief, that being deflatory gesture number nine, closed the lock, sat at the control board.

The tubes fired into a low roar. A cloud of vapor climbed around and sprinkled ground-dirt over the mob. That touch was involuntary and not recorded in the book. A pity, he thought. Everything ought to be listed. We should be systematic about such things. The showering of dirt should be duly noted under the heading of the spaceman's farewell.

The ship snored into the sky, left the Vard-world far behind. Hillder remained at the controls until free of the entire system's gravitational field. Then he headed for the beacon-area and locked the auto-pilot on that course.

For a while he sat gazing meditatively into star-spangled darkness. After a while he sighed, made notes in his log-book.

Cube K49, Sector 10, solar-grade D7, third planet. Name: Vard. Lifeform named Vards, cosmic intelligence rating BB, space-going, forty-two colonies. Comment: softened up.

He glanced over his tiny library fastened to a steel bulkhead. Two tomes were missing. They had swiped the two that were replete with diagrams and illustrations. They had left the rest, having no Rosetta Stone with which to translate cold print. They hadn't touched the nearest volume titled: *Diabologic, the Science of Driving People Nuts.*

Sighing again, he took paper from a drawer, commenced his hundredth, two hundredth or maybe three-hundredth try at concocting an Aleph number higher than A, but lower than C. He mauled his hair until it stuck out in spikes, and although he didn't know it, he did not look especially well-balanced himself.

Garbo speaks. Harpo talks. Food giggles.

Which of the above do you think would adhere like primeval chewing gum to the spongy, slightly soft cerebrum of an avid young reader of science fiction? Since I first encountered the concept of embedded giggling as an otherworldly food enhancement no stranger to an alien palate than food coloring or artificial flavoring are to us, a sort of auricular monosodium glutamate, I have never been able to regard a meal comprised of exotic constituents with quite the same nonchalant eye. Or ear. A decent writer could build an entire novelette around the concept.

To the inhumanly inventive Robert Sheckley of "Untouched by Human Hands," this rare notion is a mere belletristic bagatelle, one chip in a cookie crammed full, from a literary bakery whose assembly line never seems to take a day off. There is more innovation in a classic Sheckley short story than in your average novel. I could as easily have picked "The Last Weapon," or "Prospector's Special," or "A Wind is Rising," or "The Accountant," or any one of a hundred (yes, a hundred) other Sheckley stories to nominate for inclusion in this worthy compendium. Alas, each of us is allowed but one. So I settled on this funny-scary saga of starving stellar explorers who stumble across an overflowing alien warehouse, and when driven from desperate hunger in search of simply something to eat, encounter the true otherworldliness that dwells in only one place in the universe.

Planet Sheckley.

—Alan Dean Foster

UNTOUCHED BY HUMAN HANDS

by Robert Sheckley

Hellman plucked the last radish out of the can with a pair of dividers. He held it up for Casker to admire, then laid it carefully on the workbench beside the razor.

"Hell of a meal for two grown men," Casker said, flopping down in one of the ship's padded crash chairs.

"If you'd like to give up your share—" Hellman started to suggest.

Casker shook his head quickly. Hellman smiled, picked up the razor and examined its edge critically.

"Don't make a production out of it," Casker said, glancing at the ship's instruments. They were approaching a red dwarf, the only planet-bearing sun in the vicinity. "We want to be through with supper before we get much closer."

Hellman made a practice incision in the radish, squinting along the top of the razor. Casker bent closer, his mouth open. Hellman poised the razor delicately and cut the radish cleanly in half.

"Will you say grace?" Hellman asked.

Casker growled something and popped a half in his mouth. Hellman chewed more slowly. The sharp taste seemed to explode along his disused tastebuds.

"Not much bulk value," Hellman said.

Casker didn't answer. He was busily studying the red dwarf.

As he swallowed the last of his radish, Hellman stifled a sigh. Their last meal had been three days ago . . . if two biscuits and a cup of water could be called a meal. This radish, now resting in the vast emptiness of their stomachs, was the last gram of food on board ship.

"Two planets," Casker said. "One burned to a crisp."

"Then we'll land on the other."

Casker nodded and punched a deceleration spiral into the ship's tape.

Hellman found himself wondering for the hundredth time where the fault had been. Could he have made out the food requisitions wrong, when they took on supplies at Calao station? After all, he had been devoting most of his attention to the mining equipment. Or had the ground crew just forgotten to load those last precious cases?

He drew his belt in to the fourth new notch he had punched.

Speculation was useless. Whatever the reason, they were in a jam. Ironically enough, they had more than enough fuel to take them back to Calao. But they would be a pair of singularly emaciated corpses by the time the ship reached there.

"We're coming in now," Casker said.

And to make matters worse, this unexplored region of space had few suns and fewer planets. Perhaps there was a slight possibility of replenishing their water supply, but the odds were enormous against finding anything they could eat.

"Look at that place," Casker growled.

Hellman shook himself out of his reverie.

The planet was like a round gray-brown porcupine. The spines of a million needle sharp mountains glittered in the red dwarf's feeble light. And as they spiraled lower, circling the planet, the pointed mountains seemed to stretch out to meet them.

"It can't be *all* mountains," Hellman said.

"It's not."

Sure enough, there were oceans and lakes, out of which thrust jagged island-mountains. But no sign of level land, no hint of civilization, or even animal life.

"At least it's got an oxygen atmosphere," Casker said.

Their deceleration spiral swept them around the planet, cutting lower into the atmosphere, braking against it. And still there was nothing but mountains and lakes and oceans and more mountains.

On the eighth run, Hellman caught sight of a solitary building on a mountain top. Casker braked recklessly, and the hull glowed red hot. On the eleventh run, they made a landing approach.

"Stupid place to build," Casker muttered.

The building was doughnut-shaped, and fitted nicely over the top of the mountain. There was a wide, level lip around it, which Casker scorched as he landed the ship.

From the air, the building had merely seemed big. On the ground, it was enormous. Hellman and Casker walked up to it slowly. Hellman had his burner ready, but there was no sign of life.

"This planet must be abandoned," Hellman said almost in a whisper.

"Anyone in his right mind would abandon this place," Casker said. "There're enough good planets around, without anyone trying to live on a needle point."

They reached the door. Hellman tried to open it and found it locked. He looked back at the spectacular display of mountains.

"You know," he said, "when this planet was still in a molten state, it must have been affected by several gigantic moons that are now broken up. The strains, external and internal, wrenched it into its present spined appearance and—"

"Come off it," Casker said ungraciously. "You were a librarian before you decided to get rich on uranium."

Hellman shrugged his shoulders and burned a hole in the doorlock. They waited.

The only sound on the mountain top was the growling of their stomachs.

They entered.

The tremendous wedge-shaped room was evidently a warehouse of sorts. Goods were piled to the ceiling, scattered over the floor, stacked haphazardly against the walls. There were boxes and containers of all sizes and shapes, some big enough to hold an elephant, others the size of thimbles.

Near the door was a dusty pile of books. Immediately, Hellman bent down to examine them.

"Must be food somewhere in here," Casker said, his face lighting up for the first time in a week. He started to open the nearest box.

"This is interesting," Hellman said, discarding all the books except one.

"Let's eat first," Casker said, ripping the top off the box. Inside was a brownish dust. Casker looked at it, sniffed, and made a face.

"Very interesting indeed," Hellman said, leafing through the book.

Casker opened a small can, which contained a glittering green slime. He closed it and opened another. It contained a dull orange slime.

"Hmm," Hellman said, still reading.

"Hellman! Will you kindly drop that book and help me find some food?"

"Food?" Hellman repeated, looking up. "What makes you think there's anything to eat here? For all you know, this could be a paint factory."

"It's a warehouse!" Casker shouted.

He opened a kidney-shaped can and lifted out a soft purple stick. It hardened quickly and crumpled to dust as he tried to smell it. He scooped up a handful of the dust and brought it to his mouth.

"That might be extract of strychnine," Hellman said casually.

Casker abruptly dropped the dust and wiped his hands.

"After all," Hellman pointed out, "granted that this is a warehouse—a cache, if you wish—we don't know what the late inhabitants considered good fare. Paris Green salad, perhaps, with sulphuric acid as dressing."

"All right," Casker said, "but we gotta eat. What're you going to do about all this?" He gestured at the hundreds of boxes, cans and bottles.

"The thing to do," Hellman said briskly, "is to make a qualitative analysis on four or five samples. We could start out with a simple titration, sublimate the chief ingredient, see if it forms a precipitate, work out its molecular makeup from—"

"Hellman, you don't know what you're talking about. You're a librarian, remember? And I'm a correspondence school pilot. We don't know anything about titrations and sublimations."

"I know," Hellman said, "but we should. It's the right way to go about it."

"Sure. In the meantime, though, just until a chemist drops in, what'll we do?"

"This might help us," Hellman said, holding up the book. Do you know what it is?"

"No," Casker said, keeping a tight grip on his patience.

"It's a pocket dictionary and guide to the Helg language."

"Helg?"

"The planet we're on. The symbols match up with those on the boxes."

Casker raised an eyebrow. "Never heard of Helg."

"I don't believe the planet has ever had any contact with Earth," Hellman said. "This dictionary isn't Helg-English. It's Helg-Aloombrigian."

Casker remembered that Aloombrigia was the home planet of a small, adventurous reptilian race, out near the center of the Galaxy.

"How come you can read Aloombrigian?" Casker asked.

"Oh, being a librarian isn't a completely useless profession," Hellman said modestly. "In my spare time—"

"Yeah. Now how about—"

"Do you know," Hellman said, "the Aloombrigians probably helped the Helgans leave their planet and find another. They sell services like that. In which case, this building very likely *is* a food cache!"

"Suppose you start translating," Casker suggested wearily, "and maybe find us something to eat."

They opened boxes until they found a likely-looking substance. Laboriously, Hellman translated the symbols on it.

"Got it," he said. "It reads:—'USE SNIFFNERS—THE BETTER ABRASIVE.' "

"Doesn't sound edible," Casker said.

"I'm afraid not."

They found another, which read: VIGROOM! FILL ALL YOUR STOMACHS, AND FILL THEM RIGHT!

"What kind of animals do you suppose these Helgans were?" Casker asked.

Hellman shrugged his shoulders.

The next label took almost fifteen minutes to translate. It read: ARGOSEL MAKES YOUR THUDRA ALL TIZZY. CONTAINS THIRTY ARPS OF RAMSTAT PULZ, FOR SHELL LUBRICATION.

"There must be *something* here we can eat," Casker said with a note of desperation.

"I hope so," Hellman replied.

At the end of two hours, they were no closer. They had translated dozens of titles and sniffed so many substances that their olfactory senses had given up in disgust.

"Let's talk this over," Hellman, sitting on a box marked: VORMITASH—GOOD AS IT SOUNDS!

"Sure," Casker said, sprawling out on the floor. "Talk."

"If we could deduce what kind of creatures inhabited this planet, we'd know what kind of food they ate, and whether it's likely to be edible for us."

"All we do know is that they wrote a lot of lousy advertising copy."

Hellman ignored that. "What kind of intelligent beings would evolve on a planet that is all mountains?"

"Stupid ones!" Casker said.

That was no help. But Hellman found that he couldn't draw any references from the mountains. It didn't tell him if the late Helgans ate silicates or proteins or iodine-base foods or anything.

"Now look," Hellman said, "we'll have to work this out by pure logic—Are you listening to me?"

"Sure," Casker said.

"Okay. There's an old proverb that covers our situation perfectly: 'One man's meat is another man's poison.' "

"Yeah," Casker said. He was positive his stomach had shrunk to approximately the size of a marble.

"We can assume, first, that their meat is our meat."

Casker wrenched himself away from a vision of five juicy roast beefs dancing tantalizingly before him. "What if their meat is our *poison?* What then?"

"Then," Hellman said, "we will assume that their poison is our meat."

"And what happens if their meat *and* their poison are our poison?"

"We starve."

"All right," Casker said, standing up. "Which assumption do we start with?"

"Well, there's no sense in asking for trouble. This *is* an oxygen planet, if that means anything. Let's assume that we can eat some basic food of theirs. If we can't we'll start on their poisons."

"If we live that long," Casker said.

Hellman began to translate labels. They discarded such brands as ANDROGYNITES DELIGHT AND VERBELL—FOR LONGER, CURLIER, MORE SENSITIVE ANTENNAE, until they found a small gray box, about six inches by three by three. It was called VALKORIN'S UNIVERSAL TASTE TREAT, FOR ALL DIGESTIVE CAPACITIES.

"This looks as good as any," Hellman said. He opened the box.

Casker leaned over and sniffed. "No odor."

Within the box they found a rectangular, rubbery red block. It quivered slightly, like jelly.

"Bite into it," Casker said.

"Me?" Hellman asked. "Why not you?"

"You picked it."

"I prefer just looking at it," Hellman said with dignity. "I'm not too hungry."

"I'm not either," Casker said.

They sat on the floor and stared at the jellylike block. After ten minutes, Hellman yawned, leaned back and closed his eyes.

"All right, coward," Casker said bitterly. "I'll try it. Just remember, though, if I'm poisoned, you'll never get off this planet. You don't know how to pilot."

"Just take a little bite, then," Hellman advised.

Casker leaned over and stared at the block. Then he prodded it with his thumb.

The rubbery red block giggled.

"Did you hear that?" Casker yelped, leaping back.

"I didn't hear anything," Hellman said, his hands shaking. "Go ahead."

Casker prodded the block again. It giggled louder, this time with a disgusting little simper.

"Okay," Casker said, "what do we try next?"

"Next? What's wrong with this?"

"I don't eat anything that giggles," Casker stated firmly.

"Now listen to me," Hellman said. "The creatures who manufactured this might have been trying to create an aesthetic sound as well as a pleasant shape and color. That giggle is probably only for the amusement of the eater."

"Then bite into it yourself," Casker offered.

Hellman glared at him, but made no move toward the rubbery block. Finally he said, "Let's move it out of the way."

They pushed the block over to a corner. It lay there giggling softly to itself.

"Now what?" Casker said.

Hellman looked around at the jumbled stacks of incomprehensible alien goods. He noticed a door on either side of the room.

"Let's have a look in the other sections," he suggested.

Casker shrugged his shoulders apathetically.

Slowly they trudged to the door in the left wall. It was locked and Hellman burned it open with the ship's burner.

It was a wedge-shaped room, piled with incomprehensible alien goods.

The hike back across the room seemed like miles, but they made it only slightly out of wind. Hellman blew out the lock and they looked in.

It was a wedge-shaped room, piled with incomprehensible alien goods.

"All the same," Casker said sadly, and closed the door.

"Evidently there's a series of these rooms going completely around the building," Hellman said. "I wonder if we should explore them."

Casker calculated the distance around the building, compared it with his remaining strength, and sat down heavily on a long gray object.

"Why bother?" he asked.

Hellman tried to collect his thoughts. Certainly he should be able to find a key of some sort, a clue that would tell him what they could eat. But where was it?

He examined the object Casker was sitting on. It was about the size and shape of a large coffin, with a shallow depression on top. It was made of a hard, corrugated substance.

"What do you suppose this is?" Hellman asked.

"Does it matter?"

Hellman glanced at the symbol painted on the side of the object, then looked them up in his dictionary.

"Fascinating," he murmured, after a while.

"Is it something to eat?" Casker asked, with a faint glimmering of hope.

"No. You are sitting on something called THE MOROG CUSTOM SUPER TRANSPORT FOR THE DISCRIMINATING HELGAN WHO DESIRES THE BEST IN VERTICAL TRANSPORTATION. It's a vehicle!"

"Oh," Casker said dully.

"This is important! Look at it! How does it work?"

Casker wearily climbed off the Morog Custom Super Transport and looked it over carefully. He traced four almost invisible separations on its four corners. "Retractable wheels, probably, but I don't see—"

Hellman read on. "It says to give it three amphus of high-grain Integor fuel, then a van of Tonder lubrication, and not to run it over three thousand Ruls for the first fifty mungus."

"Let's find something to eat," Casker said.

"Don't you see how important this is?" Hellman asked. "This could solve our problem. If we could deduce the alien logic inherent in constructing this vehicle, we might know the Helgan thought pattern. This, in turn, would give us an insight into their nervous systems, which would imply their biochemical makeup."

Casker stood still, trying to decide whether he had enough strength left to strangle Hellman.

"For example," Hellman said, "what kind of vehicle would be used in a place like this? Not one with wheels, since everything is up and down. Anti-gravity? Perhaps, but what *kind* of anti-gravity? And why did the inhabitants devise a boxlike form instead—"

Casker decided sadly that he didn't have enough strength to strangle Hellman, no matter how pleasant it might be. Very quietly, he said, "Kindly stop making like a scientist. Let's see if there isn't *something* we can gulp down."

"All right," Hellman said sulkily.

Casker watched his partner wander off among the cans, bottles and cases. He wondered vaguely where Hellman got the energy, and decided that he was just too cerebral to know when he was starving.

"Here's something," Hellman called out, standing in front of a large yellow vat.

"What does it say?" Casker asked.

"Little bit hard to translate. But rendered freely, it reads: MORISHILLE'S VOOZY, WITH LACTO-ECTO ADDED FOR A NEW TASTE SENSATION. EVERYONE DRINKS VOOZY. GOOD BEFORE AND AFTER MEALS, NO UNPLEASANT AFTER-EFFECTS. GOOD FOR CHILDREN! THE DRINK OF THE UNIVERSE!"

"That sounds good," Casker admitted, thinking that Hellman might not be so stupid after all.

"This should tell us once and for all if their meat *is* our meat," Hellman said. "This Voozy seems to be the closest thing to a universal drink I've found yet."

"Maybe," Casker said hopefully, "maybe it's just plain water!"

"We'll see." Hellman pried open the lid with the edge of the burner.

Within the vat was a crystal-clear liquid.

"No odor," Casker said, bending over the vat.

The crystal liquid lifted to meet him.

Casker retreated so rapidly, that he fell over a box. Hellman helped him to his feet, and they approached the vat again. As they came near, the liquid lifted itself three feet into the air and moved toward them.

"What've you done now?" Casker asked, moving back carefully. The liquid flowed slowly over the side of the vat. It began to flow toward him.

"Hellman!" Casker shrieked.

Hellman was standing to one side, perspiration pouring

down his face, reading his dictionary with a preoccupied frown.

"Guess I bumbled the translation," he said.

"Do something!" Casker shouted. The liquid was trying to back him into a corner.

"Nothing I can do," Hellman said, reading on. "Ah, here's the error. It doesn't say 'Everyone drinks Voozy.' Wrong subject. 'Voozy drinks *everyone.*' That tells us something! The Helgans must have soaked liquid in through their pores. Naturally, they would prefer to be drunk, instead of to drink."

Casker tried to dodge around the liquid, but it cut him off with a merry gurgle. Desperately he picked up a small bale and threw it at the Voozy. The Voozy caught the bale and drank it. Then it discarded that and turned back to Casker.

Hellman tossed another box. The Voozy drank this one and a third and fourth that Casker threw in. Then, apparently exhausted, it flowed back into its vat.

Casker clapped down the lid and sat on it, trembling violently.

"Not so good," Hellman said. "We've been taking it for granted that the Helgans had eating habits like us. But, of course, it doesn't necessarily—"

"No, it doesn't. No, sir, it certainly doesn't. I guess we can see that it doesn't. Anyone can see that it doesn't—"

"Stop that," Hellman ordered sternly. "We've no time for hysteria."

"Sorry." Casker slowly moved away from the Voozy vat.

"I guess we'll have to assume that their meat is our poison," Hellman said thoughtfully. "So now we'll see if their poison is our meat."

Casker didn't say anything. He was wondering what would have happened if the Voozy had drunk him.

In the corner, the rubbery block was still giggling to itself.

"Now here's a likely-looking poison," Hellman said, half an hour later.

Casker had recovered completely, except for an occasional twitch of the lips.

"What does it say?" he asked.

Hellman rolled a tiny tube in the palm of his hand. "It's called Pvastkin's Plugger. The label reads: WARNING! HIGHLY DANGEROUS! PVASTKIN'S PLUGGER IS DESIGNED TO FILL HOLES OR CRACKS OF NOT MORE THAN TWO CUBIC VIMS. HOWEVER—

THE PLUGGER IS NOT TO BE EATEN UNDER ANY CIRCUMSTANCES. THE ACTIVE INGREDIENT, RAMOTOL, WHICH MAKES PVASTKIN'S SO EXCELLENT A PLUGGER RENDERS IT HIGHLY DANGEROUS WHEN TAKEN INTERNALLY."

"Sounds great," Casker said. "It'll probably blow us sky-high."

"Do you have any other suggestions?" Hellman asked.

Casker thought for a moment. The food of Helg was obviously unpalatable for humans. So perhaps was their poison . . . but wasn't starvation better than this sort of thing?

After a moment's communion with his stomach, he decided that starvation was *not* better.

"Go ahead," he said.

Hellman slipped the burner under his arm and unscrewed the top of the little bottle. He shook it.

Nothing happened.

"It's got a seal," Casker pointed out

Hellman punctured the seal with his fingernail and set the bottle on the floor. An evil-smelling green froth began to bubble out.

Hellman looked dubiously at the froth. It was congealing into a glob and spreading over the floor.

"Yeast, perhaps," he said, gripping the burner tightly.

"Come, come. Faint heart never filled empty stomach."

"I'm not holding *you* back," Hellman said.

The glob swelled to the size of a man's head.

"How long is that supposed to go on?" Casker asked.

"Well," Hellman said, "it's advertised as a Plugger. I suppose that's what it does—expands to plug up holes."

"Sure. But how *much?*"

"Unfortunately, I don't know how much two cubic vims are. But it can't go on much—"

Belatedly, they noticed that the Plugger had filled almost a quarter of the room and was showing no signs of stopping.

"We should have believed the label!" Casker yelled to him, across the spreading glob. "It *is* dangerous!"

As the Plugger produced more surface, it began to accelerate in its growth. A sticky edge touched Hellman and he jumped back.

"Watch out!"

He couldn't reach Casker, on the other side of the gigantic sphere of blob. Hellman tried to run around, but the Plugger had spread, cutting the room in half. It began to swell toward the walls.

"Run for it!" Hellman yelled, and rushed to the door behind him.

He flung it open just as the expanding glob reached him. On the other side of the room, he heard a door slam shut. Hellman didn't wait any longer. He sprinted through and slammed the door behind him.

He stood for a moment, panting, the burner in his hand. He hadn't realized how weak he was. That sprint had cut his reserves of energy dangerously close to the collapsing point. At least Casker had made it, too, though.

But he was still in trouble.

The Plugger poured merrily through the blasted lock, into the room. Hellman tried a practice shot on it, but the Plugger was evidently impervious . . . as, he realized, a good plugger should be.

It was showing no signs of fatigue.

Hellman hurried to the far wall. The door was locked, as the others had been, so he burned out the lock and went through.

How far could the glob expand? How much was two cubic vims? Two cubic miles, perhaps? For all he knew, the Plugger was used to repair faults in the crusts of planets.

In the next room, Hellman stopped to catch his breath. He remembered that the building was circular. He would burn his way through the remaining doors and join Casker. They would burn their way outside and . . .

Casker didn't have a burner!

Hellman turned white with shock. Casker had made it into the room on the right, because they had burned it open earlier. The Plugger was undoubtedly oozing into that room, through the shattered lock . . . and Casker couldn't get out! The Plugger was on his left, a locked door on his right!

Rallying his remaining strength, Hellman began to run. Boxes seemed to get in his way purposefully, tripping him, slowing him down. He blasted the next door and hurried on to the next. And the next. And the next.

The Plugger couldn't expand *completely* into Casker's room!

Or could it?

The wedge-shaped rooms, each a segment of a circle, seemed to stretch before him forever, a jumbled montage of locked doors, alien goods, more doors, more goods. Hellman fell over a crate, got to his feet and fell again. He had reached the limit of his strength, and passed it. But Casker was his friend.

Besides, without a pilot, he'd never get off the place.

Hellman struggled through two more rooms on trembling legs and then collapsed in front of a third.

"Is that you, Hellman?" he heard Casker ask, from the other side of the door.

"You all right?" Hellman managed to gasp.

"Haven't much room in here," Casker said, "but the Plugger's stopped growing. Hellman, get me out of here!"

Hellman lay on the floor panting. "Moment," he said.

"Moment, hell!" Casker shouted. "Get me out. I've found water!"

"What? How?"

"Get me out of here!"

Hellman tried to stand up, but his legs weren't cooperating. "What happened?" he asked.

"When I saw that glob filling the room, I figured I'd try to start up the Super Custom Transport. Thought maybe it could knock down the door and get me out. So I pumped it full of high-grain Integor fuel."

"Yes?" Hellman said, still trying to get his legs under control.

"That Super Custom Transport is an animal, Hellman! And the Integor fuel is water! Now get me out!"

Hellman lay back with a contented sigh. If he had had a little more time, he would have worked out the whole thing himself, by pure logic. But it was all very apparent now. The most efficient machine to go over those vertical, razor-sharp mountains would be an animal, probably with retractable suckers. It was kept in hibernation between trips; and if it drank water, the other products designed for it would be palatable, too. Of course they still didn't know much about the late inhabitants, but undoubtedly . . .

"Burn down that door!" Casker shrieked, his voice breaking.

Hellman was pondering the irony of it all. If one man's meat—*and* his poison—are your poison, then try eating something else. So simple, really.

But there was one thing that still bothered him.

"How did you know it was an Earth-type animal?" he asked.

"Its breath, stupid! It inhales and exhales and smells as if it's eaten onions!" There was a sound of cans falling and bottles shattering. "Now hurry!"

"What's wrong?" Hellman asked, finally getting to his feet and poising the burner.

"The Custom Super Transport. It's got me cornered behind a pile of cases. Hellman, it seems to think that I'm *its* meat!"

There aren't many short stories, in science fiction or out of it, as beautifully done as this. That doesn't mean it's merely exquisite. Real beauty has strength, and "Black Charlie" is, in its quiet way, as strong a story as you'll ever find.

This is all the more extraordinary because beauty is precisely what it is concerned with. Art is notoriously difficult to write about. In the field of the visual arts, van Loon's *R. v. R.* and Merejkovski's *The Romance of Leonardo da Vinci* are among those that have said something meaningful about the works and their creators; but these are novels. Furthermore, they deal with masters and masterpieces. "Black Charlie" gets down to the creative impulse itself.

Surely you, too, have now and then yearned for some accomplishment beyond your grasp. "Black Charlie" is for you, and about that part of your spirit.

—Poul Anderson

BLACK CHARLIE

by Gordon R. Dickson

You ask me, what is art? You expect me to have a logical answer at my fingertips because I have been a buyer for museums and galleries long enough to acquire a plentiful crop of gray hairs. It's not that simple.

Well, what is art? For forty years I've examined, felt, admired, and loved many things fashioned as hopeful vessels for that bright spirit we call art—and I'm unable to answer the question directly. The layman answers easily—beauty. But art is not necessarily beautiful. Sometimes it is ugly. Sometimes it is crude. Sometimes it is incomplete.

I have fallen back, as many men have in the business of making like decisions, on *feel* for the judgment of art. You know this business of *feel*. Let us say that you pick up something—a piece of statuary or, better, a fragment of stone, etched and colored by some ancient man of prehistoric times. You look at it. At first it is nothing, a half-developed reproduction of some wild animal, not even as good as a grade-school child could accomplish today.

But then, holding it, your imagination suddenly reaches through rock and time, back to the man himself, half squatted before the stone wall of his cave—and you see there not the dusty thing you hold in your hand—but what the man himself saw in the hour of its creation. You look beyond the physical reproduction to the magnificent accomplishment of his imagination.

This, then, may be called art—no matter what strange guise it appears in—this magic which bridges all gaps between the artist and yourself. To it, no distance, nor any difference, is too great. Let me give you an example from my own experience.

Some years back, when I was touring the newer worlds as a buyer for one of our well-known art institutions, I received a communication from a man named Cary Longan, asking me, if possible, to visit a planet named Elman's World and examine some statuary he had for sale.

Messages rarely came directly to me. They were usually referred to me by the institution I was representing at the time. Since, however, the world in question was close, being of the same solar system as the planet I was then visiting, I spacegraphed my answer that I would come. After cleaning up what remained of my business where I was, I took an interworld ship and, within a couple of days, landed on Elman's World.

It appeared to be a very raw, very new planet indeed. The port we landed at was, I learned, one of the only two suitable for deepspace vessels. And the city surrounding it was scarcely more than a village. Mr. Longan did not meet me at the port, so I took a cab directly to the hotel where I had made a reservation.

That evening, in my rooms, the annunciator rang, then spoke, giving me a name. I opened the door to admit a tall, brown-faced man with uncut, dark hair and troubled, green-brown eyes.

"Mr. Longan?" I asked.

"Mr. Jones?" he countered. He shifted the unvarnished wooden box he was carrying to his left hand and put out his right to shake mine. I closed the door behind him and led him to a chair.

He put the box down, without opening it, on a small coffee table between us. It was then that I noticed his rough, bush-country clothes, breeches, and tunic of drab plastic. Also an embarrassed air about him, like that of a man unused to city dealings. An odd sort of person to be offering art for sale.

"Your spacegram," I told him, "was not very explicit. The institution I represent—"

"I've got it here," he said, putting his hand on the box.

I looked at it in astonishment. It was no more than half a meter square by twenty centimeters deep.

"There?" I said. I looked back at him, with the beginnings of a suspicion forming in my mind. I suppose I should have been more wary when the message had come direct, instead of through Earth. But you know how it is—something of a feather in your cap when you bring in an unexpected item. "Tell me, Mr. Longan," I said, "where does this statuary come from?"

He looked at me a little defiantly. "A friend of mine made them," he said.

"A friend?" I repeated—and I must admit I was growing somewhat annoyed. It makes a man feel like a fool to be taken in that way. "May I ask whether this friend of yours has ever sold any of his work before?"

"Well, no . . ." Longan hedged. He was obviously suffering—but so was I, when I thought of my own wasted time.

"I see," I said, getting to my feet. "You've brought me on a very expensive side trip merely to show me the work of some amateur. Goodbye, Mr. Longan. And please take your box with you when you leave!"

"You've never seen anything like this before!" He was looking up at me with desperation.

"No doubt," I said.

"Look. I'll show you . . ." He fumbled, his fingers nervous on the hasp. "Since you've come all this way, you can at least look."

Because there seemed no way of getting him out of there, short of having the hotel manager eject him forcibly, I sat down with bad grace. "What's your friend's name?" I demanded.

Longan's fingers hesitated on the hasp. "Black Charlie," he replied, not looking up at me.

I stared. "I beg your pardon. Black—Charles Black?"

He looked up quite defiantly, met my eye, and shook his head. "Just Black Charlie," he said with sudden calmness. "Just the way it sounds. Black Charlie." He continued unfastening the box.

I watched rather dubiously as he finally managed to loosen the clumsy, handmade wooden bolt that secured the hasp. He was about to raise the lid, then apparently changed his mind. He turned the box around and pushed it across the coffee table.

The wood was hard and uneven under my fingers. I lifted the lid. There were five small partitions, each containing a rock of fine-grained gray sandstone of different but thoroughly incomprehensible shape.

I stared at them—then looked back at Longan to see if this weren't some sort of elaborate joke. But the tall man's eyes were severely serious. Slowly, I began to take out the stones and line them up on the table.

I studied them one by one, trying to make some sense out of their forms. But there was nothing there, absolutely nothing. One vaguely resembled a regular-sided pyramid. Another gave a foggy impression of a crouching figure. The best that could be said of the rest was that they bore a somewhat disconcerting resemblance to the kind of stones people pick up for paperweights. Yet they all had obviously been worked on. There were noticeable chisel marks on each one. And, in addition, they had been polished as well as such soft, grainy rock could be.

I looked up at Longan. His eyes were tense with waiting. I was completely puzzled about his discovery—or what he felt was a discovery. I tried to be fair about his acceptance of this as art. It was obviously nothing more than loyalty to a friend, a friend no doubt as unaware of what constituted art as himself. I made my tone as kind as I could.

"What did your friend expect me to do with these, Mr. Longan?" I asked gently.

"Aren't you buying things for that museum place on Earth?" he said.

I nodded. I picked up the piece that resembled a crouching animal figure and turned it over in my fingers. It was an awkward situation. "Mr. Longan," I said. "I have been in this business many years—"

"I know," he interrupted. "I read about you in the newsfax when you landed on the next world. That's why I wrote you."

"I see," I said. "Well, I've been in it a long time, as I say, and I think I can safely boast that I know something about art. If there is art in these carvings your friend has made, I should be able to recognize it. And I do not."

He stared at me, shock in his greenish-brown eyes.

"You're . . ." he said, finally. "You don't mean that. You're sore because I brought you out here this way."

"I'm sorry," I said. "I'm *not* sore and I *do* mean it. These things are not merely not good—there is nothing of value in them. Nothing! Someone has deluded your friend into thinking that he has talent. You'll be doing him a favor if you tell him the truth."

He stared at me for a long moment, as if waiting for me to say something to soften the verdict. Then, suddenly, he rose from the chair and crossed the room in three long strides, staring tensely out the window. His callused hands clenched and unclenched spasmodically.

I gave him a little time to wrestle it out with himself. Then I started putting the pieces of stone back into their sections of the box.

"I'm sorry," I told him.

He wheeled about and came back to me, leaning down from his lanky height to look in my face. "Are you?" he said. "*Are* you?"

"Believe me," I said sincerely, "I am." And I was.

"Then will you do something for me?" The words came in a rush. "Will you come and tell Charlie what you've told me? Will *you* break the news to him?"

"I . . ." I meant to protest, to beg off, but with his tortured eyes six inches from mine, the words would not come. "All right," I said.

The breath he had been holding came out in one long sigh. "Thanks," he said. "We'll go out tomorrow. You don't know what this means. Thanks."

I had ample time to regret my decision, both that night and the following morning, when Longan roused me at an early hour, furnished me with a set of bush clothes like his own, including high, impervious boots, and whisked me off in an old air-ground combination flyer that was loaded down with all kinds of bush-dweller's equipment. But a promise is a promise—and I reconciled myself to keeping mine.

We flew south along a high chain of mountains until we came to a coastal area and what appeared to be the swamp delta of some monster river. Here, we began to descend—much to my distaste. I have little affection for hot, muggy climates and could not conceive of anyone wanting to live under such conditions.

We set down lightly in a little open stretch of water—and Longan taxied the flyer across to the nearest bank, a tussocky mass of high brown weeds and soft mud. By myself, I would not have trusted the soggy ground to refrain from drawing me down like quicksand—but Longan stepped out onto the bank confidently enough, and I followed. The mud yielded, little pools of water springing up around my boot soles. A hot rank smell of decaying vegetation came to my nose. Under a thin but uniform blanket of cloud, the sky looked white and sick.

"This way," said Longan, and led off to the right.

I followed him along a little trail and into a small, swampy clearing with dome-shaped huts of woven branches, plastered with mud, scattered about it. And for the first time, it struck me that Black Charlie might be something other than an expatriate Earthman—might, indeed, be a native of this planet, though I had heard of no other humanlike race on other worlds before. My head spinning, I followed Longan to the entrance of one of the huts and halted as he whistled.

I don't remember now what I expected to see. Something vaguely humanoid, no doubt. But what came through the entrance in response to Longan's whistle was more like a large otter with flat, muscular grasping pads on the end of its four limbs, instead of feet. It was black with glossy, dampish hair all over it. About four feet in length, I judged, with no visible tail and a long, snaky neck. The creature must have weighed one hundred to, perhaps, one hundred and fifty pounds. The head on its long neck was also long and narrow, like the head of a well-bred collie—covered with the same black hair, with bright, intelligent eyes and a long mouth.

"This is Black Charlie," said Longan.

The creature stared at me, and I returned his gaze. Abruptly, I was conscious of the absurdity of the situation. It would have been difficult for any ordinary person to think of this being as a sculptor. To add to this a necessity, an obligation, to convince it that it was *not* a sculptor—mind you, I could not be expected to know a word of its language—was to pile Pelion upon Ossa in a madman's farce. I swung on Longan.

"Look here," I began with quite natural heat, "how do you expect me to tell—"

"He understands you," interrupted Longan.

"Speech?" I said incredulously. "Real human speech?"

"No," Longan shook his head. "But he understands actions." He turned from me abruptly and plunged into the weeds surrounding the clearing. He returned immediately with two objects that looked like gigantic puffballs and handed one to me.

"Sit on this," he said, doing so himself. I obeyed.

Black Charlie—I could think of nothing else to call him—came closer, and we sat down together. Charlie was half squatting on ebony haunches. All this time, I had been carrying the wooden box that contained his sculptures, and now that we were seated, his bright eyes swung inquisitively toward it.

"All right," said Longan, "give it to me."

I passed him the box, and it drew Black Charlie's eyes like a magnet. Longan took it under one arm and pointed toward the lake with the other—to where we had landed the flyer. Then his arm rose in the air in a slow, impressive circle and pointed northward, from the direction we had come.

Black Charlie whistled suddenly. It was an odd note, like the cry of a loon—a far, sad sound.

Longan struck himself on the chest, holding the box with one hand. Then he struck the box and pointed to me. He looked at Black Charlie, looked back at me—then put the box into my numb hands.

"Look them over and hand them back," he said, his voice tight. Against my will, I looked at Charlie.

His eyes met mine. Strange, liquid, black, inhuman eyes, like two tiny pools of pitch. I had to tear my own gaze away.

Torn between my feeling of foolishness and a real sympathy for the waiting creature, I awkwardly opened the box and I lifted the stones from their compartments. One by one, I turned them in my hand and put them back. I closed the box and returned it to Longan, shaking my head, not knowing if Charlie would understand that.

For a long moment, Longan merely sat facing me, holding the box. Then, slowly, he turned and set it, still open, in front of Charlie.

* * *

Charlie did not react at first. His head, on its long neck, dropped over the open compartments as if he was sniffing them. Then, surprisingly, his lips wrinkled back, revealing long, chisel-shaped teeth. Daintily, he reached into the box with these and lifted out the stones, one by one. He held them in his forepads, turning them this way and that, as if searching for the defects of each. Finally, he lifted one—it was the stone that faintly resembled a crouching beast. He lifted it to his mouth—and, with his gleaming teeth, made slight alterations in its surface. Then he brought it to me.

Helplessly I took it in my hands and examined it. The changes he had made in no way altered it toward something recognizable. I was forced to hand it back, with another head-shake, and a poignant pause fell between us.

I had been desperately turning over in my mind some way to explain, through the medium of pantomime, the reasons for my refusal. Now something occurred to me. I turned to Longan.

"Can he get me a piece of unworked stone?" I asked.

Longan turned to Charlie and made motions as if he were breaking something off and handing it to me. For a moment, Charlie sat still, as if considering this. Then he went into his hut, returning a moment later with a chunk of rock the size of my hand.

I had a small pocket knife, and the rock was soft. I held the rock out toward Longan and looked from him to it. Using my pocket knife, I whittled a rough, lumpy caricature of Longan seated on the puffball. When I was finished, I put the two side by side, the hacked piece of stone insignificant on the ground beside the living man.

Black Charlie looked at it. Then he came up to me—and, peering up into my face, cried softly, once. Moving so abruptly that it startled me, he turned smoothly, picked up in his teeth the piece of stone I had carved. Soon he disappeared back into his hut.

Longan stood up stiffly, like a man who has held one position too long. "That's it," he said. "Let's go."

We made our way to the combination and took off once more, headed back toward the city and the spaceship that would carry me away from this irrational world. As the mountains commenced to rise, far beneath us, I stole a glance at Longan, sitting beside me at the controls of the combination. His face was set in an expression of stolid unhappiness.

* * *

The question came from my lips before I had time to debate internally whether it was wise or not to ask it.

"Tell me, Mr. Longan," I said, "has—er—Black Charlie some special claim on your friendship?"

The tall man looked at me with something close to amazement.

"Claim!" he said. Then, after a short pause, during which he seemed to search my features to see if I was joking, "He saved my life."

"Oh," I said. "I see."

"You do, do you?" he countered. "Suppose I told you it was just after I'd finished killing his mate. They mate for life, you know."

"No, I didn't know," I answered feebly.

"I forget people don't know," he said in a subdued voice. I said nothing, hoping that, if I did not disturb him, he would say more. After a while he spoke. "This planet's not much good."

"I noticed," I answered. "I didn't see much in the way of plants and factories. And your sister world—the one I came from—is much more populated and built up."

"There's not much here," he said. "No minerals to speak of. Climate's bad, except on the plateaus. Soil's not much good." He paused. It seemed to take effort to say what came next. "Used to have a novelty trade in furs, though."

"Furs?" I echoed.

"Off Charlie's people," he went on, fiddling with the combination's controls. "Trappers and hunters used to be after them, at first, before they knew. I was one of them."

"You!" I said.

"Me!" His voice was flat. "I was doing fine, too, until I trapped Charlie's mate. Up till then, I'd been getting them out by themselves. They did a lot of traveling in those swamps. But, this time, I was close to the village. I'd just clubbed her on the head when the whole tribe jumped me." His voice trailed off, then strengthened. "They kept me under guard for a couple of months.

"I learned a lot in that time. I learned they were intelligent. I learned it was Black Charlie who kept them from killing me right off. Seems he took the point of view that I was a reasonable being and, if he could just talk things over with me, we could get together and end the war." Longan laughed, a little bitterly. "They called it a war, Charlie's people did." He stopped talking.

I waited. And when he remained quiet, I prompted him. "What happened?" I asked.

"They let me go, finally," he said. "And I went to bat for them. Clear up to the Commissioner sent from Earth. I got them recognized as people instead of animals. I put an end to the hunting and trapping."

He stopped again. We were still flying through the upper air of Elman's World, the sun breaking through the clouds at last, revealing the ground below like a huge green relief map.

"I see," I said, finally.

Longan looked at me stonily.

We flew back to the city.

I left Elman's World the next day, fully believing that I had heard and seen the last of both Longan and Black Charlie. Several years later, at home in New York, I was visited by a member of the government's Foreign Service. He was a slight, dark man, and he didn't beat about the bush.

"You don't know me," he said. I looked at his card—*Antonio Walters.* "I was Deputy Colonial Representative on Elman's World at the time you were there."

I looked up at him, surprised. I had forgotten Elman's World by that time.

"Were you?" I asked, feeling a little foolish, unable to think of anything better to say. I turned his card over several times, staring at it, as a person will do when at a loss. "What can I do for you, Mr. Walters?"

"We've been requested by the local government on Elman's World to locate you, Mr. Jones," he answered. "Cary Longan is dying—"

"Dying!" I said.

"Lung fungus, unfortunately," said Walters. "You catch it in the swamps. He wants to see you before the end—and, since we're very grateful to him out there for the work he's been doing all these years for the natives, a place has been kept for you on a government courier ship leaving for Elman's World right away—if you're willing to go."

"Why, I . . ." I hesitated. In common decency, I could not refuse. "I'll have to notify my employers."

"Of course," he said.

* * *

Luckily, the arrangements I had to make consisted of a few business calls and packing my bags. I was, as a matter of fact, between trips at the time. As an experienced traveler, I could always get under way with a minimum of fuss. Walters and I drove out to Government Port in northern New Jersey and, from there on, the authorities took over.

Less than a week later, I stood by Longan's bedside in the hospital of the same city I had visited years before. The man was now nothing more than a barely living skeleton, the hard vitality all but gone from him, hardly able to speak a few words at a time. I bent over to catch the whispered syllables from his wasted lips.

"Black Charlie . . ." he whispered.

"Black Charlie," I repeated. "Yes, what about him?"

"He's done something new," whispered Longan. "That carving of yours started him off, copying things. His tribe don't like it."

"They don't?" I said.

"They," whispered Longan, "don't understand. It's not normal, the way they see it. They're afraid—"

"You mean they're superstitious about what he carves?" I asked.

"Something like that. Listen—he's an artist . . ."

I winced internally at the last word, but held my tongue for the sake of the dying man.

". . . an artist. But they'll kill him for it, now that I'm gone. You can save him, though."

"Me?" I said.

"You!" The man's voice was like a wind rustling through dry leaves. "If you go out—take this last thing from him—act pleased . . . then they'll be scared to touch him. But hurry. Every day is that much closer . . ."

His strength failed him. He closed his eyes, and his straining throat muscles relaxed to a little hiss of air that puffed between his lips. The nurse hurried me from his room.

The local government helped me. I was surprised, and not a little touched, to see how many people knew Longan. How many of them admired his attempts to pay back the natives by helping them in any way he could. They located Charlie's tribe on a map for me and sent me out with a pilot who knew the country.

We landed on the same patch of slime. I went alone toward the clearing. With the brown weeds still walling it about, the locale showed no natural change, but Black Charlie's hut appeared broken and deserted. I whistled and waited. I called. And, finally, I got down on my hands and knees and crawled inside. But there was nothing there save a pile of loose rock and a mass of dried weeds. Feeling cramped and uncomfortable, for I am not used to such gymnastics, I backed out to find myself surrounded by a crowd.

It looked as if all the other inhabitants of the village had come out of their huts and congregated before Charlie's. They seemed agitated, milling about, occasionally whistling at each other on that one low, plaintive note which was the only sound I had ever heard Charlie make. Eventually, the excitement seemed to fade, the group fell back, and one individual came forward alone. He looked up into my face for a brief moment, then turned and glided swiftly on his pads toward the edge of the clearing.

I followed. There seemed nothing else to do. And, at that time, it did not occur to me to be afraid.

My guide led me deep into the weed patch, then abruptly disappeared. I looked around surprised and undecided, half inclined to turn about and retrace my steps by the trail of crushed weeds I had left in my floundering advance. Then a low whistle sounded close by. I went forward and found Charlie.

He lay on his side in a little circular open area of crushed weeds. He was too weak to do more than raise his head and look at me, for the whole surface of his body was crisscrossed and marked with the slashings of shallow wounds, from which dark blood seeped slowly and stained the reeds in which he lay. In Charlie's mouth I had seen the long chisel-teeth of his kind, and I knew what had made those wounds. A gust of rage went through me, and I stopped to pick him up in my arms.

He came up easily, for the bones of his kind are cartilaginous, and their flesh is far lighter than our human flesh. Holding him, I turned and made my way back to the clearing.

The others were waiting for me as we came out into the open. I glared at them—and then the rage inside me went out like a blown candle. For there was nothing there to hate. *They* had not hated Charlie. They had merely feared him—and their only crime was ignorance.

They moved back from me, and I carried Charlie to the door of his own hut. There I laid him down. The chest and arms of my jacket were soaked from his dark body fluid, and I saw that his blood was not clotting as our own does.

Clumsily, I took off my shirt and, tearing it into strips, made a poor attempt to bind up the torn flesh. But the blood came through in spite of my first aid. Charlie, lifting his head, with a great effort, from the ground, picked feebly at the bandages with his teeth, so that I gave up and removed them.

I sat down beside him then, feeling sick and helpless. In spite of Longan's care and dying effort, in spite of all the scientific developments of my own human race, I had come too late. Numbly, I sat and looked down at him and wondered why I could not have come one day earlier.

From this half stupor of self-accusation I was roused by Charlie's attempts to crawl back into his hut. My first reaction was to restrain him. But, from somewhere, he seemed to have dredged up a remnant of his waning strength—and he persisted. Seeing this, I changed my mind and, instead of hindering, helped. He dragged himself through the entrance, his strength visibly waning.

I did not expect to see him emerge. I believed some ancient instinct had called him, that he would die then and there. But, a few moments later, I heard a sound as of stones rattling from within—and, in a few seconds, he began to back out. Halfway through the entrance, his strength finally failed him. He lay still for a minute, then whistled weakly.

I went to him and pulled him out the rest of the way. He turned his head toward me, holding in his mouth what I first took to be a ball of dried mud.

I took it from him and began to scrape the mud off with my fingernails. Almost immediately, the grain and surface of the sandstone he used for his carvings began to emerge—and my hands started to shake so hard that, for a moment, I had to put the stone down while I got myself under control. For the first time, the true importance to Charlie of these things he had chewed and bitten into shape got home to me.

In that moment, I swore that whatever bizarre form this last and greatest work of his might possess, I would make certain that it was accorded a place in some respectable museum as a true work of art. After all, it had been conceived in honesty and executed in the love that took no count of labor, provided the end was achieved.

And then, the rest of the mud came free in my hands. I saw what it was, and I could have cried and laughed at the same time. For, of all the shapes he could have chosen to work in stone, he had picked the one that no critic would have selected as the choice of an artist of his race. For he had chosen no plant or animal, no structure or natural shape out of his environment, to express the hungry longing of his spirit. None of these had he chosen—instead, with painful clumsiness, he had fashioned an image from the soft and grainy rock—a statue of a standing man.

And I knew what man it was.

Charlie lifted his head from the stained ground and looked toward the lake where my flyer waited. I am not an intuitive man—but, for once, I was able to understand the meaning of a look. He wanted me to leave while he was still alive. He wanted to see me go, carrying the thing he had fashioned. I got to my feet, holding it, and stumbled off. At the edge of the clearing, I looked back. He still watched. And the rest of his people still hung back from him. I did not think they would bother him now.

And so I came home.

But there is one thing more to tell. For a long time, after I returned form Elman's World, I did not look at the crude statuette. I did not want to, for I knew that seeing it would only confirm what I had known from the start, that all the longing and desires in the world cannot create art where there is no talent, no true visualization. But at the end of one year I was cleaning up all the little details of my office. And, because I believe in system and order—and also because I was ashamed of myself for having put it off so long—I took the statuette from a bottom drawer of my desk, unwrapped it, and set it on the desk's polished surface.

I was alone in my office at the time, at the end of a day, when the afternoon sun, striking red through the tall window beside my desk, touched everything between the walls with a clear, amber light. I ran my fingers over the grainy sandstone and held it up to look at it.

And then—for the first time—I saw it, saw through the stone to the image beyond, saw what Black Charlie had seen, with Black Charlie's eyes, when he looked at Longan. I saw men as Black Charlie's kind saw men—and I saw what the worlds of men meant to Black Charlie. And, above all, overriding all, I saw art as Black Charlie saw it, through his bright alien eyes—saw the beauty he had sought at the price of his life, and had half found.

But, most of all, I saw that this crude statuette was *art.*

One more word. Amid the mud and weeds of the swamp, I had held the carving in my hands and promised myself that this work would one day stand on display. Following that moment of true insight in my office, I did my best to place it with the institution I represented, then with others who knew me as a reputable buyer.

But I could find no takers. No one, although they trusted me individually, was willing to exhibit such a poor-looking piece of work on the strength of a history that I, alone, could vouch for. There are people, close to any institution, who are only too ready to cry, "Hoax!" For several years, I tried without success.

Eventually, I gave up on the true story and sold the statuette, along with a number of other odd pieces, to a dealer of minor reputation, representing it as an object whose history I did not know.

Curiously, the statuette has justified my belief in what is art, by finding a niche for itself. I traced it from the dealer, after a time, and ran it to Earth quite recently. There is a highly respectable art gallery on this planet which has an extensive display of primitive figures of early American Indian origin.

And Black Charlie's statuette is among them. I will not tell which or where it is.

Every writer has a story about which he thinks, "Damn, I wish I'd written that one." Howard Waldrop's "The Ugly Chickens" is mine. If I'd been lucky enough to have the idea Waldrop had for the story, I might have been lucky enough to turn out a piece that looked quite a bit like the one he wrote. I could have done the research—I could have had a hell of a lot of fun doing the research—and, with the research done, the story would just about have written itself. There's only one problem: I still have this nagging suspicion (no, let's not beat around the bush—I still have this nagging certainty) that Waldrop did it better than I could have.

Dodos have fascinated people since they were discovered. What the heck were these big, ugly, stupid flightless pigeons doing on an island out in the middle of the Indian Ocean? The obvious answer is that they could survive only on an island out in the middle of the Indian Ocean, as they demonstrated by becoming extinct in jig time after European sailors discovered Mauritius. They serve as a dreadful object lesson on human ravishing of a previously pristine environment, and, in evolutionary terms, on the risks any creature that evolved in a place where there isn't much competition takes when it starts playing against the first team: and there isn't any first team tougher than men and rats.

Also, dodos are funny-looking as all get-out.

What if they'd somehow survived in the American South, on a back-country farm run by people obviously related to the ones James Agee memorialized in "Now Let Us Praise Famous Men"? That's Waldrop's premise, and he makes both the survival and the dodos' ultimate fate plausible, ironic, and highly amusing.

Damn, I wish I'd written that one. And I can't be the only person who does, too, because "The Ugly Chickens" won the Nebula for Best Novelette of 1980. Richly deserved, too.

Enjoy it, as I've done ever since.

—Harry Turtledove

THE UGLY CHICKENS

by Howard Waldrop

My car was broken, and I had a class to teach at eleven. So I took the city bus, something I rarely do.

I spent last summer crawling through the Big Thicket with cameras and tape recorder, photographing and taping two of the last ivory-billed woodpeckers on the earth. You can see the films at your local Audubon Society showroom.

This year I wanted something just as flashy but a little less taxing. Perhaps a population study on the Bermuda cahow, or the New Zealand *takahe*. A month or so in the warm (not hot) sun would do me a world of good. To say nothing of the advance of science.

I was idly leafing through Greenway's *Extinct and Vanishing Birds of the World.* The city bus was winding its way through the ritzy neighborhoods of Austin, stopping to let off the chicanas, black women and Vietnamese who tended the kitchens and gardens of the rich.

"I haven't seen any of those ugly chickens in a long time," said a voice close by.

A gray-haired lady was leaning across the aisle toward me.

I looked at her, then around. Maybe she was a shopping-bag lady. Maybe she was just talking. I looked straight at her. No doubt about it, she was talking to me. She was waiting for an answer.

"I used to live near some folks who raised them when I was a girl," she said. She pointed.

I looked down at the page my book was open to.

What I should have said was: "That is quite impossible, madam. This is a drawing of an extinct bird of the island Mauritius. It is perhaps the most famous dead bird in the world. Maybe you are mistaking this drawing for that of some rare Asiatic turkey, peafowl or pheasant. I am sorry, but you *are* mistaken."

I should have said all that.

What she said was, "Oops, this is my stop," and got up to go.

My name is Paul Lindberl. I am twenty-six years old, a graduate student in ornithology at the University of Texas, a teaching assistant. My name is not unknown in the field. I have several vices and follies, but I don't think foolishness is one of them.

The stupid thing for me to do would have been to follow her.

She stepped off the bus.

I followed her.

I came into the departmental office, trailing scattered papers in the whirlwind behind me. "Martha! Martha!" I yelled.

She was doing something in the supply cabinet.

"Jesus, Paul! What do you want?"

"Where's Courtney?"

"At the conference in Houston. You know that. You missed your class. What's the matter?"

"Petty cash. Let me at it!"

"Payday was only a week ago. If you can't . . ."

"It's business! It's fame and adventure and the chance of a lifetime! It's a long sea voyage that leaves . . . a plane ticket. To either Jackson, Mississippi or Memphis. Make it Jackson, it's closer. I'll get receipts! I'll be famous. Courtney will be famous. *You'll* even be famous! This university will make even *more* money! I'll pay you back. Give me some paper. I gotta write Courtney a note. When's the next plane out? Could you get Marie and Chuck to take over my classes Tuesday and Wednesday? I'll try to be back Thursday unless something happens. Courtney'll be back tomorrow, right? I'll call him from, well, wherever. Do you have some coffee? . . ."

And so on and so forth. Martha looked at me like I was crazy. But she filled out the requisition anyway.

"What do I tell Kemejian when I ask him to sign these?"

"Martha, babe, sweetheart. Tell him I'll get his picture in *Scientific American.*"

"He doesn't read it."

"*Nature*, then!"

"I'll see what I can do," she said.

The lady I had followed off the bus was named Jolyn (Smith) Jimson. The story she told me was so weird that it had to be true. She knew things only an expert, or someone with firsthand experience, could know. I got names from her, and addresses, and directions, and tidbits of information. Plus a year: 1927.

And a place. Northern Mississippi.

I gave her my copy of the Greenway book. I told her I'd call her as soon as I got back into town. I left her standing on the corner near the house of the lady she cleaned up for twice a week. Jolyn Jimson was in her sixties.

Think of the dodo as a baby harp seal with feathers. I know that's not even close, but it saves time.

In 1507, the Portuguese, on their way to India, found the (then unnamed) Mascarene Islands in the Indian Ocean—three of them a few hundred miles apart, all east and north of Madagascar.

It wasn't until 1598, when that old Dutch sea captain Cornelius van Neck bumped into them, that the islands received their names—names which changed several times through the centuries as the Dutch, French and English changed them every war or so. They are now known as Rodriguez, Réunion and Mauritius.

The major feature of these islands were large flightless, stupid, ugly, bad-tasting birds. Van Neck and his men named them *dod-aarsen,* stupid ass, or dodars, silly birds, or solitaires.

There were three species—the dodo of Mauritius, the real gray-brown, hooked-beak clumsy thing that weighed twenty kilos or more; the white, somewhat slimmer, dodo of Réunion; and the solitaires of Rodriguez and Réunion, which looked like very fat, very dumb light-colored geese.

The dodos all had thick legs, big squat bodies twice as large as a turkey's, naked faces, and big long downcurved beaks ending in a hook like a hollow linoleum knife. They were flightless. Long ago they had lost the ability to fly, and their wings had degenerated to flaps the size of a human hand with only three or four feathers in them. Their tails were curly and fluffy, like a child's afterthought at decoration. They had absolutely no natural enemies. They nested on the open ground. They probably hatched their eggs wherever they happened to lay them.

No natural enemies until van Neck and his kind showed up. The Dutch, French, and Portuguese sailors who stopped at the Mascarenes to replenish stores found that besides looking stupid, dodos *were* stupid. They walked right up to them and hit them on the head with clubs. Better yet, dodos could be herded around like sheep. Ship's logs are full of things like: "Party of ten men ashore. Drove half-a-hundred of the big turkey-like birds into the boat. Brought to ship where they are given the run of the decks. Three will feed a crew of 150."

Even so, most of the dodo, except for the breast, tasted bad. One of the Dutch words for them was *walghvogel,* disgusting bird. But on a ship three months out on a return for Goa to Lisbon, well, food was where you found it. It was said, even so, that prolonged boiling did not improve the flavor.

Even so, the dodos might have lasted, except that the Dutch, and later the French, colonized the Mascarenes. The islands became plantations and dumping-places for religious refugees. Sugar cane and other exotic crops were raised there.

With the colonists came cats, dogs, hogs and the cunning *Rattus norwegicus* and the Rhesus monkey from Ceylon. What dodos the hungry sailors left were chased down (they were dumb and stupid, but they could run when they felt like it) by dogs in the open. They were killed by cats as they sat on their nests. Their eggs were stolen and eaten by monkeys, rats and hogs. And they competed with the pigs for all the low-growing goodies of the islands.

The last Mauritius dodo was seen in 1681, less than a hundred years after man first saw them. The last white dodo walked off the history books around 1720. The solitaires of Rodriguez and Réunion, last of the genus as well as the species, may have lasted until 1790. Nobody knows.

Scientists suddenly looked around and found no more of the Didine birds alive, anywhere.

This part of the country was degenerate before the first Snopes ever saw it. This road hadn't been paved until the late fifties, and it was a main road between two county seats. That didn't mean it went through civilized country. I'd traveled for miles and seen nothing but dirt banks red as Billy Carter's neck and an occasional church. I expected to see Burma Shave signs, but realized this road had probably never had them.

I almost missed the turn-off onto the dirt and gravel road the man back at the service station had marked. It led onto the highway from nowhere, a lane out of a field. I turned down it and a rock the size of a golf ball flew up over the hood and put a crack three inches long in the windshield of the rent-a-car I'd gotten in Grenada.

It was a hot muggy day for this early. The view was obscured in a cloud of dust every time the gravel thinned. About a mile down the road, the gravel gave out completely. The roadway turned into a rutted dirt pathway, just wider than the car, hemmed in on both sides by a sagging three-strand barbed wire fence.

In some places the fenceposts were missing a few meters. The wire lay on the ground and in some places disappeared under it for long stretches.

The only life I saw was a mockingbird raising hell with something under a thorn bush the barbed wire had been nailed to in place of a post. To one side now was a grassy field which had gone wild, the way everywhere will look after we blow ourselves off the face of the planet. The other was fast becoming woods—pine, oak, some black gum and wild plum, fruit not out this time of the year.

I began to ask myself what I was doing here. What if Ms. Jimson were some imaginative old crank who—but no. Wrong, maybe, but even the wrong was worth checking. But I knew she hadn't lied to me. She had seemed incapable of lies—a good ol' girl, backbone of the South, of the earth. Not a mendacious gland in her being.

I couldn't doubt her, or my judgment, either. Here I was, creeping and bouncing on a dirt path in Mississippi, after no sleep for a day, out on the thin ragged edge of a dream. I *had* to take it on faith.

The back of the car sometimes slid where the dirt had loosened and gave way to sand. The back tire stuck once, but I rocked out of it. Getting back out again would be another matter. Didn't anyone ever use this road?

The woods closed in on both sides like the forest primæval, and the fence had long since disappeared. My odometer said ten kilometers and it had been twenty minutes since I'd turned off the highway. In the rearview mirror, I saw beads of sweat and dirt in the wrinkles of my neck. A fine patina of dust covered everything inside the car. Clots of it came through the windows.

The woods reached out and swallowed the road. Branches scraped against the windows and the top. It was like falling down a long dark leafy tunnel. It was dark and green in there. I fought back an atavistic urge to turn on the headlights. The roadbed must be made of a few centuries of leaf mulch. I kept constant pressure on the accelerator and bulled my way through.

Half a log caught and banged and clanged against the car bottom. I saw light ahead. Fearing for the oil pan, I punched the pedal and sped out.

I almost ran through a house.

It was maybe ten meters from the trees. The road ended under one of the windows. I saw somebody waving from the corner of my eye.

I slammed on the brakes.

A whole family was on the porch, looking like a Walker Evans Depression photograph, or a fever dream from the mind of a *Hee Haw* producer. The house was old. Strips of peeling paint a meter long tapped against the eaves.

"Damned good thing you stopped," said a voice. I looked up. The biggest man I had ever seen in my life leaned down into the driver-side window.

"If we'd have heard you sooner, I'd've sent one of the kids down to the end of the driveway to warn you," he said.

Driveway?

His mouth was stained brown at the corners. I figured he chewed tobacco until I saw the sweet-gum snuff brush sticking from the pencil pocket in the bib of his overalls. His hands were the size of catcher's mitts. They looked like they'd never held anything smaller than an ax handle.

"How y'all?" he said, by way of introduction.

"Just fine," I said. I got out of the car.

"My name's Lindberl," I said, extending my hand. He took it. For an instant, I thought of bear traps, shark's mouths, closing elevator doors. The thought went back to wherever it is they stay.

"This the Gudger place?" I asked.

He looked at me blankly with his grey eyes. He wore a diesel truck cap, and had on a checked lumberjack shirt beneath the coveralls. His rubber boots were the size of the ones Karloff wore in *Frankenstein.*

"Naw. I'm Jim Bob Krait. That's my wife Jenny, and there's Luke and Skeeno and Shirl." He pointed to the porch.

The people on the porch nodded.

"Lessee? Gudger? No Gudgers round here I know of. I'm sorta new here." I took that to mean he hadn't lived here for more than twenty years or so.

"Jennifer!" he yelled. "You know of anybody named Gudger?" To me he said, "My wife's lived around here all her life."

His wife came down onto the second step of the porch landing. "I think they used to be the ones what lived on the Spradlin place before the Spradlins. But the Spradlins left around the Korean War. I didn't know any of the Gudgers myself. That's while we was living over to Water Valley."

"You an insurance man?" asked Mr. Krait.

"Uh . . . no," I said. I imagined the people on the porch leaning toward me, all ears. "I'm a . . . I teach college."

"Oxford?" asked Krait.

"Uh, no. University of Texas."

"Well, that's a damn long way off. You say you're looking for the Gudgers?"

"Just their house. The area. As your wife said, I understand they left. During the Depression, I believe."

"Well, they musta had money," said the gigantic Mr. Krait. "Nobody around here was rich enough to *leave* during the Depression."

"Luke!" he yelled. The oldest boy on the porch sauntered down. He looked anemic and wore a shirt in vogue with the Twist. He stood with his hands in his pockets.

"Luke, show Mr. Lindbergh—"

"Lindberl."

"Mr. Lindberl here the way up to the old Spradlin place. Take him as far as the old log bridge, he might get lost before then."

"Log bridge broke down, daddy."

"When?"

"October, daddy."

"Well, hell, somethin' else to fix! Anyway, to the creek."

He turned to me. "You want him to go along on up there, see you don't get snakebit?"

"No, I'm sure I'll be fine."

"Mind if I ask what you're going up there for?" he asked. He was looking away from me. I could see having to come right out and ask was bothering him. Such things usually came up in the course of conversation.

"I'm a—uh, bird scientist. I study birds. We had a sighting—someone told us the old Gudger place—the area around here—I'm looking for a rare bird. It's hard to explain."

I noticed I was sweating. It was hot.

"You mean like a goodgod? I saw a goodgod about twenty-five years ago, over next to Bruce," he said.

"Well, no." (A goodgod was one of the names for an ivory-billed woodpecker, one of the rarest in the world. Any other time I would have dropped my jaw. Because they were thought to have died out in Mississippi by the teens, and by the fact that Krait knew they *were* rare.)

I went to lock my car up, then thought of the protocol of the situation. "My car be in your way?" I asked.

"Naw. It'll be just fine," said Jim Bob Krait. "We'll look for you back by sundown, that be all right?"

For a minute, I didn't know whether that was a command or an expression of concern.

"Just in case I get snakebit," I said. "I'll try to be careful up there."

"Good luck on findin' them rare birds," he said. He walked up to the porch with his family.

"Les go," said Luke.

Behind the Krait house was a henhouse and pigsty where hogs lay after their morning slop like islands in a muddy bay, or some Zen pork sculpture. Next we passed broken farm machinery gone to rust, though there was nothing but uncultivated land as far as the eye could see. How the family made a living I don't know. I'm told you can find places just like this throughout the South.

We walked through woods and across fields, following a sort of path. I tried to memorize the turns I would have to take on my way back. Luke didn't say a word the whole twenty minutes he accompanied me, except to curse once when he stepped into a bull nettle with his tennis shoes.

We came to a creek which skirted the edge of a woodsy hill. There was a rotted log forming a small dam. Above it the water was nearly a meter deep, below it, half that much.

"See that path?" he asked.

"Yes."

"Follow it up around the hill, then across the next field. Then you cross the creek again on the rocks, and over the hill. Take the left-hand path. What's left of the house is about three quarters the way up the next hill. If you come to a big bare rock cliff, you've gone too far. You got that?"

I nodded.

He turned and left.

The house had once been a dog-run cabin, like Ms. Jimson had said. Now it was fallen in on one side, what they call sigoglin (or was it antisigoglin?). I once heard a hymn on the radio called "The Land Where No Cabins Fall." This was the country songs like that were written in.

Weeds grew everywhere. There were signs of fences, a flattened pile of wood that had once been a barn. Further behind the house were the outhouse remains. Half a rusted pump stood in the backyard. A flatter spot showed where the vegetable garden had been; in it a single wild tomato, pecked by birds, lay rotting. I passed it. There was lumber from three outbuildings, mostly rotten and green with algae and moss. One had been a smokehouse and woodshed combination. Two had been chicken roosts. One was larger than the other. It was there I started to poke around and dig.

Where? Where? I wish I'd been on more archaeological digs, knew the places to look. Refuse piles, midden heaps, kitchen scrap piles, compost boxes. Why hadn't I been born on a farm so I'd know instinctively where to search.

I prodded around the grounds. I moved back and forth like a setter casting for the scent of quail. I wanted more, more. I still wasn't satisfied.

Dusk. Dark, in fact. I trudged into the Kraits' front yard. The toe sack I carried was full to bulging. I was hot, tired, streaked with fifty years of chicken shit. The Kraits were on their porch. Jim Bob lumbered down like a friendly mountain.

I asked him a few questions, gave them a Xerox of one of the dodo pictures, left them addresses and phone numbers where they could reach me.

Then into the rent-a-car. Off to Water Valley, acting on information Jennifer Krait gave me. I went to the postmaster's house at Water Valley. She was getting ready for bed. I asked questions. She got on the phone. I bothered people until one in the morning. Then back into the trusty rent-a-car.

On to Memphis as the moon came up on my right. Interstate 55 was a glass ribbon before me. WLS from Chicago was on the radio.

I hummed along with it, I sang at the top of my voice.

The sack full of dodo bones, beaks, feet and eggshell fragments kept me company on the front seat.

Did you know a museum once traded an entire blue whale skeleton for one of a dodo?

Driving, driving.

the dance of the dodos

I used to have a vision sometimes—I had it long before this madness came up. I can close my eyes and see it by thinking hard. But it comes to me most often, most vividly when I am reading and listening to classical music, especially Pachelbel's *Canon in D.*

It is near dusk in The Hague, and the light is that of Frans Hals, of Rembrandt. The Dutch royal family and their guests eat and talk quietly in the great dining hall. Guards with halberds and pikes stand in the corners of the room. The family is arranged around the table; the King, Queen, some princesses, a prince, a couple of other children, an invited noble or two. Servants come out with plates and cups but they do not intrude.

On a raised platform at one end of the room an orchestra plays dinner music—a harpsichordist, viola, cello, three violins and woodwinds. One of the royal dwarfs sits on the edge of the platform, his foot slowly rubbing the back of one of the dogs sleeping near him.

As the music of Pachelbel's *Canon in D* swells and rolls through the hall, one of the dodos walks in clumsily, stops, tilts its head, its eye bright as a pool of tar. It sways a little, lifts its foot tentatively, one then another, rocks back and forth in time to the cello.

The violins swirl. The dodo begins to dance, its great ungainly body now graceful. It is joined by the other two dodos who come into the hall, all three turning in sort of a circle.

The harpsichord begins its counterpoint. The fourth dodo, the white one from Réunion, comes from its place under the table and joins the circle with the others.

It is most graceful of all, making complete turns where the others only sway and dip on the edge of the circle they have formed.

The music rises in volume; the first violinist sees the dodos and nods to the King. But he and the others at the table have already seen. They are silent, transfixed—even the servants stand still, bowls, pots and kettles in their hands forgotten.

Around the dodos dance with bobs and weaves of their ugly heads. The white dodo dips, takes a half step, pirouettes on one foot, circles again.

Without a word the King of Holland takes the hand of the Queen, and they come around the table, children before the spectacle. They join in the dance, waltzing (anachronism) among the dodos while the family, the guests, the soldiers watch and nod in time with the music.

Then the vision fades, and the afterimage of a flickering fireplace and a dodo remains.

The dodo and its kindred came by ships to the ports of civilized men. The first we have record of is that of Captain van Neck who brought back two in 1599—one for the King of Holland, and one which found its way through Cologne to the menagerie of Emperor Rudolf II.

This royal aviary was at Schloss Neugebau, near Vienna. It was here the first paintings of the dumb old birds were done by Georg and his son Jacob Hoefnagel, between 1602 and 1610. They painted it among more than ninety species of birds which kept the Emperor amused.

Another Dutch artist named Roelandt Savery, as someone said, "made a career out of the dodo." He drew and painted them many times, and was no doubt personally fascinated by them. Obsessed, even. Early on, the paintings are consistent; the later ones have inaccuracies. This implies he worked from life first, then from memory as his model went to that place soon to be reserved for all its species. One of his drawings has two of the Raphidae scrambling for some goodie on the ground. His works are not without charm.

Another Dutch artist (they seemed to sprout up like mushrooms after a spring rain) named Peter Withoos also stuck dodos in his paintings, sometimes in odd and exciting places—wandering around during their owner's music lessons, or stuck with Adam and Eve in some Edenic idyll.

The most accurate representation, we are assured, comes from half a world away from the religious and political turmoil of the seafaring Europeans. There is an Indian miniature painting of the dodo which now rests in a museum in Russia. The dodo could have been brought by the Dutch or Portuguese in their travels to Goa and the coasts of the Indian subcontinent. Or they could have been brought centuries before by the Arabs who plied the Indian Ocean in their triangular-sailed craft, and who may have discovered the Mascarenes before the Europeans cranked themselves up for the First Crusade.

At one time early in my bird-fascination days (after I stopped killing them with BB guns but before I began to work for a scholarship), I once sat down and figured out where all the dodos had been.

Two with van Neck in 1599, one to Holland, one to Austria. Another was in Count Solms's park in 1600. An account speaks of "one in Italy, one in Germany, several to England, eight or nine to Holland." William Boentekoe van Hoorn knew of "one shipped to Europe in 1640, another in 1685" which he said was "also painted by Dutch artists." Two were mentioned as "being kept in Surrat House in India as pets," perhaps one of which is the one in the painting. Being charitable, and considering "several" to mean at least three, that means twenty dodos in all.

There had to be more, when boatloads had been gathered at the time.

What do we know of the Didine birds? A few ships' logs, some accounts left by travelers and colonists. The English were fascinated by them. Sir Hamon L'Estrange, a contemporary of Pepys, saw exhibited "a Dodar from the Island of Mauritius . . . it is not able to flie, being so bigge." One was stuffed when it died, and was put in the Museum Tradescantum in South Lambeth. It eventually found its way into the Ashmolean Museum. It grew ratty and was burned, all but a leg and the head, in 1750. By then there were no more dodos, but nobody had realized that yet.

Francis Willughby got to describe it before its incineration. Earlier, old Carolus Clusius in Holland studied the one in Count Solms's park. He collected everything known about the Raphidae, describing a dodo leg Pieter Pauw kept in his natural history cabinet, in *Exoticarium libri decem* in 1605, eight years after their discovery.

François Leguat, a Huguenot who lived on Réunion for some years, published an account of his travels in which he mentioned the dodos. It was published in 1690 (after the Mauritius dodo was extinct) and included the information that "some of the males weigh forty-five pound. One egg, much bigger than that of a goose is laid by the female, and takes seven weeks hatching time."

The Abbe Pingre visited the Mascarenes in 1761. He saw the last of the Rodriguez solitaires, and collected what information he could about the dead Mauritius and Réunion members of the genus.

After that, only memories of the colonists, and some scientific debate as to *where* the Raphidae belonged in the great taxonomic scheme of things—some said pigeons, some said rails—were left. Even this nitpicking ended. The dodo was forgotten.

When Lewis Carroll wrote *Alice in Wonderland* in 1865, most people thought he invented the dodo.

The service station I called from in Memphis was busier than a one-legged man in an ass-kicking contest. Between bings and dings of the bell, I finally realized the call had gone through.

The guy who answered was named Selvedge. I got nowhere with him. He mistook me for a real estate agent, then a lawyer. Now he was beginning to think I was some sort of a con man. I wasn't doing too well, either. I hadn't slept in two days. I must have sounded like a speed freak. My only progress was that I found that Ms. Annie Mae Gudger (childhood playmate of Jolyn Jimson) was now, and had been, the respected Ms. Annie Mae Radwin. This guy Selvedge must have been a secretary or toady or something.

We were having a conversation comparable to that between a shrieking macaw and a pile of mammoth bones. Then there was another click on the line.

"Young man?" said the other voice, an old woman's voice, Southern, very refined but with a hint of the hills in it.

"Yes? Hello! Hello!"

"Young man, you say you talked to a Jolyn somebody? Do you mean Jolyn Smith?"

"Hello! Yes! Ms. Radwin, Ms. Annie Mae Radwin who used to be Gudger? She lives in Austin now. Texas. She used to live near Water Valley, Mississippi. Austin's where I'm from. I . . ."

"Young man," asked the voice again, "are you sure you haven't been put up to this by my hateful sister Alma?"

"Who? No, ma'am. I met a woman named Jolyn . . ."

"I'd like to talk to you, young man," said the voice. Then offhandedly, "Give him directions to get here, Selvedge."

Click.

I cleaned out my mouth as best I could in the service station restroom, tried to shave with an old clogged Gillette disposable in my knapsack and succeeded in gapping up my jawline. I changed into a clean pair of jeans, the only other shirt I had with me and combed my hair. I stood in front of the mirror.

I still looked like the dog's lunch.

The house reminded me of Presley's mansion, which was somewhere in the neighborhood. From a shack on the side of a Mississippi hill to this, in forty years. There are all sorts of ways of making it. I wondered what Annie Mae Gudger's had been. Luck? Predation? Divine intervention? Hard work? Trover and replevin?

Selvedge led me toward the sun room. I felt like Philip Marlowe going to meet a rich client. The house was filled with that furniture built sometime between the turn of the century and the 1950s—the ageless kind. It never looks great, it never looks ratty, and every chair is comfortable.

I think I was expecting some formidable woman with sleeve blotters and a green eyeshade hunched over a roll-top desk with piles of paper whose acceptance or rejection meant life or death for thousands.

Who I met was a charming lady in a green pantsuit. She was in her sixties, her hair still a straw wheat color. It didn't look dyed. Her eyes were blue as my first-grade teacher's had been. She was wiry and looked as if the word fat was not in her vocabulary.

"Good morning, Mr. Lindberl." She shook my hand. "Would you like some coffee? You look as if you could use it."

"Yes, thank you."

"Please sit down." She indicated a white wicker chair at a glass table. A serving tray with coffeepot, cups, tea bags, croissants, napkins, and plates lay on the tabletop.

After I swallowed half a cup of coffee at a gulp, she said, "What you wanted to see me about must be important?"

"Sorry about my manners," I said. "I know I don't look it, but I'm a biology assistant at the University of Texas. An ornithologist. Working on my master's. I met Ms. Jolyn Jimson two days ago . . ."

"How is Jolyn? I haven't seen her in, oh, Lord, it must be on to fifty years. The time gets away."

"She seemed to be fine. I only talked to her half an hour or so. That was . . ."

"And you've come to see me about? . . ."

"Uh. The . . . about some of the poultry your family used to raise, when they lived near Water Valley."

She looked at me a moment. Then she began to smile.

"Oh, you mean the ugly chickens?" she said.

I smiled. I almost laughed. I knew what Oedipus must have gone through.

It is now 4:30 in the afternoon. I am sitting at the downtown Motel 6 in Memphis. I have to make a phone call and get some sleep and catch a plane.

Annie Mae Gudger Radwin talked for four hours, answering my questions, setting me straight on family history, having Selvedge hold all her calls.

The main problem was that Annie Mae ran off in 1928, the year *before* her father got his big break. She went to Yazoo City, and by degrees and stages worked her way northward to Memphis and her destiny as the widow of a rich mercantile broker.

But I get ahead of myself.

Grandfather Gudger used to be the overseer for Colonel Crisby on the main plantation near McComb, Mississippi. There was a long story behind that. Bear with me.

Colonel Crisby himself was the scion of a seafaring family with interests in both the cedars of Lebanon (almost all cut down for masts for His Majesty's and others' navies) and Egyptian cotton. Also teas, spices, and any other salable commodity which came their way.

When Colonel Crisby's grandfather reached his majority in 1802, he waved good-bye to the Atlantic Ocean at Charleston, S.C. and stepped westward into the forest. When he stopped, he was in the middle of the Chickasaw Nation, where he opened a trading post and introduced slaves to the Indians.

And he prospered, and begat Colonel Crisby's father, who sent back to South Carolina for everything his father owned. Everything—slaves, wagons, horses, cattle, guinea fowl, peacocks, and dodos, which everybody thought of as atrociously ugly poultry of some kind, one of the seafaring uncles having bought them off a French merchant in 1721. (I surmised these were white dodos from Réunion, unless they had been from even earlier stock. The dodo of Mauritius was already extinct by then.)

All this stuff was herded out west to the trading post in the midst of the Chickasaw Nation. (The tribes around there were of the confederation of the Dancing Rabbits.)

And Colonel Crisby's father prospered, and so did the guinea fowl and the dodos. Then Andrew Jackson came along and marched the Dancing Rabbits off up the Trail of Tears to the heaven of Oklahoma. And Colonel Crisby's father begat Colonel Crisby, and put the trading post in the hands of others, and moved his plantation westward still to McComb.

Everything prospered but Colonel Crisby's father, who died. And the dodos, with occasional losses to the avengin' weasel and the egg-sucking dog, reproduced themselves also.

Then along came Granddaddy Gudger, a Simon Legree role model, who took care of the plantation while Colonel Crisby raised ten companies of men and marched off to fight the War of the Southern Independence.

Colonel Crisby came back to the McComb plantation earlier than most, he having stopped much of the same volley of Minié balls that caught his commander, General Beauregard Hanlon, on a promontory bluff during the Siege of Vicksburg.

He wasn't dead, but death hung around the place like a gentlemanly bill collector for a month. The colonel languished, went slap-dab crazy and freed all his slaves the week before he died (the war lasted another two years after that). Not having any slaves, he didn't need an overseer.

Then comes the Faulkner part of the tale, straight out of *As I Lay Dying,* with the Gudger family returning to the area of Water Valley (before there was a Water Valley), moving through the demoralized and tattered displaced persons of the South, driving their dodos before them. For Colonel Crisby had given them to his former overseer for his faithful service. Also followed the story of the bloody murder of Granddaddy Gudger at the hand of Freedman's militia during the rising of the first Klan, and of the trials and tribulations of Daddy Gudger in the years between 1880 and 1910, when he was between the ages of four and thirty-four.

* * *

Alma and Annie Mae were the second and fifth of Daddy Gudger's brood, born three years apart. They seemed to have hated each other from the very first time Alma looked into little Annie Mae's crib. They were kids by Daddy Gudger's second wife (his desperation had killed the first) and their father was already on his sixth career. He had been a lumberman, a stump preacher, a plowman-for-hire (until his mules broke out in farcy buds and died of the glanders), a freight hauler (until his horses died of overwork and the hardware store repossessed the wagon), a politician's roadie (until the politician lost the election). When Alma and Annie Mae were born, he was failing as a sharecropper. Somehow Gudger had made it through the Depression of 1898 as a boy, and was too poor after that to notice more about economics than the price of Beech-Nut tobacco at the store.

Alma and Annie Mae fought, and it helped none at all that Alma, being the oldest daughter, was both her mother and father's darling. Annie Mae's life was the usual unwanted poor-white-trash-child's hell. She vowed early to run away, and recognized her ambition at thirteen.

All this I learned this morning. Jolyn (Smith) Jimson was Annie Mae's only friend in those days—from a family even poorer than the Gudgers. But somehow there was food, and an occasional odd job. And the dodos.

"My father hated those old birds," said the cultured Annie Mae Radwin, nee Gudger, in the solarium. "He always swore he was going to get rid of them someday, but just never seemed to get around to it. I think there was more to it than that. But they were so much *trouble.* We always had to keep them penned up at night, and go check for their eggs. They wandered off to lay them, and forgot where they were. Sometimes no new ones were born at all in a year.

"And they got so *ugly.* Once a year. I mean, terrible-looking, like they were going to die. All their feathers fell off, and they looked like they had mange or something. Then the whole front of their beaks fell off, or worse, hung halfway on for a week or two. They looked like big old naked pigeons. After that they'd lose weight, down to twenty or thirty pounds, before their new feathers grew back.

"We were always having to kill foxes that got after them in the turkey house. That's what we called their roost, the turkey house. And we found their eggs all sucked out by cats and dogs. They were so stupid we had to drive them into their roost at night. I don't think they could have found it standing ten feet from it."

She looked at me.

"I think much as my father hated them, they meant something to him. As long as he hung on to them, he knew he was as good as Granddaddy Gudger. You may not know it, but there was a certain amount of family pride about Granddaddy Gudger. At least in my father's eyes. His rapid fall in the world had a sort of grandeur to it. He'd gone from a relatively high position in the old order, and maintained some grace and stature after the Emancipation. And though he lost everything, he managed to keep those ugly old chickens the colonel had given him as sort of a symbol.

"And as long as he had them, too, my daddy thought himself as good as his father. He kept his dignity, even when he didn't have anything else."

I asked what happened to them. She didn't know, but told me who did and where I could find her.

That's why I'm going to make a phone call.

"Hello. Dr. Courtney. Dr. Courtney? This is Paul. Memphis. Tennessee. It's too long to go into. No, of course not, not yet. But I've got evidence. What? Okay, how do trochanters, coracoids, tarsometatarsi and beak sheaths sound? From their henhouse, where else? Where would you keep *your* dodos, then?

"Sorry. I haven't slept in a couple of days. I need some help. Yes, yes. Money. Lots of money.

"Cash. Three hundred dollars, maybe. Western Union, Memphis, Tennessee. Whichever one's closest to the airport. Airport. I need the department to set up reservations to Mauritius for me . . .

"No. No. Not wild goose chase, wild *dodo* chase. Tame dodo chase. I *know* there aren't any dodos on Mauritius! I know that. I could explain. I know it'll mean a couple of grand . . . if . . . but . . .

"Look, Dr. Courtney. Do you want *your* picture in *Scientific American,* or don't you?"

I am sitting in the airport cafe in Port Louis, Mauritius. It is now three days later, five days since that fateful morning my car wouldn't start. God bless the Sears Diehard people. I have slept sitting up in a plane seat, on and off, different planes, different seats, for twenty-four hours, Kennedy to Paris, Paris to Cairo, Cairo to Madagascar. I felt like a brand-new man when I got here.

Now I feel like an infinitely sadder and wiser brand-new man. I have just returned from the hateful sister Alma's house in the exclusive section of Port Louis, where all the French and British officials used to live.

Courtney will get his picture in *Scientific American,* me too, all right. There'll be newspaper stories and talk shows for a few weeks for me, and I'm sure Annie Mae Gudger Radwin on one side of the world and Alma Chandler Gudger Moliere on the other will come in for their share of glory.

I am putting away cup after cup of coffee. The plane back to Tananarive leaves in an hour. I plan to sleep all the way back to Cairo, to Paris, to New York, pick up my bag of bones, sleep back to Austin.

Before me on the table is a packet of documents, clippings and photographs. I have come half the world for this. I gaze from the package, out the window across Port Louis to the bulk of Mt. Pieter Boothe, which overshadows the city and its famous racecourse.

Perhaps I should do something symbolic. Cancel my flight. Climb the mountain and look down on man and all his handiworks. Take a pitcher of martinis with me. Sit in the bright semitropical sunlight (it's early dry winter here). Drink the martinis slowly, toasting Snuffo, God of Extinction. Here's one for the Great Auk. This is for the Carolina Parakeet. Mud in your eye, Passenger Pigeon. This one's for the Heath Hen. Most importantly, here's one each for the Mauritius dodo, the white dodo of Réunion, the Réunion solitaire, the Rodriguez solitaire. Here's to the Raphidae, great Didine birds that you were.

Maybe I'll do something just as productive, like climbing Mt. Pieter Boothe and pissing into the wind.

How symbolic. The story of the dodo ends where it began, on this very island. Life imitates cheap art. Like the Xerox of the Xerox of a bad novel. I never expected to find dodos still alive here (this is the one place they would have been noticed). I still can't believe Alma Chandler Gudger Moliere could have lived here twenty-five years and not *know* about the dodo, never set foot inside the Port Louis Museum, where they have skeletons, and a stuffed replica the size of your little brother.

After Annie Mae ran off, the Gudger family found itself prospering in a time the rest of the country was going to hell. It was 1929. Gudger delved into politics again, and backed a man who knew a man who worked for Theodore "Sure Two-Handed Sword of God" Bilbo, who had connections everywhere. Who introduced him to Huey "Kingfish" Long just after that gentleman lost the Louisiana governor's election one of the times. Gudger stumped around Mississippi, getting up steam for Long's Share the Wealth plan, even before it had a name.

The upshot was that the Long machine in Louisiana knew a rabble rouser when it saw one, and invited Gudger to move to the Sportsman's Paradise, with his family, all expenses paid, and start working for the Kingfish at the unbelievable salary of $62.50 a week. Which prospect was like turning a hog loose under a persimmon tree, and before you could say Backwoods Messiah, the Gudger clan was on its way to the land of pelicans, graft, and Mardi Gras.

Almost. But I'll get to that.

Daddy Gudger prospered all out of proportion with his abilities, but many men did that during the Depression. First a little, thence to more, he rose in bureaucratic (and political) circles of the state, dying rich and well-hated with his fingers in *all* the pies.

Alma Chandler Gudger became a debutante (she says Robert Penn Warren put her in his book) and met and married Jean Carl Moliere, only heir to rice, indigo, and sugar cane growers. They had a happy wedded life, moving first to the West Indies, later to Mauritius, where the family sugar cane holdings were one of the largest on the island. Jean Carl died in 1959. Alma was his only survivor.

So local family makes good. Poor sharecropping Mississippi people turn out to have a father dying with a smile on his face, and two daughters who between them own a large portion of the planet.

I open the envelope before me. Ms. Alma Moliere had listened politely to my story (the university had called ahead and arranged an introduction through the director of the Port Louis Museum, who knew Ms. Moliere socially) and told me what she could remember. Then she sent a servant out to one of the storehouses (large as a duplex) and he and two others came back with boxes of clippings, scrapbooks and family photos.

"I haven't looked at any of this since we left St. Thomas," she said. "Let's go through it together."

Most of it was about the rise of Citizen Gudger.

"There's not many pictures of us before we came to Louisiana. We were so frightfully poor then, hardly anyone we knew had a camera. Oh, look. Here's one of Annie Mae. I thought I threw all those out after Mamma died."

This is the photograph. It must have been taken about 1927. Annie Mae is wearing some unrecognizable piece of clothing that approximates a dress. She leans on a hoe, smiling a snaggle-toothed smile. She looks to be ten or eleven. Her eyes are half hidden by the shadow of the brim of a gapped straw hat she wears. The earth she is standing in barefoot has been newly turned. Behind her is one corner of the house, and the barn beyond has its upper hay-windows open. Out-of-focus people are at work there.

A few feet behind her, a huge male dodo is pecking at something on the ground. The front two thirds of it shows, back to the stupid wings and the edge of the upcurved tail feathers. One foot is in the photo, having just scratched at something, possibly an earthworm, in the new-plowed clods. Judging by its darkness, it is the gray, or Mauritius, dodo.

The photograph is not very good, one of those 3½ × 5 jobs box cameras used to take. Already I can see this one, and the blowup of the dodo, taking up a double-page spread in *S.A.* Alma told me around then they were down to six or seven of the ugly chickens, two whites, the rest gray-brown.

Besides this photo, two clippings are in the package, one from the Bruce *Banner-Times*, the other from the Oxford newspaper; both are columns by the same woman dealing with "Doings in Water Valley." Both mention the Gudger family moving from the area to seek its fortune in the swampy state to the west, and telling how they will be missed. Then there's a yellowed clipping from the front page of the Oxford paper with a small story about the Gudger Farewell Party in Water Valley the Sunday before (dated October 19, 1929).

There's a handbill in the package, advertising the Gudger Family Farewell Party, Sunday Oct. 15, 1929 Come One Come All. (The people in Louisiana who sent expense money to move Daddy Gudger must have overestimated the costs by an exponential factor. I said as much.)

"No," Alma Moliere said. "There was a lot, but it wouldn't have made any difference. Daddy Gudger was like Thomas Wolfe and knew a shining golden opportunity when he saw one. Win, lose, or draw, he was never coming back *there* again. He would have thrown some kind of soiree whether there had been money for it or not. Besides, people were much more sociable then, you mustn't forget."

I asked her how many people came.

"Four or five hundred," she said. "There's some pictures here somewhere." We searched awhile, then we found them.

Another thirty minutes to my flight. I'm not worried sitting here. I'm the only passenger, and the pilot is sitting at the table next to mine talking to an RAF man. Life is much slower and nicer on these colonial islands. You mustn't forget.

I look at the other two photos in the package. One is of some men playing horseshoes and washer-toss, while kids, dogs, and women look on. It was evidently taken from the east end of the house looking west. Everyone must have had to walk the last mile to the old Gudger place. Other groups of people stand talking. Some men, in shirtsleeves and suspenders, stand with their heads thrown back, a snappy story, no doubt, just told. One girl looks directly at the camera from close up, shyly, her finger in her mouth. She's about five. It looks like any snapshot of a family reunion which could have been taken anywhere, anytime. Only the clothing marks it as backwoods 1920s.

Courtney will get his money's worth. I'll write the article, make phone calls, plan the talk show tour to coincide with publication. Then I'll get some rest. I'll be a normal person again; get a degree, spend my time wading through jungles after animals which will all be dead in another twenty years, anyway.

Who cares? The whole thing will be just another media event, just this year's Big Deal. It'll be nice getting normal again. I can read books, see movies, wash my clothes at the laundromat, listen to Jonathan Richman on the stereo. I can study and become an authority on some minor matter or other.

I can go to museums and see all the wonderful dead things there.

"That's the memory picture," said Alma. "They always took them at big things like this, back in those days. Everybody who was there would line up and pose for the camera. Only we couldn't fit everybody in. So we had two made. This is the one with us in it."

The house is dwarfed by people. All sizes, shapes, dress and age. Kids and dogs in front, women next, then men at the back. The only exceptions are the bearded patriarchs seated toward the front with the children—men whose eyes face the camera but whose heads are still ringing with something Nathan Bedford Forrest said to them one time on a smoke-filled field. This photograph is from another age. You can recognize Daddy and Mrs. Gudger if you've seen their photographs before. Alma pointed herself out to me.

But the reason I took the photograph is in the foreground. Tables have been built out of sawhorses, with doors and boards nailed across them. They extend the entire width of the photograph. They are covered with food, more food than you can imagine.

"We started cooking three days before. So did the neighbors. Everybody brought something," said Alma.

It's like an entire Safeway had been cooked and set out to cool. Hams, quarters of beef, chickens by the tubful, quail in mounds, rabbit, butterbeans by the bushel, yams, Irish potatoes, an acre of corn, eggplant, peas, turnip greens, butter in five-pound molds, cornbread and biscuits, gallon cans of molasses, redeye gravy by the pot.

And five huge birds—twice as big as turkeys, legs capped like for Thanksgiving, drumsticks the size of Schwarzenegger's biceps, whole-roasted, lying on their backs on platters large as cocktail tables.

The people in the crowd sure look hungry.

"We ate for days," said Alma.

I already have the title for the *Scientific American* article. It's going to be called "The Dodo Is *Still* Dead."

I first read "Mathenauts" over thirty years ago, and rereading it yesterday reminds me of the mental state it induced when I was a teenager: a sharpening of the pun reflex, a vivid and exhilarating realization that some folks out there were thinking in new and scary ways. That nothing might be real, and on the other hand, to compensate, all things might be possible!

But how is *this* possible, in a story that is almost devoid of the standard merits of classic story-telling? "Mathenauts" often dips into sophomoric in-jokes and sometimes seems to have been written for a university students' magazine. There is no center, the plot lurches alarmingly, and I am never quite sure what is happening at any given moment. The result is deft and amateurish and brilliant and dizzying, and the author doesn't seem to care, and I don't mind either.

Norman Kagan has read science fiction and borrowed some of its structures and tropes—there are hints of Pohl and Kornbluth, maybe early Delany or Dick. The story was originally published in *The Magazine of Fantasy and Science Fiction*. It was anthologized by Judith Merrill. It received some focused attention and then, by and large, was forgotten. But a few remembered. Rudy Rucker resurrected the story in his collection of contemporary math stories, and names the collection after it, and incidentally included Kagan's only other story, "Four Brands of Impossible," first published in 1964 by *F&SF*.

So Kagan entered out of the blue, and vanished back into it, apparently to work in film, or so Rudy tells us.

I've never met Kagan, but I owe him an immense debt, for he was one of the first to introduce me to the philosophical concept of ideational spaces. That is, what humans can conceive of, may in fact exist or come to exist in a subjective kind of reality. Later, Vernor Vinge and others would expand on this concept, and eighteen years after "Mathenauts," the movie *Tron* would download us into the logic spaces of computers and popularize the whole virtual reality thing, which William Gibson would call cyberspace.

The base concept is older. L. Sprague de Camp and Fletcher Pratt threw the resourceful Harold Shea into a number of literary universes, fiction made real, in *The Castle of Iron* and others. But virtual reality, lucid dreaming, fictional realms, are all supposed to be briefly thought of as real, as a matter of course. We are supposed to suspend our disbelief and enter into the experience.

Norman Kagan at the very inception blows the idea to a new level. By making mathematics occupy experienced spaces, by giving abstract concepts immediate physical shape and character and consequences, he sets up an intellectual dissonance that can't help but expand one's thinking.

Kagan's genius lies in his ability to create an impression of new paradigms. *Really* new paradigms, outlandish and queer, unexpected and yet eerily convincing. The story contains a wealth of ideas that we may take further decades to mine and develop.

He is, in this story, a true heir to Lewis Carroll.

Reading "Mathenauts" again, I foresee . . . a time when consensus reality can be adjusted to accept new sensory inputs, placing us in new hypothesis spaces that actually enhance our relationship with the so-called real world—when we can dabble in extra-human perceptions like flipping through channels . . .

As Tom Disch put it, fun with your new head . . .

Hang on to your hats!

—Greg Bear

THE MATHENAUTS

by Norman Kagan

It happened on my fifth trip into the spaces, and the first ever made under the private-enterprise acts. It took a long time to get the P.E.A. through Congress for mathenautics, but the precedents went all the way back to the Telstar satellite a hundred years ago, and most of the concepts are in books anyone can buy, though not so readily understand. Besides, it didn't matter if BC-flight was made public or not. All mathenauts are crazy. Everybody knows that.

Take our crew. Johnny Pearl took a pin along whenever he went baby-sitting for the grad students at Berkeley, and three months later the mothers invariably found out they were pregnant again. And Pearl was our physicist.

Then there was Goldwasser. Ed Goldwasser always sits in those pan-on-a-post cigarette holders when we're in New York, and if you ask him, he grumbles; "Well, it's an ash tray, ain't it?" A punster and a pataphysicist. I would never have chosen him to go, except that he and I got the idea together.

Ted Anderson was our metamathematician. He's about half a nanosecond behind Ephraim Cohen (the co-inventor of BC-flight) and has about six nervous breakdowns a month trying to pass him. But he's got the best practical knowledge of the BC-drive outside Princeton—if practical knowledge means anything with respect to a pure mathematical abstraction.

And me—topologist. A topologist is a man who can't tell a doughnut from a cup of coffee. (I'll explain that some other time.) Seriously, I specialize in some of the more abstruse properties of geometric structures. "Did Galois discover that theorem before or after he died?" is a sample of my conversation.

Sure, mathenauts are mathenuts. But as we found out, not quite mathenutty enough.

The ship, the *Albrecht Dold*, was a twelve-googol scout that Ed Goldwasser and I'd picked up cheap from the N.Y.U. Courant Institute. She wasn't the Princeton I.A.S. *Von-Neumann*, with googolplex coils and a chapter of the D.A.R., and she wasn't one of those new toys you've been seeing for a rich man and his grandmother. Her coils were DNA molecules, and the psychosomatics were straight from the Brill Institute at Harvard. A sweet ship. For psychic ecology we'd gotten a bunch of kids from the Bronx College of the New York City University, commonsense types—business majors, engineers, pre-meds. But kids.

I was looking over Ephraim Cohen's latest paper, *Nymphomaniac Nested Complexes with Rossian Irrevelancies* (old Ice Cream Cohen loves sexy titles), when the trouble started. We'd abstracted, and Goldwasser and Pearl had signaled me from the lab that they were ready for the first tests. I made the *Dold* invariant, and shoved off through one of the passages that linked the isomorphomechanism and the lab. (We kept the ship in free fall for convenience.) I was about halfway along the tube when the immy failed and the walls began to close in.

I spread my legs and braked against the walls of the tube, believing with all my might. On second thought I let the walls sink in and braked with my palms. It would've been no trick to hold the walls for a while. Without the immy my own imagination would hold them, this far from the B.C.N.Y. kids. But that might've brought more trouble—I'd probably made some silly mistake, and the kids, who might not notice a simple contraction or shear, would crack up under some weirdomorphism. And if we lost the kids . . .

So anyway I just dug my feet in against the mirage and tried to slow up, on a surface that no one'd bothered to think any friction into. Of course, if you've read some of the popular accounts of math-sailing, you'd think I'd just duck back through a hole in the fiftieth dimension to the immy. But it doesn't work out that way. A ship in BC-flight is a very precarious structure in a philosophical sense. That's why we carry a psychic ecology, and that's why Brill conditioning takes six years, plus, with a Ph.D. in pure math, to absorb. Anyway, a mathenaut should never forget his postulates, or he'll find himself floating in 27-space, with nary a notion to be named.

Then the walls really did vanish—NO!—and I found myself at the junction of two passages. The other had a grabline. I caught it and rebounded, then swarmed back along the tube. After ten seconds I was climbing down into a funnel. I caught my breath, swallowed some Dramamine, and burst into the control room.

The heart of the ship was pulsing and throbbing. For a moment I thought I was back in Hawaii with my aqualung, an invader in a shifting, shimmering world of sea fronds and barracuda. But it was no immy, no immy—a rubber room without the notion of distance that we take for granted (technically, a room with topological properties but no metric ones). Instrument racks and chairs and books shrank and ballooned and twisted, and floor and ceiling vibrated with my breath.

It was horrible.

Ted Anderson was hanging in front of the immy, the isomorphomechanism, but he was in no shape to do anything. In fact, he was in no shape at all. His body was pulsing and shaking, so his hands were too big or too small to manipulate the controls, or his eyes shrank or blossomed. Poor Ted's nerves had gone again.

I shoved against the wall and bulleted toward him, a fish in a weaving, shifting undersea landsacpe, concentrating desperately on my body and the old structure of the room. (This is why physical training is so important.) For an instant I was choking and screaming in a hairy blackness, a nightmare inside-out total inversion; then I was back in the control room, and had shoved Ted away from the instruments, cursing when nothing happened, then bracing against the wall panels and shoving again. He drifted away.

The immy was all right. The twiddles circuits between the B.C.N.Y. kids and the rest of the *Dold* had been cut out. I set up an orthonormal system and punched the immy.

Across the shuddering, shifting room Ted tried to speak, but found it too difficult. Great Gauss, he was lucky his aorta hadn't contracted to a straw and given him a coronary! I clamped down on my own circulatory system viciously, while he struggled to speak. Finally he kicked off and came tumbling toward me, mouthing and flailing his notebook.

I hit the circuit. The room shifted about and for an instant Ted Anderson hung, ghostly, amid the isomorphomechanism's one-to-ones. Then he disappeared.

The invention of BC-flight was the culmination of a century of work in algebraic topology and experimental psychology. For thousands of years men had speculated as to the nature of the world. For the past five hundred, physics and the physical sciences had held sway. Then Thomas Brill and Ephraim Cohen peeled away another layer of the reality union, and the space-sciences came into being.

If you insist on an analogy—well, a scientist touches and probes the real universe, and abstracts an idealization into his head. Mathenautics allows him to grab himself by the scruff of the neck and pull himself up into the idealization. See—I *told* you.

Okay, we'll try it slowly. Science assumes the universe to be ordered, and investigates the nature of the ordering. In the "hard" sciences, mathematics is the basis of the ordering the scientist puts on nature. By the twentieth century, a large portion of the physical processes and materials in the universe were found to submit to such an ordering (e.g., analytic mechanics and the motions of the planets). Some scientists were even applying mathematical structures to aggregates of living things, and to living processes.

Cohen and Brill asked (in ways far apart), "If order and organization seem to be a natural part of the universe, why can't we remove these qualities from coarse matter and space, and study them separately?" The answer was BC-flight.

Through certain purely mathematical "mechanisms" and special psychological training, selected scientists (the term "mathenaut" came later, slang from the faddy "astronautics") could be shifted into the abstract.

The first mathenautical ships were crewed with young scientists and mathematicians who'd received Tom Brill's treatments and Ephraim Cohen's skull-cracking sessions on the BC-field. The ships went into BC-flight and vanished.

By the theory, the ships didn't *go* anywhere. But the effect was somehow real. Just as a materialist might *see* organic machines instead of people, so the mathenauts saw the raw mathematical structure of space—Riemann space, Hausdorf space, vector space—without matter. A crowd of people existed as an immensely complicated *something* in vector space. The study of these *somethings* was yielding immense amounts of knowledge. Pataphysics, patasociology, patapsychology were wild, baffling new fields of knowledge.

But the math universes were strange, alien. How could you learn to live in Flatland? The wildcat minds of the first crews were too creative. They became disoriented. Hence the immies and their power supplies—SayCows, DaughtAmRevs, the B.C.N.Y. kids—fatheads, stuffed shirts, personality types that clung to common sense where there was none, and preserved (locally) a ship's psychic ecology. Inside the BC-field, normalcy. Outside, raw imagination.

Johnny, Ted, Goldy, and I had chosen vector spaces with certain topological properties to test Goldy's commercial concept. Outside the BC-field there was dimension but no distance, structure but no shape. Inside—

"By Riemann's tensors!" Pearl cried.

He was at the iris of one of the tubes. A moment later Ed Goldwasser joined him. "What happened to Ted?"

"I—I don't know. No—yes, I do!"

I released the controls I had on my body, and stopped thinking about the room. The immy was working again. "He was doing something with the controls when the twiddles circuit failed. When I got them working again and the room snapped back into shape, he happened to be where the immy had been. The commonsense circuits rejected him."

"So where did he go?" asked Pearl.

"I don't know."

I was sweating. I was thinking of all the things that could've happened when we lost the isomorphomechanism. Some subconscious twitch and you're rotated half a dozen dimensions out of phase, so you're floating in the raw stuff of thought, with maybe a hair-thin line around you to tell you where the ship has been. Or the ship takes the notion to shrink pea-size, so you're squeezed through all the tubes and compartments and smashed to jelly when we orthonormalize. Galois! We'd been lucky.

The last thought gave me a notion. "Could we have shrunk so we're inside his body? Or he grown so we're floating in his liver?"

"No," said Goldy. "Topology is preserved. But I don't—or, hell—I really don't know. If he grew so big he was outside the psychic ecology, he might just have faded away." The big pataphysicist wrinkled up his face inside his beard. "*Alice* should be required reading for mathenauts," he muttered. "The real trouble is no one has ever been outside and been back to tell about it. The animal experiments and the *Norbert Wiener* and Wilbur on the *Paul R. Halmos*. They just disappeared."

"You know," I said, "You can map the volume of a sphere into the whole universe using the ratio IR:R equals R:OR, where IR and OR are the inside and outside distances for the points. Maybe that's what happened to Ted. Maybe he's just outside the ship, filling all space with his metamath and his acne?"

"Down boy," said Goldwasser. "I've got a simpler suggestion. Let's check over the ship, compartment by compartment. Maybe he's in it somewhere, unconscious."

But he wasn't on the ship.

We went over it twice, every tube, every compartment. (In reality, a mathenautic ship looks like a radio, ripped out of its case and flying through the air.) We ended up in the ecology section, a big Broadway-line subway car that roared and rattled in the middle of darkness in the middle of nothing. The B.C.N.Y. kids were all there—Freddi Urbont clucking happily away to her boyfriend, chubby and smily and an education major; Byron and Burbitt, electronics engineers, ecstatic over the latest copy of *C-Quantum*; Stephen Seidmann, a number-theory major, quietly proving that since Harvard is the best school in the world, and B.C.N.Y. is better than Harvard, that B.C.N.Y. is the best school in the world; two citizens with nose jobs and names I'd forgotten, engaged in a filthy discussion of glands and organs and meat. The walls were firm, the straw seats scratchy and uncomfortable. The projectors showed we were just entering the 72nd Street stop. How real, how comforting! I slid the door open to rejoin Johnny and Ed. The subway riders saw me slip into free fall, and glimpsed the emptiness of vector space.

Hell broke lose!

The far side of the car bulged inward, the glass smashing and the metal groaning. The CUNYs had no compensation training!

Freddi Urbont burst into tears. Byron and Burbitt yelled as a bubble in the floor swallowed them. The wall next to the nose jobs sprouted a dozen phallic symbols, while the seat bubbled with breasts. The walls began to melt. Seidmann began to yell about the special status of N.Y. City University Honors Program students.

Pearl acted with a speed and a surety I'd never have imagined. He shoved me out of the way and launched himself furiously at the other end of the car, now in free fall. There he pivoted, smiled horribly and at the top of his lungs began singing "The Purple and the Black."

Goldy and I had enough presence of mind to join him. Concentrating desperately on the shape and form of the car, we blasted the air with our devotion to Sheppard Hall, our love of Convent Avenue and our eternal devotion to Lewisohn Stadium. Somehow it saved us. The room rumbled and twisted and reformed, and soon the eight of us were back in the tired old subway car that brought its daily catch of Beavers to 139th Street.

The equilibrium was still precarious. I heard Goldwasser telling the nose jobs his terrible monologue about the "Volvo I want to buy. I can be the first to break the door membranes, and when I get my hands on that big, fat steering wheel, ohh!, it'll be a week before I climb out of it!"

Pearl was cooing to Urbont how wonderful she was as the valedictorian at her junior high, how great the teaching profession was, and how useful, and how interesting.

As for me: "Well, I guess you're right, Steve. I should have gone to B.C.N.Y. instead of Berkeley."

"That's right, Jimmy. After all, B.C.N.Y. has some of the best number-theory people in the world. And some of the greatest educators, too. Like Dean Cashew who started the Privileged Student Program. It sure is wonderful."

"I guess you're right, Steve."

"I'm right, all right. At schools like Berkeley, you're just another student, but at B.C.N.Y. you can be a P.S., and get all the good professors and small classes and high grades."

"You're right, Steve."

"I'm right, all right. Listen, we have people that've quit Cornell and Harvard and M.I.T. Of course, they don't do much but run home after school and sit in their houses, but their parents all say how much happier they are—like back in high school . . ."

When the scrap paper and the gum wrappers were up to our knees and there were four false panhandlers in the car, Johnny called a halt. The little psychist smiled and nodded as he walked the three of us carefully out the door.

"Standard technique," he murmured to no one in particular. "Doing *something* immediately rather than the best thing a while later. Their morale was shot, so I—" He trailed off.

"Are they really that sensitive?" Goldwasser asked. "I thought their training was better than that."

"You act like they were components in an electronics rig," said Pearl jerkily. "You know that Premedial Sensory Perception, the ability to perceive the dull routine that normal people ignore, is a very delicate talent!"

Pearl was well launched. "In the dark ages such people were called dullards and subnormals. Only now, in our enlightened age, do we realize their true ability to know things outside the ordinary senses—a talent vital for BC-flight."

The tedium and meaninglessness of life which we rationalize away—

"A ship is more mind than matter, and if you upset that mind—"

He paled suddenly. "I, I think I'd better stay with them," he said. He flung open the door and went back into the coach. Goldwasser and I looked at each other. Pearl was a trained mathenaut, but his specialty was people, not paramath.

"Let's check the lab," I muttered.

Neither of us spoke as we moved toward the lab—slap a wall, pull yourself forward, twist round some instrumentation—the "reaction swim" of a man in free fall. The walls began to quiver again, and I could see Goldy clamp down on his body and memories of this part of the ship. We were nearing the limits of the BC-field. The lab itself, and the experimental apparatus, stuck out into vector space.

"Let's make our tests and go home," I told Goldy.

Neither of us mentioned Ted as we entered the lab.

Remember this was a commercial project. We weren't patasociologists studying abstract groups, or super-purists looking for the first point. We wanted money.

Goldy thought he had a moneymaking scheme for us, but Goldy hasn't been normal since he took Polykarp Kusch's "Kusch of Death" at Columbia, "Electrodimensions and Magnespace." He was going to build four-dimensional molecules.

Go back to Flatland. Imagine a hollow paper pyramid on the surface of that two-dimensional world. To a Flatlander, it is a triangle. Flop down the sides—four triangles. Now put a molecule in each face—one molecule, four molecules. And recall that you have infinite dimensions available. Think of the storage possibilities alone. All the books of the world in a viewer, all the food in the world in your pack. A television the size of a piece of paper; circuits looped through dim-19. Loop an entire industrial plant through hyperspace, and get one the size and shape of a billboard. Shove raw materials in one side—pull finished products out the other!

But how do you make 4-dim molecules? Goldy thought he had a way, and Ted Anderson had checked over the math and pronounced it workable. The notion rested in the middle of the lab: a queer, half-understood machine of mind and matter called a Grahm-Schmidt generator.

"Jeez, Ed! This lab looks like your old room back in Diego Borough."

"Yeah," said Goldwasser. "Johnny said it would be a good idea. Orientation against *that.*"

That was the outside of the lab, raw topological space, without energy or matter or time. It was the shape and color of what you see in the back of your head.

I looked away.

Goldwasser's room was a duplicate of his old home—the metal desk, the electronics rigs, the immense bookshelves, half filled with physics and half with religious works. I picked up a copy of Stace's *Time and Eternity* and thumbed through it, then put it down, embarrassed.

"Good reading for a place like this." Goldwasser smiled.

He sat down at the desk and began to check out his "instruments" from the locked drawer where he'd kept them. Once he reached across the desk and turned on a tape of Gene Gerard's *Excelsior!* The flat midwestern voice murmured in the background.

"First, I need some hands," said Ed.

Out in the nothingness two pairs of lines met at right angles. For an instant, all space was filled with them, jammed together every which way. Then it just settled down to two.

The lab was in darkness, Goldwasser's big form crouched over the controls. He wore his engineer's boots and his hair long, and a beard as well. He might have been some medieval monk, or primitive witchdoctor. He touched a knob and set a widget, and checked his copy of *Birkhoff and MacLane.*

"Now," he said, and played with his instruments. Two new vectors rose out of the intersections. "Cross-products. Now I've a right- and a left-handed system."

All the while Gene Gerard was mumbling in the background: 'Ah, now, my pretty,' snarled the Count. 'Come to my bedchamber, or I'll leave you to Igor's mercies.' The misshapen dwarf cackled and rubbed his paws. 'Decide, decide!' cried the Count. His voice was a scream. 'Decide, my dear. SEX—ELSE, IGOR!'

"Augh," said Goldwasser, and shut it off. "Now," he said, "I've got some plasma in the next compartment."

"Holy Halmos," I whispered.

Ted Anderson stood beside the generator. He smiled, and went into topological convulsions. I looked away, and presently he came back into shape. "Hard getting used to real space again," he whispered. He looked thinner and paler than ever.

"I haven't got long," he said, "so here it is. You know I was working on Ephraim's theories, looking for a flaw. There isn't any flaw."

"Ted, you're rotating," I cautioned.

He steadied, and continued, "There's no flaw. But the theory is wrong. It's backwards. *This is the real universe,*" he said, and gestured. Beyond the lab topological space remained as always, a blank, the color of the back of your head through your own eyes.

"Now listen to me, Goldy and Johnny and Kidder." I saw

that Pearl was standing in the iris of the tube. "What is the nature of intelligence? I guess it's the power to abstract, to conceptualize. I don't know what to say beyond that—I don't know what it is. But I know where it came from! Here! In the math spaces—they're alive with thought, flashing with mind!

"When the twiddles circuits failed, I cracked. I fell apart, lost faith in it all. For I had just found what I thought was a basic error in theory. I died, I vanished . . .

"But I didn't. I'm a metamathematician. An operational philosopher, you might say. I may have gone mad—but I think I passed a threshold of knowledge. I understand . . .

"They're out there. The things we thought we'd invented ourselves. The concepts and the notions and the pure structures—if you could see them . . ."

He looked around the room, desperately. Pearl was rigid against the iris of the tube. Goldy looked at Ted for a moment, then his head darted from side to side. His hands whitened on the controls.

"Jimmy," Ted said.

I didn't know. I moved toward him, across the lab to the edge of topological space, and beyond the psychic ecology. No time, no space, no matter. But how can I say it? How many people can stay awake over a book of modern algebra; and how many of those can understand?

—I saw a set bubbling and whirling, then take purpose and structure to itself and become a group, generate a second-unity element, mount itself and become a group, generate a second unity element, mount itself and become a field, ringed by rings. Near it, a mature field, shot through with ideals, threw off a splitting field in a passion of growth, and became complex.

—I saw the life of the matrices; the young ones sporting, adding and multiplying by a constant, the mature ones mating by composition: male and female make male, female and male make female—sex through anticommunitivity! I saw them grow old, meeting false identities and loosing rows and columns into nullity.

—I saw a race of vectors, losing their universe to a newer race of tensors that conquered and humbled them.

—I watched the tyranny of the Well Ordering Principle, as a free set was lashed and whipped into structure. I saw a partially ordered set, free and happy broken before the Axiom of Zemelo.

—I saw the point sets, with their cliques and clubs, infinite numbers of sycophants clustering round a Bolzano-Weirstrauss aristocrat—the great compact medieval coverings of infinity with denumerable shires—the conflicts as closed sets created open ones, and the other way round.

—I saw the rigid castes of a society of transformation, orthogonal royalty, inner product gentry, degenerates—where intercomposition set the caste of the lower on the product.

—I saw the proud old cyclic groups, father and son and grandson, generating the generations, rebel and blacksheep and hero, following each other endlessly. Close by were the permutation groups, frolicking in a way that seemed like the way you sometimes repeat a sentence endlessly, stressing a different word each time.

There was much I saw that I did not understand, for mathematics is a deep, and even a mathenaut must choose his wedge of specialty. But that world of abstractions flamed with a beauty and meaning that chilled the works and worlds of men, so I wept in futility.

Presently we found ourselves back in the lab. I sat beside Ted Anderson and leaned on him, and I did not speak for fear my voice would break.

Anderson talked to Johnny and Ed.

"There was a—a race, here, that grew prideful. It knew the Riemann space, and the vector space, the algebras and the topologies, and yet it was unfulfilled. In some way—oddly like this craft," he murmured, gesturing—"they wove the worlds together, creating the real universe you knew in your youth.

"Yet still it was unsatisfied. Somehow the race yearned so for newness that it surpassed itself, conceiving matter and energy and entropy and creating them.

"And there were laws and properties for these: inertia, speed, potential, quantumization. Perhaps life was an accident. It was not noticed for a long time, and proceeded apace. For the proud race had come to know itself, and saw that the new concepts were . . . flawed." Anderson smiled faintly, and turned to Ed.

"Goldy, remember when we had Berkowitz for algebra?" he asked. "Remember what he said the first day?"

Goldwasser smiled. "Any math majors?"

"Hmm, that's good."

"Any physics majors?

"Physics majors! You guys are just super engineers!

"Any chemistry majors?

"Chemistry major! You'd be better off as a cook!"

Ted finished, "And so on, down to the, ahem, baloney majors."

"He was number-happy," said Ed, smiling.

"No. He was right, in a way." Ted continued. "The race had found its new notions were crudities, simple copies of algebras and geometries past. What it thought was vigor was really sloth and decay.

"It knew how to add and multiply, but it had forgotten what a field was, and what communitivity was. If entropy and time wreaked harm on matter, they did worse by this race. It wasn't interested in expeditions through the fiber bundles; rather it wanted to count apples.

"There was conflict and argument, but it was too late to turn back. The race had already degenerated too far to turn back. Then life was discovered.

"The majority of the race took matter for a bride. Its esthetic and creative powers ruined, it wallowed in passion and pain. Only remnants of reason remained.

"For the rest, return to abstraction was impossible. Time, entropy, had robbed them of their knowledge, their heritage. Yet they still hoped and expended themselves to leave, well, call it a 'seed' of sorts."

"Mathematics?" cried Pearl.

"It explains some things," mused Goldwasser softly. "Why abstract mathematics, developed in the mind, turns out fifty years or a century later to accurately describe the physical universe. Tensor calculus and relativity, for example. If you look at it this way, the math was there first."

"Yes, yes, yes. Mathematicians talked about their subject as an art form. One system is more 'elegant' than another if its logical structure is more austere. But Occam's Razor, the law of simplest hypothesis, isn't logical.

"Many of the great mathematicians did their greatest work as children and youths before they were dissipated by the sensual world. In a trivial sense, scientists and mathematicians most of all are described a 'unworldly' . . ."

Anderson bobbled his head in the old familiar way. "You have almost returned," he said quietly. "This ship is really a heuristic device, an aid to perception. You are on the threshold. You have come all the way back."

The metamathematician took his notebook, and seemed to set all his will upon it. "See Ephraim gets this," he murmured. "He, you, I . . . the oneness—"

Abruptly he disappeared. The notebook fell to the floor.

I took it up. Neither Ed nor Johnny Pearl met my eyes. We may have sat and stood there for several hours, numbed, silent. Presently the two began setting up the isomorphomechanism for realization. I joined them.

The National Mathenautics and Hyperspace Administration had jurisdiction over civilian flights then, even as it does today. Ted was pretty important, it seemed. Our preliminary debriefing won us a maximum-security session with their research chief.

Perhaps, as I'd thought passionately for an instant, I'd have done better to smash the immy, rupture the psychic ecology, let the eggshell be shattered at last. But that's not the way of it. For all of our progress, some rules of scientific investigation don't change. Our first duty was to report back. Better heads than ours would decide what to do next.

They did. Ephraim Cohen didn't say anything after he heard us out and looked at Ted's notebook. Old Ice Cream sat there, a big teddy-bear-shaped genius with thick black hair and a dumb smile, and grinned at us. It was in Institute code.

The B.C.N.Y. kids hadn't seen anything, of course. So nobody talked.

Johnny Pearl married a girl named Judy Shatz and they had fifteen kids. I guess that showed Johnny's views on the matter of matter.

Ed Goldwasser got religion. Zen-Judaism is pretty orthodox these days, yet somehow he found it suited him. But he didn't forget what happened back out in space. His book, *The Cosmic Mind*, came out last month, and it's a good summation of Ted's ideas, with a minimum of spiritual overtones.

Myself. Well, a mathematician, especially a topologist, is useless after thirty, the way progress is going along these days. But *Dim-Dustries* is a commercial enterprise, and I guess I'm good for twenty years more as a businessman.

Goldwasser's Grahm-Schmidt generator worked, but that was just the beginning. Dimensional extensions made Earth a paradise, with housing hidden in the probabilities and automated industries tucked away in the dimensions.

The biggest boon was something no one anticipated. A space of infinite dimensions solves all the basic problems of modern computer-circuit design. Now all components can be linked with short electron paths, no matter how big and complex the device.

There have been any number of other benefits. The space hospitals, for example, where topological surgery can cure the most terrible wounds—and toplogical psychiatry the most baffling syndromes. (Four years of math is required for pre-meds these days.) Patapsychology and patasociology finally made some progress, so that political and economic woes have declined—thanks, too, to the spaces, which have drained off a good deal of poor Earth's overpopulation. There are even spaces resorts, or so I'm told—I don't get away much.

I've struck it lucky. Fantastically so.

The Private Enterprise Acts had just been passed, you'll recall, and I had decided I didn't want to go spacing again. With the training required for the subject, I guess I was the only qualified man who had a peddler's pack, too. Jaffee, one of my friends down at Securities and Exchange, went so far as to say that *Dim-Dustries* was a hyperspherical trust (math is required for pre-laws too). But I placated him and I got some of my mathemateers to realign the Street on a moebius strip, so he had to side with me.

Me, I'll stick to the Earth. The "real" planet is a garden spot now, and the girls are very lovely.

Ted Anderson was recorded lost in topological space. He wasn't the first, and he was far from the last. Twiddles circuits have burned out, DaughtAmRevs have gone mad, and no doubt there have been some believers who have sought out the Great Race.

This story scared the spit out of me when I was a kid. Boomers like to reminisce about being terrified by Civil Defense movies and hiding-under-their-desk drills. Not me. It wasn't even *On the Beach* or "By the Waters of Babylon" or the dozens of other post-apocalypse stories I read that gave me nightmares.

It was this story, "Lot," which made it all seem horribly plausible, horribly real. And which stayed with me all these years. To this day, whenever I'm stuck in a northbound traffic jam, I look longingly, calculatingly at the empty southbound lanes. And when I went back to read the story again a couple of years ago, I found I remembered it almost verbatim.

Why? First of all, because Ward Moore was a wonderful writer. "Lot," like *Bring the Jubilee,* like *Greener than You Think*, is full of telling details—Jir's trying to get the ball game on the radio, the maddening refrain of "No time for niceties," the wife's insisting that they stop at a clean gas station—and flawlessly constructed, a casual, inexorable trip north on U.S. 101, from ordinariness into nightmare.

Secondly, it's a very old story. One of the things I've loved about science fiction since my first encounter is its connection to literature. (The first chapter of Heinlein's *Have Space Suit, Will Travel*, which hooked me forever, is a conversation about the moon and Jerome K. Jerome's *Three Men in a Boat.*) Greek myths, *The Prisoner of Zenda*, Shakespeare, science fiction writers had read them all and were ringing changes on them that illuminated and transfigured them. Including the Bible. I have no doubt this is the true account of what happened to Sodom and Gomorrah and poor Lot's wife, unable to keep from looking back.

Finally, like all great science fiction, the story is about more than suburbia and the Cold War. It's also about what we have to lose—not only the civilization around us but that inside us. "No time for niceties." It's a disturbing, dreadful, wonderful story. My favorite, in fact.

—Connie Willis

LOT

by Ward Moore

Mr. Jimmon even appeared elated, like a man about to set out on a vacation.

"Well, folks, no use waiting any longer. We're all set. So let's go."

There was a betrayal here; Mr. Jimmons was not the kind of man who addressed his family as "folks."

"David, you're sure . . . ?"

Mr. Jimmon merely smiled. This was quite out of character; customarily he reacted to his wife's habit of posing unfinished questions—after seventeen years the unuttered and larger part of the queries were always instantly known to him in some mysterious way, as though unerringly projected by the key in which the introduction was pitched, so that not only the full wording was communicated to his mind, but the shades and implications which circumstance and humor attached to them—with sharp and querulous defense. No matter how often he resolved to stare quietly or use the still more effective, Afraid I didn't catch your meaning, dear, he had never been able to put his resolution into force. Until this moment of crisis. Crisis, reflected Mr. Jimmon, still smiling and moving suggestively toward the door, crisis changes people. Brings out underlying qualities.

It was Jir who answered Molly Jimmon, with the adolescent's half-whine of exasperation. "Aw, furcrysay, mom, what's the idea? The highways'll be clogged tight. What's the good figuring out everything heada time and having everything all set if you're going to start all over again at the last minute? Get a grip on yourself and let's go."

Mr. Jimmon did not voice the reflexive, That's no way to talk to your mother. Instead he thought, not unsympathetically, of woman's slow reaction time. Asset in childbirth, liability behind the wheel. He knew Molly was thinking of the house and all the things in it: her clothes and Erika's, the TV set—so sullenly ugly now, with the electricity gone—the refrigerator in which the food would soon begin to rot and stink, the dead stove, the cellarful of cases of canned stuff for which there was no room in the station wagon. And the Buick, blocked up in the garage, with the air thoughtfully let out of the tires and the battery hidden.

Of course the house would be looted. But they had known that all along. When they—or rather he, for it was his executive's mind and training which were responsible for the Jimmons' preparation against this moment—planned so carefully and providentially, he had weighed property against life and decided on life. No other decision was possible. "Aren't you at least going to phone Pearl and Dan?"

Now why in the world, thought Mr. Jimmon, completely above petty irritation, should I call Dan Davisson? (Because of course it's *Dan* she means—My Old Beau. Oh, he was nobody then, just an impractical dreamer without a penny to his name; it wasn't for years that he was recognized as a Mathematical Genius; now he's a professor and all sorts of things—but she automatically says Pearl-and-Dan, not Dan.) What can Dan do with the square root of minus nothing to offset M equals whatever it is, at this moment? Or am I supposed to ask if Pearl has all her diamonds? Query, why doesn't Pearl wear pearls? Only diamonds? My wife's friend, heh heh, but even the subtlest intonation won't label them when you're entertaining an important client and Pearl and Dan.

And why should I phone? What sudden paralysis afflicts her? Hysteria?

"No," said Mr. Jimmon. "I did not phone Pearl and Dan."

Then he added, relenting. "Phone's been out since."

"But," said Molly.

She's hardly going to ask me to drive into town. He selected several answers in readiness. But she merely looked toward the telephone helplessly (she ought to have been fat, thought Mr. Jimmon, really she should, or anyway plump; her thinness gives her that air of competence), so he amplified gently, "They're unquestionably all right. As far away from it as we are."

Wendell was already in the station wagon. With Waggie hidden somewhere. Should have sent the dog to the humane society; more merciful to have it put to sleep. Too late now; Waggie would have to take his chance. There were plenty of rabbits in the hills above Malibu; he had often seen them quite close to the house. At all events there was no room for a dog in the wagon, already loaded to within a pound of its capacity.

Erika came in briskly from the kitchen, her brown jodhpurs

making her appear at first glance even younger than fourteen. But only at first glance; then the swell of hips and breasts denied the childishness the jodhpurs seemed to accent.

"The water's gone, mom. There's no use sticking around any longer."

Molly looked incredulous. "The water?"

"Of course the water's gone," said Mr. Jimmon, not impatiently, but rather with satisfaction in his own foresight. "If it didn't get the aqueduct, the mains depend on pumps. Electric pumps. When the electricity went, the water went too."

"But the water," repeated Molly, as though this last catastrophe was beyond all reason—even the outrageous logic which It brought in its train.

Jir slouched past them and outside. Erika tucked in a strand of hair, pulled her jockey cap downward and sideways, glanced quickly at her mother and father, then followed. Molly took several steps, paused, smiled vaguely in the mirror, and walked out of the house.

Mr. Jimmons patted his pockets; the money was all there. He didn't even look back before closing the front door and rattling the knob to be sure the lock had caught. It had never failed, but Mr. Jimmon always rattled it anyway. He strode to the station wagon, running his eyes over the springs to reassure himself again that they really hadn't overloaded it.

The sky was overcast; you might have thought it one of the regular morning high fogs if you didn't know. Mr. Jimmon faced southeast, but It had been too far away to see anything. Now Erika and Molly were in the front seat; the boys were in the back, lost amid the neatly packed stuff. He opened the door on the driver's side, got in, turned the key, and started the motor. Then he said casually over his shoulder, "Put the dog out, Jir."

Wendell protested, too quickly, "Waggie's not here."

Molly exclaimed, "Oh, David . . ."

Mr. Jimmon said patiently, "We're losing pretty valuable time. There's no room for the dog; we have no food for him. If we had room we could have taken more essentials; those few pounds might mean the difference."

"Can't find him," muttered Jir.

"He's not here. I tell you he's not here," shouted Wendell, tearful voiced.

"If I have to stop the motor and get him myself we'll be

wasting still more time and gas." Mr. Jimmon was still detached, judicial. "This isn't a matter of kindness to animals. It's life and death."

Erika said evenly, "Dad's right, you know. It's the dog or us. Put him out, Wend."

"I tell you—" Wendell began.

"Got him!" exclaimed Jir. "Okay, Waggie! Outside and good luck."

The spaniel wriggled ecstatically as he was picked up and put out through the open window. Mr. Jimmon raced the motor, but it didn't drown out Wendell's anguish. He threw himself on his brother, hitting and kicking. Mr. Jimmon took his foot off the gas, and as soon as he was sure the dog was away from the wheels, eased the station wagon out of the driveway and down the hill toward the ocean.

"Wendell, Wendell, stop," pleaded Molly. "Don't hurt him, Jir."

Mr. Jimmon clicked on the radio. After a preliminary hum, clashing static crackled out. He pushed all five buttons in turn varying the quality of unintelligible sound. "Want me to try?" offered Erika. She pushed the manual button and turned the knob slowly. Music dripped out.

Mr. Jimmon grunted. "Mexican station. Try something else. Maybe you can get Ventura."

They rounded a tight curve. "Isn't that the Warbinns'?" asked Molly.

For the first time since It happened Mr. Jimmon had a twinge of impatience. There was no possibility, even with the unreliable eye of shocked excitement, of mistaking the Warbinns' blue Mercury. No one else on Rambla Catalina had one anything like it, and visitors would be most unlikely now. If Molly would apply the most elementary logic!

Besides, Warbinn had stopped the blue Mercury in the Jimmon driveway five times every week for the past two months—ever since they had decided to put the Buick up and keep the wagon packed and ready against this moment—for Mr. Jimmon to ride with him to the city. Of course it was the Warbinns'.

". . . advised not to impede the progress of the military. Adequate medical staffs are standing by at all hospitals. Local civilian defense units are taking all steps in accordance . . ."

"Santa Barbara," remarked Jir, nodding at the radio with an expert's assurance.

Mr. Jimmon slowed, prepared to follow the Warbinns down to 101, but the Mercury halted and Mr. Jimmon turned out to pass it. Warbinn was driving and Sally was in the front seat with him; the back seat appeared empty except for a few things obviously hastily thrown in. No foresight, thought Mr. Jimmon.

Warbinn waved his hand vigorously out the window and Sally shouted something.

". . . panic will merely slow rescue efforts. Casualties are much smaller than originally reported . . ."

"How do they know?" asked Mr. Jimmon, waving politely at the Warbinns.

"Oh, David, aren't you going to stop? They want something."

"Probably just to talk."

". . . to retain every drop of water. Emergency power will be in operation shortly. There is no cause for undue alarm. General . . ."

Through the rearview mirror Mr. Jimmon saw the blue Mercury start after them. He had been right then, they only wanted to say something inconsequential. At a time like this.

At the junction with U.S. 101 five cars blocked Rambla Catalina. Mr. Jimmon set the handbrake, and steadying himself with the open door, stood tiptoe twistedly, trying to see over the cars ahead. 101 was solid with traffic which barely moved. On the southbound side of the divided highway a stream of vehicles flowed illegally north.

"Thought everybody was figured to go east," gibed Jir over the other side of the car.

Mr. Jimmon was not disturbed by his son's sarcasm. How right he'd been to rule out the trailer. Of course the bulk of the cars were headed eastward as he'd calculated; this sluggish mass was nothing compared with the countless ones which must now be blocking the roads to Pasadena, Alhambra, Garvey, Norwalk. Even the northbound refugees were undoubtedly taking 99 or regular 101—the highway before them was really 101 Alternate—he had picked the most feasible exit.

The Warbinns drew up alongside. "Hurry didn't do you much good," shouted Warbinn, leaning forward to clear his wife's face.

Mr. Jimmon reached in and turned off the ignition. Gas was going to be precious. He smiled and shook his head at Warbinn; no use pointing out that he'd got the inside lane by passing the Mercury, with a better chance to seize the opening on the highway when it came. "Get in the car, Jir, and shut the door. Have to be ready when this breaks."

"If it ever does," said Molly. "All that rush and bustle. We might just as well . . ."

Mr. Jimmon was conscious of Warbinn's glowering at him and resolutely refused to turn his head. He pretended not to hear him yell. "Only wanted to tell you you forgot to pick up your bumper jack. It's in front of our garage."

Mr. Jimmon's stomach felt empty. What if he had a flat now? Ruined, condemned. He knew a burning hate for Warbinn—incompetent borrower, bad neighbor, thoughtless, shiftless, criminal. He owed it to himself to leap from the station wagon and seize Warbinn by the throat . . .

"What did he say, David? What is Mr. Warbinn saying?"

Then he remembered it was the jack from the Buick; the station wagon's was safely packed where he could get at it easily. Naturally he would never have started out on a trip like this without checking so essential an item. "Nothing," he said, "nothing at all."

". . . plane dispatches indicate target was the Signal Hill area. Minor damage was done to Long Beach, Wilmington, and San Pedro. All nonmilitary air traffic warned from Mines Field . . ."

The smash and crash of bumper and fender sounded familiarly on the highway. From his lookout station he couldn't see what had happened, but it was easy enough to reconstruct the impatient jerk forward that caused it. Mr. Jimmon didn't exactly smile, but he allowed himself a faint quiver of internal satisfaction. A crash up ahead would make things worse, but a crash behind—and many of them were inevitable—must eventually create a gap.

Even as he thought this, the first car at the mouth of Rambla Catalina edged onto the shoulder of the highway. Mr. Jimmon slid back in and started the motor, inching ahead after the car in front, gradually leaving the still uncomfortable proximity of the Warbinns.

"Got to go to the toilet," announced Wendell abruptly.

"Didn't I tell you—! Well, hurry up! Jir, keep the door open and pull him in if the car starts to move."

"I can't go here."

Mr. Jimmon restrained his impulse to snap, Hold it in then. Instead he said mildly, "This is a crisis, Wendell. No time for niceties. Hurry."

". . . the flash was seen as far north as Ventura and as far south as Newport. An eyewitness who had just arrived by helicopter . . ."

"That's what we should have had," remarked Jir. "You thought of everything except that."

"That's no way to speak to your father," admonished Molly.

"Aw, heck mom, this is a crisis. No time for niceties."

"You're awful smart, Jir," said Erika. "Big, tough, brutal man."

"Go down, brat," returned Jir, "your nose needs wiping."

"As a matter of record," Mr. Jimmon said calmly, "I thought of both plane and helicopter and decided against them."

"I can't go. Honest, I just can't go."

"Just relax, darling," advised Molly. "No one is looking."

". . . fires reported in Compton, Lynwood, South Gate, Harbor City, Lomita, and other spots are now under control. Residents are advised not to attempt to travel on the overcrowded highways as they are much safer in their homes or places of employment. The civilian defense . . ."

The two cars ahead bumped forward. "Get in," shouted Mr. Jimmon.

He got the left front tire of the station wagon on the asphalt shoulder—the double lane of concrete was impossibly far ahead—only to be blocked by the packed procession. The clock on the dash said 11:04. Nearly five hours since It happened, and they were less than two miles from home. They could have done better walking. Or on horseback.

". . . All residents of the Los Angeles area are urged to remain calm. Local radio service will be restored in a matter of minutes, along with electricity and water. Reports of fifth column activities have been greatly exaggerated. The FBI has all known subversives under . . ."

He reached over and shut it off. Then he edged a daring two inches farther on the shoulder, almost grazing an aggressive Cadillac packed solid with cardboard cartons. On his left a Model A truck shivered and trembled. He knew, distantly and disapprovingly, that it belonged to two painters who called themselves man and wife. The truck bed was loaded high with household goods; poor, useless things no looter would bother to steal. In the cab the artists passed a quart beer bottle back and forth. The man waved it genially at him; Mr. Jimmon nodded discouragingly back.

The thermometer on the mirror showed 90. Hot all right. Of course if they ever got rolling . . . I'm thirsty, he thought; probably suggestion. If I hadn't seen the thermometer. Anyway I'm not going to paw around in back for the canteen. Forethought. Like the arms. He cleared his throat. "Remember there's an automatic in the glove compartment. If anyone tries to open the door on your side, use it."

"Oh, David, I . . ."

Ah, humanity. Nonresistance, Gandhi. I've never shot at anything but a target. At a time like this. But they don't understand.

"I could use the rifle from back here," suggested Jir. "Can I, dad?"

"I can reach the shotgun," said Wendell. "That's better at close range."

"Gee, you men are brave," jeered Erika. Mr. Jimmon said nothing; both shotgun and rifle were unloaded. Foresight again.

He caught the hiccuping pause in the traffic instantly, gratified at his smooth coordination. How far he could proceed on the shoulder before running into a culvert narrowing the highway to the concrete he didn't know. Probably not more than a mile at most, but at least he was off Rambla Catalina and on 101.

He felt tremendously elated. Successful.

"Here we go!" He almost added, Hold on to your hats.

Of course the shoulder too was packed solid, and progress, even in low gear, was maddening. The gas consumption was something he did not want to think about; his pride in the way the needle of the gauge caressed the F shrank. And gas would be hard to come by in spite of his pocketful of ration coupons. Black market.

"Mind if I try the radio again?" asked Erika, switching it on.

Mr. Jimmon, following the pattern of previous success, insinuated the left front tire onto the concrete, eliciting a disapproving squawk from the Pontiac alongside.

". . . sector was quiet. Enemy losses are estimated . . ."

"Can't you get something else?" asked Jir. "Something less dusty?"

"Wish we had TV in the car," observed Wendell. "Joe Tellifer's old man put a set in the back seat of their Chrysler."

"Dry up, squirt," said Jir. "Let the air out of your head."

"Jir."

"Oh, mom, don't pay attention! Don't you see that's what he wants?"

"Listen, brat, if you weren't a girl, I'd spank you."

"You mean, If I wasn't your sister. You'd probably enjoy such childish sex play with any other girl."

"Erika!"

Where do they learn it? marveled Mr. Jimmon. These progressive schools. Do you suppose . . . ?

He edged the front wheel farther in exultantly, taking advantage of a momentary lapse of attention on the part of the Pontiac's driver. Unless the other went berserk with frustration and rammed into him, he practically had a cinch on a car length of the concrete now.

"Here we go!" he gloried. "We're on our way."

"Aw, if I was driving we'd be halfway to Oxnard by now."

"Jir, that's no way to talk to your father."

Mr. Jimmon reflected dispassionately that Molly's ineffective admonitions only spurred Jir's sixteen-year-old brashness, already irritating enough in its own right. Indeed, if it were not for Molly, Jir might . . .

It was of course possible—here Mr. Jimmon braked just short of the convertible ahead—Jir wasn't just going through a "difficult" period (What was particularly difficult about it? he inquired, in the face of all the books Molly suggestively left around on the psychological problems of growth. The boy had everything he could possibly want.) but was the type who, in different circumstances drifted well into—well, perhaps not exactly juvenile delinquency, but . . .

". . . in the Long Beach—Wilmington—San Pedro area. Comparison with that which occurred at Pittsburgh reveals that this morning's was in every way less serious. All fires are now under control and all the injured are now receiving medical attention . . ."

"I don't think they're telling the truth," stated Mrs. Jimmon.

He snorted. He didn't think so either, but by what process had she arrived at that conclusion?

"I want to hear the ball game. Turn on the ball game, Rick," Wendell demanded.

Eleven sixteen, and rolling northward on the highway. Not bad, not bad at all. Foresight. Now if he could only edge his way leftward to the southbound strip they'd be beyond the Santa Barbara bottleneck by two o'clock.

"The lights," exclaimed Molly, "the taps!"

Oh no, thought Mr. Jimmon, not that too. Out of the comic strips.

"Keep calm," advised Jir. "Electricity and water are both off—remember?"

"I'm not quite an imbecile yet, Jir. I'm quite aware everything went off. I was thinking of the time it went back on."

"Furcrysay, mom, you worrying about next month's bills *now?*"

Mr. Jimmon, nudging the station wagon ever leftward, formed the sentence: You'd never worry about bills, young man, because you never have to pay them. Instead of saying it aloud, he formed another sentence: Molly, your talent for irrelevance amounts to genius. Both sentences gave him satisfaction.

The traffic gathered speed briefly, and he took advantage of the spurt to get solidly in the left-hand lane, right against the long island of concrete dividing the north- from the southbound strips. "That's using the old bean, dad," approved Wendell.

Whatever slight pleasure he might have felt in his son's approbation was overlaid with exasperation. Wendell, like Jir, was more Manville than Jimmon; they carried Molly's stamp on their faces and minds. Only Erika was a true Jimmon. Made in my own image, he thought pridelessly.

"I can't help but think it would have been at least courteous to get in touch with Pearl and Dan. At least *try.* And the Warbinns . . .

The gap in the concrete divider came sooner than he anticipated and he was on the comparatively unclogged southbound side. His foot went down on the accelerator and the station wagon grumbled earnestly ahead. For the first time Mr. Jimmon became aware how tightly he'd been gripping the wheel; how rigid the muscles in his arms, shoulders, and neck had been. He relaxed partway as he adjusted to the speed of the cars ahead and the speedometer needle hung just below 45, but resentment against Molly (at least courteous), Jir (no time for niceties), and Wendell (not to go), rode up in the saliva under his tongue. Dependent. Helpless. Everything on him. Parasites.

At intervals Erika switched on the radio. News was always promised immediately, but little was forthcoming, only vague, nervous attempts to minimize the extent of the disaster and soothe the listeners with allusions to civilian defense, military activities on the ever advancing front, and comparison with the destruction of Pittsburgh, so vastly much worse than the comparatively harmless detonation at Los Angeles. Must be pretty bad, thought Mr. Jimmon; cripple the war effort . . .

"I'm hungry," said Wendell.

Molly began stirring around, instructing Jir where to find the sandwiches. Mr. Jimmon thought grimly of how they'd have to adjust to the absence of civilized niceties; bread and mayonnaise and lunch meat. Live on rabbit, squirrel, abalone, fish. When Wendell grew hungry he'd have to get his own food. Self-sufficiency. Hard and tough.

At Oxnard the snarled traffic slowed them to a crawl again. Beyond, the juncture with the main highway north kept them at the same infuriating pace. It was long after two when they reached Ventura, and Wendell, who had been fidgeting and jumping up and down in the seat for the past hour, proclaimed, "I'm tired of riding."

Mr. Jimmon set his lips. Molly suggested, ineffectually, "Why don't you lie down, dear?"

"Can't. Way this crate is packed, ain't room for a grasshopper."

"Verry funny. Verrrry funny," said Jir.

"Now, Jir, leave him alone! He's just a little boy."

At Carpinteria the sun burst out. You might have thought it the regular dissipation of the fog, only it was almost time for the fog to come down again. Should he try the San Marcos Pass after Santa Barbara, or the longer, better way? Flexible plans, but . . . Wait and see.

It was four when they got to Santa Barbara and Mr. Jimmon faced concerted though unorganized rebellion. Wendell was screaming with stiffness and boredom; Jir remarked casually to no one in particular that Santa Barbara was the place they were going to beat the bottleneck, oh yeh; Molly said, Stop at the first clean-looking gas station. Even Erika added, "Yes, dad, you'll really have to stop."

Mr. Jimmon was appalled. With every second priceless and hordes of panic-stricken refugees pressing behind, they would rob him of all the precious gains he'd made by skill, daring, judgment. Stupidity and shortsightedness. Unbelievable. For their own silly comfort—good lord, did they think they had a monopoly on bodily weaknesses? He was cramped as they and wanted to go as badly. Time and space which could never be made up. Let them lose this half hour and it was quite likely they'd never get out of Santa Barbara.

"If we lose a half hour now we'll never get out of here."

"Well, now, David, that wouldn't be utterly disastrous, would it? There are awfully nice hotels here and I'm sure it would be more comfortable for everyone than your idea of camping in the woods, hunting and fishing . . ."

He turned off State; couldn't remember name of the parallel street, but surely less traffic. He controlled his temper, not heroically, but desperately. "May I ask how long you would propose to stay in one of these awfully nice hotels?"

"Why, until we could go home."

"My dear Molly . . ." What could he say? My dear Molly, we are never going home, if you mean Malibu? Or: My dear Molly, you just don't understand what is happening?

The futility of trying to convey the clear picture in his mind. Or any picture. If she could not of herself see the endless mob pouring out of Los Angeles, searching frenziedly for escape and refuge, eating up the substance of the surrounding country in ever-widening circles, crowding, jam-packing, overflowing every hotel, boarding-house, lodging, or private home into which they could edge, agonizedly bidding up the price of everything until the chaos they brought with them was indistinguishable from the chaos they were fleeing—if she could not see all this instantly and automatically, she could not be brought to see it at all. Any more than the other aimless, planless, improvident fugitives could see it.

So, my dear Molly; nothing.

Silence gave consent to continued expostulation. "David, do you really mean you don't intend to stop at *all?*"

Was there any point in saying, Yes, I do? He set his lips still more tightly and once more weighed San Marcos Pass against the coast route. Have to decide now.

"Why, the time we're waiting here, just waiting for the cars up ahead to move would be enough."

Could you call her stupid? He weighed the question slowly and justly, alert for the first jerk of the massed cars all around. Her reasoning was valid and logical if the laws of physics and geometry were suspended. (Was that right—physics and geometry? Body occupying two different positions at the same time?) It was the facts which were illogical—not Molly. She was just exasperating.

By the time they were halfway to Gaviota or Goleta—Mr. Jimmon could never tell them apart—foresight and relentless sternness began to pay off. Those who had left Los Angeles without preparation and in panic were dropping out or slowing down, to get gas or oil, repair tires, buy food, seek rest rooms. The station wagon was steadily forging ahead.

He gambled on the old highway out of Santa Barbara. Any kind of obstruction would block its two lanes; if it didn't he would be beating the legions on the wider, straighter road. There were stretches now where he could hit 50; once he sped a happy half-mile at 65.

Now the insubordination crackling all around gave indication of simultaneous explosion. "I really," began Molly, and then discarded this for a fresher, firmer start. "David, I don't understand how you can be so utterly selfish and inconsiderate."

Mr. Jimmon could feel the veins in his forehead begin to swell, but this was one of those rages that didn't show.

"But, Dad, would ten minutes ruin everything?" asked Erika.

"Monomania," muttered Jir. "Single track. Like Hitler."

"I want my dog," yelped Wendell. "Dirty old dog-killer."

"Did you ever hear of cumulative—" Erika had addressed him reasonably; surely he could make her understand? "Did you ever hear of cumulative . . ." What was the word? Snowball rolling downhill was the image in his mind. "Oh, what's the use?"

The old road rejoined the new; again the station wagon was fitted into the traffic like parquetry. Mr. Jimmon, from an exultant, unfettered—almost—65 was imprisoned in a treadmill set at 38. Keep calm; you can do nothing about it, he admonished himself. Need all your nervous energy. Must be wrecks up ahead. And then, with a return of satisfaction: If I hadn't used strategy back there we'd have been with those making 25. A starting-stopping 25.

"It's fantastic," exclaimed Molly. "I could almost believe Jir's right and you've lost your mind."

Mr. Jimmons smiled. This was the first time Molly had ever openly showed disloyalty before the children or sided with them in their presence. She was revealing herself. Under pressure. Not the pressure of events; her incredible attitude at Santa Barbara had demonstrated her incapacity to feel that. Just pressure against the bladder.

"No doubt those left behind can console their last moments with pride in their sanity." The sentence came out perfectly formed, with none of the annoying pauses or interpolated "ers" or "mmphs" which could, as he knew from unhappy experience, flaw the most crushing rejoinders.

"Oh, the end can always justify the means for those who want it that way."

"Don't they restrain people—"

"That's enough, Jir!"

Trust Molly to return quickly to fundamental hypocrisy; the automatic response—his mind felicitously grasped the phrase, conditioned reflex—to the customary stimulus. She had taken an explicit stand against his common sense, but her rigid code—honor they father; iron rayon the wrong side; register and vote; avoid scenes; only white wine with fish; never rehire a discharged servant—quickly substituted pattern for impulse. Seventeen years.

The road turned away from the ocean, squirmed inland and uphill for still slower miles, abruptly widened into a divided, four-lane highway. Without hesitation Mr. Jimmon took the southbound side; for the first time since they had left Rambla Catalina his foot went down to the floorboards and with a sigh of relief the station wagon jumped into smooth, ecstatic speed.

Improvisation and strategy again. And, he acknowledged generously, the defiant example this morning of those who'd done the same thing in Malibu. Now, out of reestablished habit the other cars kept to the northbound side even though there was nothing coming south. Timidity, routine, inertia. Pretty soon they would realize sheepishly that there were neither traffic nor traffic cops to keep them off, but it would be miles before they had another chance to cross over. By that time he would have reached the comparatively uncongested stretch.

"It's dangerous, David."

Obey the law. No smoking. Keep off the grass. Please adjust your clothes before leaving. Trespassers will be. Picking California wild flowers or shrubs is forbidden. Parking 45 min. Do not.

She hadn't put the protest in the more usual form of a question. Would that technique have been more irritating? *Isn't* it *dan*gerous Day-vid? His calm conclusions: it didn't matter.

"No time for niceties," chirped Jir.

Mr. Jimmon tried to remember Jir as a baby. All the bad novels he had read in the days when he read anything except *Time* and *The New Yorker*, all the movies he'd seen before they had a TV set, always prescribed such retrospection as a specific for softening the present. If he could recall David Alonzo Jimmon, Junior, at six months, helpless and lovable, it should make Jir more acceptable by discovering some faint traces of the one in the other.

But though he could re-create in detail the interminable, disgusting, trembling months of that initial pregnancy (had he really been afraid she would die?) he was completely unable to reconstruct the appearance of his firstborn before the age of . . . It must have been at six that Jir had taken his baby sister out for a walk and lost her. (Had Molly permitted it? He still didn't know for sure.) Erika hadn't been found for four hours.

The tidal screeching of sirens invaded and destroyed his thoughts. What the devil . . . ? His foot lifted from the gas pedal as he slewed obediently to the right, ingrained reverence surfacing at the sound.

"I told you it wasn't safe! Are you really trying to kill us all?"

Whipping over the rise ahead, a pair of motorcycles crackled. Behind them snapped along line of assorted vehicles, fire trucks and ambulances mostly, interspersed here and there with olive-drab army equipment. The cavalcade flicked down the central white line, one wheel in each lane. Mr. Jimmon edged the station wagon as far over as he could; it still occupied too much room to permit the free passage of the onrush without compromise.

The knees and elbows of the motorcycle policemen stuck out widely, reminding Mr. Jimmon of grasshoppers. The one on the near side was headed straight for the station wagon's left front fender; for a moment Mr. Jimmon closed his eyes as he plotted the unswerving course, knifing through the crustlike steel, bouncing lightly on the tires, and continuing unperturbed. He opened them to see the other officer shoot past, mouth angrily open in his direction while the one straight ahead came to a skidding stop.

"Going to get it now," gloated Wendell.

An old-fashioned parent, one of the horrible examples held up to shuddering moderns like himself, would have reached back and relieved his tension by clouting Wendell across the mouth. Mr. Jimmon merely turned off the motor.

The cop was not indulging in the customary deliberate and ominous performance of slowly dismounting and striding toward his victim with ever more menacing steps. Instead he got off quickly and covered the few feet to Mr. Jimmon's window with unimpressive speed.

Heavy goggles concealed his eyes; dust and stubble covered his face. "Operator's license!"

Mr. Jimmon knew what he was saying, but the sirens and the continuous rustle of the convoy prevented the sound from coming through. Again the cop deviated from the established routine; he did not take the proffered license and examine it incredulously before drawing out his pad and pencil, but wrote the citation, glancing up and down from the card to Mr. Jimmon's hand.

Even so, the last of the vehicles—*San Jose F.D.*—passed before he handed the summons through the window to be signed. "Turn around and proceed in the proper direction," he ordered curtly, pocketing the pad and buttoning his jacket briskly.

Mr. Jimmon nodded. The officer hesitated, as though waiting for some limp excuse. Mr. Jimmon said nothing.

"No tricks," said the policeman over his shoulder. "Turn around and proceed in the proper direction."

He almost ran to his motorcycle, and roared off, twisting his head for a final stern frown as he passed, siren wailing. Mr. Jimmon watched him dwindle in the rearview mirror and then started the motor. "Gonna lose a lot more than you gained," commented Jir.

Mr. Jimmon gave a last glance in the mirror and moved ahead, shifting into second. "David!" exclaimed Molly, horrified, "you're not turning around!"

"Observant," muttered Mr. Jimmon, between his teeth.

"Dad, you can't get away with it," Jir decided judicially.

Mr. Jimmon's answer was to press the accelerator down savagely. The empty highway stretched invitingly ahead; a few hundred yards to their right they could see the northbound lanes ant-clustered. The sudden motion stirred the traffic citation on his lap, floating it down to the floor. Erika leaned forward and picked it up.

"Throw it away," ordered Mr. Jimmon.

Molly gasped. "You're out of your mind."

"You're a fool," stated Mr. Jimmon calmly. "Why should I save that piece of paper?"

"Isn't what you told the cop." Jir was openly jeering now.

"I might as well have, if I'd wanted to waste conversation. I don't know why I was blessed with such a stupid family—"

"May be something in heredity after all."

If Jir had said it out loud, reflected Mr. Jimmon, it would have passed casually as normal domestic repartee, a little ill-natured perhaps, certainly callow and trite, but not especially provocative. Muttered, so that it was barely audible, it was an ultimate defiance. He had read that far back in prehistory, when the young males felt their strength, they sought to overthrow the rule of the Old Man and usurp his place. No doubt they uttered a preliminary growl or screech as challenge. They were not very bright, but they acted in a pattern; a pattern Jir was apparently following.

Refreshed by placing Jir in proper Neanderthal setting, Mr. Jimmon went on, "—none of you seem to have the slightest initiative or ability to grasp reality. Tickets, cops, judges, juries mean nothing anymore. There is no law now but the law of survival."

"Aren't you being dramatic, David?" Molly's tone was deliberately aloof adult to excited child.

"I could hear you underline words, Dad," said Erika, but he felt there was no malice in her gibe.

"You mean we can do anything we want now? Shoot people? Steal cars and things?" asked Wendell.

"There, David! You see?"

Yes, I see. Better than you. Little savage. This is the pattern. What will Wendell—and the thousands of other Wendells (for it would be unjust to suppose Molly's genes and domestic influence unique)—be like after six months of anarchy? Or after six years?

Survivors, yes. And that will be about all: naked, primitive, ferocious, superstitious savages. Wendell can read and write (but not so fluently as I or any of our generation at his age); how long will he retain the tags and scraps of progressive schooling?

And Jir? Detachedly Mr. Jimmon foresaw the fate of Jir. Unlike Wendell, who would adjust to the new conditions, Jir would go wild in another sense. His values were already set; they were those of television, high school dating, comic strips, law and order. Released from civilization, his brief future would be one of guilty rape and pillage until he fell victim to another youth or gang bent the same way. Molly would disintegrate and perish quickly. Erika . . .

The station wagon flashed along the comparatively unimpeded highway. Having passed the next crossover, there were now other vehicles on the southbound strip, but even on the northbound one, crowding had eased.

Furiously Mr. Jimmon determined to preserve the civilization in Erika. (He would teach her everything he knew [including the insurance business?]) . . . ah, if he were some kind of scientist, now—not the Dan Davisson kind, whose abstract speculations seemed always to prepare the way for some new method of destruction, but the . . . Franklin? Jefferson? Watt? protect her night and day from the refugees who would be roaming the hills south of Monterey. The rifle ammunition, properly used—and he would see that no one but himself used it—would last years. After it was gone—presuming fragments and pieces of a suicidal world hadn't pulled itself miraculously together to offer a place to return to—there were the two hunting bows whose steel-tipped shafts could stop a man as easily as a deer or mountain lion. He remembered debating long, at the time he had first begun preparing for It, how many bows to order, measuring their weight and bulk against the other precious freight and deciding at last that two was the satisfactory minimum. It must have been in his subconscious mind all along that of the whole family Erika was the only other person who could be trusted with a bow.

"There will be," he spoke in calm and solemn tones, not to Wendell, whose question was now left long behind, floating on the gas-greasy air of a sloping valley growing with live oaks, but to a large, impalpable audience, "There will be others who will think that because there is no longer law or law enforcement—"

"You're being simply fantastic!" She spoke more sharply than he had ever heard her in front of the children. "Just because It happened to Los Angeles—"

"And Pittsburgh."

"All right. And Pittsburgh, doesn't mean that the whole United States has collapsed and everyone in the country is running frantically for safety."

"Yet," added Mr. Jimmon firmly, "yet, do you suppose they are going to stop with Los Angeles and Pittsburgh, and leave Gary and Seattle standing? Or even New York and Chicago? Or do you imagine Washington will beg for armistice terms while there is the least sign of organized life left in the country?"

"We'll wipe Them out first," insisted Jir in patriotic shock. Wendell backed him up with a machine gun "brrrrr."

"Undoubtedly. But it will be the last gasp. At any rate it will be years, if at all in my lifetime, before stable communities are reestablished—"

"David, you're raving."

"Reestablished," he repeated. "So there will be many others who'll also feel that the dwindling of law and order is license to kill people and steal cars 'and things.' Naked force and cunning will be the only means of self-preservation. That was why I picked out a spot where I felt survival would be easiest; not only because of wood and water, game and fish, but because it's nowhere near the main highways, and so unlikely to be chosen by any great number."

"I wish you'd stop harping on that insane idea. You're just a little too old and flabby for pioneering. Even when you were younger you were hardly the rugged, outdoor type."

No, thought Mr. Jimmon, I was the sucker type. I would have gotten somewhere if I'd stayed in the bank, but like a bawd you pleaded; the insurance business brought in the quick money for you to give up your job and have Jir and the proper home. If you'd got rid of it as I wanted. Flabby, *Flabby!* Do you think your scrawniness is so enticing?

Controlling himself, he said aloud, "We've been through all this. Months ago. It's not a question of physique, but of life."

"Nonsense. Perfect nonsense. Responsible people who

really know its effects . . . : Maybe it was advisable to leave Malibu for a few days or even a few weeks. And perhaps it's wise to stay away from the larger cities. But a small town or village, or even one of those ranches where they take boarders—"

"Aw, mom, you agreed. You know you did. What's the matter with you anyway? Why are you acting like a drip?"

"I want to go and shoot rabbits and bears like dad said," insisted Wendell.

Erika said nothing, but Mr. Jimmon felt he had her sympathy; the boy's agreement was specious. Wearily he debated going over the whole ground again, patiently pointing out that what Molly said might work in the Dakotas or the Great Smokies but was hardly operative anywhere within refugee range of the Pacific Coast. He had explained all this many times, including the almost certain impossibility of getting enough gasoline to take them into any of the reasonably safe areas; that was why they'd agreed on the region below Monterey, on California State Highway 1, as the only logical goal.

A solitary car decorously bound in the legal direction interrupted his thoughts. Either crazy or has mighty important business, he decided. The car honked disapprovingly as it passed, hugging the extreme right of the road.

Passing through Buellton the clamor again rose for a pause at a filling station. He conceded inwardly that he could afford ten or fifteen minutes without strategic loss since by now they must be among the leaders of the exodus; ahead lay little more than the normal travel. However, he had reached such a state of irritated frustration and consciousness of injustice that he was willing to endure unnecessary discomfort himself in order to inflict a longer delay on them. In fact it lessened his own suffering to know the delay was needless, that he was doing it, and that his action was a just—if inadequate—punishment.

"We'll stop this side of Santa Maria," he said. "I'll get gas there."

Mr. Jimmon knew triumph: his forethought, his calculations, his generalship had justified themselves. Barring unlikely mechanical failure—the station wagon was in perfect shape—or accident—and the greatest danger had certainly passed—escape was now practically assured. For the first time he permitted himself to realize how unreal, how romantic the whole project had been. As any attempt to evade the fate charted for the multitude must be. The docile mass perished; the headstrong (but intelligent) individual survived.

Along with triumph went an expansion of his prophetic vision of life after reaching their destination. He had purposely not taxed the cargo capacity of the wagon with transitional goods; there was no tent, canned luxuries, sleeping bags, lanterns, candles, or any of the paraphernalia of camping midway between the urban and nomadic life. Instead, besides the weapons, tackle, and utensils, there was in miniature the List for Life on a Desert Island: shells and cartridges, lures, hooks, nets, gut, leaders, flint and steel, seeds, traps, needles and thread, government pamphlets on curing and tanning hides and the recognition of edible weeds and fungi, files, nails, a judicious stock of simple medicines. A pair of binoculars to spot intruders. No coffee, sugar, flour; they would begin living immediately as they would have to in a month or so in any case, in the old, half-forgotten human cunning.

"Cunning," he said aloud.

"What?"

"Nothing. Nothing."

"I still think you should have made an effort to reach Pearl and Dan."

"The telephone was dead, Mother."

"At the moment, Erika. You can hardly have forgotten how often the lines have been down before. And it never takes more than half an hour till they're working again."

"Mother, Dan Davisson is quite capable of looking after himself."

Mr. Jimmons shut out the rest of the conversation so completely he didn't know whether there was any more to it or not. He shut out the intense preoccupation with driving, with making speed, with calculating possible gains. In the core of his mind, quite detached from everything about him, he examined and marveled.

Erika. The cool, inflexible, adult tone. Almost indulgent, but so dispassionate as not to be. One might have expected her to be exasperated by Molly's silliness, to have answered impatiently, or not at all.

Mother. Never in his recollection had the children ever called her anything but mom. The "Mother" implied—oh, it implied a multitude of things. An entirely new relationship, for one. A relationship of aloofness, or propriety without emotion.

The ancient stump of the umbilical cord, black and shriveled, had dropped off painlessly.

She had not bothered to argue about the telephone or point out the gulf between "before" and now. She had not even tried to touch Molly's deepening refusal of reality. She had been . . . indulgent.

Not "Uncle Dan," twitteringly imposed false avuncularity, but striking through it (and the facade of "Pearl and") and aside (when I was a child I . . . something . . . but now I have put aside childish things); the wealth of implicit assertion. Ah, yes, Mother, we all know the pardonable weakness and vanity; we excuse you for your constant reminders, but Mother, with all deference, we refuse to be forced any longer to be parties to middle-age's nostalgic flirtatiousness. One could almost feel sorry for Molly.

. . . middle-age's nostalgic flirtatiousness . . .

. . . *nostalgic* . . .

Metaphorically Mr. Jimmon sat abruptly upright. The fact that he was already physically in this position made the transition, while invisible, no less emphatic. The nostalgic flirtatiousness of middle age implied—might imply—memory of something more than mere coquetry. Molly and Dan.

It all fitted together so perfectly it was impossible to believe it untrue. The impecunious young lovers, equally devoted to Dan's genius, realizing marriage was out of the question (he had never denied Molly's shrewdness; as for Dan's impracticality, well, impracticality wasn't necessarily uniform or consistent. Dan had been practical enough to marry Pearl and Pearl's money) could have renounced . . .

Or not renounced at all?

Mr. Jimmon smiled; the thought did not ruffle him. Cuckoo, cuckoo. How vulgar, how absurd. Suppose Jir were Dan's? A blessed thought.

Regretfully he conceded the insuperable obstacle of Molly's conventionality. Jir was the product of his own loins. But wasn't there an old superstition about the image in the woman's mind at the instant of conception? So, justly and rightly Jir was not his. Nor Wendy, for that matter. Only Erika, by some accident. Mr. Jimmon felt free and lighthearted.

"Get gas at the next station," he bulletined.

"The next one with a clean rest room," Molly corrected.

Invincible. The Earth Mother, using men for her purposes:

reproduction, clean rest rooms, nourishment, objects of culpability, *Better Homes and Gardens.* The bank was my life; I could have gone far but: Why, David—they pay you less than the janitor! It's ridiculous. And: I can't understand why you hesitate; it isn't as though it were a different type of work.

No, not different; just more profitable. Why didn't she tell Dan Davisson to become an accountant; that was the same type of work, just more profitable? Perhaps she had and Dan had simply been less befuddled. Or amenable. Or stronger in purpose? Mr. Jimmon probed his pride thoroughly and relentlessly without finding the faintest twinge of retrospective jealousy. Nothing like that mattered now. Nor, he admitted, had it for years.

Two close-peaked hills gulped the sun. He toyed with the idea of crossing to the northbound side now that it was uncongested and there were occasional southbound cars. Before he could decide the divided highway ended.

"I hope you're not planning to spend the night in some horrible motel," said Molly. "I want a decent bath and a good dinner."

Spend the night. Bath. Dinner. Again calm sentences formed in his mind, but they were blown apart by the unbelievable, the monumental obtuseness. How could you say, it is absolutely essential to drive till we get there? When there were no absolutes, no essentials in her concepts? My dear Molly, I—

"No," he said, switching on the lights.

Wendy, he knew, would be the next to kick up a fuss. Till he fell mercifully asleep. If he did. Jir was probably debating the relative excitements of driving all night and stopping in a strange town. His voice would soon be heard.

The lights of the combination wayside store and filling station burned inefficiently, illuminating the deteriorating false front brightly and leaving the gas pumps in shadow. Swallowing regret at finally surrendering to mechanical and human need, and so losing the hard-won position, relaxing even for a short while the fierce initiative that had brought them through in the face of all probability, he pulled the station wagon alongside the pumps and shut off the motor. About halfway—the worst half, much the worst half—to their goal. Not bad.

Molly opened the door on her side with stiff dignity. "I certainly wouldn't call this a *clean* station." She waited for a moment, hand still on the window, as though expecting an answer.

"Crummy joint," exclaimed Wendell, clambering awkwardly out.

"Why not?" asked Jir. "No time for niceties." He brushed past his mother, who was walking slowly into the shadows.

"Erika," began Mr. Jimmon, in a half-whisper.

"Yes, Dad?"

"Oh . . . never mind. Later."

He was not himself quite sure what he had wanted to say, what exclusive, urgent message he had to convey. For no particular reason he switched on the interior light and glanced at the packed orderliness of the wagon. Then he slid out from behind the wheel.

No sign of the attendant, but the place was certainly not closed. Not with the lights on and the hoses ready. He stretched, and walked slowly, savoring the comfortably painful uncramping of his muscles, toward the crude outhouse labeled MEN. Molly, he thought, must be furious.

When he returned, a man was leaning against the station wagon. "Fill it up with ethyl," said Mr. Jimmon pleasantly, "and check the oil and water."

The man made no move. "That'll be five bucks a gallon." Mr. Jimmon thought there was an uncertain tremor in his voice.

"Nonsense; I've plenty of ration coupons."

"Okay." The nervousness was gone now, replaced by an ugly truculence. "Chew'm up and spit'm in your gas tank. See how far you can run on them."

The situation was not unanticipated. Indeed, Mr. Jimmon thought with satisfaction of how much worse it must be closer to Los Angeles; how much harder the gouger would be on later supplicants as his supply of gasoline dwindled. "Listen," he said, and there was reasonableness rather than anger in his voice, "we're not out of gas. I've got enough to get to Santa Maria, even to San Luis Obispo."

"Okay. Go on then. Ain't stopping you."

"Listen. I understand your position. You have a right to make a profit in spite of government red tape."

Nervousness returned to the man's speech. "Look, whyn't you go on? There's plenty other stations up ahead."

The reluctant bandit. Mr. Jimmon was entertained. He had

fully intended to bargain, to offer $2 a gallon, even to threaten with the pistol in the glove compartment. Now it seemed mean and niggling even to protest. What good was money now? "All right," he said, "I'll pay you five dollars a gallon."

Still the other made no move. "In advance."

For the first time Mr. Jimmon was annoyed; time was being wasted. "Just how can I pay you in advance when I don't know how many gallons it'll take to fill the tank?"

The man shrugged.

"Tell you what I'll do. I'll pay for each gallon as you pump it. In advance." He drew out a handful of bills; the bulk of his money was in his wallet, but he'd put the small bills in his pockets. He handed over a five. "Spill the first one on the ground or in a can if you've got one."

"How's that?"

Why should I tell him; give him ideas? As if he hadn't got them already. "Just call me eccentric," he said. "I don't want the first gallon from the pump. Why should you care? It's just five dollars more profit."

For a moment Mr. Jimmon thought the man was going to refuse, and he regarded his foresight with new reverence. Then he reached behind the pump and produced a flatsided tin in which he inserted the flexible end of the hose. Mr. Jimmon handed over the bill, the man wound the handle round and back—it was an ancient gas pump such as Mr. Jimmon hadn't seen for years—and lifted the drooling hose from the can.

"Minute," said Mr. Jimmon.

He stuck two fingers quickly and delicately inside the nozzle and smelled them. Gas all right, not water. He held out a ten-dollar bill. "Start filling."

Jir and Wendell appeared out of the shadows. "Can we stop at a town where there's a movie tonight?"

The handle turned, a cog-toothed rod crept up and retreated, gasoline gurgled into the tank. Movies, thought Mr. Jimmon, handing over another bill; movies, rest rooms, baths, restaurants. Gouge apprehensively lest a scene be made and propriety disturbed. In a surrealist daydream he saw Molly turning the crank, grinding him on the cogs, pouring his essence into insatiable Jir and Wendell. He held out $20.

Twelve gallons had been put in when Molly appeared. "You have a phone here?" he asked casually. Knowing the answer from the blue enameled sign not quite lost among less sturdy ones advertising soft drinks and cigarettes.

"You want to call the cops?" He didn't pause in his pumping.

"No. Know if the lines to L.A."—Mr. Jimmon loathed the abbreviation—"are open yet?" He gave him another ten.

"How should I know?"

Mr. Jimmon beckoned his wife around the other side of the wagon, out of sight. Swiftly but casually he extracted the contents of his wallet. The 200 dollar bills made a fat lump. "Put this in your bag," he said. "Tell you why later. Meantime why don't you try and get Pearl and Dan on the phone? See if they're okay?"

He imagined the puzzled look on her face. "Go on," he urged. "We can spare a minute while he's checking the oil."

He thought there was a hint of uncertainty in Molly's walk as she went toward the store. Erika joined her brothers. The tank gulped: gasoline splashed on the concrete. "Guess that's it."

The man became suddenly brisk as he put up the hose, screwed the gas cap back on. Mr. Jimmon had already disengaged the hood; the man offered the radiator a squirt of water, pulled up the oil gauge, wiped it, plunged it down, squinted at it under the light, and said, "Oil's OK."

"All right," said Mr. Jimmon. "Get in, Erika."

Some of the lights shone directly on her face. Again he noted how mature and self-assured she looked. Erika would survive—and not as a savage either. The man started to wipe the windshield. "Oh, Jir," he said casually, "run in and see if your mother is getting her connection. Tell her we'll wait."

"Aw, furcrysay. I don't see why I always—"

"And ask her to buy a couple of boxes of candy bars if they've got them. Wendell, go with Jir, will you?"

He slid in behind the wheel and closed the door gently. The motor started with hardly a sound. As he put his foot on the clutch and shifted into low he thought Erika turned to him with a startled look. As the station wagon moved forward, he was sure of it.

"It's all right, Erika," said Mr. Jimmon. "I'll explain later." He'd have lots of time to do it.

I first discovered the work of Cordwainer Smith in my late teens, through the good offices of fellow Columbus, Ohio, SF fan John Ayotte, who also introduced me to the work of Zelazny, early Delany, and the arcana of fanzine publishing. I don't remember now which stories of the *Instrumentality of Mankind* I read first, but many of them still remain incandescent in my memory thirty years later; the moving "A Planet Named Shayol" ran "C'mell" a close second in the impossible winnowing for this volume. Happily, the new reader doesn't *have* to choose; the estimable NESFA Press has recently (1993) produced a beautiful collection of all of Cordwainer Smith's shorter works, titled *The Rediscovery of Man*.

"Cordwainer Smith" was the pen-name of Dr. Paul Linebarger, who was not, as I for years had assumed, a medico, but a Ph.D in Political Science (at the age of 23!) The rest of his biography gets even more interesting (among other things, he grew up in Japan, China, France, and Germany, was a godson of Sun Yat-sen, and was the author of the textbook *Psychological Warfare*.) He died far too soon, in 1966, before I even discovered his work. If he'd lived as long as Heinlein, we might have had thirty more years' worth of stories here. I don't know if angels weep, but I could.

Smith's stories first delivered the meaning of "sense of wonder" to me, with a flavor and a music never since matched. All the world is strange and new in one's teens, but the thing is, his tales still deliver, and I'm now pushing fifty. I don't think it's just nostalgia. In little more than a score of pages in "The Ballad of Lost C'mell," Smith gives us a vast and wondrous world, true love, cosmic justice, and great cat-values. You could not ask (nor get) more from most trilogies.

—Lois McMaster Bujold

THE BALLAD OF LOST C'MELL

By Cordwainer Smith

She got the which of the what-she-did,
Hid the bell with a blot, she did,
But she fell in love with a hominid,
Where is the which of the what-she-did?
from THE BALLAD OF LOST C'MELL

She was a girlygirl and they were true men, the lords of creation, but she pitted her wits against them and she won. It had never happened before, and it is sure never to happen again, but she did win. She was not even of human extraction. She was cat-derived, though human in outward shape, which explains the C in front of her name. Her father's name was C'mackintosh and her name C'mell. She won her tricks against the lawful and assembled lords of the Instrumentality.

It all happened at Earthport, greatest of buildings, smallest of cities, standing twenty-five kilometers high at the western edge of the Smaller Sea of Earth.

Jestocost had an office outside the fourth valve.

1

Jestocost liked the morning sunshine, while most of the other lords of Instrumentality did not, so that he had no trouble in keeping the office and the apartments which he had selected. His main office was ninety meters deep, twenty meters high, twenty meters broad. Behind it was the "fourth valve," almost a thousand hectares in extent. It was shaped helically, like an enormous snail. Jestocost's apartment, big as it was, was merely one of the pigeonholes in the muffler on the rim of Earthport. Earthport stood like an enormous wineglass, reaching from the magma to the high atmosphere.

Earthport had been built during mankind's biggest mechanical splurge. Though men had had nuclear rockets since the beginning of consecutive history, they had used chemical rockets to load the interplanetary ion-drive and nuclear-drive vehicles or to assembly the photonic sail-ships for interstellar cruises. Impatient with the troubles of taking things bit by bit into the sky, they had worked out a billion-ton rocket, only to find that it ruined whatever countryside it touched in landing. The Daimoni—people of Earth extraction, who came back from somewhere beyond the stars—had helped men build it of weatherproof, rustproof, timeproof, stressproof material. Then they had gone away and had never come back.

Jestocost often looked around his apartment and wondered what it might have been like when white-hot gas, muted to a whisper, surged out of the valve into his own chamber and the sixty-three other chambers like it. Now he had a back wall of heavy timber, and the valve itself was a great hollow cave where a few wild things lived. Nobody needed that much space any more. The chambers were useful, but the valve did nothing. Planoforming ships whispered in from the stars; they landed at Earthport as a matter of legal convenience, but they made no noise and they certainly had no hot gases.

Jestocost looked at the high clouds far below him and talked to himself.

"Nice day. Good air. No trouble. Better eat."

Jestocost often talked like that to himself. He was an individual, almost an eccentric. One of the top council of mankind, he had problems, but they were not personal problems. He had a Rembrandt hanging above his bed—the only Rembrandt known in the world, just as he was possibly the only person who could appreciate a Rembrandt. He had the tapestries of a forgotten empire hanging from his back wall. Every morning the sun played a grand opera for him, muting and lighting and shifting the colors so that he could almost imagine that the old days of quarrel, murder, and high drama had come back to Earth again. He had a copy of Shakespeare, a copy of Colegrove and two pages of the Book of Ecclesiastes in a locked box beside his bed. Only forty-two people in the universe could read Ancient English, and he was one of them. He drank wine, which he had made by his own robots in his own vineyards on the Sunset coast. He was a man, in short, who had arranged his own life to live comfortably, selfishly, and well on the personal side, so that he could give generously and impartially of his talents on the official side.

When he awoke on this particular morning, he had no idea that a beautiful girl was about to fall hopelessly in love with him—that he would find, after a hundred years and more of experience in government, another government on Earth just as strong and almost as ancient as his own—that he would willingly fling himself into conspiracy and danger for a cause which he only half understood. All these things were mercifully hidden from him by time, so that his only question on arising was, should he or should he not have a small cup of white wine with his breakfast. On the one hundred seventy-third day of each year, he always made a point of eating eggs. They were a rare treat, and he did not want to spoil himself by having too many, nor to deprive himself and forget a treat by having none at all. He puttered around the room, muttering, "White wine? White wine?"

C'mell was coming into his life, but he did not know it. She was fated to win; that part, she herself did not know.

Ever since mankind had gone through the Rediscovery of Man, bringing back governments, money, newspapers, national languages, sickness and occasional death, there had been the problem of the underpeople—people who were not human, but merely humanly shaped from the stock of Earth animals. They could speak, sing, read, write, work, love, and die; but they were not covered by human law, which simply defined them as "homunculi" and gave them a legal status close to animals or robots. Real people from off-world were always called "hominids."

Most of the underpeople did their jobs and accepted their half-slave status without question. Some became famous—C'makintosh had been the first Earth-being to manage a fifty-meter broad-jump under normal gravity. His picture was seen in a thousand worlds. His daughter, C'mell, was a girlygirl, earning her living by welcoming human beings and hominids from the outerworlds and making them feel at home when they reached Earth. She had the privilege of working at Earthport, but she had the duty of working very hard for a living which did not pay well. Human beings and hominids had lived so long in an affluent society that they did not know what it meant to be poor. But the lords of the Instrumentality had decreed that underpeople—derived from animal stock—should live under the economics of the Ancient World; they had to have their own kind of money to pay for their rooms, their food, their possessions, and the education of their children. If they became bankrupt, they went to the Poorhouse, where they were killed painlessly by means of gas.

It was evident that humanity, having settled all of its own basic problems, was not quite ready to let Earth animals, no matter how much they might be changed, assume a full equality with man.

The Lord Jestocost, seventh of that name, opposed the policy. He was a man who had little love, no fear, freedom from ambition, and a dedication to his job: but there are passions of government as deep and challenging as the emotions of love. Two hundred years of thinking himself right and of being outvoted had instilled in Jestocost a furious desire to get things done his own way.

Jestocost was one of the few true men who believed in the rights of the underpeople. He did not think that mankind would ever get around to correcting ancient wrongs unless the underpeople themselves had some of the tools of power—weapons, conspiracy, wealth, and (above all) organization with which to challenge man. He was not afraid of revolt, but he thirsted for justice with an obsessive yearning which overrode all other considerations.

When the lords of the Instrumentality heard that there was the rumor of a conspiracy among the underpeople, they left it to the robot police to ferret it out.

Jestocost did not.

He set up his own police, using underpeople themselves for the purpose, hoping to recruit enemies who would realize that he was a friendly enemy and who would in course of time bring him into touch with the leaders of the underpeople.

If those leaders existed, they were clever. What sign did a girlygirl like C'mell ever give that she was the spearhead of a crisscross of agents who had penetrated Earthport itself? They must, if they existed, be very, very careful. The telepathic monitors, both robotic and human, kept every thought-band under surveillance by random sampling. Even the computers showed nothing more significant than improbable amounts of happiness in minds which had no objective reason for being happy.

The death of her father, the most famous cat-athlete which the underpeople had ever produced, gave Jestocost his first definite clue.

He went to the funeral himself, where the body was packed in an ice-rocket to be shot into space. The mourners were thoroughly mixed with the curiosity-seekers. Sport is international, inter-race, inter-world, inter-species. Hominids were there: true men, one hundred percent human, they looked weird and horrible because they or their ancestors had undergone bodily modifications to meet the life conditions of a thousand worlds.

Underpeople, the animal-derived "homunculi," were there, most of them in their work clothes, and they looked more human than did the human beings from the outer worlds. None were allowed to grow up if they were less than half the size of man, or more than six times the size of man. They all had to have human features and acceptable human voices. The punishment for failure in their elementary schools was death. Jestocost looked over the crowd and wondered to himself, "We have set up the standards of the toughest kind of survival for these people and we give them the most terrible incentive, life itself, as the condition of absolute progress. What fools we are to think that they will not overtake us!" The true people in the group did not seem to think as he did. They tapped the underpeople peremptorily with their canes, even though this was an underperson's funeral, and the bear-men, bull-men, cat-men, and others yielded immediately and with a babble of apology.

C'mell was close to her father's icy coffin.

Jestocost not only watched her; she was pretty to watch. He committed an act which was an indecency in an ordinary citizen but lawful for a lord of the Instrumentality: he peeped her mind.

And then he found something which he did not expect.

As the coffin left, she cried, "Et-telly-kelly, help me! help me!"

She had thought phonetically, not in script, and he had only the raw sound on which to base a search.

Jestocost had not become a lord of the Instrumentality without applying daring. His mind was quick, too quick to be deeply intelligent. He thought by gestalt, not by logic. He determined to force his friendship on the girl.

He decided to await a propitious occasion, and then changed his mind about the time.

As she went home from the funeral, he intruded upon the circle of her grim-faced friends, underpeople who were trying to shield her from the condolences of ill-mannered but well-meaning sports enthusiasts.

She recognized him, and showed him the proper respect.

"My Lord, I did not expect you here. You knew my father?"

He nodded gravely and addressed sonorous words of consolation and sorrow, words which brought a murmur of approval from humans and underpeople alike.

But with his left hand hanging slack at his side, he made the perpetual signal of *alarm! alarm!* used within the Earthport staff—a repeated tapping of the thumb against the third finger—when they had to set one another on guard without alerting the offworld transients.

She was so upset that she almost spoiled it all. While he was still doing his pious doubletalk, she cried in a loud clear voice: "You mean *me?*"

And he went on with his condolences: ". . . and I do mean *you,* C'mell, to be the worthiest carrier of your father's name. *You* are the one to whom we turn in this time of common sorrow. *Who could I mean but you* if I say that C'mackintosh never did things by halves, and died young as a result of his own zealous conscience? Goodbye, C'mell, I go back to my office."

She arrived forty minutes after he did.

2

He faced her straightaway, studying her face.

"This is an important day in your life."

"Yes, my Lord, a sad one."

"I do not," he said, "mean your father's death and burial. I speak of the future to which we all must turn. Right now, it's you and me."

Her eyes widened. She had not thought that he was that kind of man at all. He was an official who moved freely around Earthport, often greeting important offworld visitors and keeping an eye on the bureau of ceremonies. She was a part of the reception team, when a girlygirl was needed to calm down a frustrated arrival or to postpone a quarrel. Like the geisha of ancient Japan, she had an honorable profession; she was not a bad girl but a professionally flirtatious hostess. She stared at the Lord Jestocost. He did not *look* as though he meant anything improperly personal. But, thought she, you can never tell about men.

"You know men," he said, passing the initiative to her.

"I guess so," she said. Her face looked odd. She started to give him smile No. 3 (extremely adhesive) which she had learned in the girlygirl school. Realizing it was wrong, she tried to give him an ordinary smile. She felt she had made a face at him.

"Look at me," he said, "and see if you can trust me. I am going to take both our lives in my hands."

She looked at him. What imaginable subject could involve him, a lord of the Instrumentality, with herself, an undergirl? They never had anything in common. They never would.

But she stared at him.

"I want to help the underpeople."

He made her blink. That was a crude approach, usually followed by a very raw kind of pass indeed. But his face was illuminated by seriousness. She waited.

"Your people do not have enough political power even to talk to us. I will not commit treason to the true human race, but I am willing to give your side an advantage. If you bargain better with us, it will make all forms of life safer in the long run."

C'mell stared at the floor, her red hair soft as the fur of a Persian cat. It made her head seem bathed in flames. Her eyes looked human, except that they had the capacity of reflecting when light struck them; the irises were the rich green of the ancient cat. When she looked right at him, looking up from the floor, her glance had the impact of a blow. "What do you want from me?"

He stared right back. "Watch me. Look at my face. Are you sure, *sure* that I want nothing from you personally?"

She looked bewildered. "What else is there to want from me except personal things? I am a girlygirl. I'm not a person of any importance at all, and I do not have much of an education. You know more, sir, than I will ever know."

"Possibly," he said, watching her.

She stopped feeling like a girlygirl and felt like a citizen. It made her uncomfortable.

"Who," he said, in a voice of great solemnity, "is your own leader?"

"Commissioner Teadrinker, sir. He's in charge of all outworld visitors." She watched Jestocost carefully; he still did not look as if he were playing tricks.

He looked a little cross. "I don't mean him. He's part of my own staff. Who's your leader among the underpeople?"

"My father was, but he died."

Jestocost said, "Forgive me. Please have a seat. But I don't mean that."

She was so tired that she sat down into the chair with an innocent voluptuousness which would have disorganized any ordinary man's day. She wore girlygirl clothes, which were close enough to the everyday fashion to seem agreeably modish when she stood up. In line with her profession, her clothes were designed to be unexpectedly and provocatively revealing when she sat down—not revealing enough to shock the man with their brazenness, but so slit, tripped and cut that he got far more visual stimulation than he expected.

"I must ask you to pull your clothing together a little," said Jestocost in a clinical turn of voice. "I am a man, even if I am an official, and this interview is more important to you and to me than any distraction would be."

She was a little frightened by his tone. She had meant no challenge. With the funeral that day, she meant nothing at all; these clothes were the only kind she had.

He read all this in her face.

Relentlessly, he pursued the subject.

"Young lady, I asked about your leader. You name your boss and you name your father. I want your leader."

"I don't understand," she said, on the edge of a sob, "I don't understand."

Then, he thought to himself, I've got to take a gamble. He thrust the mental dagger home, almost drove his words like steel straight into her face. "Who . . ." he said slowly and icily, "is . . . Ee . . . telly . . . kelly?"

The girl's face had been cream-colored, pale with sorrow. Now she went white. She twisted away from him. Her eyes glowed like twin fires.

Her eyes . . . like twin fires.

(No undergirl, thought Jestocost as he reeled, could hypnotize me.)

Her eyes . . . were like cold fires.

The room faded around him. The girl disappeared. Her eyes became a single white, cold fire.

Within this fire stood the figure of a man. His arms were wings, but he had human hands growing at the elbows of his wings. His face was clear, white, cold as the marble of an ancient statue; his eyes were opaque white. "I am the E'telekeli. You will believe in me. You may speak to my daughter C'mell."

The image faded.

Jestocost saw the girl staring as she sat awkwardly on the chair, looking blindly through him. He was on the edge of making a joke about her hypnotic capacity when he saw that she was still deeply hypnotized, even after he had been released. She had stiffened and again her clothing had fallen into its planned disarray. The effect was not stimulating; it was pathetic beyond words, as though an accident had happened to a pretty child. He spoke to her.

He spoke to her, not really expecting an answer.

"Who are you?" he said to her, testing her hypnosis.

"I am he whose name is never said aloud," said the girl in a sharp whisper, "I am he whose secret you have penetrated. I have printed my image and my name in your mind."

Jestocost did not quarrel with ghosts like this. He snapped out a decision. "If I open my mind, will you search it while I watch you? Are you good enough to do that?"

"I am very good," hissed the voice in the girl's mouth.

C'mell arose and put her two hands on his shoulders. She looked into his eyes. He looked back. A strong telepath himself, Jestocost was not prepared for the enormous thought-voltage which poured out of her.

Look in my mind, he commanded, for the subject of *underpeople* only.

I see it, thought the mind behind C'mell.

Do you see what I mean to do for the underpeople?

Jestocost heard the girl breathing hard as her mind served as a relay to his. He tried to remain calm so that he could see which part of his mind was being searched. Very good so far, he thought to himself. An intelligence like that on Earth itself, he thought—and we of the lords not knowing it!

The girl hacked out a dry little laugh.

Jestocost thought at the mind, Sorry. Go ahead.

This plan of yours—thought the strange mind—may I see more of it?

That's all there is.

Oh, said the strange mind, you want me to think for you. Can you give me the keys in the Bell and Bank which pertain to destroying underpeople?

You can have the information keys if I can ever get them, thought Jestocost, but not the control keys and not the master switch of the Bell.

Fair enough, thought the other mind, and what do I pay for them?

You support me in my policies before the Instrumentality. You keep the underpeople reasonable, if you can, when the time comes to negotiate. You maintain honor and good faith in all subsequent agreements. But how can I get the keys? It would take me a year to figure them out myself.

Let the girl look once, thought the strange mind, and I will be behind her. Fair?

Fair, thought Jestocost.

Break? thought the mind.

How do we re-connect? thought Jestocost back.

As before. Through the girl. Never say my name. Don't think it if you can help it. Break?

Break! thought Jestocost.

The girl, who had been holding his shoulders, drew his face down and kissed him firmly and warmly. He had never touched an underperson before, and it never had occurred to him that he might kiss one. It was pleasant, but he took her arms away from his neck, half-turned her around, and let her lean against him.

"Daddy!" she sighed happily.

Suddenly she stiffened, looked at his face, and sprang for the door. "Jestocost!" she cried. "Lord Jestocost! What am I doing here?"

"Your duty is done, my girl. You may go."

She staggered back into the room. "I'm going to be sick," she said. She vomited on his floor.

He pushed a button for a cleaning robot and slapped his desk-top for coffee.

She relaxed and talked about his hopes for the underpeople. She stayed an hour. By the time she left they had a plan. Neither of them had mentioned E'telekeli, neither had put purposes in the open. If the monitors had been listening, they would have found no single sentence or paragraph which was suspicious.

When she had gone, Jestocost looked out of his window. He saw the clouds far below and he knew the world below him was in twilight. He had planned to help the underpeople, and he had met powers of which organize mankind had no conception or perception. He was righter than he had thought. He had to go on through.

But as partner—C'mell herself!

Was there ever an odder diplomat in the history of the worlds?

3

In less than a week they had decided what to do. It was the Council of the lords of the Instrumentality at which they would work—the brain center itself. The risk was high, but the entire job could be done in a few minutes if it were done at the Bell itself.

This is the sort of thing which interested Jestocost.

He did not know that C'mell watched him with two different facets of her mind. One side of her was alertly and wholeheartedly his fellow-conspirator, utterly in sympathy with the revolutionary aims to which they were both committed. The other side of her—was feminine.

She had a womanliness which was truer than that of any hominid woman. She knew the value of her trained smile, her splendidly kept red hair with its unimaginably soft texture, her lithe young figure with firm breasts and persuasive hips. She knew down to the last millimeter the effect which her legs had on hominid men. True humans kept few secrets from her. The men betrayed themselves by their unfulfillable desires, the women by their irrepressible jealousies. But she knew people best of all by not being one herself. She had to learn by imitation, and imitation is conscious. A thousand little things which ordinary women took for granted, or thought about just once in a whole lifetime, were subjects of acute and intelligent study to her. She was a girl by profession; she was a human by assimilation; she was an inquisitive cat in her genetic nature. Now she was falling in love with Jestocost, and she knew it.

Even she did not realize that the romance would sometime leak out into rumor, be magnified into legend, distilled into romance. She had no idea of the ballad about herself that would open with the lines which became famous much later:

She got the which of the what-she-did,
Hid the bell with a blot, she did,
But she fell in love with a hominid.
Where is the which of the what-she-did?

All this lay in the future, and she did not know it.

She knew her own past.

She remembered the off-Earth prince who had rested his head in her lap and had said, sipping his glass of mott by way of farewell:

"Funny, C'mell, you're not even a person and you're the most intelligent human being I've met in this place. Do you know it made my planet poor to send me here? And what did I get out of them? Nothing, nothing, and a thousand times nothing. But you, now. If you'd been running the government of Earth, I'd have gotten what my people need, and this world would be richer too. Manhome, they call it. Manhome, my eye! The only smart person on it is a female cat."

He ran his fingers around her ankle. She did not stir. That was part of hospitality, and she had her own ways of making sure that hospitality did not go too far. Earth police were watching her; to them, she was a convenience maintained for outworld people, something like a soft chair in the Earthport lobbies or a drinking fountain with acid-tasting water for strangers who could not tolerate the insipid water of Earth. She was not expected to have feelings or to get involved. If she had ever caused an incident, they would have punished her fiercely, as they often punished animals or underpeople, or else (after a short formal hearing with no appeal) they would have destroyed her, as the law allowed and custom encouraged.

She had kissed a thousand men, maybe fifteen hundred. She had made them feel welcome and she had gotten their complaints or their secrets out of them as they left. It was a living, emotionally tiring but intellectually very stimulating. Sometimes it made her laugh to look at human women with their pointed-up noses and their proud airs, and to realize that she knew more about the men who belonged to the human women than the human women themselves ever did.

Once a policewoman had had to read over the record of two pioneers from New Mars. C'mell had been given the job of keeping in very close touch with them. When the policewoman got through reading the report she looked at C'mell and her face was distorted with jealousy and prudish rage.

"Cat, you call yourself. Cat! You're a pig, you're a dog, you're an animal. You may be working for Earth but don't ever get the idea that you're as good as a person. I think it's a crime that the Instrumentality lets monsters like you greet real human beings from outside! I can't stop it. But may the Bell help you, girl, if you ever touch a real Earth man! If you ever get near one! If you ever try tricks here! Do you understand me?"

"Yes, Ma'am," C'mell had said. To herself she thought, "That poor thing doesn't know how to select her own clothes or how to do her own hair. No wonder she resents somebody who manages to be pretty."

Perhaps the policewoman thought that raw hatred would be shocking to C'mell. It wasn't. Underpeople were used to hatred, and it was not any worse raw than it was when cooked with politeness and served like poison. They had to live with it.

But now, it was all changed.

She had fallen in love with Jestocost.

Did he love her?

Impossible. No, not impossible. Unlawful, unlikely, indecent—yes, all these, but not impossible. Surely he felt something of her love.

If he did, he gave no sign of it.

People and underpeople had fallen in love many times before. The underpeople were always destroyed and the real people brainwashed. There were laws against that kind of thing. The scientists among people had created the underpeople, had given them capacities which real people did not have (the fifty-meter jump, the telepath two miles underground, the turtle-man waiting a thousand years next to an emergency door, the cow-man guarding a gate without reward), and the scientists had also given many of the underpeople the human shape. It was handier that way. The human eye, the five-fingered hand, the human size—these were convenient for engineering reasons. By making underpeople the same size and shape as people, more or less, the scientists eliminated the need for two or three or a dozen different sets of furniture. The human form was good enough for all of them.

But they had forgotten the human heart.

And now she, C'mell had fallen in love with a man, a true man old enough to have been her own father's grandfather.

But she didn't feel daughterly about him at all. She remembered that with her own father there was an easy comradeship, an innocent and forthcoming affection, which masked the fact that he was considerably more catlike than she was. Between them there was an aching void of forever-unspoken words—things that couldn't quite be said by either of them, perhaps things that couldn't be said at all. They were so close to each other that they could get no closer. This created enormous distance, which was heart-breaking but unutterable. Her father had died, and now this true man was here, with all the kindness—

"That's it," she whispered to herself, "with all the kindness that none of these passing men have ever really shown. With all the depth which my poor underpeople can never get. Not that it's not in them But they're born like dirt, treated like dirt, put away like dirt when they die. How can any of my own men develop real kindness? There's a special sort of majesty to kindness. It's the best part there is to being people. And he has whole oceans of it in him. And it's strange, strange, strange that he's never given his real love to any human woman."

She stopped, cold.

Then she consoled herself and whispered on, "Or if he did, it's so long ago that it doesn't matter now. He's got *me*. Does he know it?"

4

The Lord Jestocost did know, and yet he didn't. He was used to getting loyalty from people, because he offered loyalty and honor in his daily work. He was even familiar with loyalty becoming obsessive and seeking physical form, particularly from women, children and underpeople. He had always coped with it before. He was gambling on the fact that C'mell was a wonderfully intelligent person, and that as a girlygirl, working on the hospitality staff of the Earthport police, she must have learned to control her personal feelings.

"We're born in the wrong age," he thought, "when I meet the most intelligent and beautiful female I've ever met, and then have to put business first. But this stuff about people and underpeople is sticky. Sticky. We've got to keep personalities out of it."

So he thought. Perhaps he was right.

If the nameless one, whom he did not dare to remember, commanded an attack on the Bell itself, that was worth their lives. Their emotions could not come into it. The Bell mattered; justice mattered; the perpetual return of mankind to progress mattered. He did not matter, because he had already done most of his work. C'mell did not matter, because their failure would leave her with mere underpeople forever. The Bell did count.

The price of what he proposed to do was high, but the entire job could be done in a few minutes if it were done at the Bell itself.

The Bell, of course, was not a Bell. It was a three-dimensional situation table, three times the height of a man. It was set one story below the meeting room, and shaped roughly like an ancient bell. The meeting table of the lords of the Instrumentality had a circle cut out of it, so that the lords could look down into the Bell at whatever situation one of them called up either manually or telepathically. The Bank below it, hidden by the floor, was the key memory-bank of the entire system. Duplicates existed at thirty-odd other places on Earth. Two duplicates lay hidden in interstellar space, one of them beside the ninety-million-mile gold-colored ship left over from the war against Raumsog and the other masked as an asteroid.

Most of the lords were off-world on the business of the Instrumentality.

Only three besides Jestocost were present—the Lady Johanna Gnade, the Lord Issan Olascoaga and the Lord William Not-from-here. (The Not-from-heres were a great Norstrilian family which had migrated back to Earth many generations before.)

The E'telekeli told Jestocost the rudiments of a plan.

He was to bring C'mell into the chambers on a summons.

The summons was to be serious.

They should avoid her summary death by automatic justice, if the relays began to trip.

C'mell would go into partial trance in the chamber.

He was then to call the items in the Bell which E'telekeli wanted traced. A single call would be enough. E'telekeli would take the responsibility for tracing them. The other lords would be distracted by him, E'telekeli.

It was simple in appearance.

The complication came in action.

The plan seemed flimsy, but there was nothing which Jestocost could do at this time. He began to curse himself for letting his passion for policy involve him in the intrigue. It was too late to back out with honor; besides, he had given his word; besides, he liked C'mell—as a being, not as a girlygirl—and he would hate to see her marked with disappointment for life. He knew how the underpeople cherished their identities and their status.

With heavy heart but quick mind he went to the council chamber. A dog-girl, one of the routine messengers whom he had seen many months outside the door, gave him the minutes.

He wondered how C'mell or E'telekeli would reach him, once he was inside the chamber with its tight net of telepathic intercepts.

He sat wearily at the table—

And almost jumped out of his chair.

The conspirators had forged the minutes themselves, and the top item was: "C'mell daughter to C'makintosh, cat stock (pure), lot 1138, confession of. Subject: conspiracy to export homuncular material. References: planet De Prinsensmacht."

The Lady Johanna Gnade had already pushed the buttons for the planet concerned. The people there, Earth by origin, were enormously strong but they had gone to great pains to maintain the original Earth appearance. One of their first-men was at the moment on Earth. He bore the title of the Twilight Prince (Prins van de Schemering) and he was on a mixed diplomatic and trading mission.

Since Jestocost was a little late, C'mell was being brought into the room as he glanced over the minutes.

The Lord Not-from-here asked Jestocost if he would preside.

"I beg you, Sir and Scholar," he said, "to join me in asking the Lord Issan to preside this time."

The presidency was a formality. Jestocost could watch the Bell and Bank better if he did not have to chair the meeting too.

C'mell wore the clothing of a prisoner. On her it looked good. He had never seen her wearing anything but girlygirl clothes before. The pale-blue prison tunic made her look very young, very human, very tender, and very frightened. The cat family showed only in the fiery cascade of her hair and the lithe power of her body as she sat, demure and erect.

Lord Issan asked her: "You have confessed. Confess again."

"This man," and she pointed at a picture of the Twilight Prince, "wanted to go to the place where they torment human children for a show."

"What!" cried three of the lords together.

"What place?" said the Lady Johanna, who was bitterly in favor of kindness.

"It's run by a man who looks like this gentleman here," said C'mell, pointing at Jestocost. Quickly, so that nobody could stop her, but modestly, so that none of them thought to doubt her, she circled the room and touched Jestocost's shoulder. He felt a thrill of contact-telepathy and heard bird-cackle in her brain. Then he knew that the E'telekeli was in touch with her.

"The man who has the place," said C'mell, "is five pounds lighter than this gentleman, two inches shorter, and he has red hair. His place is at the Cold Sunset corner of Earthport, down the boulevard and under the boulevard. Underpeople, some of them with bad reputations, live in that neighborhood."

The Bell went milky, flashing through hundreds of combinations of bad underpeople in that part of the city. Jestocost felt himself staring at the casual milkiness with unwanted concentration.

The Bell cleared.

It showed the vague image of a room in which children were playing Hallowe'en tricks.

The Lady Johanna laughed, "Those aren't people. They're robots. It's just a dull old play."

"Then," added C'mell, "he wanted a dollar and a shilling to take home. Real ones. There was a robot who had found some."

"What are those?" said Lord Issan.

"Ancient money—the real money of old America and old Australia," cried Lord William. "I have copies, but there are no originals outside the state museum." He was an ardent, passionate collector of coins.

"The robot found them in an old hiding place right under Earthport."

Lord William almost shouted at the Bell. "Run through every hiding place and get me that money."

The Bell clouded. In finding the bad neighborhoods it had flashed every police point in the northwest sector of the tower. Now it scanned all the police points under the tower, and ran dizzily through thousands of combinations before it settled on an old toolroom. A robot was polishing circular pieces of metal.

When Lord William saw the polishing, he was furious. "Get that here," he shouted. "I want to buy those myself!"

"All right," said Lord Issan. "It's a little irregular, but all right."

The machine showed the key search devices and brought the robot to the escalator.

The Lord Issan said, "This isn't much of a case."

C'mell sniveled. She was a good actress. "Then he wanted me to get a homunculus egg. One of the E-type, derived from birds, for him to take home."

Issan put on the search device.

"Maybe," said C'mell, "somebody has already put it in the disposal series."

The Bell and the Bank ran through all the disposal devices at high speed. Jestocost felt his nerves go on edge. No human being could have memorized these thousands of patterns as they flashed across the Bell too fast for human eyes, but the brain reading the Bell through his eyes was not human. It might even be locked into a computer of its own. It was, thought Jestocost, an indignity for a lord of the Instrumentality to be used as a human spy-glass.

The machine blotted up.

"You're a fraud," cried the Lord Issan. "There's no evidence."

"Maybe the offworlder tried," said the Lady Johanna.

"Shadow him," said Lord William. "If he would steal ancient coins he would steal anything."

The Lady Johanna turned to C'mell. "You're a silly thing. You have wasted our time and you have kept us from serious inter-world business."

"It *is* inter-world business," wept C'mell. She let her hand slip from Jestocost's shoulder, where it had rested all the time. The body-to-body relay broke and the telepathic link broke with it.

"We should judge that," said Lord Issan.

"You might have been punished," said Lady Johanna.

The Lord Jestocost had said nothing, but there was a glow of happiness in him. If the E'telekeli was half as good as he seemed, the underpeople had a list of checkpoints and escape routes which would make it easier to hide from the capricious sentence of painless death which human authorities meted out.

5

There was singing in the corridors that night.

Underpeople burst into happiness for no visible reason.

C'mell danced a wild cat dance for the next customer who came in from outworld stations, that very evening. When she got home to bed, she knelt before the picture of her father C'mackintosh and thanked the E'telekeli for what Jestocost had done.

But the story became known a few generations later, when the Lord Jestocost had won acclaim for being the champion of the underpeople and when the authorities, still unaware of E'telekeli, accepted the elected representatives of the underpeople as negotiators for better terms of life; and C'mell had died long since.

She had first had a long, good life.

She became a female chef when she was too old to be a girlygirl. Her food was famous. Jestocost once visited her. At the end of the meal he had asked, "There's a silly rhyme among the underpeople. No human beings know it except me."

"I don't care about rhymes," she said.

"This is called 'The what-she-did.' "

C'mell blushed all the way down to the neckline of her capacious blouse. She had filled out a lot in middle age. Running the restaurant had helped.

"Oh, that rhyme!" she said. "It's silly."

"It says you were in love with a hominid."

"No," she said. "I wasn't." Her green eyes, as beautiful as ever, stared deeply into his. Jestocost felt uncomfortable. This was getting personal. He liked political relationships; personal things made him uncomfortable.

The light in the room shifted and her cat eyes blazed at him, she looked like the magical fire-haired girl he had known.

"I wasn't in love. You couldn't call it that . . ."

Her heart cried out, *It was you, it was you, it was you.*

"But the rhyme," insisted Jestocost, "says it was a hominid. It wasn't that Prins van de Schemering?"

"Who was he?" C'mell asked the question quietly, but her emotions cried out, *Darling, will you never, never know?*

"The strong man."

"Oh, him. I've forgotten him."

Jestocost rose from the table. "You've had a good life,

C'mell. You've been a citizen, a committeewoman, a leader. And do you even know how many children you have had?"

"Seventy-three," she snapped at him. "Just because they're multiple doesn't mean we don't know them."

His playfulness left him. His face was grave, his voice kindly. "I meant no harm, C'mell."

He never knew that when he left she went back to the kitchen and cried for a while. It was Jestocost whom she had vainly loved ever since they had been comrades, many long years ago.

Even after she died, at the full age of five-score and three, he kept seeing her about the corridors and shafts of Earthport. Many of her great-granddaughters looked just like her and several of them practiced the girlygirl business with huge success.

They were not half-slaves. They were citizens (reserved grade) and they had photopasses which protected their property, their identity, and their rights. Jestocost was the godfather to them all; he was often embarrassed when the most voluptuous creatures in the universe threw playful kisses at him. All he asked was fulfillment of his political passions, not his personal ones. He had always been in love, madly in love—

With justice itself.

At last, his own time came, and he knew that he was dying, and he was not sorry. He had had a wife, hundreds of years ago, and had loved her well; their children had passed into the generations of man.

In the ending, he wanted to know something, and he called to a nameless one (or to his successor) far beneath the ground. He called with his mind till it was a scream.

I have helped your people.

"Yes," came back the faintest of faraway whispers, inside his head.

I am dying. I must know. Did she love me?

"She went on without you, so much did she love you. She let you go, for your sake, not for hers. She really loved you. More than death. More than life. More than time. You will never be apart."

Never apart?

"Not, not in the memory of man," said the voice, and was then still.

Jestocost lay back on his pillow and waited for the day to end.

The author I select is Stanley G. Weinbaum for his story "A Martian Odyssey."

Stanley G. Weinbaum (1902–35) was one of the most promising and influential of the science fiction writers who started their careers in the early 1930s. He graduated from the University of Wisconsin in 1923, and worked as a chemical engineer. When he started writing for science fiction magazines his work was quickly acclaimed for its originality and humor. His writing was more literate, mature, and scientifically sound than that of most of his competitors. He soon gave up engineering and devoted himself to fiction.

Weinbaum wrote a number of popular short stories and novels during the next few years. One of his favorite themes was the superwoman. Just as he was becoming America's leading science fiction writers, sadly at thirty-three he died of cancer.

"A Martian Odyssey," published in 1934, introduces several concepts in advance of its time. Its extraterrestrials are not improbably human beings, fighting with swords, or enjoying lives of utopian perfection, as they often had been in the works of earlier writers. Neither are they conventional bug-eyed monsters, menacing the heroine with malevolent tentacles. They are sometimes intelligent, but usually so different from mankind in their thinking that communication with human beings is difficult or impossible. In addition, the crew of Weinbaum's visiting space ship is international, as crews of astronauts may soon be.

"A Martian Odyssey" is one of the few early science fiction stories that I can still read with pleasure today.

—L. Sprague de Camp

A MARTIAN ODYSSEY

by Stanley G. Weinbaum

Jarvis stretched himself as luxuriously as he could in the cramped general quarters of the *Ares*.

"Air you can breathe!" he exulted. "It feels as thick as soup after the thin stuff out there!" He nodded at the Martian landscape stretching flat and desolate in the light of the nearer moon, beyond the glass of the port.

The other three stared at him sympathetically—Putz, the engineer; Leroy, the biologist; and Harrison, the astronomer and captain of the expedition. Dick Jarvis was chemist of the famous crew, the *Ares* expedition, first human beings to set foot on the mysterious neighbor of the earth, the planet Mars. This, of course, was in the old days, less than twenty years after the mad American Doheny perfected the atomic blast at the cost of his life, and only a decade after the equally mad Cardoza rode on it to the moon. They were true pioneers, these four of the *Ares*. Except for a half-dozen moon expeditions and the ill-fated de Lancey flight aimed at the seductive orb of Venus, they were the first men to feel other gravity than Earth's, and certainly the first successful crew to leave the Earth-moon system. And they deserved that success when one considers the difficulties and discomforts—the months spent in acclimatization chambers back on Earth, learning to breathe the air as tenuous as that of Mars, the challenging of the void in the tiny rocket driven by the cranky reaction motors of the twenty-first century, and mostly the facing of an absolutely unknown world.

Jarvis stretched and fingered the raw and peeling tip of his frost-bitten nose. He sighed again contentedly.

"Well," exploded Harrison abruptly, "are we going to hear what happened? You set out all shipshape in an auxiliary rocket, we don't get a peep for ten days, and finally Putz here picks you out of a lunatic ant-heap with a freak ostrich as your pal! Spill it, man!"

"Speel?" queried Leroy perplexedly. "Speel what?"

"He means *'spiel'*," explained Putz soberly. "It iss to tell."

Jarvis met Harrison's amused glance without the shadow of a smile. "That's right, Karl," he said in grave agreement with Putz. *"Ich spiel es!"* He grunted comfortably and began.

"According to orders," he said, "I watched Karl here take off toward the north, and then I got into my flying sweat-box and headed south. You'll remember, Cap—we had orders not to land, but just scout about for points of interest. I set the two cameras clicking and buzzed along, riding pretty high—about two thousand feet—for a couple of reasons. First, it gave the cameras a greater field, and second, the under-jets travel so far in this half-vacuum they call air here that they stir up dust if you move low."

"We know all that from Putz," grunted Harrison. "I wish you'd saved the films, though. They'd have paid the cost of this junket; remember how the public mobbed the first moon pictures?"

"The films are safe," retorted Jarvis. "Well," he resumed, "as I said, I buzzed along at a pretty good clip; just as we figured, the wings haven't much life in this air at less than a hundred miles per hour, and even then I had to use the under-jets.

"So, with the speed and the altitude and the blurring caused by the under-jets, the seeing wasn't any too good. I could see enough, though, to distinguish that what I sailed over was just more of this gray plain that we'd been examining the whole week since our landing—some blobby growths and the same eternal carpet of crawling little plant-animals, or biopods, as Leroy calls them. So I sailed along, calling back my position every hour as instructed, and not knowing whether you heard me."

"I did!" snapped Harrison.

"A hundred and fifty miles south," continued Jarvis imperturbably, "the surface changed to a sort of low plateau, nothing but desert and orange-tinted sand. I figured that we were right in our guess, then, and this gray plain we dropped on was really the Mare Cimmerium which would make my orange desert the region called Xanthus. If I were right, I ought to hit another gray plain, the Mare Chronium in another couple of hundred miles, and then another orange desert, Thyle I or II. And so I did."

"Putz verified our position a week and a half ago!" grumbled the captain. "Let's get to the point."

"Coming!" remarked Jarvis. "Twenty miles into Thyle—believe it or not—I crossed a canal!"

"Putz photographed a hundred! Let's hear something new!"

"And did he also see a city?"

"Twenty of 'em, if you call those heaps of mud cities!"

"Well," observed Jarvis, "from here on I'll be telling a few things Putz didn't see!" He rubbed his tingling nose, and continued. "I knew that I had sixteen hours of daylight at this season, so eight hours—eight hundred miles—from here, I decided to turn back. I was still over Thyle, whether I or II I'm not sure, not more than twenty-five miles into it. And right there, Putz's pet motor quit!"

"Quit? How?" Putz was solicitous.

"The atomic blast got weak. I started losing altitude right away, and suddenly there I was with a thump right in the middle of Thyle! Smashed my nose on the window, too!" He rubbed the injured member ruefully.

"Did you maybe try vashing der combustion chamber mit acid sulphuric?" inquired Putz. "Sometimes der lead giffs a secondary radiation—"

"Haw!" said Jarvis disgustedly. "I wouldn't try that, of course—not more than ten times! Besides, the bump flattened the landing gear and busted off the under-jets. Suppose I got the thing working—what then? Ten miles with the blast coming right out of the bottom and I'd have melted the floor from under me!" He rubbed his nose again. "Lucky for me a pound only weighs seven ounces here, or I'd have been mashed flat!"

"I could have fixed!" ejaculated the engineer. "I bet it vas not serious."

"Probably not," agreed Jarvis sarcastically. "Only it wouldn't fly. Nothing serious, but I had my choice of waiting to be picked up or trying to walk back—eight hundred miles, and perhaps twenty days before we had to leave! Forty miles a day! Well," he concluded, "I chose to walk. Just as much chance of being picked up, and it kept me busy."

"We'd have found you," said Harrison.

"No doubt. Anyway, I rigged up a harness from some seat straps, and put the water tank on my back, took a cartridge belt and revolver, and some iron rations, and started out."

"Water tank!" exclaimed the little biologist, Leroy. "She weigh one-quarter ton!"

"Wasn't full. Weighed about two hundred and fifty pounds earth-weight, which is eighty-five here. Then, besides, my own personal two hundred and ten pounds is only seventy on Mars, so, tank and all, I grossed a hundred and fifty-five, or fifty-five pounds less than my everyday earth-weight. I figured on that when I undertook the forty-mile daily stroll. Oh—of course I took a thermo-skin sleeping bag for these wintry Martian nights.

"Off I went, bouncing along pretty quickly. Eight hours of daylight meant twenty miles or more. It got tiresome, of course—plugging along over a soft sand desert with nothing to see, not even Leroy's crawling biopods. But an hour or so brought me to the canal—just a dry ditch about four hundred feet wide, and straight as a railroad on its own company map.

"There's been water in it sometime, though. The ditch was covered with what looked like a nice green lawn. Only, as I approached, the lawn moved out of my way!"

"Eh?" said Leroy.

"Yeah, it was relative of your biopods. I caught one—a little grasslike blade about as long as my finger, with two thin, stemmy legs."

"He is where?" Leroy was eager.

"He is let go! I had to move, so I plowed along with the walking grass opening in front and closing behind. And then I was out on the orange desert of Thyle again.

"I plugged steadily along, cussing the sand that made going so tiresome, and, incidentally, cussing that cranky motor of yours, Karl. It was just before twilight that I reached the edge of Thyle, and looked down over the gray Mare Chronium. And I knew there was seventy-five miles of *that* to be walked over, and then a couple of hundred miles of that Xanthus desert, and about as much more Mare Cimmerium. Was I pleased? I started cussing you fellows for not picking me up!"

"We were trying, you sap!" said Harrison.

"That didn't help. Well, I figured I might as well use what was left of daylight in getting down the cliff that bounded Thyle. I found an easy place, and down I went. Mare Chronium was just the same sort of place as this—crazy leafless plants and a bunch of crawlers; I gave it a glance and hauled out my sleeping bag. Up to that time, you know, I hadn't seen anything worth worrying about on this half-dead world—nothing dangerous, that is."

"Did you?" queried Harrison.

"*Did I!* You'll hear about it when I come to it. Well, I was just about to turn in when suddenly I heard the wildest sort of shenanigans!"

"Vot iss shenanigans?" inquired Putz.

He says, 'Je ne sais quoi,' " explained Leroy. "It is to say, 'I don't know what' "

"That's right," agreed Jarvis. "I didn't know what, so I sneaked over to find out. There was a racket like a flock of crows eating a bunch of canaries—whistles, cackles, caws, trills, and what have you. I rounded a clump of stumps, and there was Tweel!"

"Tweel?" said Harrison, and "Tveel?" said Leroy and Putz.

"That freak ostrich," explained the narrator. "At least, Tweel is as near as I can pronounce it without sputtering. He called it something like 'Trrrweerrlll.' "

"What was he doing?" asked the captain.

"He was being eaten! And squealing, of course, as any one would."

"Eaten! By what?"

"I found out later. All I could see then was a bunch of black ropy arms tangled around what looked like, as Putz described it to you, an ostrich. I wasn't going to interfere, naturally; if both creatures were dangerous, I'd have one less to worry about.

"But the bird-like thing was putting up a good battle, dealing vicious blows with an eighteen-inch beak, between screeches. And besides, I caught a glimpse or two of what was on the end of those arms!" Jarvis shuddered. "But the clincher was when I noticed a little black bag or case hung about the neck of the bird-thing! It was intelligent! That or tame, I assumed. Anyway, it clinched my decision. I pulled out my automatic and fired into what I could see of its antagonist.

"There was a flurry of tentacles and a spurt of black corruption, and then the thing, with a disgusting sucking noise, pulled itself and its arms into a hole in the ground. The other let out a series of clacks, staggered around on legs about as thick as golf sticks, and turned suddenly to face me. I held my weapon ready, and the two of us stared at each other.

"The Martian wasn't a bird, really. It wasn't even bird-like, except just at first glance. It had a beak all right, and a few feathery appendages, but the beak wasn't really a beak. It was somewhat flexible; I could see the tip bend slowly from side to side; it was almost like a cross between a beak and a trunk. It had four-toed feet, and four-fingered things—hands, you'd have to call them, and a little roundish body, and a long neck ending in a tiny head—and that beak. It stood an inch or so taller than I, and—well, Putz saw it!"

The engineer nodded. "*Ja!* I saw!"

Jarvis continued. "So—we stared at each other. Finally the creature went into a series of clackings and twitterings and held out its hands toward me, empty. I took that as a gesture of friendship."

"Perhaps," suggested Harrison, "it looked at that nose of yours and thought you were its brother!"

"Huh! You can be funny without talking! Anyway, I put up my gun and said 'Aw, don't mention it,' or something of the sort, and the thing came over and we were pals.

"By that time, the sun was pretty low and I knew that I'd better build a fire or get into my thermo-skin. I decided on the fire. I picked a spot at the base of the Thyle cliff, where the rock could reflect a little heat on my back. I started breaking off chunks of this desicated Martian vegetation, and my companion caught the idea and brought in an armful. I reached for a match, but the Martian fished into his pouch and brought out something that looked like a glowing coal; one touch of it, and the fire was blazing—and you all know what a job we have starting a fire in this atmosphere!

"And that bag of his!" continued the narrator. "That was a manufactured article, my friends; press an end and she popped open—press the middle and she sealed so perfectly you couldn't see the line. Better than zippers.

"Well, we stared at the fire a while and I decided to attempt some sort of communication with the Martian. I pointed at myself and said 'Dick'; he caught the drift immediately, stretched a bony claw at me and repeated. 'Tick.' Then I pointed at him, and he gave that whistle I called Tweel; I can't imitate his accent. Things were going smoothly; to emphasize the names, I repeated 'Dick,' and then, pointing at him 'Tweel.'

"There we stuck! He gave some clacks that sounded negative, and said something like 'P-p-p-root.' And that was just the beginning; I was always 'Tick,' but as for him—part of the time he was 'Tweel,' and part of the time he was 'P-p-p-root,' and part of the time he was sixteen other noises!

"We just couldn't connect. I tried 'rock,' and I tried 'star,' and 'tree,' and 'fire,' and Lord knows what else, and try as I would, I couldn't get a single word! Nothing was the same for two successive minutes, and if that's a language, I'm an alchemist! Finally I gave it up and called him Tweel, and that seemed to do.

"But Tweel hung on to some of my words. He remembered a couple of them, which I suppose is a great achievement if you're used to a language you have to make up as you go along. But I couldn't get the hang of his talk; either I missed some subtle point or we just didn't *think* alike—and I rather believe the latter view.

"I've other reasons for believing that. After a while I gave up the language business, and tried mathematics. I scratched two plus two equals four on the ground, and demonstrated it with pebbles. Again Tweel caught the idea, and informed me that three plus three equals six. Once more we seemed to be getting somewhere.

"So, knowing that Tweel had at least a grammar school education, I drew a circle for the sun, pointing first at it, and then at the last glow of the sun. Then I sketched in Mercury, and Venus, and Mother Earth, and Mars, and finally pointing to Mars, I swept my hand around in a sort of inclusive gesture to indicate that Mars was our current environment. I was working up to putting over the idea that my home was on the Earth.

"Tweel understood my diagram all right. He poked his beak at it, and with a great deal of trilling and clucking, he added Deimos and Phobos to Mars, and then sketched in the Earth's moon!

"Do you see what that proves? It proves that Tweel's race uses telescopes—that they're civilized!"

"Does not!" snapped Harrison. "The moon is visible from here as a fifth magnitude star. They could see its revolution with the naked eye."

"The moon, yes!" said Jarvis. "You've missed my point. Mercury isn't visible! And Tweel knew of Mercury because he placed the moon at the *third* planet, not the second. If he didn't know Mercury, he'd put the Earth second, and Mars third, instead of fourth! See?"

"Humph!" said Harrison.

"Anyway," proceeded Jarvis, "I went on with my lesson. Things were going smoothly, and it looked as if I could put the idea over. I pointed at the earth on my diagram, and then at myself, and then, to clinch it, I pointed to myself and then to the Earth itself shining bright green almost at the zenith.

"Tweel set up such an excited clacking that I was certain he understood. He jumped up and down, and suddenly he pointed at himself and then at the sky, and then at himself and at the sky again. He pointed at his middle and then at Arcturus, at his head and then at Spica, at his feet and then at half a dozen stars, while I just gaped at him. Then, all of a sudden, he gave a tremendous leap. Man, what a hop! He shot straight up into the starlight, seventy-five feet if an inch! I saw him silhouetted against the sky, saw him turn and come down at me head first, and land smack on his beak like a javelin! There he stuck square in the center of my sun-circle in the sand—a bull's eye!"

"Nuts!" observed the captain. "Plain nuts!"

"That's what I thought, too! I just stared at him open-mouthed while he pulled his head out of the sand and stood up. Then I figured he'd missed my point, and I went through the whole blamed rigmarole again, and it ended the same way, with Tweel on his nose in the middle of my picture!"

"Maybe it's a religious rite," suggested Harrison.

"Maybe," said Jarvis dubiously. "Well, there we were. We could exchange ideas up to a certain point, and then—blooey! Something in us was different, unrelated; I don't doubt that Tweel thought me just as screwy as I thought him. Our minds simply looked at the world from different viewpoints, and perhaps his viewpoint is as true as ours. But—we couldn't get together, that's all. Yet, in spite of all difficulties, I *liked* Tweel, and I have a queer certainty that he liked me."

"Nuts!" repeated the captain. "Just daffy!"

"Yeah? Wait and see. A couple of times I've thought that perhaps we—" He paused, and then resumed his narrative. "Anyway, I finally gave it up, and got into my thermo-skin to sleep. The fire hadn't kept me any too warm, but that damned sleeping bag did. Got stuffy five minutes after I closed myself in. I opened it a little and bingo! Some eighty-below-zero air hit my nose, and that's when I got this pleasant little frostbite to add to the bump I acquired during the crash of my rocket.

"I don't know what Tweel made of my sleeping. He sat around, but when I woke up, he was gone. I'd just crawled out of my bag, though, when I heard some twittering, and there he came, sailing down from that three-story Thyle cliff to alight on his beak beside me. I pointed to myself and toward the north, and he pointed at himself and toward the south, but when I loaded up and started away, he came along.

"Man, how he traveled! A hundred and fifty feet at a jump, sailing through the air stretched out like a spear, and landing on his beak. He seemed surprised at my plodding, but after a few moments he fell in beside me, only every few minutes he'd go into one of his leaps, and stick his nose into the sand a block ahead of me. Then he'd come shooting back at me; it made me nervous at first to see that beak of his coming at me like a spear, but he always ended in the sand at my side.

"So the two of us plugged along across the Mare Chronium. Same sort of place as this—same crazy plants and same little green biopods growing in the sand, or crawling out of your way. We talked—not that we understood each other, you know, but just for company. I sang songs, and I suspect Tweel did too; at least, some of his trillings and twitterings had a subtle sort of rhythm.

"Then, for variety, Tweel would display his smattering of English words. He'd point to an outcropping and say 'rock,' and point to a pebble and say it again; or he'd touch my arm and say 'Tick,' and then repeat it. He seemed terrifically amused that the same word meant the same thing twice in succession, or that the same word could apply to two different objects. It set me wondering if perhaps his language wasn't like the primitive speech of some earth people—you know, Captain, like the Negritoes, for instance, who haven't any generic words. No word for food or water or man—words for good food and bad food, or rain water and sea water, or strong man and weak man—but no names for general classes. They're too primitive to understand that rain water and sea water are just different aspects of the same thing. But that wasn't the case with Tweel; it was just that we were somehow mysteriously different—our minds were alien to each other. And yet—we *liked* each other!"

"Looney, that's all," remarked Harrison. "That's why you two were so fond of each other."

"Well, I like *you!*" countered Jarvis wickedly. "Anyway," he resumed, "don't get the idea that there was anything screwy about Tweel. In fact, I'm not so sure but that he couldn't teach our highly praised human intelligence a trick or two. Oh, he wasn't an intellectual superman, I guess; but don't overlook the point that he managed to understand a little of my mental workings, and I never even got a glimmering of his."

"Because he didn't have any!" suggested the captain, while Putz and Leroy blinked attentively.

"You can judge of that when I'm through," said Jarvis. "Well, we plugged along across the Mare Chronium all that day, and all the next. Mare Chronium—Sea of Time! Say, I was willing to agree with Schiaparelli's name by the end of that march! Just that gray endless plain of weird plants, and never a sign of any other life. It was so monotonous that I was even glad to see the desert of Xanthus toward the evening of the second day.

"I was fair worn out, but Tweel seemed as fresh as ever, for all I never saw him drink or eat. I think he could have crossed the Mare Chronium in a couple of hours with those block-long nose dives of his, but he stuck along with me. I offered him some water once or twice; he took the cup from me and sucked the liquid into his beak, and then carefully squirted it all back into the cup and gravely returned it.

"Just as we sighted Xanthus, or the cliffs that bounded it, one of those nasty sand clouds blew along, not as bad as the one we had here, but mean to travel against. I pulled the transparent flap of my thermo-skin bag across my face and managed pretty well, and I noticed that Tweel used some feathery appendages growing like a mustache at the base of his beak to cover his nostrils, and some similar fuzz to shield his eyes."

"He is a desert creature!" ejaculated the little biologist, Leroy.

"Huh? Why?"

"He drink no water—he is adapt' for sand storm—"

"Proves nothing! There's not enough water to waste anywhere on this desiccated pill called Mars. We'd call all of it desert on earth, you know." He paused. "Anyway, after the sand storm blew over, a little wind kept blowing in our faces, not strong enough to stir the sand. But suddenly things came drifting along from the Xanthus cliffs—small, transparent spheres, for all the world like glass tennis balls! But light—they were almost light enough to float even in this thin air—empty, too; at least, I cracked open a couple and nothing came out but a bad smell. I asked Tweel about them, but all he said was 'No, no, no.' which I took to mean that he knew nothing about them. So they went bouncing by like tumbleweeds, or like soap bubbles, and we plugged on toward Xanthus. Tweel pointed at one of the crystal balls once and said 'rock,' but I was too tired to argue with him. Later I discovered what he meant.

"We came to the bottom of the Xanthus cliffs finally, when there wasn't much daylight left. I decided to sleep on the plateau if possible; anything dangerous, I reasoned, would be more likely to prowl through the vegetation of the Mare Chronium than the sand of Xanthus. Not that I'd seen a single sign of menace, except the rope-armed black thing that had trapped Tweel, and apparently that didn't prowl at all, but lured its victims within reach. It couldn't lure me while I slept, especially as Tweel didn't seem to sleep at all, but simply sat patiently around all night. I wondered how the creature had managed to trap Tweel, but there wasn't any way of asking him. I found that out too, later; it's devilish!

"However, we were ambling around the base of the Xanthus barrier looking for an easy spot to climb. At least, I was. Tweel could have leaped it easily, for the cliffs were lower than Thyle—perhaps sixty feet. I found a place and started up, swearing at the water tank strapped to my back—it didn't bother me except when climbing—and suddenly I heard a sound that I thought I recognized!

"You know how deceptive sounds are in this thin air. A shot sounds like the pop of a cork. But this sound was the drone of a rocket, and sure enough, there went our second auxiliary about ten miles to westward, between me and the sunset!"

"Vas me!" said Putz. "I hunt for you."

"Yeah; I knew that, but what good did it do me? I hung on to the cliff and yelled and waved with one hand. Tweel saw it too, and set up a trilling and twittering, leaping to the top of the barrier and then high into the air. And while I watched, the machine droned on into the shadows to the south.

"I scrambled to the top of the cliff. Tweel was still pointing and trilling excitedly, shooting up toward the sky and coming down head-on to stick upside down on his beak in the sand. I pointed toward the south and at myself, and he said, 'Yes—Yes—Yes'; but somehow I gathered that he thought the flying thing was a relative of mine, probably a parent. Perhaps I did his intellect an injustice; I think now that I did.

"I was bitterly disappointed by the failure to attract attention. I pulled out my thermo-skin bag and crawled into it, as the night chill was already apparent. Tweel stuck his beak into the sand and drew up his legs and arms and looked for all the world like one of those leafless shrubs out there. I think he stayed that way all night."

"Protective mimicry!' ejaculated Leroy. "See! He is desert creature!"

"In the morning," resumed Jarvis, "we started off again. We hadn't gone a hundred yards into Xanthus when I saw something queer! This is one thing Putz didn't photograph, I'll wager!

"There was a line of little pyramids—tiny ones, not more than six inches high, stretching across Xanthus as far as I could see! Little buildings made of pygmy bricks, they were, hollow inside and truncated, or at least broken at the top and empty. I pointed at them and said 'What?' to Tweel, but he gave some negative twitters to indicate, I suppose, that he didn't know. So off we went, following the row of pyramids because they ran north, and I was going north.

"Man, we trailed that line for hours! After a while, I noticed another queer thing: they were getting larger. Same number of bricks in each one, but the bricks were larger.

"By noon they were shoulder high. I looked into a couple—all just the same, broken at the top and empty. I examined a brick or two as well; they were silica, and old as creation itself!"

"How you know?" asked Leroy.

"They were weathered—edges rounded. Silica doesn't weather easily even on earth, and in this climate—!"

"How old you think?"

"Fifty thousand—a hundred thousand years. How can I tell? The little ones we saw in the morning were older—perhaps ten times as old. Crumbling. How old would that make *them*? Half a million years? Who knows?" Jarvis paused a moment. "Well," he resumed, "we followed the line. Tweel pointed at them and said 'rock' once or twice, but he'd done that many times before. Besides, he was more or less right about these.

"I tried questioning him. I pointed at a pyramid and asked 'People?' and indicated the two of us. He set up a negative sort of clucking and said, 'No, no, no. No one-one-two. No two-two-four,' meanwhile rubbing his stomach. I just stared at him and he went through the business again. 'No one-one-two. No two-two-four.' I just gaped at him."

"That proves it!" exclaimed Harrison. "Nuts!"

"You think so?" queried Jarvis sardonically. "Well, I figured it out different! "No one-one-two!' You don't get it, of course, do you?"

"Nope—nor do you!"

"I think I do! Tweel was using the few English words he knew to put over a very complex idea. What, let me ask, does mathematics make you think of?"

"Why—of astronomy. Or—or logic!"

"That's it! 'No one-one-two!' Tweel was telling me that the builders of the pyramids weren't people—or that they weren't intelligent, that they weren't reasoning creatures! Get it?"

"Huh! I'll be damned!"

"You probably will."

"Why,' put in Leroy, "he rub his belly?"

"Why? Because, my dear biologist, that's where his brains are! Not in his tiny head—in his middle!"

"*C'est* impossible!"

"Not on Mars, it isn't! This flora and fauna aren't earthly; your biopods prove that!" Jarvis grinned and took up his narrative. "Anyway, we plugged along across Xanthus and in about the middle of the afternoon, something else queer happened. The pyramids ended."

"Ended!"

"Yeah; the queer part was that the last one—and now they were ten-footers—was capped! See? Whatever built it was still inside; we'd trailed 'em from their half-million-year-old origin to the present.

"Tweel and I noticed it about the same time. I yanked out my automatic (I had a clip of Boland explosive bullets in it) and Tweel, quick as a sleight-of-hand trick, snapped a queer little glass revolver out of his bag. It was much like our weapons, except that the grip was larger to accommodate his four-taloned hand. And we held our weapons ready while we sneaked up along the lines of empty pyramids.

"Tweel saw the movement first. The top tiers of bricks were heaving, shaking, and suddenly slid down the sides with a thin crash. And then—something—something was coming out!

"A long, silvery-gray arm appeared, dragging after it an armored body. Armored, I mean, with scales, silver-gray and dull-shining. The arm heaved the body out of the hole; the beast crashed to the sand.

"It was a nondescript creature—body like a big gray cask, arm and a sort of mouth-hole at one end; stiff, pointed tail at the other—and that's all. No other limbs, no eyes, ears, nose—nothing! The thing dragged itself a few yards, inserted its pointed tail in the sand, pushed itself upright, and just sat.

"Tweel and I watched it for ten minutes before it moved. Then with a creaking and rustling like—oh, like a crumbling stiff paper—its arm moved to the mouth-hole and out came a brick! The arm placed the brick carefully on the ground, and the thing was still again.

"Another ten minutes—another brick. Just one of Nature's brick-layers. I was about to slip away and move on when Tweel pointed at the thing and said 'rock'! I went 'huh?' and he said it again. Then, to the accompaniment of some of his trilling, he said, 'No—no,' and gave two or three whistling breaths.

"Well, I got his meaning, for a wonder! I said, 'No breath?' and demonstrated the word. Tweel was ecstatic; he said, 'Yes, yes, yes! No, no, no breet!' Then he gave a leap and sailed out to land on his nose about one pace from the monster!

"I was startled, you can imagine! The arm was going up for a brick, and I expected to see Tweel caught and mangled, but—nothing happened! Tweel pounded on the creature, and the arm took the brick and placed it neatly beside the first. Tweel rapped on its body again, and said 'rock,' and I got up nerve enough to take a look myself.

"Tweel was right again. The creature *was* rock, and it didn't breathe!"

"How you know?' snapped Leroy, his black eyes blazing interest.

"Because I'm a chemist. The beast was made of silica! There must have been pure silicon in the sand, and it lived on that. Get it? We, and Tweel, and those plants out there, and even the biopods are *carbon* life; this thing lived by a different set of chemical reactions. It was silicon life!"

"*La vie silicieuse!*" shouted Leroy. "I have suspect, and now it is proof! I must go see! *Il faut que je–*"

"All right! All right!" said Jarvis. "You can go see. Anyhow, there the thing was, alive and yet not alive, moving every ten minutes, and then only to remove a brick. Those bricks were its waste matter. See, Frenchy? We're carbon, and our waste is carbon dioxide, and this thing is silicon, and *its* waste is silicon dioxide—silica. But silica is a solid, hence the bricks. And it builds itself in, and when it is covered, it moves over to a fresh place to start over. No wonder it creaked! A living creature half a million years old!"

"How you know how old?" Leroy was frantic.

"We trailed its pyramids from the beginning, didn't we? If this weren't the original pyramid builder, the series would have ended somewhere before we found him, wouldn't it?—

ended and started over with the small ones. That's simple enough, isn't it?

"But he reproduces, or tries to. Before the third brick came out, there was a little rustle and out popped a whole stream of these little crystal balls. They're his spores, or eggs, or seeds—call 'em what you want. They went bouncing by across Xanthus just as they'd bounced by us back in the Mare Chronium. I've a hunch how they work, too—this is for your information, Leroy. I think the crystal shell of silica is no more than a protective covering, like an eggshell, and that the active principle is the smell inside. It's some sort of gas that attacks silicon, and if the shell is broken near a supply of that element, some reaction starts that ultimately develops into a beast like that one."

"You should try!" exclaimed the little Frenchman. "We must break one to see!"

"Yeah? Well, I did. I smashed a couple against the sand. Would you like to come back in about ten thousand years to see if I planted some pyramid monsters? You'd most like be able to tell by that time!" Jarvis paused and drew a deep breath. "Lord! That queer creature! Do you picture it? Blind, deaf, nerveless, brainless—just a mechanism, and yet—immortal! Bound to go on making bricks, building pyramids, as long as silicon and oxygen exist, and even afterwards it'll just stop. It won't be dead. If the accidents of a million years bring it its food again, there it'll be, ready to run again, while brains and civilizations are part of the past. A queer beast—yet I met a stranger one!"

"If you did, it must have been in your dreams!" growled Harrison.

"You're right!" said Jarvis soberly. "In a way, you're right. The dream-beast! That's the best name for it—and it's the most fiendish, terrifying creation one could imagine! More dangerous than a lion, more insidious than a snake!"

"Tell me!" begged Leroy. "I must go see!"

"Not *this* devil!" He paused again. "Well," he resumed, "Tweel and I left the pyramid creature and plowed along through Xanthus. I was tired and a little disheartened by Putz's failure to pick me up, and Tweel's trilling got on my nerves, as did his flying nosedives. So I just strode along without a word, hour after hour across the monotonous desert.

"Toward mid-afternoon we came in sight of a low dark line on the horizon. I knew what it was. It was a canal; I'd crossed it in the rocket and it meant that we were just one-third of the way across Xanthus. Pleasant thought, wasn't it? And still, I was keeping up to schedule.

"We approached the canal slowly; I remembered that this one was bordered by a wide fringe of vegetation and that Mud-heap City was on it.

"I was tired, as I said. I kept thinking of a good hot meal and then from that I jumped to reflections of how nice and home-like even Borneo would seem after this crazy planet, and from that, to thoughts of little old New York, and then to thinking about a girl I know there—Fancy Long. Know her?"

"Vision entertainer," said Harrison. "I've tuned her in. Nice blonde—dances and sings on the *Yerba Mate* hour."

"That's her," said Jarvis ungrammatically. "I know her pretty well—just friends, get me?—though she came down to see us off in the *Ares.* Well, I was thinking about her, feeling pretty lonesome, and all the time we were approaching that line of rubbery plants.

"And then—I said, 'What 'n Hell!' and stared. And there she was—Fancy Long, standing plain as day under one of those crack-brained tress, and smiling and waving just the way I remembered her when we left!"

"Now you're nuts, too!" observed the captain.

"Boy, I almost agreed with you! I stared and pinched myself and closed my eyes and then stared again—and every time, there was Fancy Long smiling and waving! Tweel saw something, too; he was trilling and clucking away, but I scarcely heard him. I was bounding toward her over the sand, too amazed even to ask myself questions.

"I wasn't twenty feet from her when Tweel caught me with one of his flying leaps. He grabbed my arm, yelling, 'No—no—no!' in his squeaky voice. I tried to shake him off—he was as light as if he were built of bamboo—but he dug his claws in and yelled. And finally some sort of sanity returned to me and I stopped less than ten feet from her. There she stood, looking as solid as Putz's head!"

"Vot?" said the engineer.

"She smiled and waved, and waved and smiled, and I stood there dumb as Leroy, while Tweel squeaked and chattered. I *knew* it couldn't be real, yet—there she was!

"Finally I said, 'Fancy! Fancy Long!' She just kept on smiling and waving, but looking as real as if I hadn't left her thirty-seven million miles away.

"Tweel had his glass pistol out, pointing it at her. I grabbed his arm, but he tried to push me away. He pointed at her and said, 'No breet! No breet!' and I understood that he meant that the Fancy Long thing wasn't alive. Man, my head was whirling!

"Still, it gave me the jitters to see him pointing his weapon at her. I don't know why I stood there watching him take careful aim, but I did. Then he squeezed the handle of his weapon; there was a little puff of steam, and Fancy Long was gone! And in her place was one of those writhing, black, rope-armed horrors like the one I'd saved Tweel from!

"The dream-beast! I stood there dizzy, watching it die while Tweel trilled and whistled. Finally he touched my arm, pointed at the twisting thing, and said, 'You one-one-two, he one-one-two.' After he'd repeated it eight or ten times, I got it. Do any of you?"

"*Oui!*" shrilled Leroy. "*Moi-je le comprends!* He mean you think of something, the beast he know, and you see it! *Un chien*—a hungry dog, he would see the big bone with meat! Or smell it—not?"

"Right!" said Jarvis. "The dream-beast uses its victim's longings and desires to trap its prey. The bird at nesting season would see its mate; the fox, prowling for its own prey, would see a helpless rabbit!"

"How he do?" queried Leroy.

"How do I know? How does a snake back on earth charm a bird into its very jaws? And aren't there deep-sea fish that lure their victims into their mouths? Lord!" Jarvis shuddered. "Do you see how insidious the monster is? We're warned now—but henceforth we can't trust even our eyes. You might see me—I might see one of you—and back of it may be nothing but another of those black horrors!"

"How'd your friend know?" asked the captain abruptly.

"Tweel? I wonder! Perhaps he was thinking of something that couldn't possibly have interested me, and when I started to run, he realized that I saw something different and was warned. Or perhaps the dream-beast can only project a single vision, and Tweel saw what I saw—or nothing. I couldn't ask him. But it's just another proof that his intelligence is equal to ours or greater."

"He's daffy, I tell you!" said Harrison. "What makes you think his intellect ranks with the human?"

"Plenty of things! First, the pyramid-beast. He hadn't seen one before; he said as much. Yet, he recognized it as a dead-alive automaton of silicon."

"He could have heard of it," objected Harrison. "He lives around here, you know."

"Well how about the language? I couldn't pick up a single idea of his and he learned six or seven words of mine. And do you realize what complex ideas he put over with no more than those six or seven words? The pyramid-monster—the dream-beast! In a single phrase he told me that one was a harmless automaton and the other a deadly hypnotist. What about that?"

"Huh!" said the captain.

"*Huh* if you wish! Could you have done it knowing only six words of English? Could you go even further, as Tweel did, and tell me that another creature was of a sort of intelligence so different from ours that understanding was impossible—even more impossible than that between Tweel and me?"

"Eh? What was that?"

"Later. The point I'm making is that Tweel and his race are worthy of our friendship. Somewhere on Mars—and you'll find I'm right—is a civilization and culture equal to ours, and maybe more than equal. And communication is possible between them and us; Tweel proves that. It may take years of patient trial, for thcir minds are alien, but less alien than the next minds we encountered—if they *are* minds."

"The next ones? What next ones?"

"The people of the mud cities along the canals." Jarvis frowned, then resumed his narrative. "I thought the dream-beast and the silicon-monster were the strangest beings conceivable, but I was wrong. These creatures are still more alien, less understandable than either and far less comprehensible than Tweel, with whom friendship is possible, and even, by patience and concentration, the exchange of ideas.

"Well," he continued, "we left the dream-beast dying, dragging itself back into its hole, and we moved toward the canal. There was a carpet of that queer walking-grass scampering out of our way, and when we reached the bank, there was a yellow trickle of water flowing. The mound city I'd noticed from the rocket was a mile or so to the right and I was curious enough to want to take a look at it.

"It had seemed deserted from my previous glimpse of it, and if any creatures were lurking in it—well, Tweel and I were both armed. And by the way, that crystal weapon of Tweel's was an interesting device; I took a look at it after the dream-beast episode. It fired a little glass splinter, poisoned, I suppose, and I guess it held at least a hundred of 'em to a load. The propellent was steam—just plain steam!"

"Shteam!" echoed Putz. "From vot come, shteam?"

"From water, of course! You could see the water through the transparent handle and about a gill of another liquid, thick and yellowish. When Tweel squeezed the handle—there was no trigger—a drop of water and a drop of the yellow stuff squirted into the firing chamber, and the water vaporized—pop!—like that. It's not so difficult; I think we could develop the same principle. Concentrated sulphuric acid will heat water almost to boiling, and so will quicklime, and there's potassium and sodium—

"Of course, his weapon hadn't the range of mine, but it wasn't so bad in this thin air, and it *did* hold as many shots as a cowboy's gun in a Western movie. It was effective, too, at least against Martian life; I tried it out, aiming at one of the crazy plants, and darned if the plant didn't wither up and fall apart! That's why I think the glass splinters were poisoned.

"Anyway, we trudged along toward the mud-heap city and I began to wonder whether the city builders dug the canals. I pointed to the city and then at the canal, and Tweel said 'No—no—no!' and gestured toward the south. I took it to mean that some other race had created the canal system, perhaps Tweel's people. I don't know; maybe there's still another intelligent race on the planet, or a dozen others. Mars is a queer little world.

"A hundred yards from the city we crossed a sort of road—just a hard-packed mud trial, and then, all of a sudden, along came one of the mound builders!

"Man, talk about fantastic beings! It looked rather like a barrel trotting along on four legs with four other arms or tentacles. It had no head, just body and members and a row of eyes completely around it. The top end of the barrel-body was a diaphragm stretched as tight as a drum head, and that was all. It was pushing a little coppery cart and tore right past us like the proverbial bat out of Hell. It didn't even notice us, although I thought the eyes on my side shifted a little as it passed.

"A moment later another came along, pushing another empty cart. Same thing—it just scooted past us. Well, I wasn't going to be ignored by a bunch of barrels playing train, so when the third one approached, I planted myself in the way—ready to jump, of course, if the thing didn't stop.

"But it did. It stopped and set up a sort of drumming from the diaphragm on top. And I held out both hands and said, 'We are friends!' And what do you suppose the thing did?"

"Said, 'Pleased to meet you,' I'll bet!" suggested Harrison.

"I couldn't have been more surprised if it had! It drummed on its diaphragm, and then suddenly boomed out, "We are v-r-r-riends!' and gave its pushcart a vicious poke at me! I jumped aside, and away it went while I stared dumbly after it.

"A minute later another one came hurrying along. This one didn't pause, but simply drummed out, 'We are v-r-r-riends' and scurried by. How did it learn the phrase? Were all of the creatures in some sort of communication with each other? Were they all parts of some central organism? I don't know, though I think Tweel does.

"Anyway, the creatures went sailing past us, every one greeting us with the same statement. It got to be funny; I never thought to find so many friends on this God-forsaken ball! Finally I made a puzzled gesture to Tweel; I guess he understood, for he said, 'One-one-two—yes!—two-two-four—no!' Get it?"

"Sure," said Harrison. "It's a Martian nursery rhyme."

"Yeah! Well, I was getting used to Tweel's symbolism, and I figured it out this way. 'One-one-two—yes!' The creatures were intelligent. 'Two-two-four—no!' Their intelligence was not of our order, but something different and beyond the logic of two and two is four. Maybe I missed his meaning. Perhaps he meant that their minds were of low degree, able to figure out the simple things—'One-one-two—yes!' but not more difficult things—'Two-two-four—no!' But I think from what we saw later that he meant the other.

"After a few moments, the creatures came rushing back—first one, then another. Their pushcarts were full of stones, sand, chunks of rubbery plants, and such rubbish as that. They droned out their friendly greeting, which didn't really sound so friendly, and dashed on. The third one I assumed to be my first acquaintance and I decided to have another chat with him. I stepped into his path again and waited.

"Up he came, booming out this 'We are v-r-r-riends' and stopped. I looked at him; four or five of his eyes looked at me. He tried his password again and gave a shove on his cart, but I stood firm. And then the—the dashed creature reached out one of his arms, and two finger-like nippers tweaked my nose!"

"Haw!" roared Harrison. "Maybe the things have a sense of beauty!"

"Laugh!" grumbled Jarvis. "I'd already had a nasty bump and a mean frostbite on that nose. Anyway, I yelled 'Ouch!' and jumped aside and the creature dashed away; but from then on, their greeting was 'We are v-r-r-riends! Ouch!' Queer beasts!

"Tweel and I followed the road squarely up to the nearest mound. The creatures were coming and going, paying us not the slightest attention, fetching their loads of rubbish. The road simply dived into an opening, and slanted down like an old mine, and in and out darted the barrel-people, greeting us with their eternal phrase.

"I looked in; there was a light somewhere below, and I was curious to see it. It didn't look like a flame or torch, you understand, but more like a civilized light, and I thought that I might get some clue as to the creatures' development. So in I went and Tweel tagged along, not without a few trills and twitters, however.

"The light was curious; it sputtered and flared like an old arc light, but came from a single black rod set in the wall of the corridor. It was electric, beyond doubt. The creatures were fairly civilized, apparently.

"Then I saw another light shining on something that glittered and I went on to look at that, but it was only a heap of shiny sand. I turned toward the entrance to leave, and the Devil take me if it wasn't gone!

"I suppose the corridor had curved, or I'd stepped into a side passage. Anyway, I walked back in that direction I thought we'd come, and all I saw was more dimlit corridors. The place was a labyrinth! There was nothing but twisting passages running every way, lit by occasional lights, and now and then a creature running by, sometimes with a pushcart, sometimes without.

"Well, I wasn't much worried at first. Tweel and I had only come a few steps from the entrance. But every move we made after that seemed to get us in deeper. Finally I tried following one of the creatures with an empty cart, thinking that he'd be going out for his rubbish, but he ran around aimlessly, into one passage and out another. When he started dashing around a pillar like one of these Japanese waltzing mice, I gave up, dumped my water tank on the floor, and sat down.

"Tweel was as lost as I. I pointed up and he said 'No—no—no!' in a sort of helpless trill. And we couldn't get any help from the natives. They paid no attention at all, except to assure us they were friends—ouch!

"Lord! I don't know how many hours or days we wandered around there! I slept twice from sheer exhaustion; Tweel never seemed to need sleep. We tried following only the upward corridors, but they'd run uphill a ways and then curve downwards. The temperature in that damned ant hill was constant; you couldn't tell night from day and after my first sleep I didn't know whether I'd slept one hour or thirteen, so I couldn't tell from my watch whether it was midnight or noon.

"We saw plenty of strange things. There were machines running in some of the corridors, but they didn't seem to be doing anything—just wheels turning. And several times I saw two barrel-beasts with a little one growing between them, joined to both."

"Parthenogenesis!" exulted Leroy. "Parthenogenesis by budding like *les tulipes!*"

"If you say so, Frenchy," agreed Jarvis. "The things never noticed us at all, except, as I say, to greet us with 'We are v-r-r-riends! Ouch!' They seemed to have no home-life of any sort, but just scurried around with their pushcarts, bringing in rubbish. And finally I discovered what they did with it.

"We'd had a little luck with a corridor, one that slanted upwards for a great distance. I was feeling that we ought to be close to the surface when suddenly the passage debouched into a domed chamber, the only one we'd seen. And man!—I felt like dancing when I saw what looked like daylight through a crevice in the roof.

"There was a—a sort of machine in the chamber, just an enormous wheel that turned slowly, and one of the creatures was in the act of dumping his rubbish below it. The wheel ground it with a crunch—sand, stones, plants, all into powder that sifted away somewhere. While we watched, others filed in, repeating the process, and that seemed to be all. No rhyme nor reason to the whole thing—but that's characteristic of this crazy planet. And there was another fact that's almost too bizarre to believe.

"One of the creatures, having dumped his load, pushed his cart aside with a crash and calmly shoved himself under the wheel! I watched him being crushed, too stupefied to make a sound; and a moment later, another followed him! They were perfectly methodical about it, too; one of the cartless creatures took the abandoned pushcart.

"Tweel didn't seem surprised; I pointed out the next suicide to him, and he just gave the most human-like shrug imaginable, as much as to say, 'What can I do about it?' He must have known more or less about these creatures.

"Then I saw something else. There was something beyond the wheel, something shining on a sort of low pedestal. I walked over; there was a little crystal about the size of an egg, fluorescing to beat Tophet. The light from it stung my hands and face, almost like a static discharge, and then I noticed another funny thing. Remember that wart I had on my left thumb? Look!" Jarvis extended his hand. "It dried up and fell off—just like that! And my abused nose—say, the pain went out of it like magic! The thing had the property of hard X-rays or gamma radiations, only more so; it destroyed diseased tissue and left healthy tissue unharmed!

"I was thinking what a present *that'd* be to take back to Mother Earth when a lot of racket interrupted. We dashed back to the other side of the wheel in time to see one of the pushcarts ground up. Some suicide had been careless, it seems.

"Then suddenly the creatures were booming and drumming all around us and their noise was decidedly menacing. A crowd of them advanced toward us; we backed out of what I thought was the passage we'd entered by, and they came rumbling after us, some pushing carts and some not. Crazy brutes! There was a whole chorus of 'We are v-r-r-riends! Ouch!' I didn't like the 'ouch'; it was rather suggestive.

"Tweel had his glass gun out and I dumped my water tank for greater freedom and got mine. We backed up the corridor with the barrel-beasts following—about twenty of them. Queer thing—the ones coming in with loaded carts moved past us inches away without a sign.

"Tweel must have noticed that. Suddenly, he snatched out that glowing coal cigar-lighter of his and touched a cart-load of plant limbs. Puff! The whole load was burning—and the crazy beast pushing it went right along without a change of pace! It created some disturbance among our 'v-r-r-riends,' however—and then I noticed the smoke eddying and swirling past us, and sure enough, there was the entrance!

"I grabbed Tweel and out we dashed and after us our twenty pursuers. The daylight felt like Heaven, though I saw at first glance that the sun was all but set, and that was bad, since I couldn't live outside my thermo-skin bag in a Martian night—at least, without a fire.

"And things got worse in a hurry. They cornered us in an angle between two mounds, and there we stood. I hadn't fired nor had Tweel; there wasn't any use in irritating the brutes. They stopped a little distance away and began their booming about friendship and ouches.

"Then things got still worse! A barrel-brute came out with a pushcart and they all grabbed onto it and came out with handfuls of foot-long copper darts—sharp-looking ones—and all of a sudden one sailed past my ear—zing! And it was shoot or die then.

"We were doing pretty well for a while. We picked off the ones next to the pushcart and managed to keep the darts at a minimum, but suddenly there was a thunderous booming of 'v-r-r-riends' and 'ouches,' and a whole army of 'em came out of their hole.

"Man! We were through and I knew it! Then I realized that Tweel wasn't. He could have leaped the mound behind us as easily as not. He was staying for me!

"Say, I could have cried, if there'd been time! I'd liked Tweel from the first, but whether I'd have had gratitude to do what he was doing—suppose I *had* saved him from the first dream-beast—he'd done as much for me, hadn't he? I grabbed his arm, and said 'Tweel,' and pointed up, and he understood. He said, 'No—no-no, Tick!' and popped away with his glass pistol.

"What could I do? I'd be a goner anyway when the sun set, but I couldn't explain that to him. I said, 'Thanks, Tweel. You're a man!' and felt that I wasn't paying him any compliment at all. A man! There are mighty few men who'd do that.

"So I went 'bang' with my gun and Tweel went 'puff' and his, and the barrels were throwing darts and getting ready to rush us, and booming about being friends. I had given up hope. Then suddenly an angel dropped right down from Heaven in the shape of Putz, with his under-jets blasting the barrels into very small pieces!

"Wow! I let out a yell and dashed for the rocket; Putz opened the door and in I went, laughing and crying and shouting! It was a moment or so before I remembered Tweel; I looked around in time to see him rising in one of his nosedives over the mound and away.

"I had a devil of a job arguing Putz into following! By the time we got the rocket aloft, darkness was down; you know how it comes here—like turning off a light. We sailed out over the desert and put down once or twice. I yelled 'Tweel!' and yelled it a hundred times, I guess. We couldn't find him; he could travel like the wind and all I got—or else I imagined it—was a faint trilling and twittering drifting out of the south. He'd gone, and damn it! I wish—I wish he hadn't!"

The four men of the *Ares* were silent—even the sardonic Harrison. At last little Leroy broke the stillness.

"I should like to see," he murmured.

"Yeah," said Harrison. "And the wart-cure. Too bad you missed that; it might be the cancer cure they've been hunting for a century and a half."

"Oh, that!" muttered Jarvis gloomily. "That's what started the fight!" He drew a glistening object from his pocket.

"Here it is."

This is, I think, a marvelous story—and over the past thirty years I have used it in five different anthologies, by way of demonstrating my admiration for it. It handles the theoretically impossible predicament of a space voyager who is traveling faster than light with as much scientific plausibility as any story could; it is told in an effective and dramatically moving manner; and at a certain moment it leaps into a realm of linguistic imagination that has haunted me ever since I first encountered it in the far-off year of 1953.

No human being has ever undergone an experience like the one that befalls Garrard in "Common Time." Probably none ever will. But James Blish was capable of imagining it, and bringing it forth out of his imagination in the form of this cool, precise, vivid, and curiously powerful story. For me it is an unforgettable masterpiece. May you find it as moving and strange and wonderful as I did, long ago, in the rough and shaggy pages of a now-forgotten magazine called *Science Fiction Quarterly*. I offer it to you—yours now, as the clinesterton beademung would say, with all of love.

—Robert Silverberg

COMMON TIME

by James Blish

> . . . the days went slowly round and round
> endless and uneventful as cycles in space.
> Time, and time-pieces! How many centuries did
> my hammock tell, as pendulum-like it swung
> to the ship's dull roll, and ticked the hours
> and ages.
>
> —HERMAN MELVILLE, in *Mardi*

D*on't move.*

It was the first thought that came into Garrard's mind when he awoke, and perhaps it saved his life. He lay where he was, strapped against the padding, listening to the round hum of the engines. That in itself was wrong; he should be unable to hear the overdrive at all.

He thought to himself: *Has it begun already?*

Otherwise everything seemed normal. The DFC-3 had crossed over into interstellar velocity, and he was still alive, and the ship was still functioning. The ship should at this moment be traveling at 22.4 times the speed of light—a neat 4,157,000 miles per second.

Somehow Garrard did not doubt that it was. On both previous tries, the ships had whiffed away toward Alpha Centauri at the proper moment when the overdrive should have cut in; and the split second of residual image after they had vanished, subjected to spectroscopy, showed a Doppler shift which tallied with the acceleration predicted for that moment by Haertel.

The trouble was not that Brown and Cellini hadn't gotten away in good order. It was simply that neither of them had ever been heard from again.

Very slowly, he opened his eyes. His eyelids felt terrifically heavy. As far as he could judge from the pressure of the couch against his skin, the gravity was normal; nevertheless, moving his eyelids seemed almost an impossible job.

After long concentration, he got them fully open. The instrument chassis was directly before him, extended over his diaphragm on its elbow joint. Still without moving anything but his eyes—and those only with the utmost patience—he checked each of the meters. Velocity: 22.4 c. Operating temperature: normal. Ship temperature: 37°C. Air pressure: 778 mm. Fuel: No. 1 tank full, No. 2 tank full, No. 3 tank full, No. 4 tank nine-tenths full. Gravity: 1 g. Calendar: stopped.

He looked at it closely, though his eyes seemed to focus very slowly, too. It was, of course, something more than a calendar—it was an all-purpose clock, designed to show him the passage of seconds, as well as of the ten months his trip was supposed to take to the double star. But there was no doubt about it: the second hand was motionless.

That was the second abnormality. Garrard felt an impulse to get up and see if he could start the clock again. Perhaps the trouble had been temporary and safely in the past. Immediately there sounded in his head the injunction he had drilled into himself for a full month before the trip had begun:

Don't move!

Don't move until you know the situation as far as it can be known without moving. Whatever it was that had snatched Brown and Cellini irretrievably beyond human ken was potent and totally beyond anticipation. They had both been excellent men, intelligent, resourceful, trained to the point of diminishing returns and not a micron beyond that point—the best men in the project. Preparations for every knowable kind of trouble had been built into their ships, as they had been built into the DFC-3. Therefore, if there was something wrong nevertheless, it would be something that might strike from some commonplace quarter—and strike only once.

He listened to the humming. It was even and placid and not very loud, but it disturbed him deeply. The overdrive was supposed to be inaudible, and the tapes from the first unmanned test vehicles had recorded no such hum. The noise did not appear to interfere with the overdrive's operation or to indicate any failure in it. It was just an irrelevancy for which he could find no reason.

But the reason existed. Garrard did not intend to do so much as draw another breath until he found out what it was.

Incredibly, he realized for the first time that he had not in fact drawn one single breath since he had first come to. Though he felt not the slightest discomfort, the discovery called up so overwhelming a flash of panic that he very nearly sat bolt upright on the couch. Luckily—or so it seemed, after the panic had begun to ebb—the curious lethargy which had affected his eyelids appeared to involve his whole body, for the impulse was gone before he could summon the energy to answer it. And the panic, poignant though it had been for an instant, turned out to be wholly intellectual. In a moment, he was observing that his failure to breathe in no way discommoded him as far as he could tell—it was just there, waiting to be explained. . . .

Or to kill him. But it hadn't, yet.

Engines humming; eyelids heavy; breathing absent; calendar stopped. The four facts added up to nothing. The temptation to move something—even if it were only a big toe—was strong, but Garrard fought it back. He had been awake only a short while—half an hour at most—and already had noticed four abnormalities. There were bound to be more, anomalies more subtle than these four; but available to close examination before he had to move. Nor was there anything in particular that he had to do, aside from caring for his own wants; the project, on the chance that Brown's and Cellini's failure to return had resulted from some tampering with the overdrive, had made everything in the DFC-3 subject only to the computer. In a very real sense, Garrard was just along for the ride. Only when the overdrive was off could he adjust. . . .

Pock.

It was a soft, low-pitched noise, rather like a cork coming out of a wine bottle. It seemed to have come just from the right of the control chassis. He halted a sudden jerk of his head on the cushions toward it with a flat fiat of will. Slowly, he moved his eyes in that direction.

He could see nothing that might have caused the sound. The ship's temperature dial showed no change, which ruled out a heat noise from differential contraction or expansion—the only possible explanation he could bring to mind.

He closed his eyes—a process which turned out to be just as difficult as opening them had been—and tried to visualize what the calendar had looked like when he had first come out of anesthesia. After he got a clear and—he was almost sure—accurate picture, Garrard opened his eyes again.

The sound had been the calendar, advancing one second. It was now motionless again, apparently stopped.

He did not know how long it took the second hand to make that jump, normally; the question had never come up. Certainly the jump, when it came at the end of each second, had been too fast for the eye to follow.

Belatedly, he realized what all this cogitation was costing him in terms of essential information. The calendar had moved. Above all and before anything else, he *must* know exactly how long it took it to move again. . . .

He began to count, allowing an arbitrary five seconds lost. *One-and-a six, one-and-a-seven, one-and-an-eight . . .*

Garrard had gotten only that far when he found himself plunged into hell.

First, and utterly without reason, a sickening fear flooded swiftly through his veins, becoming more and more intense. His bowels began to knot with infinite slowness. His whole body became a field of small, slow pulses—not so much shaking him as putting his limbs into contrary joggling motions and making his skin ripple gently under his clothing. Against the hum another sound became audible, a nearly subsonic thunder which seemed to be inside his head. Still the fear mounted, and with it came the pain, and the tenesmus—a boardlike stiffening of his muscles, particularly across his abdomen and his shoulders, but affecting his forearms almost as grievously. He felt himself beginning, very gradually, to double at the middle, a motion about which he could do precisely nothing—a terrifying kind of dynamic paralysis. . . .

It lasted for hours. At the height of it, Garrard's mind, even his very personality, was washed out utterly; he was only a vessel of horror. When some few trickles of reason began to return over that burning desert of reasonless emotion, he found that he was sitting up on the cushions, and that with one arm he had thrust the control chassis back on its elbow so that it no longer jutted over his body. His clothing was wet with perspiration, which stubbornly refused to evaporate or to cool him. And his lungs ached a little, although he could still detect no breathing.

What under God had happened? Was it this that had killed Brown and Cellini? For it would kill Garrard, too—of that he was sure—if it happened often. It would kill him even if it happened only twice more, if the next two such things followed the first one closely. At the very best it would make a slobbering idiot of him; and though the computer might bring Garrard and the ship back to Earth, it would not be able to tell the project about his tornado of senseless fear.

The calendar said that the eternity in hell had taken three seconds. As he looked at it in academic indignation, it said *pock* and condescended to make the total seizure four seconds long. With grim determination, Garrard began to count again.

He took care to establish the counting as an absolutely even, automatic process which would not stop at the back of his mind no matter what other problem he tackled along with it, or what emotional typhoons should interrupt him. Really compulsive counting cannot be stopped by anything—not the transports of love nor the agonies of empires. Garrard knew the dangers in deliberately setting up such a mechanism in his mind, but he also knew how desperately he needed to time that clock tick. He was beginning to understand what had happened to him—but he needed exact measurement before he could put that understanding to use.

Of course there had been plenty of speculation on the possible effect of the overdrive on the subjective time of the pilot, but none of it had come to much. At any speed below the velocity of light, subjective and objective time were exactly the same as far as the pilot was concerned. For an observer on Earth, time aboard the ship would appear to be vastly slowed at near-light speeds; but for the pilot himself there would be no apparent change.

Since flight beyond the speed of light was impossible—although for slightly differing reasons—by both the current theories of relativity, neither theory had offered any clue as to what would happen on board a translight ship. They would not allow that any such ship could even exist. The Haertel transformation, on which, in effect, the DFC-3 flew, was nonrelativistic: it showed that the apparent elapsed time of a translight journey should be identical in ship time and in the time of observers at both ends of the trip.

But since ship and pilot were part of the same system, both covered by the same expression in Haertel's equation, it had never occurred to anyone that the pilot and the ship might keep different times. The notion was ridiculous.

One-and-a-seven-hundred one, one-and-a-seven-hundred two, one-and-a-seven-hundred three, one-and-a-seven-hundred four . . .

The ship was keeping ship time, which was identical with observer time. It would arrive at the Alpha Centauri system in ten months. But the pilot was keeping Garrard time, and it was beginning to look as though he wasn't going to arrive at all.

It was impossible, but there it was. Something—almost certainly an unsuspected physiological side effect of the overdrive field on human metabolism, an effect which naturally could not have been detected in the preliminary, robot-piloted tests of the overdrive—had speeded up Garrard's subjective apprehension of time and had done a thorough job of it.

The second hand began a slow, preliminary quivering as the calendar's innards began to apply power to it. *Seventy-hundred-forty-one, seventy-hundred-forty-two, seventy-hundred-forty-three . . .*

At the count of 7,058 the second hand began the jump to the next graduation. It took it several apparent minutes to get across the tiny distance and several more to come completely to rest. Later still, the sound came to him:

Pock.

In a fever of thought, but without any real physical agitation, his mind began to manipulate the figures. Since it took him longer to count an individual number as the number became larger, the interval between the two calendar ticks probably was closer to 7,200 seconds than to 7,058. Figuring backward brought him quickly to the equivalence he wanted: one second in ship time was two hours in Garrard time.

Had he really been counting for what was, for him, two whole hours? There seemed to be no doubt about it. It looked like a long trip ahead.

Just how long it was going to be struck him with stunning force. Time had been slowed for him by a factor of 7,200. He would get to Alpha Centauri in just 72,000 months.

Which was . . .

Six thousand years!

II

Garrard sat motionless for a long time after that, the Nessus shirt of warm sweat swathing him persistently, refusing even to cool. There was, after all, no hurry.

Six thousand years. There would be food and water and air for all that time, or for sixty or six hundred thousand years; the ship would synthesize his needs, as a matter of course, for as long as the fuel lasted, and the fuel bred itself. Even if Garrard ate a meal every three seconds of objective, or ship, time (which, he realized suddenly, he wouldn't be able to do, for it took the ship several seconds of objective time to prepare and serve up a meal once it was ordered; he'd be lucky if he ate once a day, Garrard time), there would be no reason to fear any shortage of supplies. That had been one of the earliest of the possibilities for disaster that the project engineers had ruled out in the design of the DFC-3.

But nobody had thought to provide a mechanism which would indefinitely refurbish Garrard. After six thousand years, there would be nothing left of him but a faint film of dust on the DFC-3's dully gleaming horizontal surfaces. His corpse might outlast him awhile, since the ship itself was sterile—but eventually he could be consumed by the bacteria which he carried in his own digestive tract. He needed those bacteria to synthesize part of his B-vitamin needs while he lived, but they would consume him without compunction once he had ceased to be as complicated and delicately balanced a thing as a pilot—or as any other kind of life.

Garrard was, in short, to die before the DFC-3 had gotten fairly away from Sol; and when, after 12,000 apparent years, the DFC-3 returned to Earth, not even his mummy would be still aboard.

The chill that went through him at that seemed almost unrelated to the way he thought he felt about the discovery; it lasted an enormously long time, and insofar as he could characterize it at all, it seemed to be a chill of urgency and excitement—not at all the kind of chill he should be feeling at a virtual death sentence. Luckily it was not as intolerably violent as the last such emotional convulsion; and when it was over, two clock ticks later, it left behind a residuum of doubt.

Suppose that this effect of time-stretching was only mental? The rest of his bodily processes might still be keeping ship time; Garrard had no immediate reason to believe otherwise. If so, he would be able to move about only on ship time, too; it would take many apparent months to complete the simplest task.

But he would live, if that were the case. His mind would arrive at Alpha Centauri six thousand years older, and perhaps madder, than his body, but he would live.

If, on the other hand, his bodily movements were going to be as fast as his mental processes, he would have to be enormously careful. He would have to move slowly and exert as little force as possible. The normal human hand movement, in such a task as lifting a pencil, took the pencil from a state of rest to another state of rest by imparting to it an acceleration of about two feet per second—and, of course, decelerated it by the same amount. If Garrard were to attempt to impart to a two-pound weight, which was keeping ship time, an acceleration of 14,440 ft/sec^2 in his time, he'd have to exert a force of 900 pounds on it.

The point was not that it couldn't be done—but that it would take as much effort as pushing a stalled jeep. He'd never be able to lift that pencil with his forearm muscles alone; he'd have to put his back into the task.

And the human body wasn't engineered to maintain stresses of that magnitude indefinitely. Not even the most powerful professional weight lifter is forced to show his prowess throughout every minute of every day.

Pock.

That was the calendar again; another second had gone by. Or another two hours. It had certainly seemed longer than a second, but less than two hours, too. Evidently subjective time was an intensively recomplicated measure. Even in this world of microtime—in which Garrard's mind, at least, seemed to be operating—he could make the lapses between calendar ticks seem a little shorter by becoming actively interested in some problem or other. That would help during the waking hours, but it would help only if the rest of his body was *not* keeping the same time as his mind. If it was not, then he would lead an incredibly active, but perhaps not intolerable, mental life during the many centuries of his awake time and would be mercifully asleep for nearly as long.

Both problems—that of how much force he could exert with his body and how long he could hope to be asleep in his mind—emerged simultaneously into the forefront of his consciousness while he still sat inertly on the hammock, their terms still much muddled together. After the single tick of the calendar, the ship—or the part of it that Garrard could see from here—settled back into complete rigidity. The sound of the engines, too, did not seem to vary in frequency or amplitude, at least as far as his ears could tell. He was still not breathing. Nothing moved, nothing changed.

It was the fact that he could still detect no motion of his diaphragm or his rib cage that decided him at last. His body had to be keeping ship time, otherwise he would have blacked out from oxygen starvation long before now. That assumption explained, too, those two incredibly prolonged, seemingly sourceless saturnalias of emotion through which he had suffered: they had been nothing more or less than the response of his endocrine glands to the purely intellectual reactions he had experienced earlier. He had discovered that he was not breathing, had felt a flash of panic and had tried to sit up. Long after his mind had forgotten those two impulses, they had inched their way from his brain down his nerves to the glands and muscles involved, and actual, *physical* panic had supervened. When that was over, he actually *was* sitting up, though the flood of adrenaline had prevented his noticing the motion as he had made it. The later chill—less violent and apparently associated with the discovery that he might die long before the trip was completed—actually had been his body's response to a much earlier mental command; the abstract fever of interest he had felt while computing the time differential had been responsible for it.

Obviously, he was going to have to be very careful with apparently cold and intellectual impulses of any kind—or he would pay for them later with a prolonged and agonizing glandular reaction. Nevertheless, the discovery gave him considerable satisfaction, and Garrard allowed it free play; it certainly could not hurt him to feel pleased for a few hours, and the glandular pleasure might even prove helpful if it caught him at a moment of mental depression. Six thousand years, after all, provided a considerable number of opportunities for feeling down in the mouth; so it would be best to encourage all pleasure moments, and let the after-reaction last as long as it might. It would be the instants of panic, of gloom, which he would have to regulate sternly the moment they came into his mind; it would be those which would otherwise plunge him into four, five, six, perhaps even ten Garrard hours of emotional inferno.

Pock.

There now, that was very good: there had been two Garrard hours which he had passed with virtually no difficulty of any kind and without being especially conscious of their passage. If he could really settle down and become used to this kind of scheduling, the trip might not be as bad as he had at first feared. Sleep would take immense bites out of it; and during the waking periods he could put in one hell of a lot of creative thinking. During a single day of ship time, Garrard could get in more thinking than any philosopher of Earth could have managed during an entire lifetime. Garrard could, if he disciplined himself sufficiently, devote his mind for a century to running down the consequences of a single thought, down to the last detail and still have millennia left to go on to the next thought. What panoplies of pure reason could he not have assembled by the time 6,000 years had gone by? With sufficient concentration, he might come up with the solution to the problem of evil between breakfast and dinner of a single ship's day, and in a ship's month might put his finger on the first cause!

Pock.

Not that Garrard was sanguine enough to expect that he would remain logical or even sane throughout the trip. The vista was still grim in much of its detail. But the opportunities, too, were there. He felt a momentary regret that it hadn't been Haertel, rather than himself, who had been given such an opportunity . . .

Pock.

. . . for the old man could certainly have made better use of it than Garrard could. The situation demanded someone trained in the highest rigors of mathematics to be put to the best conceivable use. Still and all Garrard began to feel . . .

Pock.

. . . that he would give a good account of himself, and it tickled him to realize that (as long as he held on to his essential sanity) he would return . . .

Pock.

. . . to Earth after ten Earth months with knowledge centuries advanced beyond anything . . .

Pock.

. . . that Haertel knew or that anyone could know . . .

Pock.

. . . who had to work within a normal lifetime. *Pck.* The whole prospect tickled him. *Pck.* Even the clock tick seemed more cheerful. *Pck.* He felt fairly safe now *Pck* in disregarding his drilled-in command *Pck* against moving *Pck,* since in any *Pck* event the *Pck* had already *Pck* moved *Pck* without *Pck* being *Pck* harmed *Pck Pck Pck Pck Pck pckpckpckpckpckpckpck.* . . .

He yawned, stretched, and got up. It wouldn't do to be too pleased, after all. There were certainly many problems that still needed coping with, such as how to keep the impulse toward getting a ship-time task performed going, while his higher centers were following the ramifications of some purely philosophical point. And besides . . .

And besides, he had just moved.

More that that, he had just performed a complicated maneuver with his body *in normal time!*

Before Garrard looked at the calendar itself, the message it had been ticking away at him had penetrated. While he had been enjoying the protracted, glandular backwash of his earlier feeling of satisfaction, he had failed to notice, at least consciously, that the calendar was accelerating.

Good-by, vast ethical systems which would dwarf the Greeks. Good-by, calculuses aeons advanced beyond the spinor calculus of Dirac. Good-by, cosmologies by Garrard which would allot the Almighty a job as third-assistant waterboy in an n-dimensional backfield.

Good-by, also, to a project he had once tried to undertake in college—to describe and count the positions of love, of which, according to under-the-counter myth, there were supposed to be at least forty-eight. Garrard had never been able to carry his tally beyond twenty, and he had just lost what was probably his last opportunity to try again.

The microtime in which he had been living had worn off, only a few objective minutes after the ship had gone into overdrive and he had come out of the anesthetic. The long intellectual agony, with its glandular counterpoint, had come to nothing. Garrard was now keeping ship time.

Garrard sat back down on the hammock, uncertain whether to be bitter or relieved. Neither emotion satisfied him in the end; he simply felt unsatisfied. Microtime had been bad enough while it lasted; but now it was gone, and everything seemed normal. How could so transient a thing have killed Brown and Cellini? They were stable men, more stable, by his own private estimation, than Garrard himself. Yet he had come through it. Was there more to it than this?

And if there was—what, conceivably, could it be?

There was no answer. At his elbow, on the control chassis which he had thrust aside during that first moment of infinitely protracted panic, the calendar continued to tick. The engine noise was gone. His breath came and went in natural rhythm. He felt light and strong. The ship was quiet, calm, unchanging.

The calendar ticked, faster and faster. It reached and passed the first hour, ship time, of flight in overdrive.

Pock.

Garrard looked up in surprise. The familiar noise, this time, had been the hour hand jumping one unit. The minute hand was already sweeping past the past half-hour. The second hand was whirling like a propeller—and while he watched it, it speeded up to complete invisibility. . . .

Pock.

Another hour. The half-hour already passed. *Pock.* Another hour. *Pock.* Another, *Pock. Pock. Pock, Pock, Pock, Pock, pck-pck-pck-pck-pckpckpckpck. . . .*

The hands of the calendar swirled toward invisibility as time ran away with Garrard. Yet the ship did not change. It stayed there, rigid, inviolate, invulnerable. When the date tumblers reached a speed at which Garrard could no longer read them, he discovered that once more he could not move—and that, although his whole body seemed to be aflutter like that of a hummingbird, nothing coherent was coming to him through his senses. The room was dimming, becoming redder; or no, it was. . . .

But he never saw the end of the process, never was allowed to look from the pinnacle of macrotime toward which the Haertel overdrive was taking him.

Pseudo-death took him first.

III

That Garrard did not die completely, and within a comparatively short time after the DFC-3 had gone into overdrive, was due to the purest of accidents; but Garrard did not know that. In fact, he knew nothing at all for an indefinite period, sitting rigid and staring, his metabolism slowed down to next to nothing, his mind almost utterly inactive. From time to time, a single wave of low-level metabolic activity passed through him—what an electrician might have termed a "maintenance turnover"—in response to the urgings of some occult survival urge; but these were of so basic a nature as to reach his consciousness not at all. This was the pseudo-death.

When the observer actually arrived, however, Garrard woke. He could make very little sense out of what he saw or felt even now; but one fact was clear: the overdrive was off—and with it the crazy alterations in time rates—and there was strong light coming through one of the ports. The first leg of the trip was over. It had been these two changes in his environment which had restored him to life.

The thing (or things) which had restored him to consciousness, however, was—it was what? It made no sense. It was a construction, a rather fragile one, which completely surrounded his hammock. No, it wasn't a construction, but evidently something alive—a living being, organized horizontally, that had arranged itself in a circle about him. No, it was a number of beings. Or a combination of all of these things.

How it had gotten into the ship was a mystery, but there it was. Or there they were.

"How do you hear?" the creature said abruptly. Its voice, or their voices, came at equal volume from every point in the circle, but not from any particular point in it. Garrard could think of no reason why that should be unusual.

"I . . ." he said. "Or we—we hear with our ears. Here."

His answer, with its unintentionally long chain of open vowel sounds rang ridiculously. He wondered why he was speaking such an odd language.

"We-they wooed to pitch you-yours thiswise," the creature said. With a thump, a book from the DFC-3's ample library fell to the deck beside the hammock. "We wooed there and there and there for a many. You are the being-Garrard. We-they are the clinesterton beademung, with all of love."

"With all of love," Garrard echoed. The beademung's use of the language they both were speaking was odd; but again Garrard could find no logical reason why the beademung's usage should be considered wrong.

"Are—are you-they from Alpha Centauri?" he said hesitantly.

"Yes, we hear the twin radioceles, that show there beyond the gift-orifices. We-they pitched that the being-Garrard with most adoration these twins and had mind to them, soft and loud alike. How do you hear?"

This time the being-Garrard understood the question. "I hear Earth," he said. "But that is very soft, and does not show."

"Yes," said the beademung. "It is a harmony, not a first, as ours. The All-Devouring listens to lovers there, not on the radioceles. Let me-mine pitch you-yours so to have mind of the rodalent beademung and other brothers and lovers, along the channel which is fragrant to the being-Garrard."

Garrard found that he understood the speech without difficulty. The thought occurred to him that to understand a language on its own terms—without having to put it back into English in one's own mind—is an ability that is won only with difficulty and long practice. Yet, instantly his mind said, "But it *is* English," which of course it was. The offer the clinesterton beademung had just made was enormously hearted, and he in turn was much minded and of love, to his own delighting as well as to the beademungen; that almost went without saying.

There were many matings of ships after that, and the being-Garrard pitched the harmonies of the beademungen, leaving his ship with the many gift-orifices in harmonic for the All-Devouring to love, while the beademungen made show of they-theirs.

He tried, also, to tell how he was out of love with the overdrive, which wooed only spaces and times, and made featurelings. The rodalent beademung wooed the overdrive, but it did not pitch he-them.

Then the being-Garrard knew that all the time was devoured and he must hear Earth again.

"I pitch you-them to fullest love," he told the beademungen,

"I shall adore the radioceles of Alpha and Proxima Centauri, 'on Earth as it is in heaven.' Now the overdrive my-other must woo and win me and make me adore a featureling much like silence."

"But you will be pitched again," the clinesterton beademung said. "After you have adored Earth. You are much loved by Time, the All-Devouring. We-they shall wait for this othering."

Privately Garrard did not faith as much, but he said, "Yes, we-they will make a new wooing of the beademungen at some other radiant. With all of love."

On this the beademungen made and pitched adorations, and in the midst the overdrive cut in. The ship with the many gift-orifices and the being-Garrard him-other saw the twin radioceles sundered away.

Then, once more, came the pseudo-death.

IV

When the small candle lit in the endless cavern of Garrard's pseudo-dead mind, the DFC-3 was well inside the orbit of Uranus. Since the sun was still very small and distant, it made no spectacular display through the nearby port, and nothing called him from the postdeath sleep for nearly two days.

The computers waited patiently for him. They were no longer immune to his control; he could now tool the ship back to Earth himself if he so desired. But the computers were also designed to take into account the fact that he might be truly dead by the time the DFC-3 got back. After giving him a solid week, during which time he did nothing but sleep, they took over again. Radio signals began to go out, tuned to a special channel.

An hour later, a very weak signal came back. It was only a directional signal, and it made no sound inside the DFC-3—but it was sufficient to put the big ship in motion again.

It was that which woke Garrard. His conscious mind was still glazed over with the icy spume of the pseudo-death; and as far as he could see the interior of the cabin had not changed one whit, except for the book on the deck . . .

The book. The clinesterton beademung had dropped it there. But what under God was a clinesterton beademung? And what was he, Garrard, crying about? It didn't make sense. He remembered dimly some kind of experience out there by the Centauri twins . . .

. . . the twin radioceles . . .

There was another one of those words. It seemed to have Greek roots, but he knew no Greek—and besides, why would Centaurians speak Greek?

He leaned forward and actuated the switch which would roll the shutter off the front port, actually a telescope with a translucent viewing screen. It showed a few stars, and a faint nimbus off on one edge which might be the sun. At about one o'clock on the screen was a planet about the size of a pea which had tiny projections, like teacup handles, on each side. The DFC-3 hadn't passed Saturn on its way out; at that time it had been on the other side of the sun from the route the starship had had to follow. But the planet was certainly difficult to mistake.

Garrard was on his way home—and he was still alive and sane. Or was he still sane? These fantasies about Centaurians—which still seemed to have such a profound emotional effect upon him—did not argue very well for the stability of his mind.

But they were fading rapidly. When he discovered, clutching at the handiest fragments of the "memories," that the plural of *beademung* was *beademungen,* he stopped taking the problem seriously. Obviously a race of Centaurians who spoke Greek wouldn't also be forming weak German plurals. The whole business had obviously been thrown up by his unconscious.

But what *had* he found by the Centaurus stars?

There was no answer to that question but that incomprehensible garble about love, the All-Devouring and beademungen. Possibly, he had never seen the Centaurus stars at all, but had been lying here, cold as a mackerel, for the entire twenty months.

Or had it been 12,000 years? After the tricks the overdrive had played with time, there was no way to tell what the objective date actually was. Frantically Garrard put the telescope into action. Where was the Earth? After 12,000 years . . .

The Earth was there. Which, he realized swiftly, proved nothing. The Earth had lasted for many millions of years; 12,000 years was nothing to a planet. The moon was there, too; both were plainly visible, on the far side of the sun—but not too far to pick them out clearly, with the telescope at highest power. Garrard could even see a clear sun highlight on the Atlantic Ocean, not far east of Greenland; evidently the computers were bringing the DFC-3 in on the Earth from about twenty-three degrees north of the plane of the ecliptic.

The moon, too, had not changed. He could even see on its face the huge splash of white, mimicking the sun highlight on Earth's ocean, which was the magnesium hydroxide landing beacon, which had been dusted over the Mare Vaporum in the earliest days of space flight, with a dark spot on its southern edge which could only be the crater Monilius.

But that again proved nothing. The moon never changed. A film of dust laid down by modern man on its face would last for millennia—what, after all, existed on the moon to blow it away? The Mare Vaporum beacon covered more than 4,000 square miles; age would not dim it, nor could man himself undo it—either accidentally or on purpose—in anything under a century. When you dust an area that large on a world without atmosphere, it stays dusted.

He checked the stars against his charts. They hadn't moved; why should they have, in only 12,000 years? The pointer stars in the Dipper still pointed to Polaris. Draco, like a fantastic bit of tape, wound between the two Bears, and Cepheus and Cassiopeia, as it always had done. These constellations told him only that it was spring in the northern hemisphere of Earth.

But spring of what year?

Then, suddenly, it occurred to Garrard that he had a method of finding the answer. The moon causes tides in the Earth, and action and reaction are always equal and opposite. The moon cannot move things on Earth without itself being affected—and that effect shows up in the moon's angular momentum. The moon's distance from the Earth increases steadily by 0.6 inch every year. At the end of 12,000 years, it should be 600 feet farther away from the Earth.

Was it possible to measure? Garrard doubted it, but he got out his ephemeris and his dividers anyhow and took pictures. While he worked, the Earth grew nearer. By the time he had finished his first calculation—which was indecisive because it allowed a margin of error greater than the distances he was trying to check—Earth and moon were close enough in the telescope to permit much more accurate measurements.

Which were, he realized wryly, quite unnecessary. The computer had brought the DFC-3 back, not to an observed sun or planet, but simply to a calculated point. That Earth and moon would not be near that point when the DFC-3 returned was not an assumption that the computer could make. That the Earth was visible from here was already good and sufficient proof that no more time had elapsed than had been calculated for from the beginning.

This was hardly new to Garrard; it had simply been retired to the back of his mind. Actually he had been doing all this figuring for one reason and one reason only: because deep in his brain, set to work by himself, there was a mechanism that demanded counting. Long ago, while he was still trying to time the ship's calendar, he had initiated compulsive counting—and it appeared that he had been counting ever since. That had been one of the known dangers of deliberately starting such a mental mechanism; and now it was bearing fruit in these perfectly useless astronomical exercises.

The insight was healing. He finished the figures roughly, and that unheard moron deep inside his brain stopped counting at last. It had been pawing its abacus for twenty months now, and Garrard imagined that it was as glad to be retired as he was to feel it go.

His radio squawked and said anxiously, "DFC-3, DFC-3. Garrard, do you hear me? Are you still alive? Everybody's going wild down here. Garrard, if you hear me, call us!"

It was Haertel's voice. Garrard closed the dividers so convulsively that one of the points nipped into the heel of his hand. "Haertel, I'm here. DFC-3 to the project. This is Garrard." And then, without knowing quite why, he added: "With all of love."

Haertel, after all the hoopla was over, was more than interested in the time effects. "It certainly enlarges the manifold in which I was working," he said. "But I think we can account for it in the transformation. Perhaps even factor it out, which would eliminate it as far as the pilot is concerned. We'll see, anyhow."

Garrard swirled his highball reflectively. In Haertel's cramped old office in the project's administration shack, he felt both strange and as old, as compressed, constricted. He said, "I don't think I'd do that, Adolph. I think it saved my life."

"How?"

"I told you that I seemed to die after a while. Since I got home, I've been reading; and I've discovered that the psychologists take far less stock in the individuality of the human psyche than you and I do. You and I are physical scientists, so we think about the world as being all outside our skins—something which is to be observed, but which doesn't alter the essential *I*. But evidently, that old solipsistic position isn't quite true. Our very personalities, really, depend in large part upon *all* the things in our environment, large and small, that exist outside our skins. If by some means you could cut a human being off from every sense impression that comes to him from outside, he would cease to exist as a personality within two or three minutes. Probably he would die."

"Unquote: Harry Stack Sullivan," Haertel said, dryly. "So?"

"So," Garrard said, "think of what a monotonous environment the inside of a spaceship is. It's perfectly rigid, still, unchanging, lifeless. In ordinary interplanetary flight, in such an environment, even the most hardened spaceman may go off his rocker now and then. You know the typical spacemen's psychosis as well as I do, I suppose. The man's personality goes rigid, just like his surroundings. Usually he recovers as soon as he makes port and makes contact with a more or less normal world again.

"But in the DFC-3, I was cut off from the world around me much more severely. I couldn't look outside the ports—I was in overdrive, and there was nothing to see. I couldn't communicate with home because I was going faster than light. And then I found I couldn't move either, for an enormous long while; and that even the instruments that are in constant change for the usual spaceman wouldn't be in motion for me. Even those were fixed.

"After the time rate began to pick up, I found myself in an even more impossible box. The instruments moved, all right, but then they moved too *fast* for me to read them. The whole situation was now utterly rigid—and, in effect, I died. I froze as solid as the ship around me and stayed that way as long as the overdrive was on."

"By that showing," Haertel said dryly, "the time effects were hardly your friends."

"But they were, Adolph. Look. Your engines act on subjective time; they keep it varying along continuous curves—from far-too-slow to far-too-fast—and, I suppose, back down again. Now, this is a *situation of continuous change*. It wasn't marked enough, in the long run, to keep me out of pseudo-death; but it was sufficient to protect me from being obliterated altogether, which I think is what happened to Brown and Cellini. Those men knew that they could shut down the overdrive if they could just get to it, and they killed themselves trying. But I knew that I just had to sit and take it—and, by my great good luck, your sine-curve time variation made it possible for me to survive."

"Ah, ah," Haertel said. "A point worth considering—though I doubt that it will make interstellar travel very popular!"

He dropped back into silence, his thin mouth pursed. Garrard took a grateful pull at his drink.

At last Haertel said, "Why are you in trouble over these Centaurians? It seems to me that you have done a good job. It was nothing that you were a hero—any fool can be brave—but I see also that you *thought,* where Brown and Cellini evidently only reacted. Is there some secret about what you found when you reached those two stars?"

Garrard said, "Yes, there is. But I've already told you what it is. When I came out of the pseudo-death, I was just a sort of plastic palimpsest upon which anybody could have made a mark. My own environment, my ordinary Earth environment, was a hell of a long way off. My present surroundings were nearly as rigid as they had ever been. When I met the Centaurians—if I did, and I'm not at all sure of that—*they* became the most important thing in my world, and my personality changed to accommodate and understand them. That was a change about which I couldn't do a thing.

"Possibly I did understand them. But the man who understood them wasn't the same man you're talking to now, Adolph. Now that I'm back on Earth, I don't understand that man. He even spoke English in a way that's gibberish to me. If I can't understand myself during that period—and I can't; I don't even believe that that man was the Garrard I know—what hope have I of telling you or the project about the Centaurians? They found me in a controlled environment, and they altered me by entering it. Now that they're gone, nothing comes through; I don't even understand why I think they spoke English!"

"Did they have a name for themselves?"

"Sure," Garrard said. "They were the beademungen."

"What did they look like?"

"I never saw them."

Haertel leaned forward. "Then . . ."

"I heard them. I think." Garrard shrugged and tasted his Scotch again. He was home, and on the whole he was pleased.

But in his malleable mind he heard someone say, *On Earth, as it is in heaven;* and then, in another voice, which might also have been his own (why had he thought "him-other"?), *It is later than you think.*

"Adolph," he said, "is this all there is to it? Or are we going to go on with it from here? How long will it take to make a better starship, a DFC-4?"

"Many years," Haertel said, smiling kindly. "Don't be anxious, Garrard. You've come back, which is more than the others managed to do, and nobody will ask you to go out again. I really think that it's hardly likely that we'll get another ship built during your lifetime; and even if we do, we'll be slow to launch it. We really have very little information about what kind of playground you found out there."

"I'll go," Garrard said. "I'm not afraid to go back—I'd like to go. Now that I know how the DFC-3 behaves, I could take it out again, bring you back proper maps, tapes, photos."

"Do you really think," Haertel said, his face suddenly serious, "that we could let the DFC-3 go out again? Garrard, we're going to take that ship apart practically molecule by molecule; that's preliminary to the building of any DFC-4. And no more can we let you go. I don't mean to be cruel, but has it occurred to you that this desire to go back may be the result of some kind of posthypnotic suggestion? If so, the more badly you want to go back, the more dangerous to us all you may be. We are going to have to examine you just as thoroughly as we do the ship. If these beademungen wanted you to come back, they must have had a reason—and we have to know that reason."

Garrard nodded, but he knew that Haertel could see the slight movement of his eyebrows and the wrinkles forming in his forehead, the contractions of the small muscles which stop the flow of tears only to make grief patent on the rest of the face.

"In short," he said, *"don't move."*

Haertel looked politely puzzled. Garrard, however, could say nothing more. He had returned to humanity's common time and would never leave it again.

Not even, for all his dimly remembered promise, with all there was left in him of love.

From its first line, the authorial voice is direct, assertive: "Let me tell you of the creature called the Bork." Then we are off on a moody, grand story that encompasses time and passion with a measured tone, written in the style I've always thought of as High Romantic. Roger Zelazny had a sound education in the lyrical traditions of English literature, and from his first stories showed that he wanted to carry an air of zest, of swift intelligence without too much of the swagger to which much fantastic fiction falls prey. This story rings in memory, a marvel of compression. It achieves its tragic tone without stooping to the high diction and brooding rhetoric that are the familiar pitfalls of anyone who attempts to show the contrast between the mutable, mayfly minds of we humans and the enormous stage where we act out our dramas. More than any writer of his time, Zelazny knew how to do this; his language will echo down long corridors of time.

—Gregory Benford

THE ENGINE AT HEARTSPRING'S CENTER

by Roger Zelazny

Let me tell you of the creature called the Bork. It was born in the heart of a dying sun. It was cast forth upon this day from the river of past/future as a piece of time pollution. It was fashioned of mud and aluminum, plastic and some evolutionary distillate of seawater. It had spun dangling from the umbilical of circumstance till, severed by its will, it had fallen a lifetime or so later, coming to rest on the shoals of a world where things go to die. It was a piece of a man in a place by the sea near a resort grown less fashionable since it had become a euthanasia colony.

Choose any of the above and you may be right.

Upon this day, he walked beside the water, poking with his forked, metallic stick at the things the last night's storm had left: some shiny bit of detritus useful to the weird sisters in their crafts shop, worth a meal there or a dollop of polishing rouge for his smoother half; purple seaweed for a salty chowder he had come to favor; a buckle, a button, a shell; a white chip from the casino.

The surf foamed and the wind was high. The heavens were a blue-gray wall, unjointed, lacking the graffiti of birds or commerce. He left a jagged track and one footprint, humming and clicking as he passed over the pale sands. It was near to the point where the fork-tailed ice-birds paused for several days—a week at most—in their migrations. Gone now, portions of the beach were still dotted with their rust-colored droppings. There he saw the girl again, for the third time in as many days. She had tried before to speak with him, to detain him. He had ignored her for a number of reasons. This time, however, she was not alone.

She was regaining her feet, the signs in the sand indicating flight and collapse. She had on the same red dress, torn and stained now. Her black hair—short, with heavy bangs—lay in the only small disarrays of which it was capable. Perhaps thirty feet away was a young man from the Center, advancing toward her. Behind him drifted one of the seldom seen dispatch-machines—about half the size of a man and floating that same distance above the ground, it was shaped like a tenpin, and silver, its bulbous head-end faceted and illuminated, its three ballerina skirts tinfoil-thin and gleaming, rising and falling in rhythms independent of the wind.

Hearing him, or glimpsing him peripherally, she turned away from her pursuers, said, "Help me" and then she said a name.

He paused for a long while, although the interval was undetectable to her. Then he moved to her side and stopped again.

The man and the hovering machine halted also.

"What is the matter?" he asked, his voice smooth, deep, faintly musical.

"They want to take me," she said.

"Well?"

"I do not wish to go."

"Oh. You are not ready?"

"No, I am not ready."

"Then it is but a simple matter. A misunderstanding."

He turned toward the two.

"There has been a misunderstanding," he said. "She is not ready."

"This is not your affair, Bork," the man replied. "The Center has made its determination."

"Then it will have to reexamine it. She says that she is not ready.

"Go about your business, Bork."

The man advanced. The machine followed.

The Bork raised his hands, one of flesh, the others of other things.

"No," he said.

"Get out of the way," the man said. "You are interfering."

Slowly, the Bork moved toward them. The lights in the machine began to blink. Its skirts fell. With a sizzling sound it dropped to the sand and lay unmoving. The man halted, drew back a pace.

"I will have to report this—"

"Go away," said the Bork.

The man nodded, stooped, raised the machine. He turned and carried if off with him, heading up the beach, not looking back. The Bork lowered his arms.

"There," he said to the girl. "You have more time."

He moved away then, investigating shell-shucks and driftwood.

She followed him.

"They will be back," she said.

"Of course."

"What will I do then?"

"Perhaps by then you will be ready."

She shook her head. She laid her hand on his human part.

"No," she said. "I will not be ready."

"How can you tell, now?"

"I made a mistake," she said. "I should never have come here."

He halted and regarded her.

"That is unfortunate," he said. "The best thing that I can recommend is to go and speak with the therapists at the Center. They will find a way to persuade you that peace is preferable to distress."

"They were never able to persuade you," she said.

"I am different. The situation is not comparable."

"I do not wish to die."

"Then they cannot take you. The proper frame of mind is prerequisite. It is right there in the contract—Item Seven."

"They can make mistakes. Don't you think they ever make a mistake? They get cremated the same as the others."

"They are most conscientious. They have dealt fairly with me."

"Only because you are virtually immortal. The machines short out in your presence. No man could lay hands on you unless you willed it. And did they not try to dispatch you in a state of unreadiness?"

"That was the result of a misunderstanding."

"Like mine?"

"I doubt it."

He drew away from her, continuing on down the beach.

"Charles Eliot Borkman," she called.

That name again.

He halted once more, tracing lattices with his stick, poking out a design in the sand.

Then, "Why did you say that?" he asked.

"It is your name, isn't it?"

"No," he said. "That man died in deep space when a liner was jumped to the wrong coordinates, coming out too near a star gone nova."

"He was a hero. He gave half his body to the burning, preparing an escape boat for the others. And he survived."

"Perhaps a few pieces of him did. No more."

"It *was* an assassination attempt, wasn't it?"

"Who knows? Yesterday's politics are not worth the paper wasted on its promises, its threats."

"He wasn't just a politician. He was a statesman, a humanitarian. One of the very few to retire with more people loving him than hating him."

He made a chuckling noise.

"You are most gracious. But if that is the case, then the minority still had the final say. I personally think he was something of a thug. I am pleased, though, to hear that you have switched to the past tense."

"They patched you up so well that you could last forever. Because you deserved the best."

"Perhaps I already have. What do you want of me?"

"You came here to die and you changed your mind—"

"Not exactly. I've just never composed it in a fashion acceptable under the terms of Item Seven. To be at peace—"

"And neither have I. But I lack your ability to impress this fact on the Center."

"Perhaps if I went there with you and spoke to them . . ."

"No," she said. "They would only agree for so long as you were about. They call people like us life-malingerers and are much more casual about the disposition of our cases. I cannot trust them as you do without armor of my own."

"Then what would you have me do—girl?"

"Nora. Call me Nora. Protect me. That is what I want. You live near here. Let me come stay with you. Keep them away from me."

He poked at the pattern, began to scratch it out.

"You are certain that this is what you want?"

"Yes. Yes, I am."

"All right. You may come with me, then."

So Nora went to live with the Bork in his shack by the sea. During the weeks that followed, on each occasion when the representatives from the Center came about, the Bork bade them depart quickly, which they did. Finally, they stopped coming by.

Days, she would pace with him along the shores and help in the gathering of driftwood, for she liked a fire at night; and while heat and cold had long been things of indifference to him, he came in time and his fashion to enjoy the glow.

And on their walks he would poke into the dank trash heaps the sea had lofted and turn over stones to see what dwelled beneath.

"God! What do you hope to find in that?" she said, holding her breath and retreating.

"I don't know," he chuckled. "A stone? A leaf? A door? Something nice. Like that."

"Let's go watch the things in the tidepools. They're clean, at least."

"All right."

Though he ate from habit and taste rather than from necessity, her need for regular meals and her facility in preparing them led him to anticipate these occasions with something approaching a ritualistic pleasure. And it was later still after an evening's meal, that she came to polish him for the first time. Awkward, grotesque—perhaps it could have been. But as it occurred, it was neither of these. They sat before the fire, drying, warming, watching, silent. Absently, she picked up the rag he had let fall to the floor and brushed a fleck of ash from his flame-reflecting side. Later, she did it again. Much later, and this time with full attention, she wiped all the dust from the gleaming surface before going off to her bed.

One day she asked him, "Why did you buy the one-way ticket to this place and sign the contract, if you did not wish to die?"

"But I did wish it," he said.

"And something changed your mind after that? What?"

"I found here a pleasure greater than that desire."

"Would you tell me about it?"

"Surely. I found this to be one of the few situations—perhaps the only—where I can be happy. It is in the nature of the place itself: departure, a peaceful conclusion, a joyous going. Its contemplation here pleases me, living at the end of entropy and seeing that it is good."

"But it doesn't please you enough to undertake the treatment yourself?"

"No. I find in this reason for living, not for dying. It may seemed a warped satisfaction. But then, I am warped. What of yourself?"

"I just made a mistake. That's all."

"They screen you pretty carefully, as I recall. The only reason they made a mistake in my case was that they could not anticipate anyone finding in this place an inspiration to go on living. Could your situation have been similar?"

"I don't know. Perhaps . . ."

On days when the sky was clear they would rest in the yellow warmth of the sun, playing small games and sometimes talking of the birds that passed and of the swimming, drifting, branching, floating and flowering things in their pools. She never spoke of herself, saying whether it was love, hate, despair, weariness, or bitterness that had brought her to this place. Instead, she spoke of those neutral things they shared when the day was bright; and when the weather kept them indoors she watched the fire, slept, or polished his armor. It was only much later that she began to sing and to hum, small snatches of tunes recently popular or tunes quite old. At these times, if she felt his eyes upon her she stopped abruptly and turned to another thing.

One night then, when the fire had burned low, as she sat

buffing his plates, slowly, quite slowly, she said in a soft voice, "I believe that I am falling in love with you."

He did not speak, nor did he move. He gave no sign of having heard.

After a long while, she said, "It is most strange, finding myself feeling this way—here—under these circumstances . . ."

"Yes," he said, after a time.

After a longer while, she put down the cloth and took hold of his hand—the human one—and felt his grip tighten upon her own.

"Can you?" she said, much later.

"Yes. But I would crush you, little girl."

She ran her hands over his plates, then back and forth from flesh to metal. She pressed her lips against his only cheek that yielded.

"We'll find a way," she said, and of course they did.

In the days that followed she sang more often, sang happier things and did not break off when he regarded her. And sometimes he would awaken from the light sleep that even he required, awaken and through the smallest aperture of his lens note that she lay there or sat watching him, smiling. He sighed occasionally for the pure pleasure of feeling the rushing air within and about him, and there was a peace and a pleasure come into him of the sort he had long since relegated to the realms of madness, dream, and vain desire. Occasionally, he even found himself whistling.

One day as they sat on a bank, the sun nearly vanished, the stars coming on, the deepening dark was melted about a tiny wick of falling fire and she let go of his hand and pointed.

"A ship," she said.

"Yes," he answered, retrieving her hand.

"Full of people."

"A few, I suppose."

"It is sad."

"It must be what they want, or what they want to want."

"It is still sad."

"Yes. Tonight. Tonight it is sad."

"And tomorrow?"

"Then too, I daresay."

"Where is your old delight in the graceful end, the peaceful winding-down?"

"It is not on my mind so much these days. Other things are there."

They watched the stars until the night was all black and light and filled with cold air. Then, "What is to become of us?" she said.

"Become?" he said. "If you are happy with things as they are, there is no need to change them. If you are not, then tell me what is wrong."

"Nothing," she said. "When you put it that way, nothing. It was just a small fear—a cat scratching at my heart, as they say."

"I'll scratch your heart myself," he said, raising her as if she were weightless.

Laughing, he carried her back to the shack.

It was out of a deep, drugged-seeming sleep that he dragged himself/was dragged much later, by the sound of her weeping. His time-sense felt distorted, for it seemed an abnormally long interval before her image registered, and her sobs seemed unnaturally drawn out and far apart.

"What—is—it?" he said, becoming at the moment aware of the faint, throbbing, pinprick aftereffect in his biceps.

"I did not—want you to—awaken," she said. "Please go back to sleep."

"You are from the Center, aren't you?"

She looked away.

"It does not matter," he said.

"Sleep. Please. Do not lose the—"

"—requirements of Item Seven," he finished. "You always honor a contract, don't you?"

"That is not all that it was—to me."

"You meant what you said, that night?"

"I came to."

"Of course you would say that now. Item Seven—"

"You bastard!" she said, and she slapped him.

He began to chuckle, but it stopped when he saw the hypodermic on the table at her side. Two spent ampules lay with it.

"You didn't give me two shots," he said, and she looked away. "Come on." He began to rise. "We've got to get you to the Center. Get the stuff neutralized. Get it out of you."

She shook her head.

"Too late—already. Hold me. If you want to do something for me, do that."

He wrapped all of his arms about her and they lay that way while the tides and the winds cut, blew and ebbed, grinding their edges to an ever more perfect fineness.

I think—

Let me tell you of the creature called the Bork. It was born in the heart of a dying star. It was a piece of a man and pieces of many other things. If the things went wrong, the man-piece shut them down and repaired them. If he went wrong, they shut him down and repaired him. It was so skillfully fashioned that it might have lasted forever. But if part of it should die the other pieces need not cease to function, for it could still contrive to carry on the motions the total creature had once performed. It is a thing in a place by the sea that walks beside the water, poking with its forked, metallic stick at the other things the waves have tossed. The human piece, or a piece of the human piece, is dead.

Choose any of the above.

I read "Nerves" when I was in my first year of college. It was the first thing I read which had ordinary people in it, not Superman or movie stars or anything of that sort. At that time I did not know Lester del Rey, but later he became one of my favorite editors. The attempt to publish it as a separate novel somehow didn't come off, but the original novelette was marvelous. It was almost painlessly scientific.

—Marion Zimmer Bradley

NERVES

by Lester del Rey

The graveled walks between the sprawling, utilitarian structures of the National Atomic Products Co., Inc., were crowded with the usual five o'clock mass of young huskies just off work or going on the extra shift, and the company cafeteria was jammed to capacity and overflowing. But they made good-natured way for Doc Ferrel as he came out, not bothering to stop their horseplay as they would have done with any of the other half hundred officials of the company. He'd been just Doc to them too long for any need of formality.

He nodded back at them easily, pushed through, and went down the walk toward the Infirmary Building, taking his own time. When a man has turned fifty, with gray hairs and enlarged waistline to show for it, he begins to realize that comfort and relaxation are worth cultivating. Besides, Doc could see no good reason for filling his stomach with food and then rushing around in a flurry that gave him no chance to digest it. He let himself in the side entrance, palming his cigar out of long habit, and passed through the surgery to the door marked:

PRIVATE
ROGER T. FERREL
PHYSICIAN IN CHARGE

As always, the little room was heavy with the odor of stale smoke and littered with scraps of this and that. His assistant was already there, rummaging busily through the desk with the brass nerve that was typical of him; Ferrel had no objections to it, though, since Blake's rock-steady hands and unruffled brain were always dependable in a pinch of any sort.

Blake looked up and grinned confidently. "Hi, Doc. Where the deuce do you keep your cigarettes, anyway? Never mind, got 'em. . . . Ah, that's better! Good thing there's one room in this darned building where the 'No Smoking' signs don't count. You and the wife coming out this evening?"

"Not a chance, Blake." Ferrel stuck the cigar back in his mouth and settled down into the old leather chair, shaking his head. "Palmer phoned down half an hour ago to ask me if I'd stick through the graveyard shift. Seems the plant's got a rush order for some particular batch of dust that takes about twelve hours to cook, so they'll be running No. 3 and 4 till midnight or later."

"Hm-m-m. So you're hooked again. I don't see why any of us has to stick here—nothing serious ever pops up now. Look what I had today; three cases of athlete's foot—better send a memo down to the showers for extra disinfection—a guy with dandruff, four running noses, and the office boy with a sliver in his thumb! They bring everything to us except their babies—and they'd have them here if they could—but nothing that couldn't wait a week or a month. Anne's been counting on you and the missus, Doc; she'll be disappointed if you aren't there to celebrate her sticking ten years with me. Why don't you let the kid stick it out alone tonight?"

"I wish I could, but this happens to be my job. As a matter of fact, though, Jenkins worked up an acute case of duty and decided to stay on with me tonight." Ferrel twitched his lips in a stiff smile, remembering back to the time when his waistline had been smaller than his chest and he'd gone through the same feeling that destiny had singled him out to save the world. "The kid had his first real case today, and he's all puffed up. Handled it all by himself, so he's now Dr. Jenkins, if you please."

Blake had his own memories. "Yeah? Wonder when he'll realize that everything he did by himself came from your hints? What was it, anyway?"

"Same old story—simple radiation burns. No matter how much we tell the men when they first come in, most of them can't see why they should wear three ninety-five percent efficient shields when the main converter shield cuts off all but one-tenth percent of the radiation. Somehow, this fellow managed to leave off his two inner shields and pick up a year's burn in six hours. Now he's probably back on No. 1, still running through the hundred liturgies I gave him to say and hoping we won't get him sacked."

No. 1 was the first converter around which National Atomic had built its present monopoly in artificial radioactives, back in the days when shields were still inefficient to one part in a thousand and the materials handled were milder than the modern ones. They still used it for the gentle reactions, prices of converters being what they were; anyhow, if reasonable precautions were taken, there was no serious danger.

"A tenth percent will kill; five percent of that is one two-hundredth; five percent of that is one four-thousandth; and five percent again leaves one eighty-thousandth, safe for all but fools." Blake sing-songed the liturgy solemnly, then chuckled. "You're getting old, Doc; you used to give them a thousand times. Well, if you get the chance, you and Mrs. Ferrel drop out and say hello, even if it's after midnight. Anne's gonna be disappointed, but she ought to know how it goes. So long."

" 'Night." Ferrel watched him leave, still smiling faintly. Someday his own son would be out of medical school, and Blake would make a good man for him to start under and begin the same old grind upward. First, like young Jenkins, he'd be filled with his mission to humanity, tense and uncertain, but somehow things would roll along through Blake's stage and up, probably to Doc's own level, where the same old problems were solved in the same old way, and life settled down into a comfortable, mellow dullness.

There were worse lives, certainly, even though it wasn't like the mass of murders, kidnappings, and applied miracles played up in the current movie series about Dr. Hoozis. Come to think of it, Hoozis was supposed to be working in an atomic products plant right now—but one where chrome-plated converters covered with pretty neon tubes were mysteriously blowing up every second day, and men were brought in with blue flames all over them to be cured instantly in time to utter the magic words so the hero could dash in and put out the atomic flame barehanded. Ferrel grunted and reached back for his old copy of the *Decameron*.

Then he heard Jenkins out in the surgery, puttering around with quick, nervous little sounds. Never do to let the boy find him loafing back here, when the possible fate of the world so obviously hung on his alertness. Young doctors had to be disillusioned slowly, or they became bitter and their work suffered. Yet, in spite of his amusement at Jenkins' nervousness, he couldn't help envying the thin-faced young man's erect shoulders and flat stomach. Years crept by, it seemed.

Jenkins straightened out a wrinkle in his white jacket fussily and looked up. "I've been getting the surgery ready for instant use, Dr. Ferrel. Do you think it's safe to keep only Miss Dodd and one male attendant here—shouldn't we have more than the bare legally sanctioned staff?"

"Dodd's a one-man staff," Ferrel assured him. "Expecting accidents tonight?"

"No, sir, not exactly. But do you know what they're running off?"

"No." Ferrel hadn't asked Palmer; he'd learned long before that he couldn't keep up with the atomic engineering developments, and had stopped trying. "Some new type of atomic tank fuel for the army to use in its war games?"

"Worse than that, sir. They're making their first commercial run of Natomic I-713 in both No. 3 and 4 converters at once."

"So? Seems to me I did hear something about that. Had to do with killing off boll weevils, didn't it?" Ferrel was vaguely familiar with the process of sowing radioactive dust in a circle outside the weevil area, to isolate the pest, then gradually moving inward from the border. Used with proper precautions, it had slowly killed off the weevil and driven it back into half the territory once occupied.

Jenkins managed to look disappointed, surprised and slightly superior without a visible change of expression. "There was an article on it in the *Natomic Weekly Ray* of last issue, Dr. Ferrel. You probably know that the trouble with Natomic I-344, which they've been using, was its half life of over four months; that made the land sowed useless for planting the next year, so they had to move very slowly. I-713 has a half life of less than a week and reached safe limits in about two months, so they'll be able to isolate whole strips of hundreds of miles during the winter and still have the land usable by spring. Field tests have been highly successful, and we've just gotten a huge order from two States that want immediate delivery."

"After their legislatures waited six months debating whether to use it or not," Ferrel hazarded out of long experience. "Hm-m-m, sounds good if they can sow enough earthworms after them to keep the ground in good condition. But what's the worry?"

Jenkins shook his head indignantly. "I'm not worried. I simply think we should take every possible precaution and be ready for any accident; after all, they're working on something new, and a half life of a week is rather strong, don't you think? Besides, I looked over some of the reaction charts in the article, and— What was that?"

From somewhere to the left of the infirmary, a muffled growl was being accompanied by ground tremors; then it gave place to a steady hissing, barely audible through the insulated walls of the building. Ferrel listened a moment and shrugged. "Nothing to worry about, Jenkins. You'll hear it a dozen times a year. Ever since the Great War when he tried to commit harakiri over the treachery of his people, Hokusai's been bugs about getting an atomic explosive bomb which will let us wipe out the rest of the world. Some day you'll probably see the little guy brought in here minus his head, but so far he hasn't found anything with short enough a half life that can be controlled until needed. What about the reaction charts on I-713?"

"Nothing definite, I suppose." Jenkins turned reluctantly away from the sound, still frowning. "I know it worked in small lots, but there's something about one of the intermediate steps I distrust, sir. I thought I recognized . . . I tried to ask one of the engineers about it. He practically told me to shut up until I'd studied atomic engineering myself."

Seeing the boy's face whiten over tensed jaw muscles, Ferrel held back his smile and nodded slowly. Something funny there; of course. Jenkins' pride had been wounded, but hardly that much. Some day, he'd have to find out what was behind it. Little things like that could ruin a man's steadiness with the instruments, if he kept it to himself. Meantime, the subject was best dropped.

The telephone girl's heavily syllabized voice cut into his thoughts from the annunciator. "Dr. Ferrel. Dr. Ferrel wanted on the telephone. Dr. Ferrel, please!"

Jenkins' face blanched still further, and his eyes darted to his superior sharply. Doc grunted casually. "Probably Palmer's bored and wants to tell me all about his grandson again. He thinks that child's an all-time genius because it says two words at eighteen months."

But inside the office, he stopped to wipe his hands free of perspiration before answering; there was something contagious about Jenkins' suppressed fears. And Palmer's face on the little television screen didn't help any, though the director was wearing his usual set smile. Ferrel knew it wasn't about the baby this time, and he was right.

" 'Lo, Ferrel." Palmer's heartily confident voice was quite normal, but the use of the last name was a clear sign of some trouble. "There's been a little accident in the plant, they tell me. They're bringing a few men over to the infirmary for treatment—probably not right away, though. Has Blake gone yet?"

"He's been gone fifteen minutes or more. Think it's serious enough to call him back, or are Jenkins and myself enough?"

"Jenkins? Oh, the new doctor." Palmer hesitated, and his arms showed quite clearly the doodling operations of his hands, out of sight of the vision cell. "No, of course, no need to call Blake back, I suppose—not yet, anyhow. Just worry anyone who saw him coming in. Probably nothing serious."

"What is it—radiation burns, or straight accident?"

"Oh—radiation mostly—maybe accident, too. Someone got a little careless—you know how it is. Nothing to worry about, though. You've been through it before when they opened a port too soon."

Doc knew enough about that—if that's what it was. "Sure, we can handle that, Palmer. But I thought No. 1 was closing down at five-thirty tonight. Anyhow, how come they haven't installed the safety ports on it? You told me they had, six months ago."

"I didn't say it was No. 1, or that it was a manual port. You know, new equipment for new products." Palmer looked up at someone else, and his upper arms made a slight movement before he looked down at the vision cell again. "I can't go into it now, Dr. Ferrel; accident's throwing us off schedule, you see—details piling up on me. We can talk it over later, and you probably have to make arrangements now. Call me if you want anything."

The screen darkened and the phone clicked off abruptly, just as a muffled work started. The voice hadn't been Palmer's. Ferrel pulled his stomach in, wiped the sweat off his hands again, and went out into the surgery with careful casualness. Damn Palmer, why couldn't the fool give enough information to make decent preparations possible? He was sure 3 and 4 alone were operating, and they were supposed to be foolproof. Just what had happened?

Jenkins jerked up from a bench as he came out, face muscles tense and eyes filled with a nameless fear. Where he had been sitting, a copy of the *Weekly Ray* was lying open at a chart of symbols which meant nothing to Ferrel, except for the penciled line under one of the reactions. The boy picked it up and stuck it back on a table.

"Routine accident," Ferrel reported as naturally as he could, cursing himself for having to force his voice. Thank the Lord, the boy's hands hadn't trembled visibly when he was moving the paper; he'd still be useful if surgery were necessary. Palmer had said nothing of that, of course—he'd said nothing about entirely too much. "They're bringing a few men over for radiation burns, according to Palmer. Everything ready?"

Jenkins nodded tightly. "Quite ready, sir, as much as we can be for—routine accidents at 3 and 4! . . . Isotope R. . . . Sorry, Dr. Ferrel, I didn't mean that. Should we call in Dr. Blake and the other nurses and attendants?"

"Eh? Oh, probably we can't reach Blake, and Palmer doesn't think we need him. You might have Nurse Dodd locate Meyers—the others are out on dates by now if I know them, and the two nurses should be enough, with Jones; they're better than a flock of the others anyway." Isotope R? Ferrel remembered the name but nothing else. Something an engineer had said once—but he couldn't recall in what connection—or had Hokusai mentioned it? He watched Jenkins leave and turned back on an impulse to his office where he could phone in reasonable privacy.

"Get me Matsuura Hokusai." He stood, drumming on the table impatiently until the screen finally lighted and the little Japanese looked out of it, "Hoke, do you know what they were turning out over at 3 and 4?"

The scientist nodded slowly, his wrinkled face as expressionless as his unaccented English. "Yess, they are make I-713 for the weevil. Why you assk?"

"Nothing; just curious. I heard rumors about an Isotope R and wondered if there was any connection. Seems they had a little accident over there, and I want to be ready for whatever comes of it."

For a fraction of a second, the heavy lids on Hokusai's eyes seemed to lift, but his voice remained neutral, only slightly faster. "No connection, Dr. Ferrel, they are not make Issotope R, very much assure you. Besst you forget Issotope R. Very sorry. Dr. Ferrel, I must now see accident. Thank you for call. Goodbye." The screen was blank again, along with Ferrel's mind.

Jenkins was standing in the door, but had either heard nothing or seemed not to know about it. "Nurse Meyers is coming back," he said. "Shall I get ready for curare injections?"

"Uh—might be a good idea." Ferrel had no intention of being surprised again, no matter what the implication of the words. Curare, one of the greatest poisons, known to South American primitives for centuries and only recently synthesized by modern chemistry, was the final resort for use in cases of radiation injury that was utterly beyond control. While the infirmary stocked it for such emergencies, in the long years of Doc's practice it had been used only twice; neither experience had been pleasant. Jenkins was either thoroughly frightened or overly zealous—unless he knew something he had no business knowing.

"Seems to take them long enough to get the men here—can't be too serious, Jenkins, or they'd move faster."

"Maybe." Jenkins went on with his preparations, dissolving dried plasma in distilled, de-aerated water, without looking up. "There's the litter siren now. You'd better get washed up while I take care of the patients."

Doc listened to the sound that came in as a faint drone from outside, and grinned slightly. "Must be Beel driving; he's the only man fool enough to run the siren when the run-ways are empty. Anyhow, if you'll listen, it's the out trip he's making. Be at least five minutes before he gets back." But he turned into the washroom, kicked on the hot water and began scrubbing vigorously with the strong soap.

Damn Jenkins! Here he was preparing for surgery before he had any reason to suspect the need, and the boy was running things to suit himself, pretty much, as if armed with superior knowledge. Well, maybe he was. Either that, or he was simply half crazy with old wives' fears of anything relating to atomic reactions, and that didn't seem to fit the case. He rinsed off as

Jenkins came in, kicked on the hot-air blast and let his arms dry, then bumped against a rod that brought out rubber gloves on little holders. "Jenkins, what's all this Isotope R business, anyway? I've heard about it somewhere—probably from Hokusai. But I can't remember anything definite."

"Naturally—there isn't anything definite. That's the trouble." The young doctor tackled the area under his fingernails before looking up; then he saw Ferrel was slipping into his surgeon's whites that had come out on a hanger, and waited until the other was finished. "R's one of the big maybe problems of atomics. Purely theoretical, and none's been made yet—it's either impossible or can't be done in small control batches, safe for testing. That's the trouble, as I said; nobody knows anything about it, except that—if it can exist—it'll break down in a fairly short time into Mahler's Isotope. You've heard of that?"

Doc had—twice. The first had been when Mahler and half his laboratory had disappeared with accompanying noise. He'd been making a comparatively small amount of the new product designed to act as a starter for other reactions. Later, Maicewicz had tackled it on a smaller scale, and that time only two rooms and three men had gone up in dust particles. Five or six years later, atomic theory had been extended to the point where any student could find why the apparently safe product decided to become pure helium and energy in approximately one billionth of a second.

"How long a time?"

"Half a dozen theories, and no real idea." They'd come out of the washrooms, finished except for their masks. Jenkins ran his elbow into a switch that turned on the ultraviolets that were supposed to sterilize the entire surgery, then looked around questioningly. "What about the supersonics?"

Ferrel kicked them on, shuddering as the bone-shaking harmonic hum indicated their activity. He couldn't complain about the equipment, at least. Ever since the last accident, when the State Congress developed ideas, there'd been enough gadgets lying around to stock up several small hospitals. The supersonics were intended to penetrate through all solids in the room, sterilizing where the UV light couldn't reach. A whistling note in the harmonics reminded him of something that had been tickling around in the back of his mind for minutes.

"There was no emergency whistle, Jenkins. Hardly seems to me they'd neglect that if it were so important."

Jenkins grunted skeptically and eloquently. "I read in the papers a few days ago where Congress was thinking of moving all atomic plants—meaning National, of course—out into the Mojave Desert. Palmer wouldn't like that . . . There's the siren again."

Jones, the male attendant, had heard it, and was already running out the fresh stretcher for the litter into the back receiving room. Half a minute later, Beel came trundling in the detachable part of the litter. "Two," he announced. "More coming up as soon as they can get to 'em, Doc."

There was blood spilled over the canvas, and a closer inspection indicated its source in a severed jugular vein, now held in place with a small safety pin that had fastened the two sides of the cut with a series of little pricks around which the blood had clotted enough to stop further loss.

Doc kicked off the supersonics with relief and indicated the man's throat. "Why wasn't I called out instead of having him brought here?"

"Hell, Doc, Palmer said bring 'em in and I brought 'em—I dunno. Guess some guy pinned up this fellow so they figured he could wait. Anything wrong?"

Ferrel grimaced. "With a split jugular, nothing that stops the bleeding's wrong, orthodox or not. How many more, and what's wrong out there?"

"Lord knows, Doc. I only drive 'em. I don't ask questions. So long!" He pushed the new stretcher up on the carriage, went wheeling it out to the small two-wheeled tractor that completed the litter. Ferrel dropped his curiosity back to its proper place and turned to the jugular case, while Dodd adjusted her mask. Jones had their clothes off, swabbed them down hastily, and wheeled them out on operating tables into the center of the surgery.

"Plasma!" A quick examination had shown Doc nothing else wrong with the jugular case, and he made the injection quickly. Apparently the man was only unconscious from shock induced by loss of blood, and the breathing and heart action resumed a more normal course as the liquid filled out the depleted blood vessels. He treated the wound with a sulphonamide derivative in routine procedure, cleaned and sterilized the edges gently, applied clamps carefully, removed the pin, and began stitching with the complicated little motor needle—one of the few gadgets for which he had any real appreciation. A few more drops of blood had spilled, but not seriously, and the wound was now permanently sealed. "Save the pin, Dodd. Goes in the collection. That's all for this. How's the other, Jenkins?"

Jenkins pointed to the back of the man's neck, indicating a tiny bluish object sticking out. "Fragment of steel, clear into the medulla oblongata. No blood loss, but he's been dead since it touched him. Want me to remove it?"

"No need—mortician can do it if they want. . . . If these are a sample, I'd guess it as a plain industrial accident, instead of anything connected with radiation."

"You'll get that, too, Doc." It was the jugular case, apparently conscious and normal except for pallor. "We weren't in the converter house. Hey, I'm all right! . . . I'll be—"

Ferrel smiled at the surprise on the fellow's face. "Thought you were dead, eh? Sure, you're all right, if you'll take it easy. A torn jugular either kills you or else it's nothing to worry about. Just pipe down and let the nurse put you to sleep, and you'll never know you got it."

"Lord! Stuff came flying out of the air-intake like bullets out of a machine gun. Just a scratch, I thought; then Jake was bawling like a baby and yelling for a pin. Blood all over the place—then here I am, good as new."

"Uh-huh." Dodd was already wheeling him off to a ward room, her grim face wrinkled into a half-quizzical expression over the mask. "Doctor said to pipe down, didn't he? Well!"

As soon as Dodd vanished, Jenkins sat down, running his hand over his cap; there were little beads of sweat showing where the goggles and mask didn't entirely cover his face. " 'Stuff came flying out of the air-intake like bullets out of a machine gun,' " he repeated softly. "Dr. Ferrel, these two cases were outside the converter—just by-product accidents. Inside—"

"Yeah." Ferrel was picturing things himself, and it wasn't pleasant. Outside, matter tossed through the air ducts; inside—He left it hanging, as Jenkins had. "I'm going to call Blake. We'll probably need him."

2

"Give me Dr. Blake's residence—Maple 2337," Ferrel said quickly into the phone. The operator looked blank for a second, starting and then checking a purely automatic gesture toward the plugs. "Maple 2337, I said."

"I'm sorry, Dr. Ferrel, I can't give you an outside line. All trunk lines are out of order." There was a constant buzz from the board, but nothing showed in the panel to indicate whether from white inside lights or the red trunk indicators.

"But—this is an emergency, operator. I've got to get in touch with Dr. Blake!"

"Sorry, Dr. Ferrel. All trunk lines are out of order." She started to reach for the plug, but Ferrel stopped her.

"Give me Palmer, then—and no nonsense! If his line's busy, cut me in, and I'll take the responsibility."

"Very good." She snapped at her switches. "I'm sorry, emergency call from Dr. Ferrel. Hold the line and I'll reconnect you." Then Palmer's face was on the panel, and this time the man was making no attempt to conceal his expression of worry.

"What is it, Ferrel?"

"I want Blake here—I'm going to need him. The operator says—"

"Yeah," Palmer nodded tightly, cutting in. "I've been trying to get him myself, but his house doesn't answer. Any idea of where to reach him?"

"You might try the Bluebird or any of the other night clubs around there." Damn, why did this have to be Blake's celebration night? No telling where he could be found by this time.

Palmer was speaking again. "I've already had all the nightclubs and restaurants called, and he doesn't answer. We're paging the movie houses and theaters now—just a second. . . . Nope, he isn't there, Ferrel. Last reports, no response."

"How about sending out a general call over the radio?"

"I'd . . . I'd like to, Ferrel, but it can't be done." The manager had hesitated for a fraction of a second, but his reply was positive. "Oh, by the way, we'll notify your wife you won't be home. Operator! You there? Good, reconnect the Governor!"

There was no sense in arguing into a blank screen, Doc realized. If Palmer wouldn't put through a radio call, he wouldn't, though it had been done once before. "All trunk lines are out of order. . . . We'll notify your wife. . . . Reconnect the Governor!" They weren't even being careful to cover up. He must have repeated the words aloud as he backed out of the office, still staring at the screen, for Jenkins' face twitched into a maladjusted grin.

"So we're cut off. I knew it already; Meyers just got in with more details." He nodded toward the nurse, just coming out of the dressing room and trying to smooth out her uniform. Her almost pretty face was more confused than worried.

"I was just leaving the plant, Dr. Ferrel, when my name came up on the outside speaker, but I had trouble getting here. We're locked in! I saw them at the gate—guards with sticks. They were turning back everyone that tried to leave, and wouldn't tell why, even. Just general orders that no one was to leave until Mr. Palmer gave his permission. And they weren't going to let me back in at first. Do you suppose . . . do you know what it's all about? I heard little things that didn't mean anything, really, but—"

"I know just about as much as you do, Meyers, though Palmer said something about carelessness with one of the ports on No. 3 or 4," Ferrel answered her. "Probably just precautionary measures. Anyway, I wouldn't worry about it yet."

"Yes, Dr. Ferrel." She nodded and turned back to the front office, but there was no assurance in her look. Doc realized that neither Jenkins nor himself was a picture of confidence at the moment.

"Jenkins," he said, when she was gone, "if you know anything I don't, for the love of Mike, out with it! I've never seen anything like this around here."

Jenkins shook himself, and for the first time since he'd been there, used Ferrel's nickname. "Doc, I don't—that's why I'm in a blue funk. I know just enough to be less sure than you can be, and I'm scared as hell!"

"Let's see your hands." The subject was almost a monomania with Ferrel, and he knew it, but he also knew it wasn't unjustified. Jenkins' hands came out promptly, and there was no tremble to them. The boy threw up his arm so the sleeve slid beyond the elbow, and Ferrel nodded; there was no sweat trickling down from the armpits to reveal a worse case of nerves than showed on the surface. "Good enough, son; I don't care how scared you are—I'm getting that way myself—but with

Blake out of the picture, and the other nurses and attendants sure to be out of reach, I'll need everything you've got."

"Doc?"

"Well?"

"If you'll take my word for it, I can get another nurse here—and a good one, too. They don't come any better, or any steadier, and she's not working now. I didn't expect her—well, anyhow, she'd skin me if I didn't call when we need one. Want her?"

"No trunk lines for outside calls," Doc reminded him. It was the first time he'd seen any real enthusiasm on the boy's face, and however good or bad the nurse was, she'd obviously be of value in bucking up Jenkins' spirits. "Go to it, though; right now we can probably use any nurse. Sweetheart?"

"Wife." Jenkins went toward the dressing room. "And I don't need the phone; we used to carry ultra-short-wave personal radios to keep in touch, and I've still got mine here. And if you're worried about her qualifications, she handed instruments to Bayard at Mayo's for five years—that's how I managed to get through medical school!"

The siren was approaching again when Jenkins came back, the little tense lines about his lips still there, but his whole bearing somehow steadier. He nodded. "I called Palmer, too, and he O.K.'d her coming inside on the phone without wondering how I'd contacted her. The switchboard girl has standing orders to route all calls from us through before anything else, it seems."

Doc nodded, his ear cocked toward the drone of the siren that drew up and finally ended on a sour wheeze. There was a feeling of relief from tension about him as he saw Jones appear and go toward the rear entrance; work, even under the pressure of an emergency, was always easier than sitting around waiting for it. He saw two stretchers come in, both bearing double loads, and noted that Beel was babbling at the attendant, the driver's usually phlegmatic manner completely gone.

"I'm quitting; I'm through tomorrow! No more watching 'em drag out stiffs for me—not that way. Dunno why I gotta go back, anyhow; it won't do 'em any good to get in further, even if they can. From now on, I'm driving a truck, so help me I am!"

Ferrel let him rave on, only vaguely aware that the man was

close to hysteria. He had no time to give to Beel now as he saw the raw red flesh through the visor of one of the armor suits. "Cut off what clothes you can, Jones," he directed. "At least get the shield suits off them. Tannic acid ready, nurse?"

"Ready." Meyers answered together with Jenkins, who was busily helping Jones strip off the heavily armored suits and helmets.

Ferrel kicked on the supersonics again, letting them sterilize the metal suits—there was going to be no chance to be finicky about asepsis; the supersonics and ultraviolet tubes were supposed to take care of that, and they'd have to do it, to a large extent, little as he liked it. Jenkins finished his part, dived back for fresh gloves, with a mere cursory dipping of his hands into antiseptic and rinse. Dodd followed him, while Jones wheeled three of the cases into the middle of the surgery, ready for work; the other had died on the way in.

It was going to be messy work, obviously. Where metal from the suits had touched, or come near touching, the flesh was burned—crisped, rather. And that was merely a minor part of it, as was the more than ample evidence of major radiation burns, which had probably not stopped at the surface, but pene trated through the flesh and bones into the vital interior organs. Much worse, the writhing and spasmodic muscular contractions indicated radioactive matter that had been forced into the flesh and was acting directly on the nerves controlling the motor impulses. Jenkins looked hastily at the twisting body of his case, and his face blanched to a yellowish white; it was the first real example of the full possibilities of an atomic accident he'd seen.

"Curare," he said finally, the word forced out, but level. Meyers handed him the hypodermic and he inserted it, his hand still steady—more than normally steady, in fact, with that absolute lack of movement that can come to a living organism only under the stress of emergency. Ferrel dropped his eyes back to his own case, both relieved and worried.

From the spread of the muscular convulsions, there could be only one explanation—somehow, radioactives had not only worked their way through the air grills, but had been forced through the almost airtight joints and sputtered directly into the flesh of the men. Now they were sending out radiations into every nerve, throwing aside the normal orders from the brain and spinal column, setting up anarchic orders of their own that left the muscles to writhe and jerk, one against the other, without order or reason, or any of the normal restraints the body places upon itself. The closest parallel was that of a man undergoing metrozol shock for schizophrenia, or a severe case of strychnine poisoning. He injected curare carefully, metering out the dosage according to the best estimate he could make, but Jenkins had been acting under a pressure that finished the second injection as Doc looked up from his first. Still, in spite of the rapid spread of the drug, some of the twitching went on.

"Curare," Jenkins repeated, and Doc tensed mentally; he'd still been debating whether to risk extra dosage. But he made no counter-order, feeling slightly relieved this time at having the matter taken out of his hands; Jenkins went back to work, pushing up the injections to the absolute limit of safety, and slightly beyond. One of the cases had started a weird minor moan that hacked on and off as his lungs and vocal cords went in and out of synchronization, but it quieted under the drug, and in a matter of minutes the three lay still, breathing with the shallow flaccidity common to curare treatment. They were still moving slightly, but where before they were perfectly capable of breaking their own bones in uncontrolled efforts, now there was only motion similar to a man with a chill.

"God bless the man who synthesized curare," Jenkins muttered as he began cleaning away damaged flesh, Meyers assisting.

Doc could repeat that; with the older, natural product, true standardization and exact dosage had been next to impossible. Too much, and its action on the body was fatal; the patient died from "exhaustion" of his chest muscles in a matter of minutes. Too little was practically useless. Now that the danger of self-injury and fatal exhaustion from wild exertion was over, he could attend to such relatively unimportant things as the agony still going on—curare had no particular effect on the sensory nerves. He injected neo-heroin and began cleaning the burned areas and treating them with the standard tannic-acid routine; first with a sulphonamide to eliminate possible infection, glancing up occasionally at Jenkins.

He had no need to worry, though; the boy's nerves were frozen into an unnatural calm that still pressed through with a speed Ferrel made no attempt to equal, knowing his work would suffer for it. At a gesture, Dodd handed him the little radiation detector, and he began hunting over the skin, inch by inch, for the almost microscopic bits of matter; there was no hope of finding all now, but the worst deposits could be found and removed; later, with more time, a final probing could be made.

"Jenkins," he asked, "how about I-713's chemical action? Is it basically poisonous to the system?"

"No. Perfectly safe except for radiation. Eight in the outer electron ring, chemically inert."

That, at least, was a relief. Radiations were bad enough in and of themselves, but when coupled with metallic poisoning, like the old radium or mercury poisoning, it was even worse. The small colloidally fine particles of I-713 in the flesh would set up their own danger signal, and could be scraped away in the worst cases; otherwise, they'd probably have to stay until the isotope exhausted itself. Mercifully, its half-life was short, which would decrease the long hospitalization and suffering of the men.

Jenkins joined Ferrel on the last patient, replacing Dodd at handing instruments. Doc would have preferred the nurse, who was used to his little signals, but he said nothing, and was surprised to note efficiency of the boy's cooperation. "How about the breakdown products?" he asked.

"I-713? Harmless enough, mostly, and what isn't harmless isn't concentrated enough to worry about. That is, if it's still I-713. Otherwise—"

Otherwise, Doc finished mentally, the boy meant there'd be no danger from poisoning, at least. Isotope R, with an uncertain degeneration period, turned into Mahler's Isotope, with a complete breakdown in a billionth of a second. He had a fleeting vision of men, filled with a fine dispersion of that, suddenly erupting over their body with a violence that could never be described; Jenkins must have been thinking the same thing. For a few seconds, they stood there, looking at each other silently, but neither chose to speak of it. Ferrel reached for the probe, Jenkins shrugged, and they went on with their work and their thoughts.

It was a picture impossible to imagine, which they might or might not see; if such an atomic blowup occurred, what would happen to the laboratory was problematical. No one knew the exact amount Maicewicz had worked on, except that it was the smallest amount he could make, so there could be no good estimate of the damage. The bodies on the operating tables, the little scraps of removed flesh containing the minute globules of radioactivity, even the instruments that had come in contact with them, were bombs waiting to explode. Ferrel's own fingers took on some of the steadiness that was frozen in Jenkins as he went about his work, forcing his mind onto the difficult labor at hand.

It might have been minutes or hours later when the last dressing was in place and the three broken bones of the worst case were set. Meyers and Dodd, along with Jones, were taking care of the men, putting them into the little wards, and the two physicians were alone, carefully avoiding each other's eyes, waiting without knowing exactly what they expected.

Outside, a droning chug came to their ears, and the thump of something heavy moving over the runways. By common impulse they slipped to the side door and looked out, to see the rear end of one of the electric tanks moving away from them. Night had fallen some time before, but the gleaming lights from the big towers around the fence made the plant stand out in glaring detail. Except for the tank moving away, though, other buildings cut off their view.

Then, from the direction of the main gate, a shrill whistle cut the air and there was the sound of men's voices, though the words were indistinguishable. Sharp, crisp syllables followed, and Jenkins nodded slowly to himself. "Ten'll get you a hundred," he began, "that— Uh, no use betting. It is."

Around the corner a squad of men in state militia uniform marched briskly, bayoneted rifles on their arms. With efficient precision, they spread out under a sergeant's direction, each taking a post before the door of one of the buildings, one approaching the place where Ferrel and Jenkins stood.

"So that's what Palmer was talking to the Governor about," Ferrel muttered. "No use asking them questions, I suppose; they know less than we do. Come on inside where we can sit down and rest. Wonder what good the militia can do here—unless Palmer's afraid someone inside's going to crack and cause trouble."

Jenkins followed him back to the office and accepted a cigarette automatically as he flopped back into a chair. Doc was discovering just how good it felt to give his muscles and nerves a chance to relax, and realizing that they must have been far longer in the surgery than he had thought. "Care for a drink?"

"Uh—is it safe, Doc? We're apt to be back in there any minute."

Ferrel pulled a grin onto his face and nodded. "It won't hurt you—we're just enough on edge and tired for it to be burned up inside for fuel instead of reaching our nerves. Here." It was a generous slug of rye he poured for each, enough to send an almost immediate warmth through them, and to relax their overtensed nerves. "Wonder why Beel hasn't been back long ago?"

"That tank we saw probably explains it; it got too tough for the men to work in just their suits, and they've had to start excavating through the converters with the tanks. Electric, wasn't it, battery powered? . . . So there's enough radiation loose out there to interfere with atomic-powered machines, then. That means whatever they're doing is tough and slow work. Anyhow, it's more important that they damp the action than get the men out, if they only realize it— Sue!"

Ferrel looked up quickly to see the girl standing there, already dressed for surgery, and he was not too old for a little glow of appreciation to creep over him. No wonder Jenkins' face lighted up. She was small, but her figure was shaped like that of a taller girl, not in the cute or pert lines usually associated with shorter women, and the serious competence of her expression hid none of the liveliness of her face. Obviously she was several years older than Jenkins, but as he stood up to greet her, her face softened and seemed somehow youthful beside the boy's as she looked up.

"You're Dr. Ferrel?" she asked, turning to the older man. "I was a little late—there was some trouble at first about letting me in—so I went directly to prepare before bothering you. And just so you won't be afraid to use me, my credentials are all here."

She put the little bundle on the table, and Ferrel ran through them briefly; it was better than he'd expected. Technically she wasn't a nurse at all, but a doctor of medicine, a so-called nursing doctor; there'd been the need for assistants midway between doctor and nurse for years, having the general training and abilities of both, but only in the last decade had the actual course been created, and the graduates were still limited to a few. He nodded and handed them back.

"We can use you, Dr.—"

"Brown—professional name, Dr. Ferrel. And I'm used to being called just Nurse Brown."

Jenkins cut in on the formalities. "Sue, is there any news outside about what's going on here?"

"Rumors, but they're wild, and I didn't have a chance to hear many. All I know is that they're talking about evacuating the city and everything within fifty miles of here, but it isn't official. And some people were saying the Governor was sending in troops to declare martial law over the whole section, but I didn't see any except here."

Jenkins took her off, then, to show her the Infirmary and introduce her to Jones and the two other nurses, leaving Ferrel to wait for the sound of the siren again, and to try putting two and two together to get sixteen. He attempted to make sense out of the article in the *Weekly Ray*, but gave it up finally; atomic theory had advanced too far since the sketchy studies he'd made, and the symbols were largely without meaning to him. He'd have to rely on Jenkins, it seemed. In the meantime, what was holding up the litter? He should have heard the warning siren long before.

It wasn't the litter that came in next, though, but a group of five men, two carrying a third, and a fourth supporting the fifth. Jenkins took the carried man over, Brown helping him; it was similar to the former cases, but without the actual burns from contact with hot metal. Ferrel turned to the men.

"Where's Beel and the litter?" He was inspecting the supported man's leg as he asked, and began work on it without moving the fellow to a table. Apparently a lump of radioactive matter the size of a small pea had been driven half an inch into the flesh below the thigh, and the broken bone was the result of the violent contractions of the man's own muscles under the stimulus of the radiation. It wasn't pretty. Now, however, the strength of the action had apparently burned out the nerves around, so the leg was comparatively limp and without feeling; the man lay watching, relaxed on the bench in a half-comatose condition, his eyes popping out and his lips twisted into a sick grimace, but he did not flinch as the wound was scraped out. Ferrel was working around a small leaden shield, his arms covered with heavily leaded gloves, and he dropped the scraps of flesh and isotope into a box of the same metal.

"Beel—he's out of this world, Doc," one of the others answered when he could tear his eyes off the probing. "He got himself blotto, somehow, and wrecked the litter before he got back. Couldn't take it, watching us grapple 'em out—and we hadda go after 'em without a drop of hooch!"

Ferrel glanced at him quickly, noticing Jenkins' head jerk around as he did so. "You were getting them out? You mean you didn't come from in there?"

"Heck, no, Doc. Do we look that bad? Them two got it when the stuff decided to spit on 'em clean through their armor. Me, I got me some nice burns, but I ain't complaining—I got a look at a couple of stiffs, so I'm kicking about nothing!"

Ferrel hadn't noticed the three who had traveled under their own power, but he looked now, carefully. They were burned, and badly, by radiations, but the burns were still new enough not to give them too much trouble, and probably what they'd just been through had temporarily deadened their awareness of pain, just as a soldier on the battlefield may be wounded and not realize it until the action stops. Anyway, atomjacks were not noted for sissiness.

"There's almost a quart in the office there on the table," he told them. "One good drink apiece—no more. Then go up front and I'll send Nurse Brown in to fix up your burns as well as can be for now." Brown could apply the unguents developed to heal radiation burns as well as he could, and some division of work that would relieve Jenkins and himself seemed necessary. "Any chance of finding any more living men in the converter housings?"

"Maybe. Somebody said the thing let out a groan half a minute before it popped, so most of 'em had a chance to duck into the two safety chambers. Figure on going back there and pushing tanks ourselves unless you say no; about half an hour's work left before we can crack the chambers, I guess, then we'll know."

"Good. And there's no sense in sending in every man with a burn, or we'll be flooded here; they can wait and it looks as if we'll have plenty of serious stuff to care for. Dr. Brown, I guess you're elected to go out with the men—have one of them drive the spare litter Jones will show you. Salve down all the burn cases, put the worst ones off duty, and just send in the ones with the jerks. You'll find my emergency kit in the office, there. Someone has to be out there to give first aid and sort them out—we haven't room for the whole plant in here."

"Right, Dr. Ferrel." She let Meyers replace her in assisting Jenkins, and was gone briefly to come out with his bag. "Come on, you men. I'll hop the litter and dress down your burns on the way. You're appointed driver, mister. Somebody should have reported that Beel person before, so the litter would be out there now."

The spokesman for the others upended the glass he'd filled, swallowed, gulped, and grinned down at her. "O.K., doctor, only out there you ain't got time to think—you gotta do. Thanks for the shot, Doc, and I'll tell Hoke you're appointing her out there."

They filed out behind Brown as Jones went out to get the second litter, and Doc went ahead with the quick-setting plastic cast for the broken leg. Too bad there weren't more of those nursing doctors; he'd have to see Palmer about it after this was over—if Palmer and he were still around. Wonder how the man in the safety chambers, about which he'd completely forgotten, would make out? There were two in each converter housing, designed as an escape for the men in case of accident, and supposed to be proof against almost anything. If the men had reached them, maybe they were all right; he wouldn't have taken a bet on it, though. With a slight shrug, he finished his work and went to help Jenkins.

The boy nodded down at the body on the table, already showing extensive scraping and probing. "Quite a bit of spitting clean through the armor," he commented. "These words were just a little too graphic for me. I-713 couldn't do that."

"Hm-m-m." Doc was in no mood to quibble on the subject. He caught himself looking at the little box in which the stuff was put after they worked what they could out of the flesh, and jerked his eyes away quickly. Whenever the lid was being dropped, a glow could be seen inside. Jenkins always managed to keep his eyes on something else.

They were almost finished when the switchboard girl announced a call, and they waited to make the few last touches before answering, then filed into the office together. Brown's face was on the screen, smudged and with a spot of rouge standing out on each cheek. Another smudge appeared as she brushed the auburn hair out of her eyes with the back of her wrist.

"They've cracked the converter safety chambers, Dr. Ferrel. The north one held up perfectly, except for the heat and a little burn, but something happened in the other; oxygen valve stuck, and all are unconscious, but alive. Magma must have sprayed through the door, because sixteen or seventeen have the jerks, and about a dozen are dead. Some others need more care than I can give—I'm having Hokusai delegate men to carry those the stretchers won't hold, and they're all piling up on you in a bunch right now!"

Ferrel grunted and nodded. "Could have been worse, I guess. Don't kill yourself out there, Brown."

"Same to you." she blew Jenkins a kiss and snapped off, just as the whine of the litter siren reached their ears.

In the surgery again, they could see a truck showing behind it, and men lifting out bodies in apparently endless succession.

"Get their armor off, somehow, Jones—grab anyone else to help you that you can. Curare, Dodd, and keep handing it to me. We'll worry about everything else after Jenkins and I quiet them." This was obviously going to be a mass-production sort of business, not for efficiency, but through sheer necessity. And again, Jenkins with his queer taut steadiness was doing two for one that Doc could do, his face pale and his eyes almost glazed, but his hands moving endlessly and nervelessly on with his work.

Sometime during the night Jenkins looked up at Meyers, and motioned her back. "Go get some sleep, nurse; Miss Dodd can take care of both Dr. Ferrel and myself when we work close together. Your nerves are shot, and you need the rest. Dodd, you can call her back in two hours and rest yourself."

"What about you, doctor?"

"Me—" He grinned out of the corner of his mouth, crookedly. "I've got an imagination that won't sleep, and I'm needed here." The sentence ended on a rising inflection that was false to Ferrel's ear, and the older doctor looked at the boy thoughtfully.

Jenkins caught his look. "It's O.K., Doc; I'll let you know when I'm going to crack. It was O.K. to send Meyers back, wasn't it?"

"You were closer to her than I was, so you should know better than I." Technically, the nurses were all directly under his control, but they'd dropped such technicalities long before. Ferrel rubbed the small of his back briefly, then picked up his scalpel again.

A faint gray light was showing in the east, and the wards had overflowed into the waiting room when the last case from the chambers was finished as best he could be. During the night, the converter had continued to spit occasionally, even through the tank armor twice, but now there was a temporary lull in the arrival of workers for treatment. Doc sent Jones after breakfast from the cafeteria, then headed into the office where Jenkins was already slumped down in the old leather chair.

The boy was exhausted almost to the limit from the combined strain of the work and his own suppressed jitters, but he looked up in mild surprise as he felt the prick of the needle. Ferrel finished it, and used it on himself before explaining. "Morphine, of course. What else can we do? Just enough to keep us going, but without it we'll both be useless out there in a few more hours. Anyhow, there isn't as much reason not to use it as there was when I was younger, before the counteragent was discovered to kill most of its habit-forming tendency. Even five years ago, before they had that, there were times when morphine was useful, Lord knows, though anyone who used it except as a last resort deserved all the hell he got. A real substitute for sleep would be better, though; wish they'd finish up the work they're doing on that fatigue eliminator at Harvard. Here, eat that!"

Jenkins grimaced at the breakfast Jones laid out in front of him, but he knew as well as Doc that the food was necessary, and he pulled the plate back to him. "What I'd give an eye tooth for, Doc, wouldn't be a substitute—just half an hour of good old-fashioned sleep. Only, damn it, if I knew I had time, I couldn't do it—not with R out there bubbling away."

The telephone annunciator clipped in before Doc could answer. "Telephone for Dr. Ferrel; emergency! Dr. Brown calling Dr. Ferrel!"

"Ferrel answering!" The phone girl's face popped off the screen, and a tired-faced Sue Brown looked out at them. "What is it?"

"It's that little Japanese fellow—Hokusai—who's been running things out here, Dr. Ferrel. I'm bringing him in with an acute case of appendicitis. Prepare surgery!"

Jenkins gagged over the coffee he was trying to swallow,

and his choking voice was halfway between disgust and hysterical laughter. "Appendicitis, Doc! My God, what comes next?"

3

It might have been worse. Brown had coupled in the little freezing unit on the litter and lowered the temperature around the abdomen, both preparing Hokusai for surgery and slowing down the progress of the infection so that the appendix was still unbroken when he was wheeled into the surgery. His seamed Oriental face had a grayish cast under the olive, but he managed a faint grin.

"Verry ssorry, Dr. Ferrel, to bother you. Verry ssorry. No ether, pleasse!"

Ferrel grunted. "No need of it, Hoke; we'll use hypothermy, since it's already begun. Over here, Jones . . . And you might as well go back and sit down, Jenkins."

Brown was washing, and popped out again, ready to assist with the operation. "He had to be tied down, practically, Dr. Ferrel. Insisted that he only needed a little mineral oil and some peppermint for his stomach-ache! Why are intelligent people always the most stupid?"

It was a mystery to Ferrel, too, but seemingly the case. He tested the temperature quickly while the surgery hypothermy equipment began functioning, found it low enough, and began. Hoke flinched with his eyes as the scalpel touched him, then opened them in mild surprise at feeling no appreciable pain. The complete absence of nerve response with its accompanying freedom from post-operative shock was one of the great advantages of low-temperature work in surgery. Ferrel laid back the flesh, severed the appendix quickly, and removed it through the tiny incision. Then, with one of the numerous attachments, he made use of the ingenious mechanical stitcher and stepped back.

"All finished, Hoke, and you're lucky you didn't rupture—peritonitis isn't funny, even though we can cut down on it with the sulphonamides. The ward's full, so's the waiting room, so you'll have to stay on the table for a few hours until we can find a place for you; no pretty nurse, either—until the two other girls get here some time this morning. I dunno what we'll do about the patients."

"But, Dr. Ferrel, I am hear that now ssurgery—I sshould be up, already. There iss work I am do."

"You've been hearing that appendectomy patient aren't confined now, eh? Well, that's partly true. Johns Hopkins began it quite awhile ago. But for the next hour, while the temperature comes back to normal, you stay put. After that, if you want to move around a little, you can; but no going out to the converter. A little exercise probably helps more than it harms, but any strain wouldn't be good."

"But, the danger—"

"Be hanged, Hoke. You couldn't help now, long enough to do any good. Until the stuff in those stitches dissolves away completely in the body fluids, you're to take it easy—and that's two weeks, about."

The little man gave in, reluctantly. "Then I think I ssleep now. But besst you sshould call Mr. Palmer at once, pleasse! He musst know I am not there!"

Palmer took the news the hard way, with an unfair but natural tendency to blame Hokusai and Ferrel. "Damn it, Doc, I was hoping he'd get things straightened out somehow—I practically promised the Governor that Hoke could take care of it; he's got one of the best brains in the business. Now this! Well, no help, I guess. He certainly can't do it unless he's in condition to get right into things. Maybe Jorgenson, though, knows enough about it to handle it from a wheel chair, or something. How's he coming along—in shape to be taken out where he can give directions to the foremen?"

"Wait a minute." Ferrel stoped him as quickly as he could. "Jorgenson isn't here. We've got thirty-one men lying around, and he isn't one of them; and if he'd been one of the seventeen dead, you'd know it. I didn't know Jorgenson was working, even."

"He had to be—it was his process! Look, Ferrel, I was distinctly told that he was taken to you—foreman dumped him on the litter himself and reported at once! Better check up, and quick—with Hoke only half able, I've got to have Jorgenson!"

"He isn't here—I know Jorgenson. The foreman must have mistaken the big fellow from the south safety for him, but that man had black hair inside his helmet. What about the three hundred-odd that were only unconscious, or the fifteen-sixteen hundred men outside the converter when it happened?"

Palmer wiggled his jaw muscles tensely. "Jorgenson would

have reported or been reported fifty times. Every man out there wants him around to boss things. He's gotta be in your ward."

"He isn't, I tell you! And how about moving some of the fellows here into the city hospitals?"

"Tried—hospitals must have been tipped off somehow about the radioactives in the flesh, and they refuse to let a man from here be brought in." Palmer was talking with only the surface of his mind, his cheek muscles bobbing as if he were chewing his thoughts and finding them tough. "Jorgenson—Hoke—and Kellar's been dead for years. Not another man in the whole country that understands this field enough to make a decent guess, even; I get lost on page six myself. Ferrel, could a man in a Tomlin five-shield armor suit make the safety in twenty seconds, do you think, from—say beside the converter?"

Ferrel considered it rapidly. A Tomlin weighed about four hundred pounds, and Jorgenson was an ox of a man, but only human. "Under the stress of an emergency, it's impossible to guess what a man can do, Palmer, but I don't see how he could work his way half that distance."

"Hm-m-m, I figured. Could he live, then, supposing he wasn't squashed? Those suits carry their own air for twenty-four hours, you know, to avoid any air cracks, pumping the carbon-dioxide back under pressure and condensing the moisture out—no openings of any kind. They've got the best insulation of all kinds we know, too."

"One chance in a billion, I'd guess; but again, it's darned hard to put any exact limit on what can be done—miracles keep happening, every day. Going to try it?"

"What else can I do? There's no alternative. I'll meet you outside No. 4 just as soon as you can make it, and bring everything you need to start working at once. Seconds may count!" Palmer's face slid sideways and up as he was reaching for the button, and Ferrel wasted no time in imitating the motion.

By all logic, there wasn't a chance, even in a Tomlin. But, until they knew, the effort would have to be made; chances couldn't be taken when a complicated process had gone out of control, with now almost certainty that Isotope R was the result—Palmer was concealing nothing, even though he had stated nothing specifically. And obviously, if Hoke couldn't handle it, none of the men at other branches of National

Atomic or at the smaller partially independent plants could make even a halfhearted stab at the job.

It all rested on Jorgenson, then. And Jorgenson must be somewhere under that semi-molten hell that could drive through the tank armor and send men back into the infirmary with bones broken from their own muscular anarchy!

Ferrel's face must have shown his thoughts, judging by Jenkins' startled expression. "Jorgenson's still in there somewhere," he said quickly.

"Jorgenson! But he's the man who—Good Lord!"

"Exactly. You'll stay here and take care of the jerk cases that may come in. Brown, I'll want you out there again. Bring everything portable we have, in case we can't move him in fast enough; get one of the trucks and fit it out; and be out with it about twice as fast as you can! I'm grabbing the litter now." He accepted the emergency kit Brown thrust into his hands, dumped a caffeine tablet into his mouth without bothering to wash it down, then was out toward the litter. "No. 4, and hurry!"

Palmer was just jumping off a scooter as they cut around No. 3 and in front of the rough fence of rope strung out quite a distance beyond 4. He glanced at Doc, nodded, and dived in through the men grouped around, yelling orders to right and left as she went, and was back at Ferrel's side by the time the litter had stopped.

"O.K., Ferrel, go over there and get into armor as quickly as possible! We're going in there with the tanks, whether we can or not, and be damned to the quenching for the moment. Briggs, get those things out of there, clean out a roadway as best you can, throw in the big crane again, and we'll need all the men in armor we can get—give them steel rods and get them to probing in there for anything solid and big or small enough to be a man—five minutes at a stretch; they should be able to stand that. I'll be back pronto!"

Doc noted the confused mixture of tanks and machines of all descriptions clustered around the walls—or what was left of them—of the converter housing, and saw them yanking out everything along one side, leaving an opening where the main housing gate had stood, now ripped out to expose a crane boom rooting out the worst obstructions. Obviously they'd been busy at some kind of attempt at quenching the action, but his knowledge of atomics was too little even to guess at what it was. The equipment set up was being pushed aside by tanks without dismantling, and men were running up into the roped-in section, some already armored, others dragging on part of their armor as they went. With the help of one of the atomjacks, he climbed into a suit himself, wondering what he could do in such a casing if anything needed doing.

Palmer had a suit on before him, though, and was waiting beside one of the tanks, squat and heavily armored, its front equipped with both a shovel and a grapple swinging from movable beams. "In here, Doc." Ferrel followed him into the housing of the machine and Palmer grabbed the controls as he pulled on a shortwave headset and began shouting orders through it towards the other tanks that were moving in on their heavy treads. The dull drone of the motor picked up, and the tank began lumbering forward under the manager's direction.

"Haven't run one of these since that show-off at a picnic seven years ago," he complained, as he kicked at the controls and straightened out a developing list to left. "Though I used to be pretty handy when I was plain engineer. Damned static around here almost chokes off the radio, but I guess enough gets through. By the best guess I can make, Jorgenson should have been near the main control panel when it started, and have headed for the south chamber. Half the distance, you figure?"

"Possibly, probably slightly less."

"Yeah! And then the stuff may have tossed him around. But we'll have to try to get there." He barked into the radio again. "Briggs, get those men in suits as close as you can and have them fish with their rods about thirty feet to the left of the pillar that's still up—can they get closer?"

The answer was blurred and pieces missing, but the general idea went across. Palmer frowned. "O.K., if they can't make it, they can't; draw them back out of the reach of the stuff and hold them ready to go in. . . . No, call for volunteers! I'm offering a thousand dollars a minute to every man that gets a stick in there, double to his family if the stuff gets him, and ten times that—fifty thousand—if he locates Jorgenson! . . . Look out, you damn fool!" The last was to one of the men who'd started forward, toward the place, jumping from one piece of broken building to grab at a pillar and swing off in his suit toward something that looked like a standing position; it toppled, but he managed a leap that carried him to another lump, steadied himself, and began probing through the mess. "Oof!

You with the crane—stick it in where you can grab any of the men that pass out, if it'll reach—good! Doc, I know as well as you that the men have no business in there, even five minutes; but I'll send in a hundred more if it'll find Jorgenson!"

Doc said nothing—he knew there'd probably be a hundred or more fools willing to try, and he knew the need of them. The tanks couldn't work their way close enough for any careful investigation of the mixed mass of radioactives, machinery, building debris, and destruction, aside from which they were much too slow in such delicate probing; only men equipped with the long steel poles could do that. As he watched, some of the activity of the magma suddenly caused an eruption, and one of the men tossed up his pole and doubled back into a half circle before falling. The crane operator shoved the big boom over and made a grab, missed, brought it down again, and came out with the heaving body held by one arm, to run it back along its track and twist it outward beyond Doc's vision.

Even through the tank and the suit, heat was pouring in, and there was a faint itching in those parts where the armor was thinnest that indicated the start of a burn—though not as yet dangerous. He had no desire to think what was happening to the men who were trying to worm into the heart of it in nothing but armor; nor did he care to watch what was happening to them. Palmer was trying to inch the machine ahead, but the stuff underneath made any progress difficult. Twice something spat against the tank, but did not penetrate.

"Five minutes are up," he told Palmer. "They'd all better go directly to Dr. Brown, who should be out with the truck now for immediate treatment."

Palmer nodded and relayed the instructions. "Pick up all you can with the crane and carry them back! Send in a new bunch, Briggs, and credit them with their bonus in advance. Damn it, Doc, this can go on all day; it'll take an hour to pry around through this mess right here, and then he's probably somewhere else. The stuff seems to be getting worse in this neighborhood, too, from what accounts I've had before. Wonder if that steel plate could be pushed down?"

He threw in the clutch engaging the motor to the treads and managed to twist through toward it. There was a slight slipping of the lugs, then the tractors caught, and the nose of the tank thrust forward; almost without effort, the fragment of housing toppled from its leaning position and slid forward. The tank growled, fumbled, and slowly climbed up onto it and ran forward another twenty feet to its end; the support settled slowly, but something underneath checked it, and they were still again. Palmer worked the grapple forward, nosing a big piece of masonry out of the way, and two men reached out with the ends of their poles to begin probing, futilely. Another change of men came out, then another.

Briggs' voice crackled erratically through the speaker again. "Palmer, I got a fool here who wants to go out on the end of your beam, if you can swing around so the crane can lift him out to it."

"Start him coming!" Again he began jerking the levers, and the tank buckled and heaved, backed and turned, ran forward and repeated it all, while the plate that was holding them flopped up and down on its precarious balance.

Doc held his breath and began praying to himself; his admiration for the men who'd go out in that stuff was increasing by leaps and bounds, along with his respect for Palmer's ability.

The crane boom bobbed toward them, and the scoop came running out, but wouldn't quite reach; their own tank was relatively light and mobile compared to the bigger machine, but Palmer already had that pushed out to the limit, and hanging over the edge of the plate. It still lacked three feet of reaching.

"Damn!" Palmer slapped open the door of the tank, jumped forward on the tread, and looked down briefly before coming back inside. "No chance to get closer! Wheeoo! Those men earn their money."

But the crane operator had his own tricks, and was bobbing the boom of his machine up and down slowly with a motion that set the scoop swinging like a huge pendulum, bringing it gradually closer to the grapple beam. The man had an arm out, and finally caught the beam, swinging out instantly from the scoop that drew backward behind him. He hung suspended for a second, pitching his body around to a better position, then somehow wiggled up onto the end and braced himself with his legs. Doc let his breath out and Palmer inched the tank around to a forward position again. Now the pole of the atomjack could cover the wide territory before them, and he began using it rapidly.

"Win or lose, that man gets a triple bonus," Palmer muttered. "Uh!"

The pole had located something, and was feeling around to determine size; the man glanced at them and pointed frantically. Doc jumped forward to the windows as Palmer ran down the grapple and began pushing it down into the semi-molten stuff under the pole; there was resistance there, but finally the prong of the grapple broke under and struck on something that refused to come up. The manager's hands moved the controls gently, making it tug from side to side; reluctantly, it gave and moved forward toward them, coming upward until they could make out the general shape. It was definitely no Tomlin suit!

"Lead hopper box! Damn—Wait, Jorgenson wasn't anybody's fool; when he saw he couldn't make the safety, he might . . . maybe—" Palmer slapped the grapple down again, against the closed lid of the chest, but the hook was too large. Then the man clinging there caught the idea and slid down to the hopper chest, his armored hands grabbing at the lid. He managed to lift a corner of it until the grapple could catch and lift it the rest of the way, and his hands started down to jerk upward again.

The manager watched his motions, then flipped the box over with the grapple, and pulled it closer to the tank body; magma was running out, but there was a gleam of something else inside.

"Start praying, Doc!" Palmer worked it to the side of the tank and was out through the door again, letting the merciless heat and radiation stream in.

But Ferrel wasn't bothering with that now; he followed, reaching down into the chest to help the other two lift out the body of a huge man in a five-shield Tomlin! Somehow, they wangled the six-hundred-odd pounds out and up on the treads, then into the housing, barely big enough for all of them. The atomjack pulled himself inside, shut the door and flopped forward on his face, out cold.

"Never mind him—check Jorgenson!" Palmer's voice was heavy with the reaction from the hunt, but he turned the tank and sent it outward at top speed, regardless of risk. Contrarily, bit bucked through the mass more readily than it had crawled in through the cleared section.

Ferrel unscrewed the front plate of the armor on Jorgenson as rapidly as he could, though he knew already that the man was still miraculously alive—corpses don't jerk with force enough to move a four-hundred-pound suit appreciably. A side glance, as they drew beyond the wreck of the converter housing, showed the men already beginning to set up equipment to quell the atomic reaction again, but the armor front plate came loose at last, and he dropped his eyes back without noticing details, to cut out a section of clothing and make the needed injections; curare first, then neo-heroin, and curare again, though he did not dare inject the quantity that seemed necessary. There was nothing more he could do until they could get the man out of his armor. He turned to the atomjack, who was already sitting up, propped against the driving seat's back.

" 'Snothing much, Doc," the fellow managed. "No jerks, just burn and that damned heat! Jorgenson?"

"Alive at least," Palmer answered, with some relief. The tank stopped, and Ferrel could see Brown running forward from beside a truck. "Get that suit off you, get yourself treated for the burn, then go up to the office where the check will be ready for you!"

"Fifty thousand check?" The doubt in the voice registered over the weakness.

"Fifty thousand plus triple your minute time, and cheap; maybe we'll toss in a medal or a bottle of Scotch, too. Here, you fellows give a hand."

Ferrel had the suit ripped off with Brown's assistance and paused only long enough for one grateful breath of clean, cool air before leading the way toward the truck. As he neared it, Jenkins popped out, directing a group of men to move two loaded stretchers onto the litter, and nodding jerkily at Ferrel. "With the truck all equipped, we decided to move out here and take care of the damage as it came up—Sue and I rushed them through enough to do until we can find more time, so we could give full attention to Jorgenson. He's still living!"

"By a miracle. Stay out here, Brown, until you've finished with the men from inside, then we'll try to find some rest for you."

The three huskies carrying Jorgenson placed the body on the table set up, and began ripping off the bulky armor as the truck got under way. Fresh gloves came out of a small sterilizer, and the two doctors fell to work at once, treating the badly burned flesh and trying to locate and remove the worst of the radioactive matter.

"No use." Doc stepped back and shook his head. "It's all over him, probably clear into his bones in places. We'd have to put him through a filter to get it all out!"

Palmer was looking down at the raw mass of flesh, with all the layman's sickness at such a sight. "Can you fix him up, Ferrel?"

"We can try, that's all. Only explanation I can give for his being alive at all is that the hopper box must have been pretty well above the stuff until a short time ago—very short—and this stuff didn't work in until it sank. He's practically dehydrated now, apparently, but he couldn't have perspired enough to keep from dying of heat if he'd been under all that for even an hour—insulation or no insulation." There was admiration in Doc's eyes as he looked down at the immense figure of the man. "And he's tough; if he weren't, he'd have killed himself by exhaustion, even confined inside that suit and box, after the jerks set in. He's close to having done so, anyway. Until we can find some way of getting that stuff out of him, we don't dare risk getting rid of the curare's effect—that's a time-consuming job, in itself. Better give him another water and sugar intravenous, Jenkins. Then, if we do fix him up, Palmer, I'd say it's a fifty-fifty chance that all this hasn't driven him stark crazy."

The truck had stopped, and the men lifted the stretcher off and carried it inside as Jenkins finished the injection. He went ahead of them, but Doc stopped outside to take Palmer's cigarette for a long drag, and let them go ahead.

"Cheerful!" The manager lighted another from the butt, his shoulders sagging. "I've been trying to think of one man who might possibly be of some help to us, Doc, and there isn't such a person—anywhere. I'm sure now, after being in there, that Hoke couldn't do it. Kellar, if he were still alive, could probably pull the answer out of a hat after three looks—he had an instinct and genius for it; the best man the business ever had, even if his tricks did threaten to steal our work out from under us and give him the lead. But—well, now there's Jorgenson—either he gets in shape, or else!"

Jenkins' frantic yell reached them suddenly. "Doc! Jorgenson's dead! He's stopped breathing entirely!"

Doc jerked forward into a full run, a white-faced Palmer at his heels.

4

Dodd was working artificial respiration and Jenkins had the oxygen mask in his hands, adjusting it over Jorgenson's face, before Ferrel reached the table. He made a grab for the pulse that had been fluttering weakly enough before, felt it flicker feebly again, and then stop completely. "Adrenaline!"

"Already shot it into his heart, Doc! Cardiacine, too!" The boy's voice was bordering on hysteria, but Palmer was obviously closer to it than Jenkins.

"Doc, you gotta—"

"Get the hell out of here!" Ferrel's hands suddenly had a life of their own as he grabbed frantically for instruments, ripped bandages off the man's chest, and began working against time, when time had all the advantages. It wasn't surgery—hardly good butchery; the bones that he cut through so ruthlessly with savage strokes of an instrument could never heal smoothly after being so mangled. But he couldn't worry about minor details now.

He tossed back the flap of flesh and ribs that he'd hacked out. "Stop the bleeding, Jenkins!" Then his hands plunged into the chest cavity, somehow finding room around Dodd's and Jenkins', and were suddenly incredibly gentle as they located the heart itself and began working on it, the skilled, exact massage of a man who knew every function of the vital organ. Pressure here, there, relax, pressure again; take it easy, don't rush things! It would do no good to try to set it going as feverishly as his emotions demanded. Pure oxygen was feeding into the lungs, and the heart could safely do less work. Hold it steady, one beat a second, sixty a minute.

It had been perhaps half a minute from the time the heart stopped before his massage was circulating blood again; too little time to worry about damage to the brain, the first part to be permanently affected by stoppage of the circulation. Now, if the heart could start again by itself within any reasonable time, death would be cheated again. How long? He had no idea. They'd taught him ten minutes when he was studying medicine, then there'd been a case of twenty minutes once, and while he was interning it had been pushed up to a record of slightly over an hour, which still stood; but that was an exceptional case. Jorgenson, praise be, was a normally healthy and vigorous specimen, and his system had been in first-class condition, but with the torture of those long hours, the radioactive, narcotic and curare all fighting against him, still one more miracle was needed to keep his life going.

Press, massage, relax, don't hurry it too much. There! For a second, his fingers felt a faint flutter, then again; but it stopped. Still, as long as the organ could show such signs, there was hope, unless his fingers grew too tired and he muffed the job before the moment when the heart could be safely trusted by itself.

"Jenkins!"

"Yes, sir!"

"Ever do any heart massage?"

"Practiced it in school, sir, on a model, but never actually. Oh, a dog in dissection class, for five minutes. I . . . I don't think you'd better trust me, Doc."

"I may have to. If you did it on a dog for five minutes, you can do it on a man, probably. You know what hangs on it—you saw the converter and know what's going on."

Jenkins nodded, the tense nod he'd used earlier. "I know—that's why you can't trust me. I told you I'd let you know when I was going to crack—well, it's damned near here!"

Could a man tell his weakness, if he were about finished? Doc didn't know; he suspected that the boy's own awareness of his nerves would speed up such a break, if anything, but Jenkins was a queer case, having taut nerves sticking out all over him, yet a steadiness under fire that few older men could have equaled. If he had to use him, he would; there was no other answer.

Doc's fingers were already feeling stiff—not yet tired, but showing signs of becoming so. Another few minutes, and he'd have to stop. There was the flutter again, one—two—three! Then it stopped. There had to be some other solution to this; it was impossible to keep it up for the length of time probably needed, even if he and Jenkins spelled each other. Only Michel at Mayo's could—Mayo's! If they could get it here in time, that wrinkle he'd seen demonstrated at their last medical convention was the answer.

"Jenkins, call Mayo's—you'll have to get Palmer's O.K., I guess—ask for Kubelik, and the extension where I can talk to him!"

He could hear Jenkins' voice, level enough at first, then with a depth of feeling he'd have thought impossible in the boy. Dodd looked at him quickly and managed a grim smile, even as she continued with the respiration; nothing could make her blush, though it should have done so.

The boy jumped back. "No soap, Doc! Palmer can't be

located—and that post-mortem misconception at the board won't listen."

Doc studied his hands in silence, wondering, then gave it up; there'd be no hope of his lasting while he sent out the boy. "O.K., Jenkins, you'll have to take over here, then. Steady does it, come on in slowly, get your fingers over mine. Now, catch the motion? Easy, don't rush things. You'll hold out—you'll have to! You've done better than I had any right to ask for so far, and you don't need to distrust yourself. There, got it?

"Got it, Doc. I'll try, but for Pete's sake, whatever you're planning, get back here quick! I'm not lying about cracking! You'd better let Meyers replace Dodd and have Sue called back in here; she's the best nerve tonic I know."

"Call her in then, Dodd." Doc picked up a hypodermic syringe, filled it quickly with water to which a drop of another liquid added a brownish-yellow color, and forced his tired old legs into a reasonably rapid trot out of the side door and toward Communications. Maybe the switchboard operator was stubborn, but there were ways of handling people.

He hadn't counted on the guard outside the Communications Building, though. "Halt!"

"Life or death; I'm a physician."

"Not in here—I got orders." The bayonet's menace apparently wasn't enough; the rifle went up to the man's shoulder, and his chin jutted out with the stubbornness of petty authority and reliance on orders." Nobody sick here. There's plenty of phones elsewhere. You get back—and fast!"

Doc started forward and there was a faint click from the rifle as the safety went off; the darned fool meant what he said. Shrugging, Ferrel stepped back—and brought the hypodermic needle up inconspicuously in line with the guard's face. "Ever see one of these things squirt curare? It can reach before your bullet hits!"

"Curare?" The guard's eyes flicked to the needle, and doubt came into them. The man frowned. "That's the stuff that kills people on arrows, ain't it?"

"It is—cobra venom, you know. One drop on the outside of your skin and you're dead in ten seconds." Both statements were out-and-out lies, but Doc was counting on the superstitious ignorance of the average man in connection with poisons." This little needle can spray you with it very nicely, and it may be a fast death, but not a pleasant one. Want to put down the rifle?"

A regular might have shot; but the militiaman was taking no chances. He lowered the rifle gingerly, his eyes on the needle, then kicked the weapon aside at Doc's motion. Ferrel approached, holding the needle out, and the man shrank backward and away, letting him pick up the rifle as he went past to avoid being shot in the back. Lost time! But he knew his way around this little building, at least, and went straight toward the girl at the board.

"Get up!" His voice came from behind her shoulder and she turned to see the rifle in one of his hands; the needle in the other, almost touching her throat. "This is loaded with curare, deadly poison, and too much hangs on getting a call through to bother with physician's oaths right now, young lady. Up! No plugs! That's right; now get over there, out of the cell—there, on your face, cross your hands behind your back, and grab your ankles—right! Now if you move, you won't move long!"

Those gangster picture he'd seen were handy, at that. She was throughly frightened and docile. But, perhaps, not so much so she might not have bungled his call deliberately. He had to do that himself. Darn it, the red lights were trunk lines, but which plug—try the inside one, it looked more logical; he'd seen it done, but couldn't remember. Now, you flip back one of these switches—uh-uh, the other way. The tone came in assuring him he had it right, and he dialed operator rapidly, his eyes flickering toward the girl lying on the floor, his thoughts on Jenkins and the wasted time running on.

"Operator, this is an emergency. I'm Walnut, 7654; I want to put in a long-distance call to Dr. Kubelik, Mayo's Hospital, Rochester, Minnesota. If Kubelik isn't there, I'll take anyone else who answers from his department. Speed is urgent."

"Very good, sir." Long-distance operators, mercifully, were usually efficient. There were the repeated signals and clicks of relays as she put it through, the answer from the hospital board, more wasted time, and then a face appeared on the screen; but not that of Kubelik. It was a much younger man.

Ferrel wasted no time in introduction. "I've got an emergency case here where all Hades depends on saving a man, and it can't be done without that machine of Dr. Kubelik's; he knows me, if he's there—I'm Ferrel, met him at the convention, got him to show me how the thing worked."

"Kubelik hasn't come in yet, Dr. Ferrel; I'm his assistant. But, if you mean the heart and lung exciter, it's already boxed and supposed to leave for Harvard this morning. They've got a rush case out there, and may need it—"

"Not as much as I do."

"I'll have to call— Wait a minute, Dr. Ferrel, seems I remember your name now. Aren't you the chap with National Atomic?"

Doc nodded. "The same. Now, about that machine, if you'll stop the formalities—"

The face on the screen nodded, instant determination showing, with an underlying expression of something else. "We'll ship it down to you instantly, Ferrel. Got a field for a plane?"

"Not within three miles, but I'll have a truck sent out for it. How long?"

"Take too long by truck if you need it down there, Ferrel; I'll arrange to transship in air from our special speedster to a helicopter, have it delivered wherever you want. About—um, loading plane, flying a couple hundred miles, transshipping—about half an hour's the best we can do."

"Make it the square of land south of the infirmary, which is crossed visibly from the air. Thanks!"

"Wait, Dr. Ferrel!" The younger man checked Doc's cut-off. "Can you use it when you get it? It's tricky work."

"Kubelik gave quite a demonstration and I'm used to tricky work. I'll chance it—have to. Too long to rouse Kubelik himself, isn't it?"

"Probably. O.K., I've got the telescript reply from the shipping office, it's starting for the plane. I wish you luck!"

Ferrel nodded his thanks, wondering. Service like that was welcome, but it wasn't the most comforting thing, mentally, to know that the mere mention of National Atomic would cause such an about-face. Rumors, it seemed, were spreading, and in a hurry, in spite of Palmer's best attempts. Good Lord, what was going on here? He'd been too busy for any serious worrying or to realize, but—well, it had gotten him the exciter, and for that he should be thankful.

The guard was starting uncertainly off for reinforcements when Doc came out, and he realized that the seemingly endless call must have been over in short order. He tossed the rifle well out of the man's reach and headed back toward the infirmary at a run, wondering how Jenkins had made out—it had to be all right!

Jenkins wasn't standing over the body of Jorgenson; Brown was there instead, her eyes moist and her face pinched in and white around the nostrils that stood out at full width. She looked up, shook her head at him as he started forward, and went on working at Jorgenson's heart.

"Jenkins cracked?"

"Nonsense! This is woman's work, Dr. Ferrel, and I took over for him, that's all. You men try to use brute force all your life and then wonder why a woman can do twice as much delicate work where strong muscles are a nuisance. I chased him out and took over, that's all." But there was a catch in her voice as she said it, and Meyers was looking down entirely too intently at the work of artificial respiration.

"Hi, Doc!" It was Blake's voice that broke in. "Get away from there; when this Dr. Brown needs help, I'll be right in there. I've been sleeping like a darned fool all night, from four this morning on. Didn't hear the phone, or something, didn't know what was going on until I got to the gate out there. You go rest."

Ferrel grunted in relief; Blake might have been dead drunk when he finally reached home, which would explain his not hearing the phone, but his animal virility had soaked it out with no visible sign. The only change was the absence of the usual cocky grin on his face as he moved over beside Brown to test Jorgenson. "Thank the Lord you're here, Blake. How's Jorgenson doing?"

Brown's voice answered in a monotone, words coming in time to the motions of her fingers. "His heart shows signs of coming around once in a while, but it doesn't last. He isn't getting worse from what I can tell, though."

"Good. If we can keep him going half an hour more, we can turn all this over to a machine. Where's Jenkins?"

"A machine? Oh, the Kubelik exciter, of course. He was working on it when I was there. We'll keep Jorgenson alive until then, anyway, Dr. Ferrel."

"Where's Jenkins?" he repeated sharply, when she stopped with no intention of answering the former question.

Blake pointed toward Ferrel's office, the door of which was now closed. "In there. But lay off him, Doc. I saw the whole thing, and he feels like the deuce about it. He's a good kid, but only a kid, and this kind of hell could get any of us."

"I know all that." Doc headed toward the office, as much for a smoke as anything else. The sight of Blake's rested face was somehow an island of reassurance in this sea of fatigue and nerves. "Don't worry, Brown, I'm not planning on lacing him down, so you needn't defend your man so carefully. It was my fault for not listening to him."

Brown's eyes were pathetically grateful in the brief flash she threw him, and he felt like a heel for the gruffness that had been his first reaction to Jenkins' absence. If this kept on much longer, though, they'd all be in worse shape than the boy, whose back was toward him as he opened the door. The still, huddled shape did not raise its head from its arms as Ferrel put his hand onto one shoulder, and the voice was muffled and distant.

"I cracked, Doc—high, wide and handsome, all over the place. I couldn't take it! Standing there, Jorgenson maybe dying because I couldn't control myself right, the whole plant blowing up, all my fault. I kept telling myself I was O.K., I'd go on, then I cracked. Screamed like a baby! Dr. Jenkins—*nerve* specialist!"

"Yeah. . . . Here, are you going to drink this, or do I have to hold your blasted nose and pour it down your throat?" It was crude psychology, but it worked, and Doc handed over the drink, waited for the other to down it, and passed a cigarette across before sinking into his own chair. "You warned me, Jenkins, and I risked it on my own responsibility, so nobody's kicking. But I'd like to ask a couple of questions."

"Go ahead—what's the difference?" Jenkins had recovered a little, obviously, from the note of defiance that managed to creep into his voice.

"Did you know Brown could handle that kind of work? And did you pull your hands out before she could get hers in to replace them?"

"She told me she could. I didn't know before. I dunno about the other; I think . . . yeah, Doc, she had her hands over mine. But—"

Ferrel nodded, satisfied with his own guess. "I thought so. You didn't crack, as you put it, until your mind knew it was safe to do so—and then you simply passed the work on. By that definition, I'm cracking, too. I'm sitting in here, smoking, talking to you, when out there a man needs attention. The fact that he's getting it from two others, one practically fresh, the other at least a lot better off than we are, doesn't have a thing to do with it, does it?"

"But it wasn't that way, Doc. I'm not asking for grand-stand stuff from anybody."

"Nobody's giving it to you, son. All right, you screamed—why not? It didn't hurt anything. I growled at Brown when I came in for the same reason—exhausted, overstrained nerves. If I went out there and had to take over from them, I'd probably scream myself, or start biting my tongue—nerves have to have an outlet; physically, it does them no good, but there's a psychological need for it." The boy wasn't convinced, and Doc sat back in the chair, staring at him thoughtfully. "Ever wonder why I'm here?"

"No, sir."

"Well, you might. Twenty-seven years ago, when I was about your age, there wasn't a surgeon in this country—or the world, for that matter—who had the reputation I had; any kind of surgery, brain, what have you. They're still using some of my techniques . . . uh-hum, thought you'd remember when the association of names hit you. I had a different wife then, Jenkins, and there was a baby coming. Brain tumor—I had to do it, no one else could. I did it, somehow, but I went out of that operating room in a haze, and it was three days later when they'd tell me she'd died; not my fault—I know that now—but I couldn't realize it then.

"So, I tried setting up as a general practitioner. No more surgery for me! And because I was a fair diagnostician, which most surgeons aren't, I made a living, at least. Then, when this company was set up, I applied for the job, and got it; I still had a reputation of sorts. It was a new field, something requiring study and research, and damned near every ability of most specialists plus a general practitioner's, so it kept me busy enough to get over my phobia of surgery. Compared to me, you don't know what nerves or cracking means. That little scream was a minor incident."

Jenkins made no comment, but lighted the cigarette he'd been holding. Ferrel relaxed farther into the chair, knowing that he'd be called if there was any need for his work, and glad to get his mind at least partially off Jorgenson. "It's hard to find a man for this work, Jenkins. It takes too much ability at too many fields, even though it pays well enough. We went through plenty of applicants before we decided on you, and I'm not regretting our choice. As a matter of fact, you're better equipped for the job than Blake was—your record looked as if you'd deliberately tried for this kind of work."

"I did."

"Hm-m-m." That was the one answer Doc had least expected; so far as he knew, no one deliberately tried for a job at Atomics—they usually wound up trying for it after comparing their receipts for a year or so with the salary paid by National. "Then you knew what was needed and picked it up in toto. Mind if I ask why?"

Jenkins shrugged. "Why not? Turnabout's fair play. It's kind of complicated, but the gist of it doesn't take much telling. Dad had an atomic plant of his own—and a darned good one, too, Doc, even it it wasn't as big as National. I was working in it when I was fifteen, and I went through two years of university work in atomics with the best intentions of carrying on the business. Sue—well, she was the neighbor girl I followed around, and we had money at the time; that wasn't why she married me, though. I never did figure that out—she'd had a hard enough life, but she was already holding down a job at Mayo's, and I was just a raw kid. Anyway—

"The day we came home from our honeymoon, Dad got a big contract on a new process we'd worked out. It took some swinging, but he got the equipment and started it. . . . My guess is that one of the controls broke though faulty construction; the process was right! We'd been over it too often not to know what it would do. But, when the estate was cleared up, I had to give up the idea of a degree in atomics, and Sue was back working at the hospital. Atomic courses cost real money. Then one of Sue's medical acquaintances fixed it for me to get a scholarship in medicine that almost took care of it, so I chose the next best thing to what I wanted."

"National and one of the biggest competitors—if you can call it that—are permitted to give degrees in atomics," Doc reminded the boy. The field was still too new to be a standing university course, and there were no better teachers in the business than such men as Palmer, Hokusai and Jorgenson. "They pay a salary while you're learning, too."

"Hm-m-m. Takes ten years that way, and the salary's just

enough for a single man. No, I'd married Sue with the intention she wouldn't have to work again; well, she did until I finished internship, but I knew if I got the job here I could support her. As an atomjack, working up to an engineer, the prospects weren't so good. We're saving a little money now, and someday maybe I'll get a crack at it yet. . . . Doc, what's this all about? You babying me out of my fit?"

Ferrel grinned at the boy. "Nothing else, son, though I was curious. And it worked. Feel all right now, don't you?"

"Mostly, except for what's going on out there—I got too much of a look at it from the truck. Oh, I could use some sleep, I guess, but I'm O.K. again."

"Good." Doc had profited almost as much as Jenkins from the rambling off-trail talk, and had managed more rest from it than from nursing his own thoughts. "Suppose we go out and see how they're making out with Jorgenson? Um, what happened to Hoke, come to think of it?"

"Hoke? Oh, he's in my office now, figuring out things with a pencil and paper since we wouldn't let him go back out there. I was wondering—"

"Atomics? . . . Then suppose you go in and talk to him; he's a good guy, and he won't give you the brush-off. Nobody else around here apparently suspected this Isotope R business, and you might offer a fresh lead for him. With Blake and the nurses here and the men out of the mess except for the tanks, there's not much you can do to help on my end."

Ferrel felt more at peace with the world than he had since the call from Palmer as he watched Jenkins head off across the surgery toward his office; and the glance that Brown threw, first toward the boy, then back at Doc, didn't make him feel worse. That girl could say more with her eyes than most women could with their mouths! He went over toward the operating table where Blake was now working the heart massage with one of the fresh nurses attending to respiration and casting longing glances toward the mechanical lung apparatus; it couldn't be used in this case, since Jorgenson's chest had to be free for heart attention.

Blake looked up, his expression worried. "This isn't so good, Doc. He's been sinking in the last few minutes. I was just going to call you. I—"

The last words were drowned out by the bull-throated drone that came dropping down from above them, a sound peculiarly characteristic of the heavy Sikorsky freighters with their modified blades to gain lift. Ferrel nodded at Brown's questioning glance, but he didn't choose to shout as his hands went over those of Blake and took over the delicate work of simulating the natural heart action. As Blake withdrew, the sound stopped, and Doc motioned him out with his head.

"You'd better go to them and oversee bringing in the apparatus—and grab up any of the men you see to act as porters—or send Jones for them. The machine is an experimental model, and pretty cumbersome; must weigh seven–eight hundred pounds."

"I'll get them myself—Jones is sleeping."

There was no flutter to Jorgenson's heart under Doc's deft manipulations, though he was exerting every bit of skill he possessed. "How long since there was a sign?"

"About four minutes, now. Doc, is there still a chance?"

"Hard to say. Get the machine, though, and we'll hope."

But still the heart refused to respond, though the pressure and manipulation kept the blood circulating and would at least prevent any starving or asphyxiation of the body cells. Carefully, delicately, he brought his mind into his fingers, trying to woo a faint quiver. Perhaps he did, once, but he couldn't be sure. It all depended on how quickly they could get the machine working now, and how long a man could live by manipulation alone. That point was still unsettled.

But there was no question about the fact that the spark of life burned faintly and steadily lower in Jorgenson, while outside the man-made hell went on ticking off the minutes that separated it from becoming Mahler's Isotope. Normally, Doc was an agnostic, but now, unconsciously, his mind slipped back into the simple faith of his childhood, and he heard Brown echoing the prayer that was on his lips. The second hand of the watch before him swung around and around and around again before he heard the sound of men's feet at the back entrance, and still there was no definite quiver from the heart under his fingers. How much time did he have left, if any, for the difficult and unfamiliar operation required?

His side glance showed the seemingly innumerable filaments of platinum that had to be connected into the nerves governing Jorgenson's heart and lungs, all carefully coded, yet almost terrifying in their complexity. If he made a mistake anywhere, it was at least certain there would be no time for a second trial; if his fingers shook or his tired eyes clouded at the wrong instant, there would be no help from Jorgenson. Jorgenson would be dead!

5

"Take over massage, Brown," he ordered. "And keep it up no matter what happens. Good. Dodd, assist me, and hang onto my signals. If it works, we can all rest afterward."

Ferrel wondered grimly with that part of his mind that was off by itself whether he could justify his boast to Jenkins of having been the world's greatest surgeon; it had been true once, he knew with no need for false modesty, but that was long ago, and this was at best a devilish job. He'd hung on with a surge of the old fascination as Kubelik had performed it on a dog at the convention, and his memory for such details was still good, as were his hands. But something else goes into the making of a great surgeon, and he wondered it that were still with him.

Then, as his fingers made the microscopic little motions needed and Dodd became another pair of hands, he ceased wondering. Whatever it was, he could feel it surging through him, and there was a pure joy to it somewhere, over and above the urgency of the work. This was probably the last time he'd ever feel it, and if the operation succeeded, probably it was a thing he could put with the few mental treasures that were still left from his former success. The man on the table ceased to be Jorgenson, the excessively gadgety infirmary became again the main operating theater of that same Mayo's which had produced Brown and this strange new machine, and his fingers were again those of the Great Ferrel, the miracle boy from Mayo's, who could do the impossible twice before breakfast without turning a hair.

Some of his feeling was devoted to the machine itself. Massive, ugly, with parts sticking out in haphazard order, it was more like something from an inquisition chamber than a scientist's achievement, but it worked—he'd seen it functioning. In that ugly mass of assorted pieces, little currents were generated and modulated to feed out to the heart and lungs and replace the orders given by a brain that no longer worked or could not get through, to coordinate breathing and beating according to the need. It was a product of the combined genius of surgery and electronics, but wonderful as the exciter was, it was distinctly secondary to the technique Kubelik had evolved for selecting and connecting only those nerves and nerve bundles necessary, and bringing the almost impossible into the limits of surgical possibility.

Brown interrupted, and that interruption in the midst of such an operation indicated clearly the strain she was under. "The heart fluttered a little then, Dr. Ferrel."

Ferrel nodded, untroubled by the interruption. Talk, which bothered most surgeons, was habitual in his own little staff, and he always managed to have one part of his mind reserved for that while the rest went on without noticing. "Good. That gives us at least double the leeway I expected."

His hands went on, first with the heart which was the more pressing danger. Would the machine work, he wondered, in this case? Curare and radioactives, fighting each other, were an odd combination. Yet, the machine controlled the nerves close to the vital organ, pounding its message through into the muscles, where the curare had a complicated action that paralyzed the whole nerve, establishing a long block to the control impulses from the brain. Could the nerve impulses from the machine be forced through the short paralyzed passages? Probably—the strength of its signals was controllable. The only proof was in trying.

Brown drew back her hands and stared down uncomprehendingly. "It's beating, Dr. Ferrel! By itself . . . it's beating!"

He nodded again, though the mask concealed his smile. His technique was still not faulty, and he had performed the operation correctly after seeing it once on a dog! He was still the Great Ferrel! Then, the ego in him fell back to normal, though the lift remained, and his exultation centered around the more important problem of Jorgenson's living. And, later, when the lungs began moving of themselves as the nurse stopped working them, he had been expecting it. The detail work remaining was soon over, and he stepped back, dropping the mask from his face and pulling off his gloves.

"Congratulations, Dr. Ferrel!" The voice was guttural, strange. "A truly great operation—truly great. I almost stopped you, but now I am glad I did not; it was a pleasure to observe you, sir." Ferrel looked up in amazement at the bearded smiling face of Kubelik, and he found no words as he accepted the other's hand. But Kubelik apparently expected none.

"I, Kubelik, came, you see; I could not trust another with the machine, and fortunately I made the plane. Then you seemed so sure, so confident—so when you did not notice me, I remained in the background, cursing myself. Now, I shall return, since you have no need of me—the wiser for having watched you. . . . No, not a word; not a word from you, sir. Don't destroy your miracle with words. The 'copter awaits me, I go; but my admiration for you remains forever!"

Ferrel still stood looking down at his hand as the roar of the 'copter cut in, then at the breathing body with the artery on the neck now pulsing regularly. That was all that was needed; he had been admired by Kubelik, the man who thought all other surgeons were fools and nincompoops. For a second or so longer he treasured it, then shrugged it off.

"Now," he said to the others, as the troubles of the plant fell back on his shoulders, "all we have to do is hope that Jorgenson's brain wasn't injured by the session out there, or by this continued artifically maintained life, and try to get him in condition so he can talk before it's too late. God grant us time! Blake, you know the detail work as well as I do, and we can't both work on it. You and the fresh nurses take over, doing the bare minimum needed for the patients scattered around the wards and waiting room. Any new ones?"

"None for some time; I think they've reached a stage where that's over with," Brown answered.

"I hope so. Then go round up Jenkins and lie down somewhere. That goes for you and Meyers, too, Dodd. Blake, give us three hours if you can, and get us up. There won't be any new developments before then, and we'll save time in the long run by resting. Jorgenson's to get first attention!"

The old leather chair made a fair sort of bed, and Ferrel was too exhausted physically and mentally to be choosy—too exhausted to benefit as much as he should from sleep of three hours' duration, for that matter, though it was almost imperative he try. Idly, he wondered what Palmer would think of all his safeguards had he known that Kubelik had come into the place so easily and out again. Not that it mattered; it was doubtful whether anyone else would want to come near, let alone inside the plant.

In that, apparently, he was wrong. It was considerably less than the three hours when he was awakened to hear the bullroar of a helicopter outside. But sleep clouded his mind too much for curiosity and he started to drop back into his slumber. Then another sound cut in jerking him out of his drowsiness. It was the sharp sputter of a machine gun from the direction of the gate, a pause and another burst; an eddy of sleep-memory indicated that it had begun before the helicopter's arrival, so it could not be that they were gunning. More trouble, and while it was none of his business, he could not go back to sleep. He got up and went out into the surgery, just as a gnomish little man hopped out from the rear entrance.

The fellow scooted toward Ferrel after one birdlike glance at Blake, his words spilling out with a jerky self-importance that should have been funny, but missed it by a small margin; under the surface, sincerity still managed to show. "Dr. Ferrel? Uh, Dr. Kubelik—Mayo's, you know—he reported you were shorthanded; stacking patients in the other rooms. We volunteered for duty—me, four other doctors, nine nurses. Probably should have checked with you, but couldn't get a phone through. Took the liberty of coming through directly, fast as we could push our 'copters."

Ferrel glanced through the back, and saw that there were three of the machines, instead of the one he'd thought, with men and equipment piling out of them. Mentally he kicked himself for not asking for help when he'd put through the call; but he'd been used to working with his own little staff for so long that the ready response of his profession to emergencies had been almost forgotten. "You know you're taking chances coming here, naturally? Then, in that case, I'm grateful to you and Kubelik. We've got about forty patients here, all of whom should have considerable attention, though I frankly doubt whether there's room for you to work."

The man hitched his thumb backward jerkily. "Don't worry about that. Kubelik goes the limit when he arranges things. Everything we need with us, practically all the hospital's atomic equipment; though maybe you'll have to piece us out there. Even a field hospital tent, portable wards for every patient you have. Want relief in here or would you rather have us simply move out the patients to the tent, leave this end to you? Oh, Kubelik sent his regards. Amazing of him!"

Kubelik, it seemed, had a tangible idea of regards, however dramatically he was inclined to express them; with him directing the volunteer force, the wonder was that the whole staff and equipment hadn't been moved down. "Better leave this end," Ferrel decided. "Those in the wards will probably be better off in your tent as well as the men now in the waiting room; we're equipped beautifully for all emergency work, but not used to keeping the patients here any length of time, so our accommodations that way are rough. Dr. Blake will show you around and help you get organized in the routine we use here. He'll get help for you in erecting the tent, too. By the way, did you hear the commotion by the entrance as you were landing?"

"We did, indeed. We saw it, too—bunch of men in some kind of uniform shooting a machine gun; hitting the ground, though. Bunch of other people running back away from it, shaking tneir fists, looked like. We were expecting a dose of the same, maybe; didn't notice us, though."

Blake snorted in half amusement. "You probably would have gotten it if our manager hadn't forgotten to give orders covering the air approach; they must figure that's an official route. I saw a bunch from the city arguing about their relatives in here when I came in this morning, so it must have been that." He motioned the little doctor after him, then turned his neck back to address Brown. "Show him the results while I'm gone, honey."

Ferrel forgot his new recruits and swung back to the girl. "Bad?"

She made no comment, but picked up a lead shield and placed it over Jorgenson's chest so that it cut off all radiation from the lower part of his body, then placed the radiation indicator close to the man's throat. Doc looked once; no more was needed. It was obvious that Blake had already done his best to remove the radioactive from all parts of the body needed for speech, in the hope that they might strap down the others and block them off with local anesthetics; Then the curare could have been counteracted long enough for such information as was needed. Equally obviously, he'd failed. There was no sense in going through the job of neutralizing the drug's block only to have him under the control of the radioactive still present. The stuff was too finely dispersed for surgical removal. Now what? He had no answer.

Jenkins' lean-sinewed hand took the indicator from him for inspection. The boy was already frowning as Doc looked up in faint surprise, and his face made no change. He nodded slowly. "Yeah. I figured as much. That was a beautiful piece of work you did, too. Too bad. I was watching from the door and you almost convinced me he'd be all right, the way you handled it. But— So we have to make out without him; and Hoke and Palmer haven't even cooked up a lead that's worth a good test. Want to come into my office, Doc? There's nothing we can do here."

Ferrel followed Jenkins into the little office off the now emptied waiting room; the men from the hospital had worked rapidly, it seemed. "So you haven't been sleeping, I take it? Where's Hokusai now?"

"Out there with Palmer; he promised to behave, if that'll comfort you. . . . Nice guy, Hoke; I'd forgotten what it felt like to talk to an atomic engineer without being laughed at. Palmer, too. I wish—" There was a brief lightening to the boy's face and the first glow of normal human pride Doc had seen in him. Then he shrugged, and it vanished back into his taut cheeks and reddened eyes. "We cooked up the wildest kind of a scheme, but it isn't so hot."

Hoke's voice came out of the doorway, as the little man came in and sat down carefully in one of the three chairs.

"No, not sso hot! It iss fail, already. Jorgensson?"

"Out, no hope there! What happened?"

Hoke spread his arms, his eyes almost closing. "Nothing. We knew it could never work, not sso? Misster Palmer, he iss come ssoon here, then we make planss again, I am think now, besst we sshould move from here. Palmer, I—mosstly we are theoreticianss; and, excusse, you alsso, doctor. Jorgensson wass the production man. No Jorgensson, no—ah—ssoap!"

Mentally, Ferrel agreed about the moving—and soon! But he could see Palmer's point of view; to give up the fight was against the grain, somehow. And besides, once the blowup happened, with the resultant damage to an unknown area, the pressure groups in Congress would be in, shouting for the final abolition of all atomic work; now they were reasonably quiet, only waiting an opportunity—or, more probably, at the moment were already seizing on the rumors spreading to turn this into their coup. If, by some streak of luck, Palmer could save the plant with no greater loss of life and property than already existed, their words would soon be forgotten, and the benefits from the products of National would again outweigh all risks.

"Just what will happen if it all goes off?" he asked.

Jenkins shrugged, biting at his inner lip as he went over a sheaf of papers on the desk, covered with the scrawling symbols of atomics. "Anybody's guess. Suppose three tons of the army's new explosives were to explode in a billionth—or at least, a millionth—of a second? Normally, you know, compared to atomics, that stuff burns like any fire, slowly and quietly, giving its gases plenty of time to get out of the way in an orderly fashion. Figure it one way, with this all going off together, and the stuff could drill a hole that'd split open the whole continent from Hudson Bay to the Gulf of Mexico, and leave a lovely sea where the Middle West is now. Figure it another, and it might only kill off everything within fifty miles of here. Somewhere in between is the chance we count on. This isn't U-235, you know."

Doc winced. He'd been picturing the plant going up in the air violently, with maybe a few buildings somewhere near it, but nothing like this. It had been purely a local affair to him, but this didn't sound like one. No wonder Jenkins was in that state of suppressed jitters; it wasn't too much imagination, but too much cold, hard knowledge that was worrying him. Ferrel looked at their faces as they bent over the symbols once more, tracing out point by point their calculations in the hope of finding one overlooked loophole, then decided to leave them alone.

The whole problem was hopeless without Jorgenson, it seemed, and Jorgenson was his responsibility; if the plant went, it was squarely on the senior physician's shoulders. But there was no apparent solution. If it would help, he could cut it down to a direct path from brain to speaking organs, strap down the body and block off all nerves below the neck, using an artificial larynx instead of the normal breathing through vocal cords. But the indicator showed the futility of it; the orders could never get through from the brain with the amount of radioactive still present throwing them off track—even granting that the brain itself was not affected, which was doubtful.

Fortunately for Jorgenson, the stuff was all finely dispersed around the head, with no concentration at any one place that was unquestionably destructive to his mind; but the good fortune was also the trouble, since it could not be removed by any means known to medical practice. Even so simple a thing as letting the man read the questions and spell out the answers by winking an eyelid as they pointed to the alphabet was hopeless.

Nerves! Jorgenson had his blocked out, but Ferrel wondered if the rest of them weren't in as bad a state. Probably, somewhere well within their grasp, there was a solution that was being held back because the nerves of everyone in the plant were blocked by fear and pressure that defeated its own purpose. Jenkins, Palmer, Hokusai—under purely theoretical conditions, any one of them might spot the answer to the problem, but sheer necessity of finding it could be the thing that hid it. The same might be true with the problem of Jorgenson's treatment. Yet, though he tried to relax and let his mind stray idly around the loose ends, and seemingly disconnected knowledge he had, it returned incessantly to the necessity of doing something, and doing it now!

Ferrel heard weary footsteps behind him and turned to see Palmer coming from the front entrance. The man had no business walking into the surgery, but such minor rules had gone by the board hours before.

"Jorgenson?" Palmer's conversation began with the same old question in the usual tone, and he read the answer from Doc's face with a look that indicated it was no news. "Hoke and that Jenkins kid still in the there?"

Doc nodded, and plodded behind him toward Jenkins' office; he was useless to them, but there was still the idea that in filling his mind with other things, some little factor he had overlooked might have a chance to come forth. Also, curiosity still worked on him, demanding to know what was happening. He flopped into the third chair, and Palmer squatted down on the edge of the table.

"Know a good spiritualist, Jenkins?" the manager asked. "Because if you do, I'm about ready to try calling back Kellar's ghost. The Steinmetz of atomics—so he had to die before this Isotope R came up, and leave us without even a good guess at how long we've got to crack the problem. Hey, what's the matter?"

Jenkins' face had tensed and his body straightened back tensely in the chair, but he shook his head, the corner of his mouth twitching wryly. "Nothing. Nerves, I guess. Hoke and I dug out some things that give an indication on how long this runs, though. We still don't know exactly, but from observations out there and the general theory before, it looks like something between six and thirty hours left; probably ten's closer to being correct!"

"Can't be much longer. It's driving the men back right now! Even the tanks can't get in where they can do the most good, and we're using the shielding around No. 3 as a headquarters for the men; in another half hour, maybe they won't be able to stay that near the thing. Radiation indicators won't register any more, and it's spitting all over the place, almost constantly. Heat's terrific; it's gone up to around three hundred centigrade and sticks right there now, but that's enough to warm up 3, even."

Doc looked up. "No. 3?"

"Yeah. Nothing happened to that batch—it ran through and came out I-713 right on schedule, hours ago. Palmer reached for a cigarette, realized he had one in his mouth, and slammed the package back on the table. "Significant data, Doc; if we get out of this, we'll figure out just what caused the change in No. 4—if we get out! Any chance of making those variable factors work, Hoke?"

Hoke shook his head, and again Jenkins answered from the notes. "Not a chance; sure, theoretically, at least, R should have a period varying between twelve and sixty hours before turning into Mahler's Isotope, depending on what chains of reaction or subchains it goes through; they all look equally good, and probably are all going on in there now, depending on what's around to soak up neutrons or let them roam, the concentration and amount of R together, and even high or low temperatures that change their activity somewhat. It's one of the variables, no question about that."

"The sspitting iss prove that," Hoke supplemented.

"Sure. But there's too much of it together, and we can't break it down fine enough to reach any safety point where it won't toss energy around like rain. The minute one particle manages to make itself into Mahler's, it'll crash through with energy enough to blast the next over the hump and into the same thing instantly, and that passes it on to the next, at about light speed! If we *could* get it juggled around so some would go off first, other atoms a little later, and so on, fine—only we can't do it unless we can be sure of isolating every blob bigger than a tenth of a gram from every other one! And if we start breaking it down into reasonably small pieces, we're likely to have one decide on the short transformation subchain and go off at any time; pure chance gave us a concentration to begin with that eliminated the shorter chains, but we can't break it down into small lots and those into smaller lots, and so on. Too much risk!"

Ferrel had known vaguely that there were such things as variables, but the theory behind them was too new and too complex for him; he'd learned what little he knew when the simpler radioactives proceeded normally from radium to lead, as an example, with a definite, fixed half-life, instead of the super-heavy atoms they now used that could jump through several different paths, yet end up the same. It was over his head, and he started to get up and go back to Jorgenson.

Palmer's words stopped him. "I knew it, of course, but I hoped maybe I was wrong. Then—we evacuate! No use fooling ourselves any longer. I'll call the Governor and try to get him to clear the country around; Hoke, you can tell the men to get the hell out of here! All we ever had was the counteracting isotope to hope on, and no chance of getting enough of that. There was no sense in making I-231 in thousand-pound batches before. Well—"

5

He reached for the phone, but Ferrel cut in. "What about the men in the wards? They're loaded with the stuff, most of them with more than a gram apiece dispersed through them. They're in the same class with the converter, maybe, but we can't just pull out and leave them!"

Silence hit them, to be broken by Jenkins' hushed whisper. "My God! What damned fools we are. I-231 under discussion for hours, and I never thought of it. Now you two throw the connection in my face, and I still almost miss it!"

"I-231? But there iss not enough. Maybe twenty-five pound, maybe less. Three and a half days to make more. The little we have would be no good, Dr. Jenkinss. We forget that already." Hoke struck a match to a piece of paper, shook one drop of ink onto it, and watched it continue burning for a second before putting it out. "Sso. A drop of water for sstop a foresst fire. No."

"Wrong, Hoke. A drop to short a switch that'll turn on the real stream—maybe. Look, Doc, I-231's an isotope that reacts atomically with R—we've checked on that already. It simply gets together with the stuff and the two break down into non-radioactive elements and a little heat, like a lot of other such atomic reactions; but it isn't the violent kind. They simply swap parts in a friendly way and open up to simpler atoms that are stable. We have a few pounds on hand, can't make enough in time to help with No. 4, but we do have enough to treat every man in the wards, *including Jorgenson!*"

"How much heat?" Doc snapped out of his lethargy into the detailed thought of a good physician. "In atomics you may call it a little; but would it be small enough in the human body?"

Hokusai and Palmer were practically riding the pencil as Jenkins figured. "Say five grams of the stuff in Jorgenson, to be on the safe side, less in the others. Time for reaction . . . hm-m. Here's the total heat produced and the time taken by the reaction, probably, in the body. The stuff's water-soluble in the chloride we have of it, so there's no trouble dispersing it. What do you make of it, Doc?"

"Fifteen to eighteen degrees temperature rise at a rough estimate. Uh!"

"Too much! Jorgenson couldn't stand ten degrees right now!" Jenkins frowned down at his figures, tapping nervously with his hand.

Doc shook his head. "Not too much! We can drop his whole body temperature first in the hypothermy bath down to eighty degrees, then let it rise to a hundred, if necessary, and still be safe. Thank the Lord, there's equipment enough. If they'll rip out the refrigerating units in the cafeteria and improvise baths, the volunteers out in the tent can start on the other men while we handle Jorgenson. At least that way we can get the men all out, even if we don't save the plant."

Palmer stared at them in confusion before his face galvanized into resolution. "Refrigerating units—volunteers—tent? What—O.K., Doc, what do you want?" He reached for the telephone and began giving orders for the available I-231 to be sent to the surgery, for men to rip out the cafeteria cooling equipment, and for such other things as Doc requested. Jenkins had already gone to instruct the medical staff in the field tent without asking how they'd gotten there, but was back in the surgery before Doc reached it with Palmer and Hokusai at his heels.

"Blake's taking over out there," Jenkins announced. "Says if you want Dodd, Meyers, Jones, or Sue, they're sleeping."

"No need. Get over there out of the way, if you must watch," Ferrel ordered the two engineers, as he and Jenkins began attaching the freezing units and bath to the sling on the exciter. "Prepare his blood for it, Jenkins; we'll force it down as low as we can to be on the safe side. And we'll have to keep tabs on the temperature fall and regulate his heart and breathing to what it would be normally in that condition; they're both out of his normal control, now."

"And pray," Jenkins added. He grabbed the small box out of the messenger's hand before the man was fully inside the door and began preparing a solution, weighing out the whitish powder and measuring water carefully, but with the speed that was automatic to him under tension. "Doc, if this doesn't work—if Jorgenson's crazy or something—you'll have another case of insanity on your hands. One more false hope would finish me."

"Not one more case; four! We're all in the same boat. Temperature's falling nicely—I'm rushing it a little, but it's safe enough. Down to ninety-six now." The thermometer under Jorgenson's tongue was one intended for hypothermy work, capable of rapid response, instead of the normal fever thermometer. Slowly, with agonizing reluctance, the little needle on the dial moved over, down to ninety, then on. Doc kept his eyes glued to it, slowing the pulse and breath to the proper speed. He lost track of the number of times he sent Palmer back out of the way, and finally gave up.

Waiting, he wondered how those outside in the field hospital were doing? Still, they had ample time to arrange their makeshift cooling apparatus and treat the men in groups—ten hours probably; and hypothermy was a standard thing, now. Jorgenson was the only real rush case. Almost imperceptibly to Doc, but speedily by normal standards, the temperature continued to fall. Finally it reached seventy-eight.

"Ready, Jenkins, make the injection. That enough?"

"No. I figure it's almost enough, but we'll have to go slow to balance out properly. Too much of this stuff would be almost as bad as the other. Gauge going up, Doc?"

It was, much more rapidly than Ferrel liked. As the injection coursed through the blood vessels and dispersed out to the fine deposits of radioactive, the needle began climbing past eighty, to ninety, and up. It stopped at ninety-four and slowly began falling as the cooling bath absorbed heat from the cells of the body. The radioactivity meter still registered the presence of Isotope R, though much more faintly.

The next shot was small, and a smaller one followed. "Almost," Ferrel commented. "Next one should about do the trick."

Using partial injections, there had been need for less drop in temperature than they had given Jorgenson, but there was small loss to that. Finally, when the last minute bit of the I-213 solution had entered the man's veins and done its work, Doc nodded. "No sign of activity left. He's up to ninety-five, now that I've cut off the refrigeration, and he'll pick up the little extra temperature in a hurry. By the time we can counteract the curare, he'll be ready. That'll take about fifteen minutes, Palmer."

The manager nodded, watching them dismantling the hypothermy equipment and going through the routine of cancelling out the curare. It was always a slower job than treatment with the drug, but part of the work had been done already by the normal body processes, and the rest was a simple, standard procedure. Fortunately, the neo-heroin would be nearly worn off, or that would have been a longer and much harder problem to eliminate.

"Telephone for Mr. Palmer. Calling Mr. Palmer. Send Mr. Palmer to the telephone." The operator's words lacked the usual artificial exactness, and were only a nervous sing-song. It was getting to her, and she wasn't bothered by excess imagination, normally. "Mr. Palmer is wanted on the telephone."

"Palmer." The manager picked up an instrument at hand, not equipped with vision, and there was no indication to the caller. But Ferrel could see what little hope had appeared at the prospect of Jorgenson's revival disappearing. "Check! Move out of there, and prepare to evacuate, but keep quiet about that until you hear further orders! Tell the men Jorgenson's about out of it, so they won't lack for something to talk about."

He swung back to them. "No use, Doc, I'm afraid. We're already too late. The stuff's stepped it up again, and they're having to move out of No. 3 now. I'll wait on Jorgenson, but even if he's all right and knows the answer, we can't get in to use it!"

6

"Healing's going to be a long, slow process, but they should at least grow back better than silver ribs; never take a pretty X-ray photo, though." Doc held the instrument in his hand, staring down at the flap opened in Jorgenson's chest, and his shoulders came up in a faint shrug. The little platinum filaments had been removed from around the nerves to heart and lungs, and the man's normal impulses were operating again, less steadily than under the exciter, but with no danger signals. "Well, it won't much matter if he's still sane."

Jenkins watched him being stitching the flap back, his eyes centered over the table out toward the converter. "Doc, he's got to be sane! If Hoke and Palmer find it's what it sounds like out there, we'll have to count on Jorgenson. There's an answer somewhere, has to be! But we won't find it without him."

"Hm-m-m. Seems to me you've been having ideas yourself, son. You've been right so far, and if Jorgenson's out—" He shut off the stitcher, finished the dressings, and flopped down on a bench, knowing that all they could do was wait for the drugs to work on Jorgenson and bring him around. Now that he relaxed the control over himself, exhaustion hit down with full force; his fingers were uncertain as he pulled off the gloves. "Anyhow, we'll know in another five minutes or so."

"And heaven help us, Doc, if it's up to me. I've always had a flair for atomic theory; I grew up on it. But he's the production man who's been working at it week in and week out, and it's his process, to boot. . . . There they are now! All right for them to come back here?"

But Hokusai and Palmer were waiting for no permission. At the moment, Jorgenson was the nerve center of the plant, drawing them back, and they stalked over to stare down at him, then sat where they could be sure of missing no sign of returning consciousness. Palmer picked up the conversation where he'd dropped it, addressing his remarks to both Hokusai and Jenkins.

"Damn that Link-Stevens postulate! Time after time it fails, until you figure there's nothing to it; then, this! It's black magic, not science, and if I get out, I'll find some fool with more courage than sense to discover why. Hoke, are you positive it's the *theta* chain? There isn't one chance in ten thousand of that happening, you know; it's unstable, hard to stop, tends to revert to the simpler ones at the first chance."

Hokusai spread his hands, lifted one heavy eyelid at Jenkins questioningly, then nodded. The boy's voice was dull, almost uninterested. "That's what I thought it had to be, Palmer. None of the others throws off that much energy at this stage, the way you described conditions out there. Probably the last thing we tried to quench set it up in that pattern, and it's in a concentration just right to keep it going. We figured ten hours was the best chance, so it had to pick the six-hour short chain."

"Yeah." Palmer was pacing up and down nervously again, his eyes swinging toward Jorgenson from whatever direction he moved. "And in six hours, maybe all the population around here can be evacuated, maybe not, but we'll have to try it. Doc, I can't even wait for Jorgenson now! I've got to get the Governor started at once!"

"They've been known to practice lynch law, even in recent years," Ferrel reminded him grimly. He'd seen the result of one such case of mob violence when he was practicing privately, and he knew that people remain pretty much the same year after year; they'd move, but first they'd demand a sacrifice. "Better get the men out of here first, Palmer, and my advice is to get yourself a good long distance off; I heard some of the trouble at the gate, and that won't be anything compared to what an evacuation order will do."

Palmer grunted. "Doc, you might not believe it, but I don't give a continental about what happens to me or the plant right now."

"Or the men? Put a mob in here, hunting your blood, and the men will be on your side, because they know it wasn't your fault, and they've seen you out there taking chances yourself. That mob won't be too choosy about its targets, either, once it gets worked up, and you'll have a nice vicious brawl all over the place. Besides, Jorgenson's practically ready."

A few minutes would make no difference in the evacuation, and Doc had no desire to think of his partially crippled wife going through the hell evacuation would be; she'd probably refuse, until he returned. His eyes fell on the box Jenkins was playing with nervously, and he stalled for time. "I thought you said it was risky to break the stuff down into small particles, Jenkins. But that box contains the stuff in various sizes, including one big piece we scraped out, along with the contaminated instruments. Why hasn't it exploded?"

Jenkins' hand jerked up from it as if burned, and he backed away a step before checking himself. Then he was across the room toward the I-231 and back, pouring the white powder over everything in the box in a jerky frenzy. Hokusai's eyes had snapped fully open, and he was slopping water in to fill up the remaining space and keep the I-231 in contact with everything else. Almost at once, in spite of the low relative energy release, it sent up a white cloud of steam faster than the air conditioner could clear the room; but that soon faded down and disappeared.

Hokusai wiped his forehead slowly. "The ssuits—armor of the men?"

"Sent 'em back to the converter and had them dumped into the stuff to be safe long ago," Jenkins answered. "But I forgot that box, like a fool. Ugh! Either blind chance saved us or else the stuff spit out was all one kind, some reasonably long chain. I don't know nor care right—"

"S'ot! Nnnuh . . . Whmah nahh?"

"Jorgenson!" They swung from the end of the room like one man, but Jenkins was the first to reach the table. Jorgenson's eyes were open and rolling in a semiorderly manner, his hands moving sluggishly. The boy hovered over his face, his own practically glowing with the intensity behind it. "Jorgenson, can you understand what I'm saying?"

"Uh." The eyes ceased moving and centered on Jenkins. One hand came up to his throat, clutching at it, and he tried unsuccessfully to lift himself with the other, but the aftereffects of what he'd been through seemed to have left him in a state of partial paralysis.

Ferrel had hardly dared hope that the man could be rational, and his relief was tinged with doubt. He pushed Palmer back, and shook his head. "No, stay back. Let the boy handle it; he knows enough not to shock the man now, and you don't. This can't be rushed too much."

"I—uh. . . . Young Jenkins? Whasha doin' here? Tell y'ur dad to ge' busy ou' there!" Somewhere in Jorgenson's huge frame, and untapped reserve of energy and will sprang up, and he forced himself into a sitting position, his eyes on Jenkins, his hand still catching at the reluctant throat that refused to cooperate. His words were blurry and uncertain, but sheer determination overcame the obstacles and made the words understandable.

"Dad's dead now, Jorgenson. Now—"

" 'Sright. 'N' you're grown up—'bout twelve years old, y'were. . . . The plant!"

"Easy, Jorgenson." Jenkins' own voice managed to sound casual, though his hands under the table were white where they clenched together. "Listen, and don't try to say anything until I finish. The plant's still all right, but we've got to have your help. Here's what happened."

Ferrel could make little sense of the cryptic sentences that followed, though he gathered that they were some form of engineering shorthand; apparently, from Hokusai's approving nod, they summed up the situation briefly but fully, and Jorgenson sat rigidly still until it was finished, his eyes fastened on the boy.

"Hellova mess! Gotta think . . . yuh tried—" He made an attempt to lower himself back, and Jenkins assisted him, hanging on feverishly to each awkward, uncertain change of expression on the man's face. "Uh . . . da' sroat! Yuh . . . uh . . . urrgh!"

"Got it?"

"Uh!" The tone was affirmative, unquestionably, but the clutching hands around his neck told their own story. The temporary burst of energy he'd forced was exhausted, and he couldn't get through with it. He lay there, breathing heavily and struggling, then relaxed after a few more half-whispered words, none intelligently articulated.

Palmer clutched at Ferrel's sleeve. "Doc, isn't there anything you can do?"

"Try." He metered out a minute quantity of drug doubtfully, felt Jorgenson's pulse, and decided on half that amount. "Not much hope, though; that man's been through hell, and it wasn't good for him to be forced around in the first place. Carry it too far, and he'll be delirious if he does talk. Anyway, I suspect it's partly his speech centers as well as the throat."

But Jorgenson began a slight rally almost instantly, trying again, then apparently drawing himself together for a final attempt. When they came, the words spilled out harshly in forced clearness, but without inflection.

"First . . . variable . . . at . . . twelve . . . water . . . stop." His eyes, centered on Jenkins, closed, and he relaxed again, this time no longer fighting of the inevitable unconsciousness.

Hokusai, Palmer, and Jenkins were staring back and forth at one another questioningly. The little Japanese shook his head negatively at first, frowned, and repeated it, to be imitated almost exactly by the manager. "Delirious ravings!"

"The great white hope Jorgenson!" Jenkins' shoulders dropped and the blood drained from his face, leaving it ghastly with fatigue and despair. "Oh, damn it, Doc stop staring at me! I can't pull a miracle out of a hat!"

Doc hadn't realized that he was staring, but he made no effort to change it. "Maybe not, but you happened to have the most active imagination here, when you stop abusing it to scare yourself. Well, you're on the spot now, and I'm still giving odds on you. Want to bet, Hoke?"

It was an utterly stupid thing, and Doc knew it; but somewhere during the long hours together, he'd picked up a queer respect for the boy and a dependence on the nervousness that wasn't fear but closer akin to the reaction of a rear-running thoroughbred on the home stretch. Hoke was too slow and methodical, and Palmer had been too concerned with outside worries to give anywhere nearly full attention to the single most urgent phase of the problem; that left only Jenkins, hampered by his lack of self-confidence.

Hoke gave no sign that he caught the meaning of Doc's heavy wink, but he lifted his eyebrows faintly. "No, I think I am not bet. Dr. Jenkins, I am to be command!"

Palmer looked briefly at the boy, whose face mirrored in credulous confusion, but he had neither Ferrel's ignorance of atomic technique nor Hokusai's fatalism. With a final glance at the unconscious Jorgenson, he started across the room toward the phone. "You men play, if you like. I'm starting evacuation immediately!"

"Wait!" Jenkins was shaking himself, physically as well as mentally. "Hold it, Palmer! Thanks, Doc. You knocked me out of the rut, and bounced my memory back to something I picked up somewhere; I think it's the answer! It has to work—nothing else can at this stage of the game!"

"Give me the Governor, operator." Palmer had heard, but he went on with the phone call. "This is no time to play crazy hunches until after we get the people out, kid. I'll admit you're a darned clever amateur, but you're no atomicist!"

"And if we get the men out, it's too late—there'll be no one left in here to do the work!" Jenkins' hand snapped out and jerked the receiver of the plug-in telephone from Palmer's hand. "Cancel the call, operator; it won't be necessary. Palmer, you've got to listen to me; you can't clear the whole middle of the continent, and you can't depend on the explosion to limit itself to less ground. It's a gamble, but you're risking fifty million people against a mere hundred thousand. Give me a chance!"

"I'll give you exactly one minute to convince me, Jenkins, and it had better be good! Maybe the blowup won't hit beyond the fifty-mile limit!"

"Maybe. And I can't explain in a minute." The boy scowled tensely. "O.K., you've been bellyaching about a man named Kellar being dead. If he were here, would you take a chance on him? Or on a man who'd worked under him on everything he tried?"

"Absolutely, but you're not Kellar. And I happen to know he was a lone wolf; didn't hire outside engineers after Jorgenson had a squabble with him and came here." Palmer reached for the phone. "It won't wash, Jenkins."

Jenkins' hand clamped down on the instrument, jerking it out of reach. "I wasn't *outside* help, Palmer. When Jorgenson was afraid to run one of the things off and quit, I was twelve; three years later, things got too tight for him to handle alone, but he decided he might as well keep it in the family, so he started me in. I'm Kellar's stepson!"

Pieces clicked together in Doc's head then, and he kicked himself mentally for not having seen the obvious before. "That's why Jorgenson knew you, then? I thought that was funny. It checks, Palmer."

For a split second, the manager hesitated uncertainly. Then he shrugged and gave in. "O.K., I'm a fool to trust you, Jenkins, but it's too late for anything else, I guess. I never forgot that I was gambling the locality against half the continent. What do you want?"

"Men—construction men, mostly, and a few volunteers for dirty work. I want all the blowers, exhaust equipment, tubing, booster blowers and everything ripped from the other three converters and connected as close to No. 4 as you can get. Put them up some way so they can be shoved in over the stuff by crane—I don't care how; the shop men will know better than I do. You've got sort of a river running off behind the plant; get everyone within a few miles of it out of there, and connect the blower outlets down to it. Where does it end, anyway—some kind of a swamp, or morass?"

"About ten miles farther down, yes; we didn't bother keeping the drainage system going, since the land meant nothing to us, and the swamps made as good a dumping ground as anything else." When the plant had first used the little river as an outlet for their waste products, there'd been so much trouble that National had been forced to take over all adjacent land and quiet the owners' fears of the atomic activity in cold cash. Since then, it had gone to weeds and rabbits, mostly. "Everyone within a few miles is out, anyway, except a few fishers or tramps that don't know we use it. I'll have militia sent in to scare them out."

"Good. Ideal, in fact, since the swamps will hold stuff longer in there where the current's slow. Now, what about that superthermite stuff you were producing last year? Any around?"

"Not in the plant. But we've got tons of it at the warehouse, still waiting for the army's requisition. That's pretty hot stuff to handle, though. Know much about it?"

"Enough to know it's what I want." Jenkins indicated the copy of the *Weekly Ray* still lying where he'd dropped it, and Doc remembered skimming through the nontechnical part of the description. It was made up of two superheavy atoms, kept separate. By itself, neither was particularly important or active, but together they reacted with each other atomically to release a tremendous amount of raw heat and comparatively little unwanted radiation. "Goes up around twenty thousand centigrade, doesn't it? How's it stored?"

"In ten-pound bombs that have a fragile partition; it breaks with shock, starting the action. Hoke can explain it—it's his baby." Palmer reached for the phone. "Anything else? Then, get out and get busy! The men will be ready for you when you get there! I'll be out myself as soon as I can put through your orders."

Doc watched them go out, to be followed in short order by the manager, and was alone in the infirmary with Jorgenson and his thoughts. They weren't pleasant; he was both too far outside the inner circle to know what was going on and too much mixed up in it not to know the dangers. Now he could have used some work of any nature to take his mind off useless speculations, but aside from a needless check of the foreman's condition, there was nothing for him to do.

He wriggled down in the leather chair, making the mistake of trying to force sleep, while his mind chased out after the sounds that came in from outside. There were the drones of crane and tank motors coming to life, the shouts of hurried orders, and above all, the jarring rhythm of pneumatic hammers on metal, each sound suggesting some possibility to him without adding to his knowledge. The *Decameron* was boring, the whiskey tasted raw and rancid, and solitaire wasn't worth the trouble of cheating.

Finally, he gave up and turned out to the field hospital tent. Jorgenson would be better off out there, under the care of the staff from Mayo's, and perhaps he could make himself useful. As he passed through the rear entrance, he heard the sound of a number of helicopters coming over with heavy loads, and looked up as they began settling over the edge of the buildings. From somewhere, a group of men came running forward, and disappeared in the direction of the freighters. He wondered whether any of those men would be forced back into the stuff out there to return filled with radioactivity; though it didn't matter so much, now that the isotope could be eliminated without surgery.

Blake met him at the entrance of the field tent, obviously well satisfied with his duty of bossing and instructing the others. "Scram, Doc. You aren't necessary here, and you need some rest. Don't want you added to the casualties. What's the latest dope from the pow-wow front?"

"Jorgenson didn't come through, but the kid had an idea, and they're out there working on it." Doc tried to sound more hopeful than he felt. "I was thinking you might as well bring Jorgenson in here; he's still unconscious, but there doesn't seem to be anything to worry about. Where's Brown? She'll probably want to know what's up, if she isn't asleep."

"Asleep when the kid isn't? Uh-huh. Mother complex, has to worry about him." Blake grinned. "She got a look at him running out with Hoke tagging at his heels, and hiked out after him, so she probably knows everything now. Wish Anne'd chase me that way, just once—Jenkins, the wonder boy! Well, it's out of my line; I don't intend to start worrying until they pass out the order. O.K., Doc, I'll have Jorgenson out here in a couple of minutes, so you grab yourself a cot and get some shut-eye."

Doc grunted, looking curiously at the refinements and well-equipped interior of the field tent. "I've already prescribed that, Blake, but the patient can't seen to take it. I think I'll hunt up Brown, so give me a call over the public speaker if anything turns up."

He headed toward the center of action, knowing that he'd been wanting to do it all along, but hadn't been sure of not being a nuisance. Well, if Brown could look on, there was no reason why he couldn't. He passed the machine shop, noting the excited flurry of activity going on, and went past No. 2, where other men were busily ripping out long sections of big piping and various other devices. There was a rope fence barring his way, well beyond No. 3, and he followed along the edge, looking for Palmer or Brown.

She saw him first. "Hi, Dr. Ferrel, over here in the truck. I thought you'd be coming soon. From up here we can get a look over the heads of all these other people, and we won't be tramped on." She stuck down a hand to help him up, smiled faintly as he disregarded it and mounted more briskly than his muscles wanted to. He wasn't so old that a girl had to help him yet.

"Know what's going on?" he asked, sinking down onto the plank across the truck body, facing out across the men below toward the converter. There seemed to be a dozen different centers of activity, all crossing each other in complete confusion, and the general pattern was meaningless.

"No more than you do. I haven't seen my husband, though Mr. Palmer took time enough to chase me here out of the way."

Doc centered his attention on the 'copters, unloading, rising, and coming in with more loads, and he guessed that those boxes must contain the little thermodyne bombs. It was the one thing he could understand, and consequently the least interesting. Other men were assembling the big sections of piping he'd seen before, connecting them up in almost endless order, while some of the tanks hooked on and snaked them off in the direction of the small river that ran off beyond the plant.

"Those must be the exhaust blowers, I guess," he told Brown, pointing them out. "Though I don't know what any of the rest of the stuff hooked on is."

"I know—I've been inside the plant Bob's father had." She

lifted an inquiring eyebrow at him, went on as he nodded. "The pipes are for exhaust gases, all right, and those big square things are the motors and fans—they put in one at each five hundred feet or less of piping. The things they're wrapping around the pipe must be the heaters to keep the gases hot. Are they going to try to suck all that out?"

Doc didn't know, though it was the only thing he could see. But he wondered how they'd get around the problem of moving in close enough to do any good. "I heard your husband order some thermodyne bombs, so they'll probably try to gassify the magma; then they're pumping it down the river."

As he spoke, there was a flurry of motion at one side, and his eyes swung over instantly, to see one of the cranes laboring with a long framework stuck from its front, holding up a section of pipe with a nozzle on the end. It tilted precariously, even though heavy bags were piled everywhere to add weight, but an inch at a time it lifted its load, and began forcing its way forward, carrying the nozzle out in front and rather high.

Below the main exhaust pipe was another smaller one. As it drew near the outskirts of the danger zone, a small object ejaculated from the little pipe, hit the ground, and was a sudden blazing inferno of glaring blue-white light, far brighter than it seemed, judging by the effect on the eyes. Doc shielded his, just as someone below put something into his hands.

"Put 'em on. Palmer says the light's actinic."

He heard Brown fussing beside him, then his vision cleared, and he looked back through the goggles again to see a glowing cloud spring up from the magma, spread out near the ground, narrowing down higher up, until it sucked into the nozzle above, and disappeared. Another bomb slid from the tube, and erupted with blazing heat. A sideways glance showed another crane being fitted, and a group of men near it wrapping what might have been oiled rags around the small bombs; probably no tubing fitted them exactly, and they were padding them so pressure could blow them forward and out. Three more dropped from the tube, one at a time, and the fans roared and groaned, pulling the cloud that rose into the pipe and feeding it down toward the river.

Then the crane inched back out carefully as men uncoupled its piping from the main line, and a second went in to replace it. The heat generated must be too great for the machine to stand steadily without the pipe fusing, Doc decided; though they couldn't have kept a man inside the heavily armoured cab for any length of time, if the metal had been impervious. Now another crane was ready, and went in from another place; it settled down to a routine of ingoing and outcoming cranes, and men feeding materials in, coupling and uncoupling the pipes and replacing the others who came from the cabs. Doc began to feel like a man at a tennis match, watching the ball without knowing the rules.

Brown must have had the same idea, for she caught Ferrel's arm and indicated a little leather case that came from her handbag. "Doc, do you play chess? We might as well fill our time with that as sitting here on edge, just watching. It's supposed to be good for nerves."

He seized on it gratefully, without explaining that he'd been city champion three years running; he'd take it easy, watch her game, handicap himself just enough to make it interesting by the deliberate loss of a rook, bishop or knight, as was needed to even the odds— Suppose they got all the magma out and into the river; how did that solve the problem? It removed it form the plant, but far less than the fifty-mile minimum danger limit.

"Check," Brown announced. He castled, and looked up at the half-dozen cranes that were now operating. "Check! Checkmate!"

He looked back again hastily, then, to see her queen guarding all possible moves, a bishop checking him. Then his eye followed down toward her end. "Umm. Did you know you've been in check for the last half-dozen moves?" Because I didn't."

She frowned, shook her head, and began setting the men up again. Doc moved out the queen's pawn, looked out at the workers, and then brought out the king's bishop, to see her take it with her king's pawn. He hadn't watched her move it out, and had counted on her queen's to block his. Things would require more careful watching on this little portable set. The men were moving steadily and there was a growing clear space, but as they went forward, the violent action of the thermodyne had pitted the ground, carefully as it had been used, and going became more uncertain. Time was slipping by rapidly now.

"Checkmate!" He found himself in a hole, started to nod; but she caught herself this time. "Sorry, I've been playing my king for a queen. Doctor, let's see if we can play at least one game right."

Before it was half finished, it became obvious that they couldn't. Neither had chess very much on the mind, and the pawns and men did fearful and wonderful things, while the knights were as likely to jump six squares as their normal L. They gave it up, just as one of the cranes lost its precarious balance and toppled forward, dropping the long extended pipe into the bubbling mass below. Tanks were in instantly, hitching on and tugging backward until it came down with a thump as the pipe fused, releasing the extreme forward load. It backed out on its own power, while another went in. The driver, by sheer good luck, hobbled from the cab, waving an armored hand to indicate he was all right. Things settled back to an excited routine again that seemed to go on endlessly, though seconds were dropping off too rapidly, turning into minutes that threatened to be hours far too soon.

"Uh!" Brown had been staring for some time, but her little feet suddenly came down with a bang and she straightened up, her hand to her mouth. "Doctor, I just thought; it won't do any good—all this!"

"Why?" She couldn't know anything, but he felt the faint hopes he had go downward sharply. His nerves were dulled, but still ready to jump at the slightest warning.

"The stuff they were making was a superheavy—it'll sink as soon as it hits the water, and all pile up right there! It won't float down river!"

Obvious, Ferrel thought; too obvious. Maybe that was why the engineers hadn't thought of it. He started from the plank, just as Palmer stepped up, but the manager's hand on his shoulder forced him back.

"Easy, Doc, it's O.K. Ummm, so they teach women *some* science nowadays, eh, Mrs. Jenkins . . . Sue . . . Dr. Brown, whatever your name is? Don't worry about it, though—the old principle of Brownian movement will keep any colloid suspended, if it's fine enough to be a real colloid. We're sucking it out and keeping it pretty hot until it reaches the water—then it cools off so fast it hasn't time to collect in particles big enough to sink. Some of the dust that floats around in the air is heavier than water, too. I'm joining the bystanders, if you don't mind;

the men have everything under control, and I can see better here than I could down there, if anything does come up."

Doc's momentary despair reacted to leave him feeling more sure of things than was justified. He pushed over on the plank, making room for Palmer to drop down beside him. "What's to keep it from blowing up anyway, Palmer?"

"Nothing! Got a match?" He sucked in on the cigarette heavily, relaxing as much as he could. "No use trying to fool you, Doc, at this stage of the game. We're gambling, and I'd say the odds are even; Jenkins thinks they're ninety to ten in his favor, but he has to think so. What we're hoping is that by lifting it out in a gas, thus breaking it down at once from full concentration to the finest possible form, and letting it settle in the water in colloidal particles, there won't be a concentration at any one place sufficient to set it all off at once. The big problem is making sure we get every bit of it cleaned out here, or there may be enough left to take care of us and the nearby city! At least, since the last change, it's stopped spitting, so all the men have to worry about is burn!"

"How much damage, even if it doesn't go off all at once?"

"Possibly none. If you can keep it burning slowly, a million tons of dynamite wouldn't be any worse than the same amount of wood, but a stick going off at once will kill you. Why the dickens didn't Jenkins tell me he wanted to go into atomics? We could have fixed all that—it's hard enough to get good men as it is!"

Brown perked up, forgetting the whole trouble beyond them, and went into the story with enthusiasm, while Ferrel only partly listened. He could see the spot of magma growing steadily smaller, but the watch on his wrist went on ticking off minutes remorselessly, and the time was growing limited. He hadn't realized before how long he'd been sitting there. Now three of the crane nozzles were almost touching, and around them stretched the burned-out ground, with no sign of converter, masonry, or anything else; the heat from the thermodyne had gassified everything indiscriminately.

"Palmer!" The portable ultrawave set around the manager's neck came to life suddenly. "Hey, Palmer, those blowers are about shot; the pipe's pitting already. We've been doing everything we can to replace them, but that stuff eats faster than we can fix. Can't hold up more'n fifteen minutes more."

"Check, Briggs. Keep 'em going the best you can." Palmer flipped a switch and looked out toward the tank standing by behind the cranes. "Jenkins, you get that?"

"Yeah. Surprised they held out this long. How much time till deadline?" The boy's voice was completely toneless, neither hope nor nerves showing up, only the complete weariness of a man almost at his limit.

Palmer looked and whistled. "Twelve minutes, according to the minimum estimate Hoke made! How much left?"

"We're just burning around now, trying to make sure there's no pocket left; I hope we've got the whole works, but I'm not promising. Might as well send out all the I-231 you have and we'll boil it down the pipes to clear out any deposits on them. All the old treads and parts that contacted the R gone into the pile?"

"You melted the last, and your cranes haven't touched the stuff directly. Nice pile of money's gone down that pipe—converter, machinery, everything!"

Jenkins made a sound that was expressive of his worry about that. "I'm coming in now and starting the clearing of the pipe. What've you been paying insurance for?"

"At a lovely rate, too! O.K., come on in, kid; and if you're interested, you can start sticking A.E. after the M.D., anytime you want. Your wife's been giving me your qualifications, and I think you've passed the final test, so you're now an atomic engineer, duly graduated from National!"

Brown's breath caught, and her eyes seemed to glow, even through the goggles, but Jenkin's voice was flat. "O.K., I expected you to give me one if we don't blow up. But you'll have to see Dr. Ferrel about it; he's got a contract with me for medical practice. Be there shortly."

Nine of the estimated twelve minutes had ticked by when he climbed up beside them, mopping off some of the sweat that covered him, and Palmer was hugging the watch. More minutes ticked off slowly, while the last sound faded out in the plant, and the men stood around, staring down toward the river or at the hole that had been No. 4. Silence. Jenkins stirred and grunted.

"Palmer, I know where I got the idea, now. Jorgenson was trying to remind me of it, instead of raving, only I didn't get it, at least consciously. It was one of Dad's, the one he told Jorgenson was a last resort, in case the thing they broke up about went haywire. It was the first variable Dad tried. I was twelve, and he insisted water would break it up into all its chains and kill the danger. Only Dad didn't really expect it to work!"

Palmer didn't look up from the watch, but he caught his breath and swore. "Fine time to tell me that!"

"He didn't have your isotopes to heat it up with, either," Jenkins answered mildly. "Suppose you look up from that watch of yours for a minute, down the river."

As Doc raised his eyes, he was aware suddenly of a roar from the men. Over to the south, stretching out in a huge mass, was a cloud of steam that spread upward and out as he watched, and the beginnings of a mighty hissing sound came in. Then Palmer was hugging Jenkins and yelling until Brown could pry him away and replace him.

"Ten miles or more of river, plus the swamps, Doc!" Palmer was shouting in Ferrel's ear. "All that dispersion, while it cooks slowly from now until the last chain is finished, atom by atom! The *theta* chain broke, unstable and now there's everything there, too scattered to set itself off! It'll cook the river bed up and dry it, but that's all!"

Doc was still dazed, unsure of how to take the relief. He wanted to lie down and cry or to stand up with the men and shout his head off. Instead, he sat loosely, gazing at the cloud. "So I lose the best assistant I ever had! Jenkins, I won't hold you; you're free for whatever Palmer wants."

"Hoke wants him to work on R—he's got the stuff for his bomb now!" Palmer was clapping his hands together slowly, like an excited child watching a steam shovel. "Heck, Doc, pick out anyone you want until your own boy gets out next year. You wanted a chance to work him in here, now you've got it. Right now I'll give you anything you want."

"You might see what you can do about hospitalizing the injured and fixing things up with the men in the tent behind the infirmary. And I think I'll take Brown in Jenkins' place, with the right to grab him in an emergency, until that year's up."

"Done." Palmer slapped the boy's back, stopping the protest, while Brown winked at him. "Your wife likes working, kid; she told me that herself. Besides, a lot of the women work here where they can keep an eye on their men; my own wife does, usually. Doc, take these two kids and head for home, where I'm going myself. Don't come back until you get good and ready, and don't let them start fighting about it."

Doc pulled himself from the truck and started off with Brown and Jenkins following, through the yelling, relief-crazed men. The three were too thoroughly worn out for any exhibition themselves, but they could feel it. Happy ending! Jenkins and Brown where they wanted to be, Hoke with his bomb, Palmer with proof that atomic plants were safe where they were, and he—well, his boy would start out right, with himself and the widely differing but competent Blake and Jenkins to guide him. It wasn't a bad life, after all.

Then he stopped and chuckled. "You two wait for me, will you? If I leave here without making out that order of extra disinfection at the showers, Blake'll swear I'm growing old and feeble-minded. I can't have that."

Old? Maybe a little tired, but he'd been that before, and with luck would be again. He wasn't worried. His nerves were good for twenty years and fifty accidents more, and by that time Blake would be due for a little ribbing himself.

> Peoples and governments never have learned anything from history, or acted on principles deduced from it.
>
> —Hegel, from the Introduction to *The Philosophy of History*

In my opinion, Cyril M. Kornbluth was the best short-story writer working only in the SF/fantasy genres. (The limitation excepts Kipling and Wells, both of whom worked extensively in SF and fantasy but were world-class mainstream writers as well.)

Not everybody would agree with my position, but I think most folks who've read widely in the field would accept that Kornbluth was arguably the best short-story writer in the field just as boxing fans would agree that Rocky Marciano might be the best boxer of all time, even if they personally think Muhammad Ali was better. It's harder to explain why "The Only Thing We Learn" is my favorite of all sf stories, though.

I first read the story in an anthology when I was fifteen. I didn't recognize the Hegel-derived title aphorism ("The only thing we learn from history is that we never learn") and Kornbluth's name didn't mean anything to me either. Nonetheless the story really blew me away.

I've reread "The Only Thing We Learn" a number of times since then, both before and after I began writing myself. My undergraduate majors were history and Latin, so I understand the story's background much better, Among other things I understand that it's influenced by Spengler to the extent of being a fictional illustration of *The Decline of the West*; a thesis that has been pretty much disproven by scholars who may lack Spengler's breadth of intellect but have the advantage of a stationary target to shoot at.

Whatever the merits of the historical theory which provides the framework or the space-opera idiom in which it's written, "The Only Thing We Learn" comes close to being a flawless example of telling a complex story in a compressed form. In 5,000 words Kornbluth crystalizes a thesis that took Asimov three volumes—and there are more real characters in "The Only Thing We Learn" than in the entire Foundation Trilogy besides.

Kornbluth was first and last a craftsman. He never forgot people, characters, and he never forgot he was telling a story. These are virtues which any writer could benefit by remembering. What "The Only Thing We Learn" has for me in particular is that it's about change and the fact that enemies *though they may very truly be demons* are no different from ourselves as we were or may become.

In retrospect, and as a veteran myself, I find it interesting that "The Only Thing We Learn" is the first story Cyril Kornbluth sold when he returned to civilian life after fighting the Nazis.

—David Drake

THE ONLY THING WE LEARN

by C. M. Kornbluth

The Professor, though he did not know the actor's phrase for it, was counting the house—peering through a spyhole in the door through which he would in a moment appear before the class. He was pleased with what he saw. Tier after tier of young people, ready with notebooks and styli, chattering tentatively, glancing at the door against which his nose was flattened, waiting for the pleasant interlude known as "Archaeo-Literature 203" to begin.

The professor stepped back, smoothed his tunic, crooked four books in his left elbow and made his entrance. Four swift strides brought him to the lectern and, for the thousandth-odd time, he impassively swept the lecture hall with his gaze. Then he gave a wry little smile. Inside, for the thousandth-odd time, he was nagged by the irritable little thought that the lectern really ought to be a foot or so higher.

The irritation did not show. He was out to win the audience, and he did. A dead silence, the supreme tribute, gratified him. Imperceptibly, the lights of the lecture hall began to dim and the light on the lectern to brighten.

He spoke.

"Young gentlemen of the Empire, I ought to warn you that this and the succeeding lectures will be most subversive."

There was a little rustle of incomprehension from the audience—but by then the lectern light was strong enough to show the twinkling smile about his eyes that belied his stern mouth, and agreeable chuckles sounded in the gathering darkness of the tiered seats. Glow-lights grew bright gradually at the student's tables, and they adjusted their notebooks in the narrow ribbons of illumination. He waited for the small commotion to subside.

"Subversive—" He gave them a link to cling to. "Subversive because I shall make every effort to tell both sides of our ancient beginnings with every resource of archaeology and with every clue my diligence has discovered in our epic literature.

"There *were* two sides, you know—difficult though it may be to believe that if we judge by the Old Epic alone—such epics as the noble and tempestuous *Chant of Remd*, the remaining fragments of *Krall's Voyage*, or the gory and rather out-of-date *Battle for the Ten Suns*." He paused while styli scribbled across the notebook pages.

"The Middle Epic is marked, however, by what I might call the rediscovered ethos." From his voice, every student knew that that phrase, surer than death and taxes, would appear on an examination paper. The styli scribbled. "By this I mean an awakening of fellow-feeling with the Home Suns People, which had once been filial loyalty to them when our ancestors were few and pioneers, but which turned into contempt when their numbers grew.

"The Middle Epic writers did not despise the Home Suns People, as did the bards of the Old Epic. Perhaps this was because they did not have to—since their long war against the Home Suns was drawing to a victorious close.

"Of the New Epic I shall have little to say. It was a literary fad, a pose, and a silly one. Written within historic times, the some two score pseudo-epics now moulder in their cylinders, where they belong. Our ripening civilization could not with integrity work in the epic form, and the artistic failures produced so indicate. Our genius turned to the lyric and to the unabashedly romantic novel.

"So much, for the moment, of literature. What contribution, you must wonder, have archaeological studies to make in an investigation of the wars from which our ancestry emerged?

"Archaeology offers—one—a check in historical matter in the epics—confirming or denying. Two—it provides evidence glossed over in the epics—for artistic or patriotic reasons.

Three—it provides evidence which has been lost, owing to the fragmentary nature of some of the early epics."

All this he fired at them crisply, enjoying himself. Let them not think him a dreamy litterateur, nor, worse, a flat precisionist, but let them be always a little off-balance before him, never knowing what came next, and often wondering, in class and out. The styli paused after heading Three.

"We shall examine first, by our archaeo-literary technique, the second book of the *Chant of Remd.* As the selected youth of the Empire, you know much about it, of course—much that is false, some that is true and a great deal that is irrelevant. You know that Book One hurls us into the middle of things, aboard ship with Algan and his great captain, Remd, on their way from the triumph over a Home Suns stronghold, the planet Telse. We watch Remd on his diversionary action that splits the Ten Suns Fleet into two halves. But before we see the destruction of those halves by the Horde of Algan, we are told in Book Two of the battle for Telse."

He opened one of his books on the lectern, swept the amphitheater again and read sonorously.

"Then battle broke
And high the blinding blast
Sight-searing leaped
While folk in fear below.
Cowered in caverns
From the wrath of Remd—

"Or, in less sumptuous language, one fission bomb—or a stick of time-on-target bombs—was dropped. An unprepared and disorganized populace did not take the standard measure of dispersing, but huddled foolishly to await Algan's gunfighters and the death they brought.

"One of the things you believe because you have seen them in notes to elementary-school editions of *Remd* is that Telse was the fourth planet of the star, Sol. Archaeology denies it by establishing that the fourth planet—actually called Marse, by the way—was in those days weather-roofed at least, and possibly atmosphere-roofed as well. As potential warriors, you know that one does not waste fissionable material on a roof, and there is no mention of chemical explosives being used to crack the roof. Marse, therefore, was not the locale of *Remd*, Book Two.

"Which planet was? The answer to that has been established by X-radar, differential decay analyses, video-coring and every other resource of those scientists still quaintly called 'diggers.' We know and can prove that Telse was the *third* planet of Sol. So much for the opening of the attack. Let us jump to Canto Three, the Storming of the Dynastic Palace.

"Imperial purple wore they
Fresh from the feast
Grossly gorged
They sought to slay—

"And so on. Now, as I warned you, Remd is of the Old Epic, and makes no pretense at fairness. The unorganized huddling of Telse's population was read as cowardice instead of poor A.R.P. The same is true of the Third Canto. Video-cores show on the site of the palace a hecatomb of dead in once-purple livery, but also shows impartially that they were not particularly gorged and that digestion of their last meals had been well advanced. They didn't give such a bad accounting of themselves, either. I hesitate to guess, but perhaps they accounted for one of our ancestors apiece and were simply outnumbered. The study is not complete.

"That much we know." The professor saw they were tiring of the terse scientist and shifted gears. "But if the veil of time were rent that shrouds the years between us and the Home Suns People, how much more would we learn? Would we despise the Home Suns People as our frontiersman ancestors did, or would we cry: '*This* is our spiritual home—this world of rank and order, this world of formal verse and exquisitely patterned arts'?"

If the veil of time were rent—?

We can try to rend it . . .

Wing Commander Arris heard the clear jangle of the radar net alarm as he was dreaming about a fish. Struggling out of his too-deep, too-soft bed, he stepped into a purple singlet, buckled on his Sam Browne belt with its holstered .45 automatic and tried to read the radar screen. Whatever had set it off was either too small or too distant to register on the five-inch C.R.T.

He rang for his aide, and checked his appearance in a wall-mirror while waiting. His space tan was beginning to fade, he saw, and made a mental note to get it renewed at the parlor. He stepped into the corridor as Evan, his aide, trotted up—younger, browner, thinner, but the same officer type that made the Service what it was, Arris thought with satisfaction.

Evan gave him a bone-cracking salute, which he returned. They set off for the elevator that whisked them down to a large, chilly, dark underground room where faces were greenly lit by radar screens and the lights of plotting tables. Somebody yelled "Attention!" and the tecks snapped. He gave them "At ease" and took the brisk salute of the senior teck, who reported to him in flat, machine-gun delivery:

"Object-becoming-visible-on-primary-screen-sir."

He studied the sixty-inch disk for several seconds before he spotted the intercepted particle. It was coming in fast from zenith, growing while he watched.

"Assuming it's now traveling at maximum, how long will it be before it's within striking range?" he asked the teck.

"Seven hours, sir."

"The interceptors at Idlewild alerted?"

"Yessir."

Arris turned on a phone that connected with Interception. The boy at Interception knew the face that appeared on its screen, and was already capped with a crash helmet.

"Go ahead and take him, Efrid," said the wing commander.

"Yessir!" and a punctilious salute, the boy's pleasure plain at being known by name and a great deal more at being on the way to a fight that might be first-class.

Arris cut him off before the boy could detect a smile that was forming on his face. He turned from the pale lunar glow of the sixty-incher to enjoy it. Those kids—when every meteor was an invading dreadnaught, when every ragged scouting ship from the rebels was an armada!

He watched Efrid's squadron roar off on the screen and then he retreated to a darker corner. This was his post until the meteor or scout or whatever it was got taken care of. Evan joined him, and they silently studied the smooth, disciplined functioning of the plot room, Arris with satisfaction and Evan doubtless with the same. The aide broke silence, asking:

"Do you suppose it's a Frontier ship, sir?" He caught the wing commander's look and hastily corrected himself: "I mean rebel ship, sir, of course."

"Then you should have said so. Is that what the junior officers generally call those scoundrels?"

Evan conscientiously cast his mind back over the last few junior messes and reported unhappily: "I'm afraid we do, sir. We seem to have got into the habit."

"I shall write a memorandum about it. How do you account for that very peculiar habit?"

"Well, sir, they do have something like a fleet, and they did take over the Regulus Cluster, didn't they?"

What had got into this incredible fellow, Arris wondered in amazement. Why, the thing was self-evident! They had a few ships—accounts differed as to how many—and they had, doubtless by raw sedition, taken over some systems temporarily.

He turned from his aide, who sensibly became interested in a screen and left with a murmured excuse to study it very closely.

The brigands had certainly knocked together some ramshackle league or other, but— The wing commander wondered briefly if it could last, shut the horrid thought from his head, and set himself to composing mentally a stiff memorandum that would be posted in the junior officer's mess and put an end to this absurd talk.

His eyes wandered to the sixty-incher, where he saw the interceptor squadron climbing nicely toward the particle—which, he noticed, had become three particles. A low crooning distracted him. Was one of the tecks singing at work? It couldn't be!

It wasn't. An unsteady shape wandered up in the darkness, murmuring a song and exhaling alcohol. He recognized the Chief Archivist, Glen.

"This is Service country, mister," he told Glen.

"Hullo, Arris," the round little civilian said, peering at him. "I come down here regularly—regularly against regulations—to wear off my regular irregularities with the wine bottle. That's all right, isn't it?"

He was drunk and argumentative. Arris felt hemmed in. Glen couldn't be talked into leaving without loss of dignity to the wing commander, and he couldn't be chucked out because he was writing a biography of the chamberlain and could, for the time being, have any head in the palace for the asking. Arris sat down unhappily, and Glen plumped down beside him.

The little man asked him.

"Is that a fleet from the Frontier League?" He pointed to the big screen. Arris didn't look at his face, but felt that Glen was grinning maliciously.

"I know of no organization called the Frontier League," Arris said. "If you are referring to the brigands who have recently been operating in Galactic East, you could at least call them by their proper names." Really, he thought—civilians!

"So sorry. But the brigands should have the Regulus Cluster by now, shouldn't they?" he asked, insinuatingly.

This was serious—a grave breach of security. Arris turned to the little man.

"Mister, I have no authority to command you," he said measuredly. "Furthermore, I understand you are enjoying a temporary eminence in the non-service world which would make it very difficult for me to—ah—tangle with you. I shall therefore refer only to your altruism. How did you find out about the Regulus Cluster?"

"Eloquent!" murmured the little man, smiling happily. "I got it from Rome."

Arris searched his memory. "You mean Squadron Commander Romo broke security? I can't believe it!"

"No, commander. I mean Rome—a place—a time—a civilization. I got it also from Babylon, Assyria, the Mogul Raj—every one of them. You don't understand me, of course.

"I understand that you're trifling with Service security and that you're a fat little, malevolent, worthless drone and scribbler!"

"Oh, commander!" protested the archivist. "I'm not so little!" He wandered away, chuckling.

Arris wished he had the shooting of him, and tried to explore the chain of secrecy for a weak link. He was tired and bored by this harping on the Fron—on the brigands.

His aide tentatively approached him. "Interceptors in striking range, sir," he murmured.

"Thank you," said the wing commander, genuinely grateful to be back in the clean, etched-line world of the Service and out of that blurred, water-color, civilian land where long-dead Syrians apparently retailed classified matter to nasty little drunken warts who had no business with it. Arris confronted the sixty-incher. The particle that had become three particles was now—he counted—eighteen particles. Big ones. Getting bigger.

He did not allow himself emotion, but turned to the plot on the interceptor squadron.

"Set up Lunar relay," he ordered.

"Yessir."

Half the plot room crew bustled silently and efficiently about the delicate job of applied relativistic physics that was "lunar relay." He knew that the palace power plant could take it for a few minutes, and he wanted to *see*. If he could not believe radar pips, he might believe a video screen.

On the great, green circle, the eighteen—now twenty-four—particles neared the thirty-six smaller particles that were interceptors, led by the eager young Efrid.

"Testing Lunar relay, sir," said the chief teck.

The wing commander turned to a twelve-inch screen. Unobtrusively, behind him, tecks jockeyed for position. The picture on the screen was something to see. The chief let mercury fill a thick-walled, ceramic tank. There was a sputtering and contact was made.

"Well done," said Arris. "Perfect seeing."

He saw, upper left, a globe of ships—what ships! Some were Service jobs, with extra turrets plastered on them wherever there was room. Some were orthodox freighters, with the same porcupine-bristle of weapons. Some were obviously home-made crates, hideously ugly—and as heavily armed as the others.

Next to him, Arris heard his aide murmur, "It's all wrong, sir. They haven't got any pick-up boats. They haven't got any hospital ships. What happens when one of them gets shot up?"

"Just what ought to happen, Evan," snapped the wing commander. "They float in space until they desiccate in their suits. Or if they get grappled inboard with a boat hook, they don't get any medical care. As I told you, they're brigands, without decency even to care for their own." He enlarged on the theme. "Their morale must be insignificant compared with our men's. When the Service goes into action, every rating and teck knows he'll be cared for it he's hurt. Why, if we didn't have pick-up boats and hospital ships the men wouldn't—" He almost finished it with "fight," but thought, and lamely ended—"wouldn't like it."

* * *

Evan nodded, wonderingly, and crowded his chief a little as he craned his neck for a look at the screen.

"Get the hell away from here!" said the wing commander in a restrained yell, and Evan got.

The interceptor squadron swam into the field—a sleek, deadly needle of vessels in perfect alignment, with its little cloud of pick-ups trailing, and farther astern a white hospital ship with the ancient red cross.

The contact was immediate and shocking. One of the rebel ships lumbered into the path of the interceptors, spraying fire from what seemed to be as many points as a man has pores. The Service ships promptly riddled it and it should have drifted away—but it didn't. It kept on fighting. It rammed an interceptor with a crunch that must have killed every man before the first bulwark, but aft of the bulwark the ship kept fighting.

It took a torpedo portside and its plumbing drifted through space in a tangle. Still the starboard side kept squirting fire. Isolated weapon blisters fought on while they were obviously cut off from the rest of the ship. It was a pounded tangle of wreckage, and it had destroyed two interceptors, crippled two more, and kept fighting.

Finally, it drifted away, under feeble jets of power. Two more of the fantastic rebel fleet wandered into action, but the wing commander's horrified eyes were on the first pile of scrap. It was going *somewhere—*

The ship neared the thin-skinned, unarmored, gleaming hospital vessel, rammed it amidships, square in one of the red crosses, and then blew itself up, apparently with everything left in its powder magazine, taking the hospital ship with it.

The sickened wing commander would never have recognized what he had seen as it was told in a later version, thus:

"The crushing course they took
And nobly knew
Their death undaunted
By heroic blast
The hospital's host
They dragged to doom
Hail! Men without mercy
From the far frontier!"

Lunar relay flickered out as overloaded fuses flashed into vapor. Arris distractedly paced back to the dark corner and sank into a chair.

"I'm sorry," said the voice of Glen next to him, sounding quite sincere. "No doubt it was quite a shock to you."

"Not to you?" asked Arris bitterly.

"Not to me."

"Then how did they do it?" the wing commander asked the civilian in a low, desperate whisper. "They don't even wear .45s. Intelligence says their enlisted men have hit their officers and got away with it. They *elect* ship captains! Glen, what does it all mean?"

"It means," said the fat little man with a timbre of doom in his voice, "that they've returned. They always have. They always will. You see, commander, there is always somewhere a wealthy, powerful city, or nation, or world. In it are those whose blood is not right for a wealthy, powerful place. They must seek danger and overcome it. So they go out—on the marshes, in the desert, on the tundra, the planets, or the stars. Being strong, they grow stronger by fighting the tundra, the planets or the stars. They—they change. They sing new songs. They know new heroes. And then, one day, they return to their old home.

"They return to the wealthy, powerful city, or nation or world. They fight its guardians as they fought the tundra, the planets or the stars—a way that strikes terror to the heart. Then they sack the city, nation or world and sing great, ringing sagas of their deeds. They always have. Doubtless they always will."

"But what shall we do?"

"We shall cower, I suppose, beneath the bombs they drop on us, and we shall die, some bravely, some not, defending the palace within a very few hours. But you will have your revenge."

"How?" asked the wing commander, with haunted eyes.

The fat little man giggled and whispered in the officer's ear. Arris irritably shrugged it off as a bad joke. He didn't believe it. As he died, drilled through the chest a few hours later by one of Algan's gunfighters he believed it even less.

The professor's lecture was drawing to a close. There was time for only one more joke to send his students away happy. He was about to spring it when a messenger handed him two slips of paper. He raged inwardly at his ruined exit and poisonously read from them:

"I have been asked to make two announcements. One, a bulletin from General Sleg's force. He reports that the so-called Outland Insurrection is being brought under control and that there is no cause for alarm. Two, the gentlemen who are members of the S.O.T.C. will please report to the armory at 1375 hours—whatever that may mean—for blaster inspection. The class is dismissed."

Petulantly, he swept from the lectern and through the door.

ABOUT THE AUTHORS

Theodore Sturgeon (1918–1985) influenced many authors with his penetrating insight into the psychology of human behavior applied to science fiction and fantasy. Better known for his many short stories than his novels, he had the ability to distill novel-length ideas into clear, crisp stories. Notable works include "Fear Is a Business," "A Saucer of Loneliness," and "Killdozer!" the latter made into a movie of the same name. He was the Guest of Honor at the 20th World Science Fiction Convention, and was awarded the Life Achievement Award by the World Fantasy Association in 1985.

Keith Laumer (1925–1993) is best known for his series of stories and novels about the interstellar diplomat Jaime Retief, but he had written all types of science fiction in his career, from razor-sharp military fiction in his *Bolo* series to alternate reality fiction in his Imperium novels. His experience in the U.S. Army and Air Force served him well in extrapolating what the military of the future might be like. His diplomatic Retief stories were also grounded in real life experience from his tour of duty as a Foreign Service Vice-Consul in Rangoon.

Frederik Pohl has written over forty novels in his 45-year career, collaborating with such luminaries in the field as C.M. Kornbluth and Jack Williamson. He has also edited literally dozens of anthologies which have often brought classic science fiction and fantasy stories to a whole new generation of readers. He has edited books at such publishing companies as Ace Books and Bantam Books, and won the Hugo Award three times for editing and twice for fiction.

C.M. Kornbluth (1923–1958) primarily collaborated with Frederick Pohl on novels of social science fiction, but it is his shorter stories that are considered his more excellent work. Often combining a humorous look at social conventions with a strange sense of piercing the veils of common perception, many of his stories straddle the boundary between fantasy and science fiction. Other works include "The Silly Season" and "The Mindworm."

Before turning to speculative fiction, Barry N. Malzberg edited such magazines as *Amazing* and *Fantastic*, and worked as an editor and agent for the Scott Meredith Literary Agency, a position he holds today. A prolific writer and editor, he has written in every genre, but is known for his harrowing science fiction stories which examine the basic nature of reality as it is perceived by his various protagonists. His novels examining the space program during the early 1970s are exceptional, with *Beyond Apollo* winning the John W. Campbell award. The satirical *Gather in the Hall of the Planets*, a lampooning of the goings-on at science-fiction conventions and *Galaxies*, one of his forays into postmodern fiction, show his talent at examining the present through extrapolating the future.

Eric Frank Russell (1905–1978) first achieved recognition in the science fiction field with the publication of *Sinister Barrier*, the novel that launched John W. Campbell's *Unknown* magazine in 1939. Usually at the forefront of the science fiction scene during the next two decades, he was adept at tackling such humanistic issues as race relations and transposing them to the science fictional realms. His story "Allamagoosa" won the Hugo award in 1955.

Robert Sheckley is a writer who is constantly pursuing the unknown in his writing, making his reader rethink the most ordinary situations. He has written almost 20 novels, and has collaborated with such authors as Harry Harrison and the late Roger Zelazny. He was the fiction editor of *Omni* magazine from 1980 to 1982, and has also written many television and radio plays. A winner of the Jupiter award, he lives in Oregon.

Gordon R. Dickson has written more than 50 novels in many genres, from the humorous fantasy of his *Dragon* books to a massive, ambitious science fiction chronicle of human evolution in his *Childe Cycle* series. His novels often assert that, as free-willed entities, living beings, whether human or alien, can control their own destiny. Other standalone novels include *Way of the Pilgrim*, *Wolf and Iron*, and *The Final Encyclopedia*. He has also edited several anthologies, including *Combat SF* and *Nebula Winners 12*. A former president of the Science Fiction and Fantasy Writers of America, he has won three Hugo Awards, as well as the Nebula, Derleth, and Jupiter Awards.

Howard Waldrop fuses such diverse elements as alternate history, UFOs, and rock and roll into finely researched and detailed stories unlike anything else being written today. He primarily writes short stories, which have been collected in anthologies such as *Howard Who?: Twelve Outstanding Stories of Speculative Fiction*. His novels include *A Dozen Tough Jobs*, in which the Twelve Labors of Hercules is recast in Mississippi in the 1920s. A winner of the Nebula and World Fantasy Awards, he lives in Washington.

Norman Kagan uses his PhD in mathematics to explore worlds many would just pass by without seeing. He produced a handful of short stories in the 1960s, “Four Brands of Impossible” and “Laugh Along With Franz” among them. He has also written nonfiction as well, mainly about the cinema. Other books include *The War Film* and *The Cinema of Stanley Kubrick*.

Ward Moore (1903–1978) was a self-educated author whose small but impressive body of work examined human determination at its finest. His chief work is the novel *Bring the Jubilee*, an alternate history tale where the South had won the Civil War, only to have their victory undone by a time-traveling historian. His other novels were primarily collaborations, such as *Joyleg: A Folly* with Avram Davidson. He has also worked in many careers while writing, such as shipbuilder, copy editor, and book review editor.

Writing under the pseudonym Cordwainer Smith, Paul Linebarger (1915–1966) used his years of experience in the U.S. Army Intelligence Service and his degree in psychiatry to create a universe-spanning empire called the Instrumentality of

Mankind. His short stories deal almost exclusively with this timeline, telling of a future humanity which rises from near self-destruction to success and decadence. Pivotal stories in the series include "Scanners Live in Vain," and "The Game of Rat and Dragon." He was educated at schools such as the University of Nanking and George Washington University, and served as the President of the American Peace Society.

Stanley G. Weinbaum (1902–1935) was just starting to emerge as one of the pulp era's genuine craftsmen before his untimely death. His portrayal of alien life-forms as sympathetic creatures with thought processes markedly different from humans was a groundbreaking step in the advancement of science fiction. His best novel, *The New Adam*, portrays a superman character as a man adrift among mere humans. Unfortunately, his short career has not garnered him the study and acclaim of better-known authors.

James Blish (1921–1975) spent his career writing stories about certain aspects of science fiction, psychic powers, miniature humans, and antigravity, for example, and then expanded those stories into longer pieces with the broader scope of a novel. The finished pieces *The Seedling Stars*, *A Case of Conscience*, and *Jack of Eagles* are prime examples of how his novels grew from short stories. He also did excellent television novelizations, most notably the *Star Trek* Logs 1–12 and the classic novel *Spock Must Die!*

Roger Zelazny (1937–1995) burst onto the science-fiction writing scene as part of the "New Wave" group of writers in the mid to late 1960s. His novels *This Immortal* and *Lord of Light* met universal praise, the latter winning a Hugo Award for best novel. His work is notable for its lyrical style and innovative use of language both in description and dialogue. The Amber novels are his most recognized series, about a parallel universe which is the one true world, with all others, Earth included, being mere reflections of his created universe. Besides the Hugo for *Lord of Light*, he was also awarded three Nebulas, three more Hugos and two Locus Awards.

Lester del Rey (1915–1993) began his writing career submitting only to John W. Campbell, editor of *Astounding* magazine.

He sold 38 stories there, and began writing novels and juvenile science fiction. Notable novels include *The Sky Is Falling*, *Siege Perilous*, and *Pstalemate*. He also edited some of the top science fiction magazines during the Golden Age, including *Galaxy* and *If*. In 1977 he began his own imprint at Ballantine Books. That imprint, Del Rey Books, is still publishing today.